FORGOTTEN LIVES

Wes Markin

For Hugo and Bea

About the Author

Wes Markin is the bestselling author of The Yorkshire Murders, which stars the compassionate and relentless DCI Emma Gardner. He is also the author of Whitby's Forgotten Victims, the DCI Michael Yorke Thrillers set in Salisbury, and the Jake Pettman Thrillers set in New England. Wes lives in Harrogate with his wife, two children, and his cheeky cockapoo, Rosie, close to the crime scenes in The Yorkshire Murders and Whitby's Forgotten Victims.

You can find out more at:
www.wesmarkinauthor.com

facebook.com/wesmarkinauthor

By Wes Markin

DCI Yorke Thrillers
One Last Prayer
The Repenting Serpent
The Silence of Severance
Rise of the Rays
Dance with the Reaper
Christmas with the Conduit
The Killing Pit
Fire in Bone
Blue Falls
The Rotten Core
Rock and a Hard Place
Better the Devil
The Secret Diary of Lacey Ray

The Yorkshire Murders
The Viaduct Killings
The Lonely Lake Killings
The Crying Cave Killings
The Graveyard Killings
The Winter Killings

Whitby's Forgotten Victims
Forgotten Bones

Forgotten Lives

Forgotten Souls

Forgotten Graves

∼

Details of how to claim your **FREE** DCI Michael Yorke quick read, **A lesson in Crime**, can be found at the end of this book.

This story is a work of fiction. All names, characters, organizations, places, events and incidents are products of the author's imagination or are used fictitiously. Any resemblance to any persons, alive or dead, events or locals is entirely coincidental.

Text copyright © 2024 Wes Markin

First published 2024

ISBN: 9798338749845

Edited by: Candida Bradford

Published by: WFM Publishing Ltd

All rights reserved.

No part of this book should be reproduced in any way without the express permission of the author.

Chapter One

The Rusty Anchor public house was the cream of the crop – if the crop being called into question happened to be a harvest of derelict husks.

Ethan Crawley stared up at boarded windows, jagged holes gaping in the roof, and crumbling brickwork, wondering which sadistic idiot he'd aggravated to land this job. Surveying derelict buildings was never a barrel of laughs, but this place took the right royal piss.

It had to be a mistake.

Ethan double-checked the date on the clipboard in his gloved hands.

No mistake.

Un-bloody-believable. Five years since last orders! Nobody could have frequented this place as recently as that? Surely?

Common sense told Ethan he should call it in as a two-man job and delay the survey.

He turned around. The slate grey sky pressed down, smothering the moors in a dreary half-light, but it was still as picturesque as ever. No wonder the call to have the Rusty

Anchor razed to the ground was so incessant. The old pub was a true blot on the landscape, stuffing up watercolours everywhere, and scaring the sheep.

He refocused on the Anchor. He'd a job to do and people to impress. Scarring his reputation was unthinkable now. The recent increase in interest rates had turned his mortgage from an inconvenience to a positively life-threatening burden.

His clipboard tucked securely under one arm, Ethan snapped on plastic gloves and then grappled with the rusted padlock which secured the front door. There was a moment of disappointment when the key didn't snap off in the corroded mechanism.

Just his luck! *Looks like I'm going in after all.* Gritting his teeth, he shouldered the door open.

Christ. He reeled back, one hand clamped over his mouth and nose. An animal had died in here. Not unusual in derelict properties, but not something you could ever get used to. Still, Ethan could cope. He muttered a thanks to his mum, whose earthy adherence to traditional Yorkshire cuisine had gifted him a truly cast-iron stomach. Then he knelt to set an overturned chair upright and propped the front door open with it. Most of the windows were boarded over, so he didn't want to close off any more of the sun – light was limited enough in November as it was. He removed his backpack, rummaged for a torch, clicked it on and cast a powerful beam around the gloomy interior of the pub—

A skittering sound erupted over on the bar, and he nearly shat himself.

Heart slamming against his ribs, he swung the torch beam towards the noise. A pair of beady eyes flashed in the darkness. A rat.

FORGOTTEN LIVES

Par for the course in his line of work, but God how he hated them.

He let out a shaky laugh. 'How's the beer, fella?'

The mangy creature twitched its whiskers at him and streaked off into the shadows.

'Do come back. You're the only regular this place has seen in years.'

He sighed and, torch gripped in one sweat-slicked palm, Ethan began a cautious circuit of the ruined pub. In the wavering light, it was almost possible to imagine the place as it might once have been.

Formica tabletops gleaming, scattered with half-empty pint glasses and salt-dusted crisp packets. Vinyl bar stools, yet unravaged by time and piss-poor upkeep, holding up the sagging arses of hardened regulars. The mingled scents of spilled lager, stale smoke, and the odd ploughman's lunch gone rogue.

In his schedule, he'd a sweep planned for this afternoon and another one for tomorrow morning. He shone his torch up at the ceiling, which he'd be later checking for asbestos, and then took his beam down onto the walls, knowing the paint would be full of lead.

Testing each step for weak spots on the water-stained floor, Ethan approached the bar. Going through the rotten wood into the cellar was not on his agenda. He had checked he'd a signal on his mobile phone earlier, just in case.

Some of Ethan's colleagues were more laissez-faire with these surveys, especially when the building was slated for demolition. Why risk crawling through an asbestos-riddled shithole when it would be rubble by next Tuesday?

Ethan thought back to his father, who'd always approached his work with integrity, even if he never dealt with dirty jobs like this. He'd taught Ethan to do the same, and the lesson had stuck with him throughout his career.

There were regulations, and he'd follow them. Didn't mean he had to set any land speed records, mind. He'd be taking his sweet time in this deathtrap, thank you very much. Slow and steady, with an emphasis on not plummeting through the sodding floorboards.

He smiled when he glimpsed the faded chalkboard above the bar. It still bore the ghostly outlines of the daily specials. 'Chef's Special: Yorkshire Rarebit.' That would usually have him salivating, but there was a dead animal being consumed by bacteria close by, generating some rather off-putting fumes.

Ethan walked the length of the bar, standing on abandoned beer mats, and kicking aside broken glass with his sturdy Doc Martens.

Behind the bar, two doors stood sentinel on far sides. Both would lead down into the dank, miserable bowels of the pub. The door on the left was nearer. He'd start there.

The door resisted his tug at first, so he gave it a solid yank. A tortured squeal made him flinch. Another rat? He held his breath as he looked at his feet to see if he was standing on the tail of one. No, thank Christ. It was probably just the hinges. *Last time I'm doing one of these on my own.*

He inched forward and stopped, gagging. Even with its dead animal, the upstairs was far more tolerable than down there. At least up here, there was a steady breeze courtesy of the front door and poorly boarded windows, but lord knew what was going on down there.

Time to break out the big guns.

From his bag, he pulled out a half-face respiratory mask. Groaning, he put it on. The rubber seal jamming against his cheeks and jaw was horrible, the elastic straps dug into the back of his head like a pair of over-tightened vices, and the acrid tang of rubber and chemicals, underscored by the faint, unmistakable odour of his own recycled breath, was overwhelming. He drew a deep, experimental breath, feeling the resistance of the filters. Although it protected him, it closed off one of his senses in what was a hazardous area. Over the years, he'd developed a habit of relying on his sense of smell – the eggy stench of a gas leak, the burnt-copper tang of faulty wiring.

Still, needs must.

He descended the stone steps.

The torch beam sliced through the heavy darkness, illuminating a cramped corridor with a low, barrel-vaulted ceiling. Three doors – two on the left wall, one on the right. The one on the right was closest; odds were good that it led to the main cellar where the kegs and bottles had once been kept. A quick peek confirmed his suspicions. Barrels littered the floor. Moisture dripped from the ceiling. There were puddles of stagnant water. Black mould furred the brick walls. This respiratory mask was a small price to pay for not taking a lungful of that shite!

He closed the door and then tried the first of the two doors on the left. It was locked, so he took the bunch of keys he'd been supplied with from his pocket. He cycled through them until he found one that fit into the door and opened it.

This room was large but had a lower ceiling. No sign of dripping or mould in here. He took several steps inside. A large oak table occupied the centre of the room, surrounded by chairs. Dog-eared playing cards and a scattering of poker chips lay strewn about its surface.

Smiling, Ethan put the clipboard down on the table and picked up the King of Hearts. 'This place is not fit for you, your Majesty.' His voice sounded tinny in the respirator. 'The establishment has taken a rather precipitous turn.'

He chucked the card back onto the table and continued his circuit of the room, clipboard in hand. He tried to conjure the scene that may've played out here so many times over the years: a gaggle of grizzled old men hunched over their cards, wreathed in smoke, the air thick with obscenities and the reek of spilled beer. There'd have been money changing hands, old grudges being aired, ancient jokes told and retold.

A cold draught brought him from his reverie. He put the clipboard back down and spun to the crumbling expanse of brick – the wall shared by the room behind the last door he was yet to open. A jagged gap yawned where several bricks had shaken loose from the decaying mortar, ugly as a knocked-out tooth. It was clear even in the uneven light that this wall had seen some recent disturbance; several of the bricks were notably less weathered, the surrounding mortar paler than the rest.

Hunkering down, Ethan ran gloved hands over the bricks.

A patch-up job.

He pulled out a chunk of loose brick and placed it on the table behind him.

Not a good patch-up job either.

Then, using his torch, he identified a shadowy void behind the damaged wall. A gap that existed between the two rooms. Not unusual. Insulation helped to maintain temperatures for storing beer. It could also serve as a conduit for pipework.

The bright beam fell upon an expanse of faded blue fabric – a canvas of some kind, perhaps? No. The shape was irregular. A chill rippled through him as he leaned closer, heart suddenly beating far too fast.

A backpack. There was an ancient mouldering backpack wedged into the gap behind the bricks.

Laying the torch down, so it was illuminating the wall, he worked the loose bricks free, widening the hole. It was hard with the clumsy respiratory mask on, but he was filled with curiosity. The older bricks crumbled beneath his questing fingers, their mortar dried to little more than reddish dust, but the newer ones took a bit more persuading. It took him a few minutes to make the gap large enough.

He dragged the blue backpack out by its frayed straps and turned the torch on it. The faded and hole-riddled find was in poor nick. He sat up, lifted the respiratory mask off for a moment just so he could cool down.

The old backpack stank. When the reek settled at the back of his throat, he put the mask back on.

Swallowing hard, Ethan tugged at the zip on the backpack. But years of grime and oxidation had damaged the metal teeth. Eventually, though, the zipper gave way by painful increments until it was open.

Ethan reached in and pulled out a paperback, swollen and warped with damp. *The Hitchhiker's Guide to the Galaxy*. Christ, now there was a blast from the past! He'd devoured that book as a teenager, adoring its absurd take on the cold, uncaring universe.

Still smiling faintly, the surveyor set the book aside and reached into the bag again, fingers brushing the slick, decaying fabric until they closed on the sharp-edged rectangle of a plastic sleeve. He drew it out. It was a comic book sleeve. He blinked, registering the familiar logo. Superman. Another relic of his younger days. The cover, faded and mottled with damp, was achingly familiar.

He then shook out the backpack—

A knife hit the floor with a clatter, and his breath caught in his throat.

The knife was a cruel-looking thing with its wicked blade fully extended. It had flecks of a substance that could only be old, dried blood.

Ethan's eyes widened, and he sucked in a mammoth breath.

He turned the torch back on the gap. The beam fell upon a swathe of grimy pale cloth.

No, not cloth – plastic.

A tarp of some kind, or maybe a heavy-duty bin bag?

Wrapped around something.

Heart pounding in his ears, Ethan reached in.

He drew his fingers over the cold, unyielding contours beneath the plastic, knowing with a bone-deep, sickening certainty what it was.

He snatched his hand back and scrambled. The torch tumbled from the fingers of his other hand. It rolled across the floor, its beam strobing. He scrabbled backwards, grit gouging his palms through plastic gloves.

Ethan's back hit the table's edge, and he hauled himself upright, latching onto the torch beside him.

He exited the room, only realising after that he'd left the clipboard on the table.

He didn't wish to return and took the stairs three at a time, respirator mask still in place, his heart hammering against his ribs, desperately trying to make sense of what he'd seen.

A card game gone wrong, maybe? An accusation of cheating, a thrown punch, a moment of red-misted madness? And then a body cooling on the floor. Hasty hands stuffing the damning evidence of their sins into a bag, a tarp, a hole in the wall like a makeshift tomb...

Ethan burst through the cellar door and back into the husk of the pub, tearing off his respirator mask and gasping for breath.

A skitter of claws on the bar caught his attention. He directed the torch beam at the rat. The rodent twitched its whiskers at him, inscrutable and uncaring.

Ethan fumbled his mobile from his pocket with shaking hands. The demolition of the Rusty Anchor wouldn't take place next Tuesday. In fact, until the police had scoured and catalogued every grisly inch of it, the demolition of the Anchor wouldn't take place at all. This derelict pub, this rotten, sagging monument to a bygone age, held secrets far more dangerous than mere physical decay.

With a trembling finger, Ethan dialled the emergency services.

And as he waited for the call to connect, the rat watched him with one beady, unblinking eye.

Chapter Two

'Easy now, lass.' DCI Frank Black eased Bertha, his 1980s Volvo Estate, to a stop by the pavement, the shocks protesting in their usual chaotic way. He cut the engine, plunging the car into silence, and squinted out of his windscreen.

Dusk had already fallen, which meant that this stretch of pavement was heaving. And because of Bertha, every eye was now on him.

After sucking his roll-up to the filter, he wound down his window and threw it out onto the squalid street. He smelled the desperation mingling with the acrid tang of exhaust fumes.

Sighing, Frank observed young men and women along the street. Dressed in a mishmash of styles, from torn fishnets to faux leather. Society's casualties. Their eyes, though heavy with fatigue and the weight of untold stories, still flickered with a resilient spirit that refused to be extinguished.

He removed his glasses from his brow, tossed them onto the passenger seat, and massaged his temples. The ache behind his eyes was an absolute bastard. It pulsed in time with his heartbeat.

It was also a daily occurrence and only passed when he'd had a drink. But that would come later. He may be a mess of a man, but he wasn't about to sacrifice what little remained of his integrity by drinking and driving.

Sex workers gravitated towards his vehicle. He knew the drill. Within seconds, there'd be a knock on the window. He'd wind it down, and the questioning concerning sexual preferences would begin.

A tall brunette peeled away from the pack. She opted to knock on the passenger window. *Smart move, lass. Except I've no electric windows on Bertha!*

He leaned over, grunting, his bad back on fire, and wound the window down. By the time he'd righted himself, he was out of breath, sweating and looking, as was quite usual, on the verge of a heart attack.

She leaned in and looked at him.

Jesus wept, he thought, *I'm old enough to be your great grandad.*

'Hello, handsome. What you—'

He cut her off. 'It's okay.' He'd heard the spiel before. It sickened him to the depths of his soul. 'I'm looking for someone.'

A wry smile stretched across her face. 'Aren't we all?'

He stared at her. 'No, really.' He picked the photograph up off his passenger seat and held it out to her. 'This lass here. She's in her early thirties. Older than you. Her name is Maddie Black.' He leaned in, suppressing a groan, lifting the photograph so she could pluck it from his hands. 'I haven't seen her in months.'

Frank watched her heavy eyebrow wander up and down, and he felt his adrenaline surge.

Dare he hope?

'Sorry, no. I don't recognise her.'

Frank inwardly sighed, nodded, and reached into his jacket pocket for a twenty-pound note he had ready and leaned over again. 'Could you just show it around to some of your friends?'

She took the money and nodded.

She moved among the crowd. Frank scoured their faces, desperate to see one of them light up in recognition.

After five minutes, she returned and dropped the photograph onto the seat.

She shrugged. 'Sorry. If she'd been here, Cheryl would know.'

Frank sighed. 'Thank you.' He reached for the ignition.

'Who is she, anyway?'

Frank kept his fingers on the key as he looked at her. This lass was so young. It was so wrong. 'My daughter.'

'You trying to take her home?'

He nodded and looked forward. 'Aye.' Up ahead, he saw a sex worker climbing into a dark blue Audi. 'I'd like that more than anything.'

'I think you're wasting your time.'

He looked back at her. *Probably*. He smiled. 'Thanks. I know it's a long shot. But she's in Leeds somewhere. And, while I know that, well...' He broke off. *I can't stop*, he thought.

'How old is she?'

'Thirty-two.'

'Don't you think she can make up her own mind where she wants to be?'

Her question irritated him, but he wasn't about to take it out on a young lass whose life was in the gutter. Besides, it was true. 'Aye. But I can't give up.'

The weight of her nod suggested she appreciated this. 'At least you're trying. Can't remember my dad ever driving around trying to find me!'

Don't make me dad of the year. I'd a chance, and I completely fucked it up. Again.

'I'd like to move on now,' he said. 'And keep trying.'

'Okay.' She gave him the name of a road about five minutes away. 'Lots of newbies around there. Might be worth a squint.'

She turned away to join the others.

Frank sighed and fired up Bertha.

Everyone on the street watched him rattling away.

Chapter Three

DI GERRY CARVER rested her hands on the top of the closed menu with Rylan's leash looped around one wrist.

She hadn't needed to open the menu. She always ordered the same thing. Steak, well-done. No sauce. Boiled potatoes and sauteed broccoli. She had fed Rylan, her Golden Labrador, before coming out.

Tom Foley, her sandy-haired date, fidgeted in his chair opposite. She looked up and watched his eyes darting between the menu in his hands and Rylan. 'Is Rylan making you uncomfortable?'

Tom shook his head vigorously as he continued to read the menu, *too vigorously*. 'No... no. Course not...' He turned the page on the menu and then locked eyes with Gerry. 'It's just I've never seen someone bring a pet on a first date before.'

'Rylan isn't a pet.'

Tom dropped his eyes. 'Sorry... you explained before. He's a comfort dog.'

'A therapy dog.'

'Yes, that's right...'

Gerry felt irritated. She had, indeed, explained Rylan to Tom. In fact, she'd sent him a three-page document prior to their date, addressing her needs.

She took a sip of water. Had he even read the document? Or had he done what her boss, Frank, had done when they'd first started working together, and completely ignored it?

Tom closed the menu. 'Rylan is essential for maintaining your equilibrium in social situations.'

Gerry made brief eye contact with him.

Word for word. He had read the memo, after all.

Finally, a promising sign.

'I suggest we order immediately. The food is good, and it's the most inclusive place in Whitby.' Gerry glanced down at Rylan, allowed to sit beside her for that very reason. 'But they aren't the quickest. In six of my last eight dates here, the meal took over an hour to arrive.'

Tom coughed. He put a pint glass down and patted his chest. 'Sorry... wrong hole. Eight dates, you say? That seems a lot of dates.'

Gerry thought about it. 'Maybe. But they were over a forty-six-day period.'

Tom had beer froth on his top lip.

'I guess you're looking for something very particular. I understand that. I've yet to really hit it off with anyone.' Tom sounded downbeat.

She often found it interesting how many people suffered from loneliness, as well as how easily they'd share their sadness. Loneliness wasn't something that had ever really plagued her, even before she had a therapy dog. Still, if she was ever lonely or sad, she doubted she'd wear it like some kind of badge.

Her parents had raised her well, though. They'd tried

hard to instil values in her. And, although they weren't always natural to her, she always tried. She didn't want to hurt anyone's feelings. She touched her top lip. 'You've beer on your face.'

Flushing, Tom swiped at his mouth with the back of his hand. 'Cheers.'

The server came over and Tom ordered Spaghetti Bolognese. A messy choice. The sauce could splash.

If Tom speckled his white shirt with red, she wouldn't be able to see him again.

She reached down to Rylan. Sensing her anxiety, he nuzzled her hand.

Gerry ordered her usual.

'On separate plates, ma'am?'

'Yes, please.'

After the server left, Gerry launched into her questions regarding interests and habits. Obviously, she'd already done her research on Tom. He worked for the council, and his social profile showed a keen interest in golf. She needed a lot more than that. 'Do you like listening to music?'

'As much as the next person.'

'Do you go to live concerts?'

'I've seen Ed Sheeran.'

'I find them too noisy, but I do like Ed Sheeran. Do you have a favourite song?'

'I've a few, but I'm no good at remembering the names of them.'

'I see. Do you watch a lot of television?'

Tom paused, and he suddenly looked overwhelmed.

This wasn't the first time she'd had this reaction. Why did people always find her questions so jarring? They were straightforward and obvious!

He eventually answered. 'I prefer to read.'

'So, you watch no television?'

'Obviously... some... the news, the occasional quiz show, but like I said, I love books. I like autobiographies, mainly. I'm interested in other people.'

Gerry nodded. That was a suitable answer. She, too, was interested in what made others tick, she supposed. That was why she'd joined the police. 'How many times a week do you exercise?'

Tom laughed.

'What's funny?' Gerry asked.

'You're joking, right?'

'Why is exercise funny?'

'No, I mean, surely the next question should be: what kinds of people?'

Gerry thought about this. She understood his point. In terms of social interaction, which she studied at length, locating the common ground, their nuanced links in interests, was key. Still, she felt impatient. After all, even if he preferred autobiographies written by world leaders rather than sports personalities, like she did, that wouldn't be enough for her. There needed to be a range of broader similarities before delving into the nuances.

'Three times a week,' he answered, clearly growing impatient with the silence.

Not bad. Four would be better. Still, maybe she should reward him with a question he'd like now? 'Not including the golf. I don't count golf.'

'There's a lot of walking in golf,' Tom said.

'Meandering,' she said.

He laughed. 'Three times a week. Not golf.'

'What kind of exercise?'

'Swimming and running.'

Good.

'Oh, and football.'

Not so good. Competitive games. And a potential attachment to an aggressive culture.

'My turn,' Tom said. 'What do you do in the police, then? Your profile didn't specify.'

She smiled. 'I'm a detective inspector.'

He offered a weak grin. 'Blimey. I suppose that explains your, er, rather intense interrogation technique.'

Gerry frowned. 'I wasn't interrogating you. I was attempting to find the blend between showing interest and finding out our suitability – as is the social convention on a date.'

'Right, right, of course.' Tom tugged at his collar. 'Well, I appreciate the effort. Top marks. Why didn't you say you were a detective inspector on your profile?'

'I used to,' Gerry said. 'But no one was responding. I asked my superior at work, Frank, and he said it was probably intimidating. I was loath to take it out, though. I'm looking for compatibility. But it just wasn't working. I'd paid a year's subscription to the forum, so I didn't want to waste my money.'

'I see,' Tom said.

Gerry thought she'd give him a brief break from the questions and restrained herself. However, the date quickly lapsed into an uncomfortable silence. The clatter of cutlery and murmur of conversation from the neighbouring tables became suddenly overwhelming.

Gerry stroked Rylan and noticed Tom was gulping back beer. *Not great.* But it may've been a sign of nerves. That wouldn't be a black mark just yet. 'Are you ready for more questions?'

'If you wish.'

She asked him another three, and was pleased to hear he enjoyed travelling, animals, and long walks.

He was really ticking those boxes!

Eventually, Tom cleared his throat. 'I have to say, this has to be the most unique date I've ever been on.'

'Are you referring to the questioning?' Gerry said.

'The directness, yes, among other things. You can also be quite blunt.'

'I believe honesty is the best policy in all interpersonal dealings.'

He nodded with a furrowed brow. 'Ah. Good to know.'

The food arrived. Tom requested his next pint. He asked Gerry if she wanted anything, but she declined. She was happy with water and never drank alcohol.

Tom laid a napkin down on his lap. The trousers would go unscathed from the Bolognese sauce... but how about the shirt? She watched him wind spaghetti around the fork, and after he'd put it in his mouth, she looked for splashes. Nothing. *Good.* A careful eater.

Gerry chopped her steak into small pieces.

Tom paused, his fork halfway to his mouth. 'Why is your dog staring at me like that?'

Gerry glanced down at Rylan.

Rylan sat up, ears pricked, keeping his eyes fixed on Tom.

'Oh, he's probably just hoping you'll drop something. One of my colleagues, Reggie, started feeding him in the incident room against my wishes. It's made him more food orientated. I'm having to work on it.'

'Ah. Right.' Tom popped the spaghetti into his mouth and chewed slowly. Rylan tracked the motion, tongue lolling. After Tom swallowed, he asked, 'Why's he not watching you, then?'

'Ah, he knows that there's no chance I'll drop anything from the table.'

'Can you not tell him I won't either?'

Gerry laughed. 'Seriously?'

Tom didn't smile.

'It doesn't work like that, I'm afraid,' Gerry said. 'Like I said, I'm working on it.'

Swallowing hard, Tom set down his cutlery. 'I can't. It's just too off-putting.'

This concerned Gerry. 'When I asked you before, you said you liked animals?'

'I do... although, I never specified dogs.'

'You don't like dogs?'

Tom rolled his eyes. 'I'm not saying that... but they wouldn't be my first choice.'

Gerry chewed on a large piece of steak.

'But I still like them... dogs...' Tom said.

Good.

'But' – he put his fork down and sighed – 'I just, you know, have needs too, I guess. I don't like dogs begging me while I eat.'

'He isn't begging,' Gerry assured him. 'I well and truly trained that out of him.'

'Gazing then?'

'He's gazing at you in hope. I can't control hope, and I can't control his gaze.'

Tom sighed and picked up his knife and fork again. He mumbled under his breath. 'Brilliant.'

'But it's nice to know about your needs, too,' Gerry said. 'It's important for partners to be mindful of each other and their triggers.'

They ate in silence for a few minutes.

Gerry glanced at Rylan. His unwavering *gaze* was

indeed boring into the side of Tom's head. She looked up at her date.

Good, he was eating now, although she noticed that the second pint was almost gone already.

They finished their meals in silence, and then Tom ordered a third pint. This made him more talkative. 'What made you decide to try online dating?'

'My parents were together and happy for a long time. They understood one another. I felt it should be something I aimed for in my life, despite the challenges. My father always said that there was someone out there for everyone. I didn't see any reason to doubt him. Online dating offered me a chance to gather data. It seemed the most efficient method of dating for me.'

Tom raised an eyebrow. 'Gather data?'

'Learn about the person first.'

'Ah...' He took a mouthful of beer. 'You realise many people are full of shit on that site?'

'Of course.' Gerry nodded. 'I'm very good at spotting inconsistencies. Identifying falsehoods. In fact, the falsehoods themselves can be very educational when learning about someone.'

'How did you find me?'

'Refreshingly honest. Still do.'

Tom laughed. 'Refreshingly honest.' He raised his glass. 'I'll take that.'

'Yes. Black and white. I'm similar. Makes everything easier.'

He drank and wiped his mouth with the back of his hand.

You're going to have to stop that, though, she thought.

'Easier?' Tom smirked. 'I rarely find myself lost for words on a date like tonight. Until now, maybe.' He nodded down at his pint. 'Loosening up a little.' He laughed. 'Do you know what, Gerry? I quite like being refreshingly honest.'

Gerry took a sip of water. 'Then this has been successful.'

'Has it?' Tom's brow furrowed. He snorted. 'Then why does it feel like a business transaction?'

Gerry thought about it for a moment. She saw his point. 'It's better that way, I feel. Better to know what you're getting, what you're signing up for.'

Tom took a few more mouthfuls. Did he know when to stop?

'Dessert?' he asked.

Gerry shook her head. 'Not for me. Too many additives and colours.'

'You're right.' Tom nodded. 'Too many additives. You know, it's been different, but I *think* I've had a good night.'

Gerry nodded. 'Me too. But please be aware that we won't be having sex.'

Tom's eyebrows shot up, and he set his glass down. 'I... wasn't suggesting that.' His voice sounded strained.

'Not tonight, anyway. There's still a lot for both of us to find out, but hopefully, by the end of the month, sex will be permissible.'

Tom signalled the server for a fourth pint, his hand slightly unsteady.

I hope you stop after this one, Tom. If you go for a fifth, it's back to the drawing board.

Chapter Four

Frank drove through another dilapidated area of Leeds.

As he neared the road that the sex worker had mentioned, a group of bedraggled individuals caught his eye. They huddled together in front of a derelict shop. They'd wrapped tattered blankets around their thin shoulders. A shit defence against a November chill.

He'd no evidence suggesting that Maddie had turned to prostitution – that was merely fear. However, he was certain that she was homeless. Colleagues in Yorkshire had been keeping an eye out for him, and one had reported a sighting of her a month earlier among a wandering crowd of homeless people in Leeds.

Frank parked Bertha and climbed out, his joints cracking. In contrast to his previous stop, no one had their eyes on him. He suspected they were intoxicated.

Up close, he caught the acrid stench of marijuana.

Bairns again. He sighed. *Always so bloody young. Already chewed up by this godforsaken world.*

A lanky boy in his early twenties, wearing a threadbare hoodie and ripped jeans, looked up as Frank drew near. His face was gaunt, and his eyes were bloodshot, with deep shadows under them. Frank suppressed a second sigh. The kid looked as if he'd been to hell and back.

'Can I help you, mate?'

Frank kept his tone soft, non-threatening. 'I'm just looking for someone.'

'Who?'

'My daughter.'

The boy snorted, spat on the ground, and looked around at his companions. He said nothing else.

'Could I show you a photo?' Frank asked.

'Why? She ain't here, is she?'

'No... but maybe if you pass it around.' He took the picture from his jacket pocket. 'One of you might have seen her at some point.'

The boy's lip curled. 'She's not 'ere. Now piss off.'

The others remained silent, their eyes glazed. Frank's stomach churned as he wondered what substances were in their bodies. The thought of Maddie falling back into the clutches of heroin made his blood run cold.

Frank reached into his pocket for a twenty-pound note, but realised he'd already given it to the girl in the last place. He pulled his wallet from his back pocket and slipped two ten-pound notes free. He held them up. 'Please.'

The lad was on his feet in an instant. He approached, his movements sharp and jerky, and snatched the money from Frank's hand. Frank held out the photograph. When the kid took it, Frank felt his cold, clammy fingers brush against his skin.

The lad examined the picture while Frank regarded his face. A map of hardship and suffering. A jagged scar ran down his left cheek, and his teeth were yellow and crooked.

'Nah.' The kid shook his head. 'Don't know her.'

FORGOTTEN LIVES

'How about your friends?' Frank gestured to the others.

The lad snorted. 'They're not my mates. Just sold 'em some gear, that's all. Look at 'em. The only thing they're good for right now is dribbling on your photo.' He eyed Frank. 'Yer after something to take the edge off? Saw you'd some cash in that wallet...'

'No... thank you.' Frank turned to leave, his heart heavy.

'Hang on,' the boy called after him. 'Let me have another look.'

Frank paused, feeling a faint spark of hope in his chest. He turned and the lad reached for the photo. His sudden grin told Frank what he needed to know. He'd cocked up. Exhaustion and despair had made him sloppy.

The lad's fist slammed into his face, pain exploding behind his eyes. He staggered backwards.

Through the haze, Frank saw the lad coming at him again. He tried to raise his hands, to block the blow, but he was too slow. The second punch hit him on the lip. He tasted blood, hot and coppery. The third strike caught him square in the nose, which had only just recovered from being hit with a spade several months back.

Frank crashed into the ground, face down. The lad plucked Frank's wallet from his back pocket. 'Fuck,' he muttered, blood dribbling from his mouth. *You idiot.* He shook his head, face on fire. *You bloody idiot.*

He felt the wallet hit him on the back. He must have opted for the cash, and not his cards. That was something.

By the time Frank had staggered to his feet, the lad had sprinted away. And to think, before tonight, he'd been moaning about a headache! Now, his entire face was throbbing in time with his pulse.

At least the lad had dropped the photo along with his wallet. He knelt, groaned, and swiped them both up. He stumbled back over to Bertha and slumped behind the wheel.

The drive home passed in a blur of pain. Lumbering into his dark, quiet house felt like the purest sort of defeat. He grabbed a four-pack of beer from the fridge, collapsed into his favourite chair, and drank them while he stared at the television screen.

Maddie.

Nothing could take his mind off her.

Not even his battered face.

Eventually, Frank returned to the fridge for more to drink.

He dreamt of Maddie that night, as he always did. She stood on a bustling street corner, her long, dark hair whipping across her pale, gaunt face in the chilly wind. Her eyes, once bright with laughter, were now wide and haunted, pleading silently for help. Frank tried to shout at her, but the noise of the traffic swallowed his voice. He reached for her, his fingers straining to grasp her thin, trembling hand, but she seemed to be drifting away, her image growing fainter with each passing second. Panic surged through him, his heart pounding in his chest as he fought to close the distance between them. But it was like grasping at smoke. She slipped away, fading into the grey, unforgiving city, leaving him alone with an aching emptiness in his soul. He woke with a start, a half-empty can of beer still clutched in his hand. His face throbbed with a dull, persistent pain.

But that was nothing, really.

The true agony was deep inside.

Maddie.

He finished the lukewarm beer and stumbled to bed, her name still echoing in his mind.

Chapter Five

Frank didn't know what was causing his head to hurt the most. Was it the battering, which had blackened one eye, dented his already dodgy nose and split his top lip? Was it the beer that he'd consumed to drown out the pain? Or was it option three? Being woken by the irritating voice of humourless cubicle farmer, Chief Constable Donald Oxley?

Whatever the reason, he did all he could, which was take two paracetamol, and bury the packet in his pocket for when they'd worn off.

As much as he loved Bertha, he couldn't face her rattle in his current condition so he caught a taxi.

After confirming the destination was the Rusty Anchor, Frank clocked the driver, scrutinising him in the rear-view mirror. 'Everything okay?'

'Aye.'

'Maybe stop by the hospital?'

Frank responded with a grunt, and the driver knew better than to press it.

Frank hopped out of the taxi two minutes' walk from the derelict pub. His eye socket was throbbing to buggery, and dried blood clogged his nose.

A quick blast of cool November air was called for, and this was the perfect spot for it.

The Rusty Anchor was nestled in a shallow valley between two rolling hills, while the vast expanse of the moors stretched out behind it like a dark, forbidding sea. The pub's isolation had been a draw for those who liked to escape tourism, but it had also attracted unsavoury types who liked to escape the watchful eyes that operated in more populated areas.

Remote pubs such as the Anchor often attracted local families, and with that came historical feuds. In his much younger years, when Frank had been part of uniform, he'd been called to this spot frequently to divide warring bloodlines. When the Anchor had finally popped its clogs five years back, there'd been a lot of happy bobbies in North Yorkshire. That was, until the feuds and the scrapping started moving closer to home, and everyone realised it'd been better contained in the middle of nowhere.

The wind carried with it the scent of heather, peat, and something else: a whiff of decay, faint but unmistakable.

He stared out over the moors. Out here, the vastness of the landscape seemed to dwarf all human concerns.

His injuries... Maddie's disappearance... the dead man squashed into a cavity behind a brick wall in the cellar of a derelict pub...

Did any of it *really* matter?

Were we all just flotsam? Inconsequential? Litter blowing over this heath?

Probably.

But that didn't pay the rent. And murder really pissed him off.

With a sigh, Frank turned his back on the moors and trudged towards the Rusty Anchor, a decaying remnant of the past, holding secrets that demanded to be uncovered.

Chapter Six

As he neared the pub, Frank shook his head. The lonely, decaying husk stood in stark contrast to the gleaming police vehicles and incident vans.

He hated to be late to the party.

Early was best. Before the more inexperienced youngsters raced about at breakneck speed, making mistakes and contaminating scenes with their excitement over the potential of it being the investigation that would get them noticed.

But Frank was late here for a valid reason.

The pedantic prick, Chief Constable Donald Oxley, had waited until the last minute to let it be known that Frank was the Senior Investigating Officer. Donald had done this to steer clear of a debate over whether Frank could go into the pub.

The Chief Constable didn't want him in there. He didn't want to shoulder the responsibility of sending an ageing detective, so close to retirement, into a potentially hazardous environment. So Donald simply waited until the crime scene had been harvested before telling Frank, leaving him with no real argument.

After all, there was no need to wear a hazmat suit, hard hat, respirator mask and crawl through debris and grime, if the cellar had already been excavated.

Besides, there would be rats in there!

Once, Mary had pulled out the washing machine in their utility room and unleashed a hundred baby mice. They'd scurried over the kitchen while he'd stood on a chair, and Mary had brushed them out the front door. She'd laughed for days, but he was certain it'd left him with undiagnosed trauma of some kind.

Rats in mind, Frank now wondered if Donald had unwittingly done him a favour. He'd never admit that to the prick, though.

He approached a baby-faced constable standing alongside a cordon strung up between two trees across the dirt road. This was the only way in and out of the crime scene by vehicle, but you could reach it on foot from other directions. He hoped they'd taped off the pub perimeter but would give it the once over, regardless. Never assume.

'Are you all right, sir?' the constable asked.

'Aye. Reason you asked?' Frank knew full well that his injured face alarmed the lad.

The constable fumbled his logbook open. 'Nothing sir, you just look... tired... is all.'

'Tired? I've been at this job since you were in nappies, son.' Frank showed his identification. 'Knackered is my baseline state.'

The lad made a note of him. 'Have to admit, sir, it's a knackering job.'

'Don't think it gets any better.' Frank snorted and made his way in.

Up ahead, near the entrance to the Anchor, he spied a

group of suited figures. A familiar face detached from the crowd.

Familiar, but not welcome.

Jesus Christ. Here we go…

'How do, Reggie?'

'Bloody hell, boss,' DS Reggie Moyes said. 'You look like you've been ten rounds with Muhammad Ali.'

'Ten rounds? He wouldn't have lasted that long.' Frank grinned, but a flash of pain made him wince.

Reggie regarded him with concern. 'Are you in any condition to—'

Frank held up his hand. 'Let me worry about that.'

Not only was Reggie his longest serving colleague, he was also the longest serving irritant in his life.

It probably wasn't so much Reggie's fault as Frank's own. Reggie had a superb approach to health, and had what verged on a beach body, at least a mature man's version of a beach body – think Hugh Jackman or Tom Cruise.

Frank didn't have a beach body.

Actually, he didn't know what kind of body he had. He suspected there'd be a definition, but he'd no desire to know it.

Reggie's eyes were boring into him now, and Frank couldn't hack it. 'Look… I fell. Par for the sodding course for old men like us.'

None of the concern drained from Reggie's face.

But why would it? Men like Reggie didn't fall, not physically, anyway. Too bloody sturdy for that. Plus, he'd never wrap his head around any fall doing that kind of damage, unless it was from a helicopter.

Reggie wasn't relenting. 'Frank…' He was even using his first name. Unusual for him. A real sign of worry. 'That's not a fall.'

FORGOTTEN LIVES

'I bounced… a few times,' Frank said. 'And now the conversation ends.' He pointed over to a small tent near the entrance. A couple of SOCOs were milling around it. 'Have you seen the body yet?'

'No. Same as you. Only just arrived.'

'Thought you'd have been first on the list for excavation.' Frank suppressed a grin, knowing the pain it would cause.

'No chance they're getting me in there. Full of black mould, I reckon.' He pounded his chest. 'Can't run a marathon without these at full capacity.'

Frank rolled his eyes. 'Yes, was thinking the same thing.' He touched his own chest. 'Need these for the tobacco.' He raised an eyebrow. 'Still, if I remember correctly, this place was full of black mould back when it was open, too.'

Reggie laughed.

Frank nodded at the tent. 'Take me over, Reggie.'

Chapter Seven

As they neared the tent, Frank noted the acrid tang of mould and damp emanating from the pub, mingling with the fresh breeze off the moors. The SOCOs bustled around with purposeful energy, a hive of activity against the pub's dilapidated façade. He lifted back the canvas doorway and saw the skeleton laid out on the tarp. A suited woman was leaning over, examining the bones.

Frank turned to Reggie and nodded at the unopened bag in his hands. 'Lend me your suit?'

Knowing that you didn't lend a suit, as it would be disposed of afterwards, Reggie sighed and held it out. While Reggie looked around for someone to grab another from, Frank tore the suit from its packet, wrestled into it and ducked into the tent. An unfamiliar woman glanced up at him, her expression inscrutable behind her mask.

He nodded to her. 'DCI Frank Black. I'm assuming you're the forensic pathologist?'

The woman nodded back. She'd a mask on, so he couldn't tell if she was smiling or grimacing. 'Dr Nasreen Quereshi.' Her voice was muffled.

He made a gesture for her to pull down her mask. She did so.

Frank studied her for a moment, taking in her intelligent eyes and the confident set of her shoulders beneath the protective suit. She seemed young for a forensic pathologist, but there was a keen sharpness to her gaze that suggested a wealth of experience.

Frank knelt alongside her, most of his joints creaking, and focused on the yellowed bones laid out on a black mat.

'Who do we have here then?' He ran his eyes over the curve of the jaw, the angle of the cheekbones, trying to conjure up a face. Impossible, of course. The spark of life that animated this person was long gone. This was simply a yellowing scaffold.

Nasreen's gloved fingers traced the curve of the skull. 'Male. Pelvic bone and skull shape make that clear. As for age, well, looking at the wear on his teeth and joints, I'd go for middle-aged. Mid-thirties at a push. No older than early fifties.'

Frank nodded. The Anchor, in its day, had attracted such a diverse crowd.

Was he looking at a family man, or an old rogue, choking on a lifetime of sins? Frank preferred the more savoury of the two options. It would help stoke his fires and keep him interested for the long days ahead.

'I was told a knife was recovered?' Frank said.

Nasreen pointed to some ragged, splintered bone on the left side of the rib cage. 'Just below the fourth rib. This would have pierced his lung, causing it to collapse. And this one' – she pointed out another puncture, slightly lower and angled upward – 'went right into his heart. Either wound can be fatal. Together? Well, he'd have bled out in minutes, if not seconds.'

Frank rocked back on his heels. 'A frenzied attack. Sudden. Violent.'

'He didn't go quietly... no.'

'He's certainly been quiet since, though, eh?'

Nasreen took a deep breath and sighed. 'I was down there earlier, overseeing the excavation.'

'Brave. I guess I've you to thank for the good condition of the remains.'

'It was a laborious task.'

'How long do you reckon he was there?'

Nasreen shrugged. 'Look, in that space, sealed off from sunlight and scavengers. Stable temp and humidity... it could really slow down decay. The bones are dry and brittle but would be more so if exposed to the elements...' She clucked her tongue. 'We're talking years.'

'How many? Five? Ten? Twenty?'

Nasreen shook her head, sighing again. 'It's really hard to say without further testing, and I don't want to lead you down any paths that—'

'Best guess,' Frank interrupted.

'The discolouration of the bones – the yellowing – suggests significant age. The complete lack of any soft tissue remnants, even in the most protected joint spaces. I'd go a minimum of a decade.' She lifted a skeletal hand with gloved fingers. 'Ligaments and tendons are fully decomposed. Notice the misalignment in the bones of the fingers?' She clucked her tongue a second time. 'No longer perfectly articulate... so, I'm going to go longer than a decade, actually.' She fixed him with a stare. 'But it could be, potentially, much longer.'

'Bloody hell, the place only shut five years ago.' *How many punters had laughed, drunk and brawled here, all unaware of the grim secret mouldering beneath their feet?*

Frank narrowed his eyes.

Someone did this to you and walked free. You, left to rot. Them, with blood on their hands. Don't add up, fella, does it?

Whether this man had been a family man or an old rogue had to be irrelevant. Whoever this was had led a life. And yes, he may've been old enough to have made his fair share of mistakes, but...

Christ, how many sodding mistakes have I made? he thought.

With a groan, he heaved himself back to standing, his resolve hardening along with his ageing joints.

He looked at the skeleton.

Who are you? What happened?

A thousand possible lives, a thousand possible ends, all narrowed down to this sad, ignoble finish.

I'll find whoever did this to you.

Chapter Eight

As Frank emerged from the tent, his eyes were immediately drawn to DI Gerry Carver, who stood alone, studying the derelict pub with an intensity that seemed to pierce through the very walls. He knew that look well – it was the same one that had led to countless breakthroughs in their previous cases together.

Despite her intricate understanding of the physical world, Gerry projected little confidence and always looked rather lost without Rylan by her side. A crime scene was one situation that really didn't allow for a therapy dog. Despite Frank knowing that Rylan would never run off with a victim's ankle bone, there were many who didn't, and would be justifiably paranoid.

Approaching, Frank called to her. 'Gerry.'

She turned, and every single one of Frank's injuries burned under her clinical stare.

He tried to shield his face as if he was suddenly a bloody vampire hiding from the sun, but it was too late. She came towards him at a fast pace. Words were about to be had.

FORGOTTEN LIVES

He was readying his lies when he was blindsided.

'Frank?' Chief Forensic Officer Helen Taylor had flanked him.

He spun to face her. Her stare was just as stinging.

Helen had been his late wife, Mary's, best friend. Age had been kind to her, leaving only faint lines around her eyes and mouth, but at this precise moment, those lines seemed deeper and more pronounced than ever before.

He looked between the two colleagues, now closing him down in a pincer movement. He took a deep breath and stood up straight, ready to defend himself, despite knowing that without a steel cage, there was no defence.

Helen sounded stunned. 'What the absolute—'

He cut her off. 'How do?'

She grunted.

Gerry was looking him up and down. *Assessing* him.

'Look, it's not what you think,' he said.

'And what should we think?' Helen folded her arms.

Frank sighed. They'd both seen him in rough shape before, but this was a new low. Usually, it was just his excess weight and his dishevelled appearance.

'Three pints in the local and I ran into a lamppost.' Frank raised his eyebrows. It caused an unbearable pain in his swelling eye. He groaned.

'Liar,' Helen said.

'Bit strong, Hel. It's the truth.'

'When have you ever stopped at three pints, Frank?'

He laughed, battling the pain. 'Fair point.'

'Sarcasm never helps in making a situation any less serious,' Gerry said.

He looked at his colleague. 'Your assessment is complete?'

'Yes... I assume you've been to the hospital.'

'Assume nothing, Gerry.'

'Okay then. Have you been to the hospital?'

'Look, it's nothing that a few healing licks from Rylan back at HQ won't fix.' He moved his eyes between the two angry expressions. 'Now can we crack on... *please?*'

Frank already knew the basics. Ethan Crawley, a surveyor, had been assessing the site when he'd discovered the body. Donald had put an immediate hold on Tuesday's demolition.

'The council closed down the place five years ago, after deeming the site unsafe,' Gerry said. 'The landlord was Rory Calverdale.'

Frank nodded. 'I know Rory. He now owns the Whitby Arms. Not too far from the bottom of the 199 steps leading up to the Abbey. Nice enough...'

'Aye.' Reggie had now joined them. 'A real man's man.'

'What's a man's man?' Gerry asked.

'You know,' Reggie said. 'A man that gets along well with other men.'

'And how does he get along with women?' Gerry's brow furrowed.

'I don't know...' Reggie's face reddened. 'Well, I imagine? He's friendly. Married though if that's what you meant?'

'That's not what she meant,' Helen said.

Gerry shook her head. 'But what's the relevance of the term? Does it show that Rory Calverdale prefers the company of men?'

Frank had to force back a smile. He looked at Reggie, loving that the attention was off him for a change.

'Not exactly. It's more like... I don't know... that he's a bloke...'

'A bloke?' Gerry raised her eyebrow. 'But isn't that obvious?'

'It's a bollocks, old-fashioned stereotype,' Helen said to Gerry. 'Reggie is suggesting he's a *traditional* man, behaving in certain ways. Macho... manly...' She patted Frank on his arm and pointed at his face. 'Aggressive, perhaps?'

'Give over! Don't drag me into this.' Frank looked at Reggie. 'Could you bring yourself into the twenty-first century, lad? Stop winding everyone up, so we can get back to it.'

Reggie glowered at Frank, but then lowered his head.

'Good. Look, I know about this place. Rory inherited it from his father.' Frank nodded at the pub. 'Kept it in order, mainly, although there were a few skirmishes over the years. When he clocked how much it was going to cost him to settle the council's nerves, he shut up shop and used his savings to buy the Whitby Arms.'

'Done a good job of it. Truth be told,' Reggie said. 'The quiz night and the pool tournaments are a crack.'

Helen sneered at Reggie. 'Well, it seems your man's man had a body in the wall of the cellar.'

'Aye. It puts a blot on a rather good reputation,' Frank said. 'Okay, I know about the knife, but were there some other items recovered?'

'Yes,' Helen said. 'This way.'

She led the detectives over to a group of SOCOs, who were logging the evidence. With gloved hands, she plucked a plastic bag containing a comic book from one of her staff. 'This was in the recovered backpack.'

'You've got to be kidding me,' Frank said.

The cover depicted a cartoon image of Superman and Muhammed Ali engaged in an intense boxing match in a crowded stadium ring.

'Bloody hell, boss,' Reggie said. 'We were just talking about Muhammed Ali. Coincidence or—'

Frank looked at him and shook his head, silencing him. He didn't care about coincidences, and he certainly didn't care to have his battered face under the spotlight again.

'A middle-aged man and a kid's comic. Does that make sense?' Frank said.

'Men and women of all ages read comic books.' Gerry was matter of fact. As always.

Helen smiled. 'Stereotypes again.'

'Okay, I'm as bad as Reggie.' Frank grunted. 'A product of a long dead era. Forgive me.'

'And I read comic books,' Gerry said. 'In fact, I've read that one. It's from 1978. A classic. It would cost you a few hundred pounds on eBay.'

Frank looked at her. 'When did you look at the evidence?'

'I haven't.'

'Then how did you know the date?'

Gerry shrugged.

'Is there anything you don't know?'

She shrugged again.

'Okay,' Frank said. 'So could that body date right back to 1978 then?'

'Possible.' Gerry came closer. 'But probably not. Notice, it's in a protective plastic cover. People do that to preserve comics. Is that a label?' Gerry pointed.

Helen looked closely. 'Yes. It says VG- £30-BC.'

'This comic wasn't purchased new,' Gerry said. 'Most comic dealers mark the plastic sleeves with an indication of the comic's quality. And how much it's worth. I'd say this was bought a fair while ago as it's worth a lot more now.'

'VG?' Frank said.

Gerry thought about it. 'Very good.'

Frank nodded. 'Makes sense. BC?'

'Well, it's nothing to do with the year.' Reggie laughed. 'Pretty sure comic books were invented after Christ.'

Frank rolled his eyes. 'You think you can work your magic with this, Gerry?'

Gerry was typing notes into her mobile phone, nodding at the same time.

'What else do we have?' Frank asked.

Helen pointed out the backpack, which had seen better days. He looked at Gerry, hopefully. For once, she offered nothing. This in itself was more stunning than some of her revelations. They took a quick look at the knife, which was caked in dried blood. Finally, Helen pointed out *The Hitchhiker's Guide to the Galaxy*.

'I'm not a big reader, but I've heard of that,' Frank said. 'Isn't it a comedy set in space?'

'It's social satire,' Gerry said. 'A scathing critique of bureaucratic incompetence and the inherent absurdity of existence.'

Frank just stared at her. Gerry blinked back, indifferent to his bafflement and usual admiration.

'It was a radio drama first,' Helen interjected. 'Then a series of books. I remember grappling with the concepts as a philosophy student. That there's no inherent meaning to life, that we're all just bumbling through, trying to make sense of random happenstance...'

Reggie frowned. 'Sounds a bit depressing.'

'I don't know.' Frank spoke slowly. 'A murdered man, sealed away and forgotten, his earthly possessions a random jumble... Seems to fit with the whole "no meaning" bit.' He shook himself, trying to physically dislodge the morose thoughts. It didn't help that his head was pounding worse than ever, his tongue thick and sour from last night's booze. 'Okay, Gerry, you have the comic book angle, and are you able to produce a list of every missing person in this area that covers our age range and gender for the last forty years or so? Reggie, can you start digging into the Anchor's history?'

Reggie and Gerry didn't make too big of a deal around their farewells before traipsing away – Frank would be seeing them back at Scarborough HQ in next to no time, anyway.

He turned to look at the dilapidated pub. 'I heard there were playing cards down there?'

'They're all bagged up,' Helen said.

'Never understood cards, me. Or any games, for that matter. I always just feel pissed off when I lose. You think that's what happened here? Someone was pissed off at losing at a game of cards?'

Helen didn't answer. He knew why. After drawing in a long and deep breath, he sighed. 'Do we have to do this now?'

'You look bloody awful.'

'I always look bloody awful.'

'Never quite this bad.'

Frank joined his palms and shook them, pleading. 'I've got a banging headache, Hel. Please.'

'One day, it will be worse than a banging headache.'

Frank nodded. 'Aye, there's no greater truth! But it's the same for everyone.'

'No reason to hurry it along.'

'I'm sixty-four!'

'Be nice to retire first though. Eh?'

He shrugged.

'You were talking about it earlier this year.'

'Aye.' He wondered if he should just get it off his chest: *Yes, when I got Maddie off the drugs, but then I went and messed it up again, didn't I? Hid her phone because she had the numbers of a load of scrotes in it. Stopped her getting an important phone call. She felt betrayed and disappeared again. And now, I've no idea where she is. She's pissed off and living on the streets in Leeds...*

He decided not to. Burdening Helen wouldn't solve any problems. She'd been close to Mary. If she knew about this, she'd want to get involved. Immediately. And Frank didn't know if he could cope with dragging someone else into the cesspit of his life.

'Okay,' Frank said. 'I'll make you a promise... if you get off my back.'

'When was the last time you kept a promise?'

He smiled. 'I promise to keep this one.'

Helen grinned, shaking her head. 'Go on...'

'I'll look into it.'

'Into what?'

'Retirement! I promise. I'll book a cruise or something. Give myself a date to aim for.'

Helen wrinkled her nose. 'Believe it when I see it.'

'You'll see it.'

She shook her head, sighed and turned away. A moment later, she turned back and touched his arm again. 'You've still got a chance, Frank.' She nodded at the tent. 'It's good you care. That you stop these people being forgotten about. But I think somewhere along the line, you've forgotten about yourself, too. You know you matter.'

Frank smiled, thinking to himself: *Do I?*

Chapter Nine

CHIEF CONSTABLE DONALD OXLEY hadn't stopped shaking his head since Frank had entered his office.

After sitting, Frank was unable to hold back any longer. 'Just say what's on your mind, sir.'

'Fine. You look like shit!'

If it didn't hurt to do so, Frank would've smiled. 'No one else has been quite as blunt.'

'What happened?'

He wasn't going to use the lamppost story. He was bored with lying. It only dug him into a dispute. And to be honest, he didn't really care what Donald thought. He didn't respect the man. And, at sixty-four, he was long past buttering up his superiors. 'Someone hit me a few times,' he said.

'I can see that. Who?'

'It's private.'

Donald rolled his eyes. 'Can't help you if you don't tell me who.'

Don't want your help. 'I know, sir.'

'Stubborn as ever.'

Aye.

'Will it affect your ability to do your job, Frank?' Donald asked.

'Unfortunately, not. I'm running on full, and available for service.'

The chief constable narrowed his eyes and prodded his desk. 'Fighting could bring us into disrepute, Frank.'

Frank sighed. His head was pounding too much for this. 'I'm sixty-four years old.' He bit back the urge to add: *twenty years older than you.* 'Name me one time that I've brought the place into disrepute.'

'Your record is good, Frank, I'm not disputing—'

'However...' Frank took a pen and a notebook from his pocket. 'I could make a list of all those people I've encountered over the years who've *most definitely* brought the force into disrepute. Are you ready, sir? We may be here a while.'

'You're so dramatic.' Donald waved him away. 'Put your pen down. I only said you looked in bad shape.'

And any second now you'll be angling for my retirement, Frank thought. *You've wanted me gone for as long as I can remember, Donald. You're desperate to get a younger, fresher, cheaper officer through the door...*

Frank closed his book and slipped it back into his pocket.

'Before you ask, I've approved the team you've requested.' Donald's tone was triumphant, as if he'd worked really hard to pull this off. Nonsense, of course. The task had been simple. Frank had requested the detectives no one else wanted. 'Are you content with that?'

'Aye.'

Donald frowned. 'And I always thought you hated DS Moyes.'

'Not sure I'd use the word hate, sir. He's okay. He came good last time.'

Donald maintained his frown, making it clear he bought nothing Frank said. 'And you said DC Groves moved less than a sloth and DC Miller could suck the joy out of a room faster than a Dementor at a child's birthday party.'

'Aye, I remember.'

'So, why request them?'

'Because at the final hurdle they didn't let me down, and they won't do again. And I'm a sucker for lost causes. Not like I've ever been the most popular person.'

Donald nodded.

The pompous prick was agreeing!

'Well, I suppose you have Gerry,' Donald said. 'She's effective.'

'They don't get any more effective.'

Donald looked off in the distance with a confused expression.

'Something the matter?' Frank asked.

'Just strange... unexpected...'

'Sir?'

'That Gerry settled with you. No offence, but you two are like chalk and cheese.'

'We get on very well as a matter of fact. She gets me, and I get her.'

Donald tilted his head from side to side as if not quite believing it. 'To be honest, I was expecting her to request a transfer by now!'

'Sorry to disappoint, sir.' Frank tried to keep irritation from his voice, reminding himself that he didn't care what Donald thought of him. His superior was wrong anyway. Frank's relationship with Gerry had already proven productive, and he was certain they were developing a fondness for one another.

'You were always good at reading people, Frank, if not so good at interacting with them.'

'I take that as a compliment, sir. I've always been good at reading you, I feel.'

Donald laughed. 'Best we end this conversation there, DCI. Anyway, before you go... there's one more thing.'

Your wish is my command, dickhead, Frank thought.

'Rory Calverdale, former owner of the Rusty Anchor,' Donald said.

And Reggie's man's man. 'I know who he is.'

Donald raised an eyebrow. 'Go easy.'

'Easy?'

Donald nodded. 'Yep. Easy as you can, Frank.'

'He was the owner of a pub with a body in the wall, sir.'

'I know. But we both know he'll have nothing to do with that—'

'Sir, how can we possibly bloody know that?'

'His services to the community. He's done a lot for the police, you know?'

Frank inwardly sighed. 'And he's your friend.'

'He's *our* friend. The community's friend. Look, I'm not saying give him a pass, Frank. I'm just saying don't go in like a bull in a china shop. Do what you must, but professional, like.'

Frank frowned. 'Is this why I got the team I wanted so quickly?'

Donald shrugged. 'Professional please, Frank. All I ask.'

Something else occurred to Frank. He looked down at his fists, clenched on his lap. 'Sir?'

'Yes.'

'Have you warned Rory Calverdale that we're coming?' Frank looked up.

'Of course not!' Donald narrowed his eyes and slammed his palm on the table. 'Look, I don't know what you think's happening here, but it's nothing sinister! And here was me praising you only moments ago on reading people. Just be bloody careful. Don't drag him in wearing handcuffs. His bloody pub hosts our annual Christmas party. Think media!'

Frank stood and touched his head. 'Always.' He headed for the door.

'Oh and Frank.'

'Yes?'

'Clean yourself up a bit first.'

'Why? In case I end up on the front of the newspaper?'

Donald smiled.

While leaving, Frank thought that the retirement cruise he'd suggested to Helen sounded more appealing than ever.

If it didn't run the risk of making Donald's week, or even his year, Frank would have done it there and then.

Chapter Ten

Frank wanted another pair of eyes on Rory Calverdale during the initial interview.

Not just any old eyes, mind.

Frank was loath to interrupt Gerry, who was bashing away on her keyboard, tracing the origins of the comic, but those eyes were some of the best in the business.

He requested her assistance. At first, she looked hesitant, but then he promised that she wouldn't have to go anywhere near Bertha. She immediately looked at ease.

His noisy old Volvo really did unnerve her!

Frank signed out an Audi from the carpool, and they drove to Whitby. After parking, they made the journey on foot into the old side of town with Rylan on his lead.

The Whitby Arms was based near the bottom of Whitby's 199 steps up to the Abbey. Frank stopped and gazed at the stone steps, recalling a time when he used to climb them regularly with Mary and a young Maddie in tow.

Gerry noticed Frank had stopped. 'Are you coming?'

'Aye. Just giving a silent thanks to our Lord that we don't have to go up these steps.'

'Did you know, Frank, that the average life expectancy for a male in the UK is seventy-nine?'

Frank regarded her out of the corner of his eye, thinking, *Jesus, lass. Don't start up with my health again.*

'And that regular exercise,' Gerry continued, 'such as climbing steps, can increase that by up to seven years?'

Frank did the sums in his head. 'Fifteen happy years without, twenty-two unhappy years with.' He turned and entered the pub.

The interior was all dark wood and gleaming brass, the air thick with the scent of ale. Rory Calverdale, a barrel-chested man with a thatch of silver hair, stood behind the bar, polishing a glass. He looked up as they entered, his ruddy face splitting into a welcoming grin.

'Frank!' He came around the bar, freezing in his tracks when he caught an eyeful of Frank's war wounds. 'What happened to your face?' He'd a thick Yorkshire accent.

'Occupational hazard.'

Rory's eyebrows shot up. 'Occupational hazard? Looks more like you went a few rounds with a brick wall, and the wall won.'

Frank wasn't in any way amused, but forced a laugh, regardless.

'Would you like an ale, Frank?'

'As I said on the phone, Rory, it's not a social call.'

'A shame... I won't tell if you don't...' He wriggled his eyebrows. 'The Whitby Whaler IPA that won the Regatta Brew Fest has made an appearance.'

Christ, that sounds nice. Might just take the edge off this hangover and throbbing in his face. He glanced at Gerry. She'd tear him to strips afterwards if he accepted. He inwardly sighed. 'No thanks, fella.'

'Duty calls an' all?'

'Aye,' Frank said.

Rory went over to Rylan, knelt and rubbed his ears. 'Who's this fine lad, then?' He looked up at Gerry.

'Rylan,' Gerry said. 'And I'm DI Gerry Carver.'

'Well, pleased to meet you both. Would Rylan like a biscuit?'

'No thanks,' Frank answered before Gerry. He knew her response to this could be quite cold and dismissive. No one fed her dog but her. 'Is there somewhere we can talk in private?'

'Of course, of course. Come through to the back.' Rory ushered them into a small office, the walls lined with shelves groaning under the weight of ledgers and binders. He gestured to a couple of worn leather chairs. 'Have a seat. Now, what's so important that it brings Whitby's finest to my door?'

Frank and Gerry settled into the chairs. The leather creaked under Frank's weight. Rylan sat between them, his eyes fixed on Rory. Frank suspected he was dreaming about that biscuit and what could have been.

'It's about the Rusty Anchor,' Frank said.

Rory cocked his head. 'You know it's not mine any more, don't you? I gifted it to the council. Last I heard, it was coming down in a week or two, so they could build an information centre for hikers and nature enthusiasts.'

'It's not coming down any longer.' Frank took a notebook from his inside pocket. 'At least for the foreseeable.'

Rory leaned forward. 'Eh?'

'Look, there's no easy way to say this, Rory, but the surveyor readying it for demolition discovered some human remains in the cellar.'

Rory's eyes widened. 'You've got to be kidding me!' He slumped back in his chair.

'And they've been there for quite some time,' Gerry added. 'Most certainly back when it was trading.'

Rory guffawed, half a smile on his face. Then he looked between both, over and over, until the smile faded. 'Behave, you two!'

'Aye, it's true,' Frank said.

'Which part?'

'Not the main room. The remains were in the cavity wall between the two rooms on the left side of the cellar.'

'Really? In the wall?' Rory put a hand to his mouth, and his eyes widened.

'Aye.'

Eventually, Rory dropped his hand. 'Shit. How long exactly?'

Frank exchanged a glance with Gerry. 'Decades? Since the late eighties, nineties perhaps? We're still waiting to identify the body.'

Rory ran a hand over his face, his eyes still wide and not settling. He shivered. 'Fucking hell.' He looked at Gerry. 'Sorry... Are you telling me that there was a body right beneath me... all that time?'

Frank described how the surveyor had uncovered the body.

'That room...' He was shaking his head, still processing it. 'I hadn't used that room for donkeys.'

'Can you be more specific?' Gerry asked.

'It was a games room, of sorts. Except...' He was paling now. The gravity of the situation was weighing on him. It'd been a shock, but that didn't make him innocent. 'It was only ever really used for cards... poker... games... mainly on the weekends.'

Frank nodded. 'That would explain the playing cards strewn on the table.'

FORGOTTEN LIVES

'Aye,' Rory said. 'See... I locked the door to that cellar when I stopped the games... let me think...' He bounced his head up and down as he circled dates in his head. 'Wasn't the nineties...' He paused. 'Late eighties... very late eighties... I have August in my mind.'

Frank made a note. 'Is there any chance of a more specific date?'

'I'll have a think on it. Speak to the wife.'

'Thank you,' Frank said.

'Why did you stop the poker nights?' Gerry asked.

Rory took a deep breath and straightened up, looking more enthused. Frank had always known him as a good-natured individual. He'd want to help. Unless he was the murderer, of course.

'On account of that wall. It wasn't in the best of nick down there. Especially considering the new era of health and safety that was being ushered in. I shut off the poker nights. Was always planning to get the wall done and get the card games back up and running. But with one thing and another, it just fell by the wayside. I locked that door to keep the folk out. I was never short on space, and I knew the wall was shot in there, so I just kept using the cellar's main room. You know, I don't think I went back in there until the council started sniffing around. Would I have smelled that body?'

'Hard to know for sure,' Gerry said. 'Work had been done to that wall. The gap as it was wouldn't have been large enough for the body, so it makes sense that someone made enough space to get the body behind, and then resealed the wall. I guess, as long as the wall was intact, the smell could have been masked, somewhat.'

Rory puffed out his chest. 'Well, it wasn't me. Like I said, I never touched that sodding wall.'

'Someone did,' Frank said. 'Any idea who? I mean, they didn't do such a good job. It started decaying again, mainly because they left some of the older, crumbling structure in place.'

'A rush job?' Rory said.

'Precisely,' Frank said. 'You said that the council came sniffing around?'

'Yes. They inspected me. They wanted me to close it down until the place was safe. But the costs to get it back up and running safely were astronomical. To be honest, I'd had my eye on this area for a while now. Something more pleasant. It could get rough there and a man gets old, you know? Tired.'

Frank nodded, knowing exactly how that felt.

'I dangled it in the market for a while,' Rory said, 'But there wasn't much appetite. Eventually, I ended up gifting it to the council. They're going to put a plaque up at the planned visitor's centre with our family name on it, you know, just as a sort of tribute to a bygone era.'

'And you opened that door for the council when they did those first checks?' Gerry asked.

'Aye. But I smelled nothing, and I didn't go over to inspect the wall. I guess they must have inspected it, but they mustn't have spotted whatever was behind it.'

'The surveyor the other night had to do a bit of digging,' Frank said. 'Like I said, someone had tried to plug those gaps.'

Frank made a few notes, allowing time for Gerry to ask some questions. She didn't use the opportunity. By the time he looked back up, Rory was as white as a sheet. 'Does this mean I'm a suspect? Do you think I put this person behind the wall?'

Frank held up a hand. 'Rory, it's okay. It's still very early. We're just asking questions.'

Rory put his hand to his chest. 'I swear I never went in there after I closed it down. We always stored all the kegs in the massive room over on the right. I kept all my tools and whatnot in the other smaller room. I just kept planning to go back and do the wall at some point, but never did. Over the years, I kept meaning to do something with the room, but life got in the way. I was always so bloody busy.'

Frank nodded. 'Who else had access to that room in the cellar?'

'Anyone I guess,' Rory said. 'Bar staff. My wife, I suppose, when she helped.'

'Did anyone else have a key?' Gerry said.

'No... but I did keep it on site. In the drawer in an office behind the bar.' He gestured around himself. 'Much like this room... I suppose anyone could have got access to it.'

'Punters?' Frank asked.

'It's possible.'

'Is it possible you simply locked the door after someone concealed the body there and no one opened it again until the council came?' Frank asked.

'I guess. I couldn't tell you whether the body was already there when I locked that door. Since I already knew the wall was a mess, there was no need for me to reinspect it. If the wall had been fixed, I may not have noticed.'

'Would we be able to get a list of all your employees while you were in business?' Gerry asked.

'I'll try my best. I've some old ledgers somewhere. Can I email you later?'

'That would be good,' Frank said.

Rory rubbed his temples and then fixed Frank with a stare. 'Look, Frank. I love this community.'

So? Frank thought. *What's that got to do with anything?* He merely nodded.

'I've hosted charity events, sponsored local sports team.'

He was laying it on thick. It was like being back in the room with Donald.

'Your chief constable drinks here,' Rory said.

Frank suppressed a groan. *Here we go.*

He felt like saying, *How does that prove your innocence?* Instead, he nodded again. 'Back to the poker nights. How did they work?'

'Mainly weekend nights, since the early eighties. Anywhere between four and six players. There were a core few, but quite a few locals gave it a go at some point. They often ran late, after hours.' He winked. 'Different time. Easier to get away with a lock-in. You must remember, Frank?'

'Aye.' Frank suppressed another groan. 'I used to police them.'

'Well, that doesn't go on now... *here.*'

'Did you not keep a record of who played?' Gerry asked.

'Yes, but that information is going to be hard to dig up. I'll try.'

'That would be good,' Frank said. 'Could you give us some names in the meantime? Punters who played? Could you put that in your email about the employees?'

Rory nodded.

Later, after the interview, Rory tried to return to his usual jovial self, but it now seemed forced. Having forgotten that he'd already been knocked back once before, Rory tried to offer another biscuit to Rylan.

'Haven't seen you in a long time, Frank,' Rory said as they were leaving.

The reality was Frank had been opting for the Black

Horse Inn more and more. He enjoyed working his way through a bag of Wilson's snuff and gorging on Yapas – Yorkshire Tapas. It was also a place he'd frequented regularly with Mary and it reminded him of her.

'Stop by for a drink,' Rory said. 'On the house.' He looked at Gerry. 'Both of you.' Then, down at Rylan. 'Actually, all three of you!'

Don't worry, Rory, Frank thought, *I'm absolutely certain we'll be stopping by again soon.*

Chapter Eleven

Frank suggested they stretch their legs along the pier – it would provide an unobstructed vista across the ancient port's tiled rooftops to the rugged headlands and the North Sea's restless waters.

'What do you make of him?' Frank asked.

'Genuine shock,' Gerry said.

'But that tells us nothing,' Frank said. 'It'd been so long. He would've thought he'd got away with it. There would be shock.'

'True, but wouldn't he be afraid the demolition itself would uncover the body? Would he really have gifted it to the council? And, if he had done it, then surely he'd have taken the body out first.'

Frank looked at her, impressed as always. 'I agree. So, we buy that he locked that door and didn't go back in for decades.'

Gerry shrugged. 'It's odd. But not as odd as handing his murder victim over to the council.'

'It's the lesser of two odds,' Frank said. 'He was so defensive though, wasn't he?'

'Yes. Although you could maybe see why.'

'I don't like this Donald Oxley connection. Did you notice him mention it?'

She gave him a rare moment of eye contact. 'The intimidation tactic? I'm not blind.'

He smiled. He'd never heard her use that sarcastic expression before. She'd assimilated that from him.

'But none of that rules him in or out. We could just have a community-minded fella who doesn't want to be dragged through the mud. But, I didn't like the way that Donald was nice to me.'

'I thought you said Chief Constable Oxley couldn't be nice?'

'Well, that's what I thought. He's always seen me as shit on his shoe... an old piece of shit, too, you know? The kind that's dried on and can't be pried off... But today he gave me a team I asked for. For him, that's Mother Teresa territory!'

'Does that make you want to tread carefully?' Gerry asked.

A sharp wind bit into his battered face. He smiled, trying to ignore the pain. 'Tread carefully? Ha! It makes me want to shake the bloody floor with my size twelves.' He reached into his pocket for a pre-rolled cigarette.

Chapter Twelve

Frank admired the rugged cliffs and churning sea as he navigated the coastal road. Beside him, Gerry's profile was illuminated by intermittent flashes of sunlight that broke through the clouds, highlighting the determined set of her jaw as she focused on her phone. He suspected she was researching the comic angle. The interior of the car was filled with the faint scent of salt air. At one point, she lifted her head and looked at Frank. Thinking she'd discovered something, he shuddered with excitement.

'You need a shower.' Gerry returned to her phone.

Delivered with such subtlety!

However, he did a quick calculation in his head of how many days it'd been and realised she was right.

When Frank stopped for a traffic light, he turned and stroked Rylan's head poking between the seats. 'You still love me, don't you, fella?'

'If he recognises you,' Gerry said.

Frank sighed as the lights changed. 'You're really giving this acerbic wit of yours a whirl, aren't you?' He turned his attention back to driving. 'I thought we'd maybe moved forward from that friction this morning...'

'I really think you need to take better care of yourself.'

Irritation flashed through him. 'Gerry, you're sounding like a broken record.'

Her phone buzzed, and her screen lit up. She stared down at it, gave a swift nod, and swiftly tapped out a response.

'So the comic.' Frank was determined to change the subject. 'Where are you up to?'

The phone buzzed again.

He waited patiently for her to read and respond, drumming his fingers on the steering wheel.

Afterwards, he tried again. 'Any closer with the comic angle—'

The phone buzzed a third time.

'I give up!' He glanced at her, tapping away, making no effort to stop and engage with him. 'Unbelievable. It must be bloody important!'

She finished and looked at him. 'Why do you say that?'

'Well...' He took one hand off the wheel and pointed at himself. 'Your SIO here asked you a question, so I'm guessing that *whoever* that is' – he pointed at her phone now, but kept his eyes on the road – 'must be delivering some earth-shaking news.'

She didn't respond. From the corner of his eye, he watched her type another message.

Give me strength.

Eventually, she graced him with a response. 'Regarding the comic, I scheduled a call earlier. Alvin Prendergast. I'll speak to him in an hour. He's an expert on comics. The best I could find.'

'A guru on comics, eh? Good call, Gerry—'

Her phone beeped again—

'Who the bloody hell is *that*?' Frank realised too late he'd raised his voice. That was a no-go where Gerry was involved, so he lowered it again, quick. 'Have you got a stalker or something?'

She typed her message, giving Frank some relief that his outburst hadn't scared her. After, she said, 'Tom Foley.'

'Who? Is he to do with the case?'

'No. Personal. He's a potential new partner.'

'Partner?'

'Companion.'

Frank furrowed his brow, but it made his eye hurt to hell, so he quickly put an end to that. 'Like a boyfriend?'

She looked at him. 'Yes, but I don't like that term. Opposite genders can be friends without being in a sexual relationship.'

Surprises came thick and fast where Gerry was concerned. No doubt about that. 'So you're in a relationship?'

'No. Not yet. Still in the consideration stage.'

Wow. The consideration stage? Was this a younger generation thing or a Gerry thing?

'Well, consider this,' he said. 'The lad is keen!'

'Keen on what?'

'On you, Gerry, lass, *you!*'

'I'm not sure how you reached that conclusion.'

'Four buzzes in what? Four bloody minutes? He types faster than I can think...' He pointed at her. 'And no acerbic comments, thank you.'

'We're simply organising our second meeting,' Gerry said.

'Second date?'

'Yes.'

FORGOTTEN LIVES

He forced back a smile, the muscles in his cheeks twitching with the effort. 'Well, don't get all loved up on me, Gerry... we've got some old bones to identify.'

Gerry kept her eyes on him for a sustained time. It made for a rather piercing gaze. 'Love has absolutely nothing to do with it, Frank.' She broke off the stare.

'If you say so. Not a bad thing, though. It's kind of important in the grand scheme of things.'

'Is it? I'm merely looking for efficiency and reliability. Emotions complicate matters unnecessarily. They also don't ensure a satisfactory companionship.'

He couldn't force back the smile any longer, the corners of his mouth curling upward, causing his damaged lip to sting. 'And how does our gentleman, Tom Foley, feel about the lack of emotion?'

'I don't know.' Gerry's voice was even. 'That will be a topic of discussion on our second meeting.'

'Date.'

'Yes. I'll assess his pragmatism.'

Bloody hell, Frank thought, shaking his head. *The lad doesn't know what's coming.* Gone with the Wind, *this is not.*

Chapter Thirteen

Gerry sat at her desk in Frank's personal office, the late afternoon sun casting long shadows across the cluttered space. She fiddled with a pen, her eyes fixed on the clock as she waited for Alvin Prendergast's call. Gerry's mobile phone felt heavy in her hand. She waited until the clock ticked two minutes past the time that Alvin Prendergast had promised to call her.

Too late.

She called him. 'Mr Prendergast?'

'Yes... DI Carver?'

'That's right.'

'Oh, I was just about to ring...'

'You missed our appointment.'

'Did I?'

'Yes. It was at four.'

'Ah... It's only just gone four.'

Gerry didn't grace this with a response. Her lips pressed into a thin line. Punctuality was essential. If you didn't adhere to it, how could you hope to get anything done?

'Okay. Good news.' Alvin's voice crackled over the line.

'For confirmation, VG- stands for Very Good minus. Thirty pounds is the price it was, which would fit with its valuation between 1988 and 1989. BC stood for the original owner's initials. I was also right about the dealer that used this code format. Excelsior Comics. Alas, it doesn't exist any more. I spoke to Riley Thorpe, the former owner. Unfortunately, Riley no longer has the records for the comics he traded back in the eighties. However, he could tell me that BC stands for Bernie Charms.'

Gerry nodded as she noted down Bernie Charms. It stood out starkly on the white page. Was he the man recovered from the cellar? She guessed that wouldn't make sense, though, as he was the original owner. Unless he'd bought it back?

'I remember Bernie well,' Alvin said. 'He used to work at Charms' Comics in Scarborough.'

'Is Mr Charms alive?'

'I spoke to him over a year back.'

Definitely not his body then. 'Do you know how I can get in touch with him?'

'I do, as a matter of fact. You have a pen?'

Gerry jotted down the contact information, a sense of anticipation building in her chest. She thanked Alvin for his help and ended the call, her mind already racing with the possibilities of what Bernie Charms might know.

After thanking Alvin, Gerry contacted Bernie. His wife answered the phone, her voice soft and hesitant. She explained Bernie had Alzheimer's, but he still had lucid moments. She went to talk to him. When she returned, she said he was keen to help as much as he could and put him on.

Bernie came onto the phone sounding more jovial than she'd expected. His voice was warm and friendly, despite the occasional pause as he searched for the right words. One of his lucid days, Gerry hoped. He sighed, the sound heavy with a mixture of wistfulness and frustration. 'Superman vs Muhammad Ali... bear with me.' For a short time, the only sound was the faint crackle of static. 'I'm sorry, but my head really isn't what it once was. There was a time I'd remember every cover and every comic that I bought and sold in my shop. Sharp as a tack, I was. Photographic memory, my wife, Rose, said. What year is the comic from again?'

'1978.' Gerry could feel the lead evaporating, disappointment settling like a lead weight in her stomach. She looked up to see that Frank had returned and was sitting down. She sensed his impatience, but not from his expression – she couldn't read anything from his face in its current state.

He doubted the outcome of this lead was going to improve his mood.

'1978.' Bernie's voice was distant, as if he were reaching back through the years. 'And I sold it for what?'

'Thirty pounds?'

There was a lengthy silence, followed by a sigh. 'It's a bloody nightmare.' His voice sounded weighed down with sadness.

Gerry had an idea. She told him to locate a computer and google the comic in question.

'Look at that artwork!' Bernie's voice was now animated, filled with a childlike wonder. 'Muhammad Ali. I remember thinking that if anyone could beat Superman, then that man could... look at the definition around his torso...' He broke off, a sharp intake of breath echoing down the line. 'Wait a moment. I've had this conversation before.'

Gerry sat up straight. A glimmer of hope. Something in Bernie's weakened memory had been triggered.

'And he said no one is beating Superman, he said... Adrian said! I remember! Adrian Hughes. Adrian was a regular! Bought his fair share from my store. Nice guy. Quiet, but many were that came in. So knowledgeable about comics. Again, maybe not too uncommon. I remember him now. I really do!'

Gerry looked up at Frank. He raised an eyebrow, a silent question in his eyes. She gave him a swift nod, and he rose to his feet, Rylan padding along beside him, tail wagging.

'Okay,' Gerry said. 'It's going to be hard, but can you remember when you last saw him?'

'Ah... God. I don't know. That's hard. Let me think...' Bernie's voice trailed off, and Gerry could almost hear the gears turning in his mind as he struggled to recall the details. 'Yes, he did suddenly stop coming. I remember that bothered me. Let me think... why?' There was a pause, the silence stretching out between them. 'Oh yes, I remember. He said he was going to bring me a box of classics to flog at a comic convention that was... that was...' He clapped his hands. He clearly enjoyed remembering things. The thrill of recollection was palpable even over the phone. 'In August. We always had a comic convention in North Yorkshire that month... and, I remember, he didn't show, and you know what, I was disappointed, because he'd promised some right rarities in that box. You know, I don't believe I ever saw him again...'

'But August of what year?'

He thought about it. 'You know, I really can't...'

'The comic was valued at thirty pounds between '88 and '89,' Gerry said.

'In that case, it must have been August '89, because I started trading in November '88.'

Gerry circled August 1989.

Frank leaned over her shoulder, studying the notes she'd made. She glanced up at him, and he gave her a nod of approval, a glimmer of excitement in his eyes despite his battered face.

Chapter Fourteen

The hum of the computer and the clicking of Gerry's keyboard filled the otherwise silent office. Frank shifted his weight from one foot to the other, his muscles stiff from standing in one position for too long.

Gerry brought up a picture on her screen. A gaunt man with pale skin, slicked back hair, and a thoughtful, sad look in his eyes, as if he somehow knew the fate that had awaited him in a damp, dark cellar.

Hello Adrian Hughes.

'How old was he Gerry?'

'Forty years old on the date he was reported missing: 30th August 1989. He was a social worker.'

'Okay.' Frank leaned in, studying the picture, recalling those ribs, chipped by the knife, that Dr Quereshi had pointed out on the body. 'Let's get it confirmed with dental records. Who reported him missing?'

Gerry clicked through a few more screens. 'Moira Hennessey. Manager at Sunnybrook House. A home for children in care who are in the transition between foster parents and adoptions.' Her hands flew over the keyboard, her speed and precision an impressive feat. He knelt and stroked Rylan until Gerry had more. 'He started working there in 1980. Moira reported him missing when he failed to turn up for work on the Monday and Tuesday. She called it on the Wednesday.'

'Okay, we could do with getting in touch with Moira.'

Gerry glanced up at him, briefly. 'She died four years back.'

He sighed. 'Others connected with Sunnybrook?'

'We need to dig. It closed in 2002.'

He groaned. 'Over twenty years ago. Print out the missing person's report please, Gerry.'

They both read through it.

Frank underlined key details about Adrian as he read. Quiet... reserved... not much of a talker... efficient at his job... kept himself to himself at work and read comics to himself at break. 'Comics. Sounds like our man. How much of the investigation is on the system, Gerry?'

'A fair chunk. There's a flag that there's some more on the hard copy in storage.'

'Okay, let's get what we can printed, and I'll organise the rest to be brought up. Let's take a quick peek at the opening, though, find out where Adrian was last sighted, who he lived with...'

As usual, Gerry was already one step ahead. 'It appears he has a surviving older sister. Rowena Hughes. They shared the house they'd inherited from their parents together. Let me check...' Her fingers danced. 'She's still alive and in that same house. He was born two years after her. She's seventy-seven now.'

'Quick question,' Frank said, thinking out loud. 'If he lived with his sister, then why was it the manager at work reporting him missing? Why not her?'

FORGOTTEN LIVES

Gerry flicked through the files. Her brow furrowed in concentration. 'Because she was outside of the country on the week he disappeared. She was on some kind of meditation retreat in Thailand and couldn't be contacted. When he was reported missing, the police checked his home, but they found no sign of him.'

Frank nodded. 'Did they get confirmation she was in Thailand when he disappeared?'

Gerry nodded. 'Yes. Passport check.'

'Let's get to Rowena's then.'

Gerry looked up at him, her expression questioning. 'Now?'

'No time like the present.'

'Do you not think it best to confirm it first?'

'And wait another day or so for dental records? Nah. It's him. Bernie Charms? Reading comics in the missing person's report? Let's get a head start. After that, we can come back here and process the original investigation and call a briefing.'

'Okay,' Gerry said. 'But I need to take Rylan.'

He knew better now than to question this. If she needed Rylan, she needed Rylan.

Frank glanced down at the Lab, who was now sitting attentively at Gerry's feet. 'What do you say, boy? Ready for a road trip?'

Rylan's tail thumped against the floor. Frank grabbed his coat from the back of his chair. 'That settles it then.' He popped two paracetamol from a blister pack in his pocket and used the dregs of a cup of coffee to wash them down. 'Let's find out who Adrian Hughes was.'

He felt purpose enter his stride. Here was another forgotten life about to be remembered.

Chapter Fifteen

It was getting harder and harder for Mike Bailey to stay still. His back and joints would no longer have it. The sofa creaked as he shifted about, groaning. He reached for the towel to dab sweat from his head.

It'd been less than an hour since he'd last eaten, yet he caught himself looking at the fridge again. He sighed. The journey across the open plan lounge and kitchen was no small task, and he needed to get his blog finished. His audience were expecting a full account of the legend of the Cottingley Fairies based around a series of photographs taken in the early 20th century which appeared to show them dancing in a garden.

He tried to force his fingers onto the laptop but diverted them at the last second to the open takeaway pizza box on the sofa beside him. The pizza was gone, but he reached in for the unopened garlic dip. He peeled off the lid, tipped the sauce into his mouth, savouring the tangy flavour. Using his finger, he spooned out some of the remaining contents and eventually cleaned it out with his tongue.

FORGOTTEN LIVES

He threw the empty pot back in the box and shut the lid.

'You're fucking disgusting.'

He clenched his teeth and forced his fingers onto the keys and typed: *The photographs, taken by Elsie Wright and Frances Griffiths, caused a sensation when they were first published in 1917.*

After this single sentence, he closed his eyes, feeling the full weight of sleep deprivation.

'Come on,' he said, opening his eyes. The number of subscribers to *Yorkshire Folklore* had been flourishing. Now was not the time to let it slip.

He wrote the next sentence: *Many believed the images to be genuine, including Sir Arthur Conan Doyle, creator of Sherlock Holmes.*

The shrill ring of his mobile broke his concentration. 'Bloody hell!' Pissed off, he slammed the laptop cover down.

He reached for his mobile, sighing when he saw who was calling.

'Laurie.'

'Jesus! You answered.'

'Don't,' Mike said. 'You know I can't always answer.'

'So you say.'

Mike inwardly groaned. She was in one of *those* moods. 'It's true.' He tried to massage his forehead, but his fingers were slick with sweat and slipped back and forth. He reached for the towel again. 'How's Noah?'

His wife snorted.

He dabbed his forehead with the towel.

'Why I'm phoning, actually,' Laurie said. 'I mean why else? You're not interested in me.'

'That's not true,' he said.

'Whatever,' she said. 'And I'm not phoning because I'm worried about you, either.'

'Good. I don't want you to worry,' he said. And he meant it. With all his heart.

'That ship sailed when you walked out of our lives two years ago,' Laurie said. 'So, what the fuck is worrying going to achieve?'

He stopped himself short of apologising. There was no point. They'd been down this road too many times. 'Is Noah okay?'

'I don't know.' The sadness in her voice was palpable. 'Is there any point? Are you interested?'

'Yes, of course.' He put his hand flat on the closed laptop. His large, swollen fingers made him grimace. 'What's wrong with Noah?'

She sighed. 'Just the usual. A kid that needs a father.'

Mike needed to be rational. Calm. Doctor's orders. He allowed himself several long breaths before replying. 'He's got a father. I love him very much.'

'But yet you won't see him?'

His heart sank. *Don't, Mike. Just don't give in to emotion. Be rational.* 'He's a child. He shouldn't ever see me like this. I don't want that for him. How many times have we discussed it? Only last week, you said you agreed.'

'I've changed my mind.'

He shook his head. 'I won't poison our son... I won't destroy his memories of me.'

'His imagination is probably worse than the reality.'

'Is it though, Laurie? Really?'

She didn't respond.

'I can speak to him... anytime... on the phone,' Mike said. 'Now if you want?'

'Christ almighty! If that were only enough! Listen, Mike, he's getting in trouble. At school. He's hanging with the wrong crowd. Tilly said they're a bad lot.' Tilly was Laurie's best friend. 'Into drugs, apparently.'

Mike's blood ran cold. He reached for the towel and dabbed himself again. The towel was already wet. Needing a fresh one, he threw it away from him. 'He's a good lad.' His voice trembled. 'He won't do that. I'll talk to him—'

'Are you not listening to a word I'm bloody saying?' Her voice rose in anger. 'He wants to see you. You won't be able to talk to him on the phone any more. He told me this weekend that he thinks it's an excuse. That you're not interested in him. Part of me wonders if—'

'Don't say it, Laurie, *please*. Look. He can't come here.' Mike looked to his side at the pizza box and the empty sauce container, the sweat-drenched towel on the floor, and his fat fucking fingers on top of the laptop. 'Listen to me. You're not to tell him where I live.'

Laurie was sobbing.

Mike rubbed tears from his own eyes. 'I'll phone him later, I promise.'

'I'm running out of options, Mike.'

'Please. I'm worse now than when you last saw me. Far worse. If he comes here, it'll hurt him. Hurt him more than it already does.'

'I'm just not sure it would,' Laurie said, and then the phone went dead.

He sighed and looked at the front door, imagining what it would feel like to have his son knocking, desperate to come in, to *see* him.

The dread was overwhelming... as was his appetite...

He put the laptop to his side and reached up to the

handle of the bariatric rollator. After sucking in a deep breath, he forced himself upwards with all his might, exhaling as he did so. Once he was upright, holding both handles, he leaned his bulk forward slightly and panted. Sweat ran into his eyes, but he didn't want to take his hands from the handles, so he let them sting.

As he inched forward, leaning on the rollator, gasping for air, his legs trembled. The journey from the sofa to the kitchenette, mere feet, felt like miles to a man who weighed 215 kg. His heart pounded, but he imagined it as a frantic drumbeat urging him on.

After what seemed like an eternity, Mike reached the kitchen work surface. He grasped the fitted railings gratefully, allowing them to support his bulk as he caught his breath. Then, with shaking hands, he opened the tabletop fridge, and pulled out another takeaway pizza box.

Flipping the lid, he looked at the untouched food. He'd been thinking about it all day. He took a mouthful. The cold, congealed cheese and greasy pepperoni slid down his throat. The momentary comfort immediately lifted after swallowing. So, he ate at speed. Halfway through the pizza, his stomach revolted, and he gagged, fighting the urge to vomit. He paused, and when he felt well enough to continue, he ploughed through the rest of the food until the box was empty.

Afterwards, he wiped his mouth with the back of his hand and leaned on the railing, panting and shaking.

When the trembling lifted, he worked his way around to a drawer, from which he retrieved a worn photo album. With his clumsy fingers, he flipped through the pages, his eyes misting. There was Noah, two, grinning gap-toothed at the camera as Mike, slim and healthy, pushed him on a swing. Noah, seven, sitting by a sandcastle, while Mike worked a spade with lean, muscular arms. Noah, nine, holding a fish he'd caught; beside him, Mike, beaming, standing tall with a perfect posture.

Mike slammed the album shut. Painfully, he turned and leaned over the sink, his stomach heaving, and vomited.

Chapter Sixteen

'Absolutely, George.' Eyes wide, Phoebe Turner stood up behind her desk. She waved over Mandy Briggs, who was sitting on the sofa at the back of her office.

Her perky financial director flew across the room, wide eyed, mouthing her question. 'We got it?'

Phoebe put her thumb in the air and winked. 'There're children everywhere today who've you to thank for their future in science.'

She put the phone down and smiled at Mandy. 'One multi-million-pound STEM outreach programme courtesy of Soltech.' She made a ticking gesture in the air. 'Check.'

Mandy clapped. 'You knew he'd come good! You *said* he would!'

'Never in doubt. Have you not seen old George in front of the cameras? That blond quiff? That thousand-pound suit! He lives for the media. And helping thousands of underprivileged children to an education buys you a shed load of media coverage.'

'Can we tell the team *now*?' Mandy asked.

Phoebe smiled. As CEO of Brighter Horizons, she'd hit many home runs in the past, but none quite like this one. Soltech was one of the 'Big Three' – a major player. A bloody superpower! Thanking her team ASAP was essential. 'Yes.'

'I'll get them all together in the front suite.' Mandy clapped again as she left the room.

Phoebe sat behind her desk, eager to phone Brad, her husband. Her most staunch supporter. He'd be as nervous as anyone about the outcome right now. But it'd only take Mandy a minute to round up the team, and she'd want to give her conversation with Brad longer than that.

Her computer beeped. An email. Instinctively, she leaned over her desktop. The subject line on this new email was blank, and the sender's address was unfamiliar. Frowning, Phoebe clicked.

She put a fist to her mouth.

Twisted and charred metal. A picture of a burned-out car.

Memories came flooding back. The acrid smoke, the searing flames, the screams.

She squeezed her eyes shut, trying to block out the images, trying not to go under—

A knock.

She opened her eyes, sucked in a deep breath, and saw that Mandy was poking her head in. 'Ready?'

Phoebe stared at her. She couldn't speak.

'Pheebs?'

She felt as if her heart was about to burst from her body.

Mandy was now several steps into the room with a concerned eyebrow raised.

Get yourself together, Phoebe.

Now.

'Yes, just came over all faint... must be the excitement?'

'Stay sat down then.' Mandy gestured with her hands. 'It was an intense phone conversation. Let me give your apologies? I'll fill them in...'

'No, I'm fine now. This is *our* greatest achievement.' Phoebe stood. 'I'm coming.'

Mandy smiled and left. Phoebe looked down to see if there was a message attached to the image. There wasn't. She looked at the email: goodietwoshoes@hotmail.com. Who the hell was goodietwoshoes?

Who'd sent her this bloody image?

The urge to reply was strong, but she closed the email down. *Nothing impulsive now, Phoebe.*

As she left the room, she realised that someone had just torn the rug from beneath her, and she was all over the place.

Still, she wouldn't fall.

She wouldn't let herself.

Whoever you are, she thought, *if you think I'm crawling on my hands and knees to you like some pathetic fucking creature, you've another thing coming.*

I haven't operated that way in a long time now.

I'm a CEO.

Choose your targets more wisely.

Steeling herself, Phoebe marched to the suite to address her staff. No one was going to take this moment away from her. She smiled at her team, showing gratitude for their presence and their dedication.

'I just got off the phone with Mr Standish from Soltech. They've agreed to fund our STEM outreach programme in full.'

A cheer erupted from the gathered employees. Phoebe felt a strange mixture of emotions.

Tears pricked the corners of her eyes.

Was this because she and her team had made a difference in a society that was often broken and unequal?

Or was it to do with that burned-out car?

'Thank you, everyone.' She realised her voice was trembling.

She hoped they'd see a person overwhelmed by happiness, rather than one crumbling. Inside, she felt like she was being torn apart, the past and present colliding in a dizzying whirlwind of emotion. 'This programme is going to make such a difference for so many children. Children who might have never had the chance to discover their passion for science, for technology, for innovation. Children who might have slipped through the cracks, their potential gone unrealised.'

Twisted and charred metal. The acrid smoke, the searing flames, the screams.

She felt as if the ground might suddenly give way. Desperately, she tried to focus on the faces of her team, on the importance of this moment, but she didn't have long left before she'd need to find somewhere to be alone, to let the mask slip and the trauma take hold.

A toilet cubicle, maybe?

A dark room in the top corner of her four-floor house?

Anywhere, but here.

She forced herself on, finding words she'd used before in chaos. Relaying her vision had become such a habit for her. She hoped it didn't sound too rehearsed. 'Because of your hard work, your commitment, your belief in our mission... those children are going to have a chance. A chance to learn, to grow, to become the leaders and innovators of tomorrow.' Her words felt hollow, as if they belonged to someone else.

She clapped for them all. Everyone joined in. The sound rang in her ears.

Then, she made it out of the room, and their applause became a distant echo, drowned out by the roar of the flames and the screams that wouldn't let her go.

Chapter Seventeen

THE FRONT WINDOW of Rob Johnson's second-floor office overlooked the entire showroom. He tried not to spend too much time at it. It only seemed like yesterday that he'd been down on that showroom floor, *on the front line*, selling cars, and he could vividly recall how intimidating it felt to have the boss watching you like a hawk.

However, he couldn't resist a peek now, because *this* was unbelievable.

Derek Reynolds was about to close a sale on an Audi A8.

His third in one day!

Derek, his salesperson of the month, for five consecutive months, was cleaning up again, and how could he miss that? Besides, Derek didn't mind an audience. The man simply thrived on it.

Derek's smooth smile and practiced hand gestures fascinated Rob. He reminded him so much of himself when he was a hungry and determined twenty-five-year-old, revelling in that moment when you finally realised you were actually good at something.

Derek glided around the A8, the well-dressed middle-aged couple eating out of the palm of his hand. At a price point of over £80,000, the Audi was a significant investment, but Derek seemed to have the couple thoroughly convinced.

Rob again recalled his own heady days on the sales floor, and that first time he realised he possessed the power to persuade and influence people. From that point on, he became almost unstoppable, and then it was a breathless blur as he raced up the ranks. He turned away and looked at his plush office.

But it can't go on forever, pal. And one day, no doubt, this will be all yours, Derek, and just like it was with me, it will be well-deserved.

He walked to his desk and looked down at the picture of him with his wife, Sarah, and three children at Lapland, around Santa Claus, five years back, when the youngest still believed. His kids were much older now, and far less cute and naïve, but to him, they'd always be the same. He and his Sarah would always be there for them. Naivety didn't vanish in your teens, or even in your twenties. It just took on different forms.

There was a knock at his door. The frosted door prevented him from seeing who it was. Usually, Harry would phone up to alert him to a visitor, which meant it would be Sophie, his fifteen-year-old daughter, who always insisted on surprising him, Harry, his receptionist, happy to play along.

'Come in,' Rob called.

Sophie walked in. She usually burst in, laughing and announcing herself. 'Surprise, it's your favourite child!'

Today, she didn't. Something must have been up. 'That was a subdued entrance.'

'Uh-huh.'

'Was just thinking about that trip to Lapland,' Rob said.

'Eh?' Fifteen-year-olds were great with monosyllabic responses.

'The time we met Santa?'

'Random.'

He chuckled. 'Remember when you set traps for him on Christmas Eve because you couldn't believe anyone, no matter how supernatural, could cover the distance from Lapland to Scarborough in one night?'

'I don't think you'll ever let me forget.'

Rob noticed a nervousness in Sophie's demeanour. He approached her and placed his hands on her shoulders. 'What's on your mind, baby girl? Been a while since you stopped here on the way back from school. Usually, the world of TikTok is demanding your presence around now.'

Sophie's gaze dropped to the floor, her fingers fidgeting with the hem of her shirt. 'Tomorrow.'

'Jitters?'

'Yep.'

'We discussed this.'

'I know.'

'We said they were natural, but almost irrelevant, because you've completely and utterly got this in the bag.'

She shook her head. 'I went through the lines today at school. I'd forgotten some of them.'

'Standard.' He gave her shoulders a gentle squeeze and waited for her to look up and meet his gaze. 'In reality, you know the words like the back of your hand. I know, don't I? How many times have you been through them with me?'

'I know, but it's like when you're not there, I just forget them.'

Rob puffed out his chest, rubbing his fingers against his

shirt and blowing on them in a playful display of pride. 'Well, I'm an inspiration.' He was trying to lighten the mood.

Sophie cracked a smile, but the worry lingered in her eyes. 'What if I can't see you tomorrow night? What if you're late or you get called away?'

'I won't be late, I won't get called away, and come on, front row, as if you won't be able to see me.'

She nodded, trying to look reassured and determined. 'Okay... can we go through my lines now? Just once?'

'Of course.' He gestured to the chair opposite his over the desk.

Sophie reached into her backpack, pulling out a well-worn script. She flipped to a dog-eared page, the title 'Romeo and Juliet' visible at the top. As she recited her lines, her voice gaining confidence with each word, Rob watched with a mix of pride and admiration.

'O Romeo, Romeo, wherefore art thou Romeo? Deny thy father and refuse thy name, or if thou wilt not, be but sworn my love, and I'll no longer be a Capulet.' Sophie's delivery was passionate, her natural talent shining through.

Rob leaned forward, his elbows resting on the desk, fully engrossed in his daughter's performance. However, the sudden ringing of the office phone interrupted their moment. With an apologetic smile, Rob picked up the receiver.

Harry spoke on the other end, his voice hesitant. 'Rob, there's a lady here who insists on speaking with you. She's not an existing or interested customer.'

'Okay. Did she say what it was concerning?'

'No. Gave her name. Louise Parkes. And merely said that you'd want to take the call.'

Rob mouthed 'won't be long' to Sophie. 'Sounds like Louise is trying to sell me something, Harry. Tell her to leave her details, and I'll get back to her.'

'Will do.' Harry hung up, leaving Rob to focus on his daughter once more.

'Now, where were we?' Rob scanned the script, finding their place. 'Ah, here we go. Ready, honey?'

Sophie nodded, taking a deep breath to centre herself. However, before she could utter a word, the phone rang again. Rob sighed, a flicker of annoyance crossing his face. He snatched up the receiver, his tone clipped. 'Yes?'

'Sorry, Rob. She's adamant. She's insisting on speaking with you.' Harry's voice was strained.

Rob pinched the bridge of his nose, his patience wearing thin. 'If she leaves her details, I'll phone back, okay?'

'She told me to tell you it's regarding her father, Bryan Parkes,' Harry said.

The name hit Rob like a thunderbolt. His breath caught in his throat and the world suddenly felt as if it was tilting on its axis.

He shook his head. He must have misheard. 'Could you repeat that?'

'Bryan Parkes. Said you'd know.'

Rob was suddenly in a dark room, face down, pressed down, feeling as if he was going to suffocate.

'Dad... Dad...'

He pulled himself back from his vision, heart racing, palms clammy, and glanced at Sophie. Her eyes were wide.

'Put her through, Harry,' he said.

As the line clicked, Rob took a steadying breath. 'Hello?'

'Is this Rob Wake?' The woman's voice was unfamiliar, but that name wasn't.

His mind reeled. 'No, you've made a mistake... this is Rob Johnson.'

'My father is dead.' Louise's words were blunt, cutting through the static of the phone line. 'Bryan is dead.'

Rob felt the blood drain from his face. He gripped the receiver so hard his fingers ached. Sophie's eyes were boring into him, but he couldn't bring himself to meet her gaze.

'I'm sorry...' He shook his head, desperate for all this to be a figment of his imagination. 'I think you have the wrong number.' He put the phone down, his heart pounding even harder now.

The room spun, and that suffocating memory clawed at him. He focused on the Lapland picture, giving himself a fixed point, willing himself to keep control. Sophie had come to his side.

He could feel her hand on his shoulder. 'Dad, are you okay? What's wrong?'

Rob looked up, forcing himself to meet his daughter's gaze. Her eyes, so full of love and concern. They'd raised her so well. He hated lying to her. 'I'm fine, sweetie. Just a little dizzy spell. Nothing to worry about. I barely ate today.'

'Maybe you should take a break, get some fresh air.'

'No, I'm all right. Let's get back to your lines, shall we? You've got a big night tomorrow.'

Sophie hesitated, her eyes searching his face for any sign of distress. But Rob gave her a swift nod, insisting she continue. As she launched back into her performance, her voice ringing out with the passion of a young Juliet, Rob tried to push the phone call from his mind.

But even as he listened to his daughter's words, the

feeling that his fantastically constructed world was about to come crashing down around him lingered, and he was about to be dragged, painfully, back to those dark, *suffocating* moments.

Chapter Eighteen

Rowena Hughes was a dog lover who'd recently lost her beloved Cocker Spaniel, Daniel, and was over the moon to accommodate Rylan. She was a petite woman in her late seventies, with silver hair pulled back into a neat bun. Despite the lines etched on her face, her blue eyes sparkled with youth and energy. She welcomed Frank and Gerry with a gentle smile.

Soft afternoon light filtered through the lace curtains, bathing the living room in a soft glow. Carefully tended houseplants adorned the cosy space.

From the moment they all took a seat, Rylan had his head on Rowena's lap and was being petted to within an inch of his life.

'He can smell Daniel all over me, no doubt,' Rowena said. 'I only lost him last month. He's still very much around here.'

Frank nodded slowly. 'Sorry to hear that, Ms Hughes.'

'Rowena, please.' She stroked Rylan as she spoke. 'And it's okay. He had a good, long, healthy life. I'm struggling with the idea of another. No one could replace him.' She gazed into the Lab's eyes. 'Although you'd fit in here nicely, wouldn't you? Golden young man like you!'

Frank glanced at Gerry, wondering how she felt about having her dog's attention seized. She'd already taken out her notebook and looked ready, so he assumed it was fine. He imagined she found comfort in seeing Rylan contented.

As long as she doesn't feed him, Frank thought, *then things could get messy.*

Rowena was tickling Rylan under the chin when Frank decided it was time to explain why they were here, but she got there before he had a chance. 'I know it's about Adrian.'

Frank nodded. 'Aye.'

'What made you think that?' Gerry asked.

She smiled at Gerry. 'I've two senior detectives in my home, dear. And it's not on account of the money laundering.'

Frank almost laughed, but held it back. He wasn't worried about Gerry taking that at face value, but decided he didn't want to risk her quizzing it, so he hopped in quick smart. 'Aye, Rowena. We think we found him.'

She raised an eyebrow at Frank. 'Think?'

'Not confirmed yet. But... we suspect, strongly, that it may be your brother. I'm sorry.'

'I see.' She returned her attention to stroking Rylan's silky, floppy ears. 'How?'

'They found his remains at the Rusty Anchor pub. Do you know it?'

'Sorry, no,' Rowena said.

'Overlooking the North York Moors?'

She shook her head. 'Sorry. Quite a way out, then?'

'Aye.'

'Strange name for a place far from the coast?' Rowena asked.

'Someone connected to whaling founded the pub I believe. A long time ago,' Frank said.

'I see. Well, it's nice and scenic on those moors. Used to take Daniel. But, sorry, no, the pub doesn't ring any bells.'

'Any ideas how your brother could have ended up there?' Frank asked.

She raised both eyebrows this time. 'My brother? Adrian? My word. Adrian was never a pub going man. In fact, he wasn't much of a going anywhere kind of man! He barely left the house except for work. Shopping, sometimes. He visited comic stores. How certain are you it's Adrian? Would you like me to look at a photo of the body... I'd be able to tell you.'

'The remains are skeletal,' Gerry said. 'We will use dental records to make the identification.'

'Ah.' Her tone of voice suggested Gerry's usual brusque tone had taken her aback.

'Thank you for the offer, Rowena,' Frank said. 'But we've some good indicators. We've a comic book which was purchased around the time he disappeared.'

She smiled. 'He loved his comics.' She stared off into space.

Frank clocked some tissues poking from a box just off to his right. He'd be quick on the draw if she became tearful. 'We were hoping you could tell us more about your brother and the time he disappeared.'

'Of course.' She squinted, her voice faltering slightly. 'Was it suicide?'

She swallowed hard, her eyes glistening. 'What makes you say that?' Gerry asked.

'I just always assumed it was. Like I said, he was rather reclusive. He never really fitted in with society. It always felt like the most likely reason he suddenly disappeared.' Her voice was barely above a whisper by the end.

Frank nodded, his expression softening. 'We don't believe it was suicide.'

Her eyes widened, a mix of shock and disbelief crossing her face. 'So... someone murdered him?'

'The condition of the remains and the location of them would suggest so,' Gerry said.

'Good Lord.' A tear streaked down Rowena's face.

Frank plucked her out a tissue.

'Thank you.' She dabbed at her eyes with one hand while she stroked Rylan with the other.

'Take your time,' Frank said.

'I'm okay... just a little stunned. I'd always accepted he wasn't coming home. That someone would find him one day. But I suspected nothing but suicide. The thought of anyone wanting to hurt my brother... it's absurd, really.'

'Could you explain why, please?'

Frank noted that although Gerry's choice of language was polite, the tone sounded anything but.

'He was his own person,' Rowena continued. 'Very quiet. And very reserved. He read a lot of comics when he wasn't working and did very little else.'

Frank made notes – this tallied up with what his manager at Sunnybrook, Moira Hennessey, had said in the missing person's report.

'What was your relationship like?' Frank asked.

She stared off into space, considering for a moment. 'Good... kind of... He was a home bird, so he felt comfortable around me. He never really spoke at length about much. That was just his nature. So, conversations were rather short, and quite... what's the word? Functional? Arrange deliveries, splitting bills, and all that kind of stuff.

But we watched television together. Often, we'd sit in the lounge while he read comics and I read books. We had different tastes in food, so we often ate separately.' Her tears were heavier now.

'Do you need a break, Rowena, before we talk further?' Frank asked. 'A drink, perhaps?'

Rowena shook her head. 'No. I'm fine. Just the idea of murder. It's thrown me.'

Murder has a habit of doing that, Frank thought. *It's never expected, except, maybe, by the murderer.*

'Please continue. I don't want to slow down your investigation.'

'His manager, Moira Hennessey, reported him missing on Wednesday August 30th, 1989,' Gerry said. 'This was the third day on which he'd failed to show for work. He was at work on the previous Friday. August 25th, 1989. So, at the moment, it's reasonable to assume he disappeared over that weekend.'

Rowena nodded. 'I remember, but I wasn't here. I was outside the country. I only found all of this out after I'd returned.' Rowena explained she was on a two-week meditation retreat at the Wat Phra Dhammakaya temple in Bangkok, Thailand. 'I'd been away before, frequently, for shorter periods, within the UK, but this was a two-week trip outside the country. I'd been extremely worried about leaving him for such a long time, but he assured me he'd be fine.' She looked down and sighed. 'You know, he was a capable social worker. He didn't need a carer.' She looked back up. 'Yes, these days they might label him as autistic or something similar, but he was functioning well in society. He just preferred his own company. I'd no clue that anything like this could happen. And I needed those trips, you know? Still do...'

'I don't feel there's a need to justify those trips, Rowena. Like you said, he didn't need a carer, and you weren't caring for him,' Frank said.

'Hard not to feel some guilt, you know? I was his older sister.'

Frank, no stranger to the insidious nature of guilt, nodded.

'You said that you needed these trips,' Gerry said. 'What did you mean by that, please?'

She sighed. 'I suffer badly from anxiety and depression. Have done since I was a child. Meditation has always helped. More so than medication. The retreats in Asia are second to none. I saved for years to go. But other than that one trip, most retreats have been here, in the UK. They're much better these days. The world has opened up, somewhat. I doubt I'll go overseas again. I don't have the money for that kind of thing.'

'And you returned home on 4th September 1989?'

'Around then. I'd need to check my dates. There was a note to contact the police through the door. So, I did. Two detectives came straight to me. I didn't know what it was about until they told me. It was a weekday, so I'd just assumed Adrian was at work.'

'And what was your initial reaction to the fact that he was missing?' Frank asked.

'Stunned. This was unexpected.'

'What were your thoughts?'

She looked down, shaking her head. 'I'm an anxious person so I immediately jumped to the worst scenario. I told you before. Suicide. Where else could he have gone?'

'So, because he was reclusive, you immediately assumed suicide?' Gerry's tone of voice suggested she didn't buy that as a reason for suicide.

'Among other things.' Rowena sighed and looked down.

'What other things?'

There was a lingering silence. Frank glanced at Gerry to warn her not to press her again just yet. To give her some time. Gerry was too busy eyeing Rowena to notice his concerned look, though.

Then Rylan whined and lifted his paws onto the sofa cushion Rowena was sitting on. He raised his head higher, so it was level with her shoulder, and whined a second time.

Rowena looked up, tearfully, and stroked his head. She then smiled.

Rylan's keen awareness of people's emotions was staggering.

Rowena's fingers tensed slightly, and she drew a measured breath before continuing. 'My brother had been badly damaged by his childhood.'

Rylan whined a third time. Rowena kissed his head. 'Don't you worry yourself, darling,' she whispered. She eased him back down and brought his head back onto her lap. She continued to stroke him while looking between Frank and Gerry. 'In fact, we both suffered damage,' she said. 'Our father.' Her voice wavered, and she pressed her lips together, as if steeling herself against a flood of painful memories.

Frank's heart sank, but he tried to keep it from his expression and body language. 'I'm sorry to hear that. We weren't aware.'

'There's no record of any abuse,' Gerry said. 'And the previous investigation never mentioned it.'

Rowena nodded. 'That would be correct, dear.'

'Why didn't you mention it?' Gerry asked.

'I don't know,' Rowena said. 'This is the first time I've ever spoken of it.'

'Surely, you would've realised it was relevant?' Gerry pressed.

Frank could feel Gerry's pressure getting out of hand. 'It's okay, Rowena, we—'

She held up her hand. 'No. The question is fair. Of course it was relevant, but... the pain was still very raw then. I just couldn't.' Rowena's deep breath was audible. 'We experienced abuse in the fifties, and society wasn't what it is now. It wasn't transparent, and it was far less forgiving. We'd learned from a very young age to close it in, and keep it closed in. I certainly wasn't ready in 1989. In fact, I'm not ready now.' She stroked Rylan. 'If not for this young man, I think I still may've struggled.'

Frank nodded. The world had, indeed, moved on dramatically from that era. There hadn't been many places for a pair of terrified youngsters to run to back then. It saddened him to think that there'd be many people around here with untold stories like this.

Rowena continued. 'My father died of a heart attack quite young. I was twenty-two and Adrian was twenty. You try to convince yourself that you can bury the truth with them, and that you can't hold them accountable, anyway. All nonsense, of course.'

'Did your mother know?' Frank asked.

Rowena nodded. 'No one ever spoke about it, but of course she knew. But, like I said, it was a different time. She was just as terrified. The knowledge of what had happened tore her to pieces. By the time he died, she was a shell of herself. And she died less than two years later.'

Frank suppressed a sigh.

'I know I should have told the police back then... I know.' Rowena dabbed at her tears. 'I'm sorry... I just remember the police being so convinced that it was suicide, too. He'd a history of anxiety and depression, like me. And he'd reported suicidal thoughts to the doctor before. I stupidly decided it was best not to drag our living hell back up. All I could think about was letting him rest in peace. But maybe I was being selfish. In fact, I think I was. I just wanted to protect myself. Not have to talk about that horrible time. But I was so desperate for them to find him, so I could bury him and say goodbye to him. It can take a long time to recover bodies, they told me. Especially if he jumped into the sea or a river. I was patient. I mean, murder? How? Why? He didn't have enemies, people who'd hurt him... honestly. He loved children. Wouldn't hurt a fly. Unless he was working, he was here, in this house, with me.'

'But you cannot confirm that, because you were away?' Gerry asked.

'Well... no... but why would he wait until I wasn't here before leaving the house?'

'To protect you from something?' Gerry suggested. 'Something about himself that he didn't want you to know about, perhaps? Can you think of anything that would draw Adrian out of the house?'

Rowena shook her head. 'Apart from the comic obsession. Nothing. I just can't see it. No. He never seemed to have that drive.'

It's amazing what people can mask, Frank thought. 'Was there anyone at work he ever talked about?' Frank asked. 'Someone he got on well with? Someone he didn't, perhaps?'

'No,' Rowena said. 'He'd only ever talk about the children he helped. He was in awe of those children. The problems they faced and overcame. This was mainly all he ever talked about with me, apart from the functional stuff I mention before.'

'Did you ever talk about the abuse itself?' Gerry asked.

'No.' She shook her head to reinforce this. 'But it damaged him. The anxiety, the suicidal thoughts, his introverted nature... it all stemmed from that. I knew it because I felt it, too. Inside me. Eating me. Destroying me. The only good that ever came from our hell – if it's even appropriate to say that – is that we both wanted to help children. He became a social worker, and me a primary school teacher.'

'Are you okay with talking about the abuse?' Frank asked. 'At least regarding your brother? I understand if you don't wish to talk about yourself.'

She nodded, stroked both of Rylan's ears, and provided details of what had happened. The abuse had been sexual.

Frank maintained a sympathetic expression throughout, but inside, he was in turmoil. He wanted to scream at the top of his lungs and pound the walls with his fists. At sixty-four, he'd heard it all, but the levels of depravity that a fellow member of humanity would sink to still filled him with anguish and rage.

Afterwards, she cried.

He leaned forward, his head tilted slightly to one side. 'Thank you, Rowena. That couldn't have been easy.' He offered her another tissue. He pressed his lips together in a tight line, and nodded slowly, both sympathetic and proud of this brave lady.

He then looked at Gerry, who was feverishly making notes, glad she could. His shaking hands wouldn't be able to control a pen at this current moment.

'I always worried that Adrian blamed me,' Rowena said.
'Why?' Gerry asked.
'I was two years older. It was only after he'd lost interest

in me that he moved onto Adrian. I knew it was happening. Just like my mother did. Yet, I did nothing to stop it.' She looked up at Frank. 'Does that make me complicit? Stupid question, really. I was, wasn't I? A monster, too. No wonder I was too ashamed to talk about it.'

'No.' Frank shook his head adamantly. 'You were terrified, Rowena. A terrified *child*. It was your father who was the monster. And, as you pointed out before, it was a different time. A man, then, had so much control. A man like that would be hard to stop.' He desperately hoped he'd got through to her. He didn't want her blaming herself. The idea was unbearable.

'I used to walk into Adrian's room the day after it'd happened,' Rowena said. 'And he'd be reading his comic books. He'd look at me and wouldn't smile. Not talk to me. Not acknowledge I was there. He just wanted to be alone. With his comics.'

'But when he grew up, you say he felt comfortable around you, Rowena,' Frank said. 'That he was a home bird when he wasn't working. That doesn't sound like someone who was bitter.' *And,* Frank thought to himself, *he may've kept things from you, to protect you.*

She smiled and nodded. 'Thanks.'

Frank wondered what these secrets he had could have been. Undoubtedly, there must have been some. He had been in that cellar at the Rusty Anchor. Maybe playing cards? Definitely dying at the end of a knife and sealed behind a wall.

'How often were you away on these retreats?' Gerry asked.

'It varied, but I'd say twice a month was the average,' Rowena said.

'How long were your trips?' Gerry asked.

'Always weekends because of work. Friday night to Sunday night.'

'And when did you become interested in retreats?'

'I've been going since my early twenties. Still do. More regularly now I'm retired.'

'So,' Frank said. 'He could have been going out on the nights you were away, and you wouldn't have known?'

She shook her head. 'It's possible, but you know my thoughts on that.'

'So, he had no relationships? Girlfriends, boyfriends?' Frank asked.

She shook her head.

'Friends?' Gerry asked.

Again, she shook her head. 'I know it sounds unrealistic, but that was the case.'

'Was he ever late home from work?' Frank asked.

Rowena thought. 'Sometimes… but if he was, he'd phone. It would usually revolve around a problem at work. He was very conscientious. Looking back, I guess he must have seen me as a mother figure.'

Gerry continued pressing, and Frank allowed this. He shared his colleague's doubts that Adrian didn't have any secrets. If he'd had another life, then he could have kept it from Rowena. Late nights at work? Weekends unsupervised?

The investigators in 1989 hadn't found a body pocked with knife wounds stuffed into the wall of a disreputable pub. Suicide may've looked the likeliest option. But it was still unforgivable that they'd moved on so quickly.

People have secret lives. It was a tale as old as time.

The investigators should have done more.

Eventually, when it became clear that they were struggling to build on what they already had, Frank called time on the interview.

'You can leave him if you want,' Rowena said at the door, gesturing Rylan.

'I can't do that,' Gerry said.

Frank, sensing how literally Gerry had taken the comment, hurried in with a laugh. 'The station would be a glum place without him.'

Rowena laughed, and Frank saw that he'd stamped out any awkwardness.

'I'll let you know as soon as we've confirmation that it's Adrian,' Frank said.

'Thank you,' Rowena said.

While Frank walked away, Rowena called him back. 'DCI Black?'

He turned. 'Frank, please.'

'Frank. I never asked. How did my brother die?'

He came closer so as not to alert the neighbours. 'Knife wound.'

'Oh God.' She put her hands to her mouth. 'Did he suffer?'

'It would have been quick.'

'Who'd do such a thing?'

'We'll find out, Rowena.'

Rowena dropped her hands. 'He was a good man, my brother.'

Chapter Nineteen

Mike Bailey scooped up some snow, patted it into a ball, then began rolling it over his garden. The crisp, cold air nipped at his cheeks. Noah ran alongside, cheering as the snowball grew.

Eventually, out of breath, Mike swept the snowman's torso up into his arms and deposited it close to the patio door.

'Mike?' A female voice... Not his wife, Laurie.

Mike opened his eyes and stared up at Nurse Emma Holloway. She held a damp towel in one hand.

Blinking while the dream faded, and reality reasserted itself, he murmured, 'What's happened?'

'Cold compress.' Emma signalled the towel. 'You were asleep and boiling.'

'Ah.' He looked down at the open laptop on his large legs. 'Must have nodded off. Sorry. Shit. I'm getting more and more knackered.'

Emma regarded him, her eyes full of concern. 'Are you feeling any cooler now?'

'Yes. I'm fine. I don't have a fever.'

'I know. I took your temperature.'

'I should be freezing. I just dreamt about playing in the snow.'

Emma raised an eyebrow. 'A grown man like you?'

'You're never too old to build a snowman.'

'You know, I don't know if I've ever built a snowman.' Emma's Australian accent was more pronounced with her amusement. She'd only moved over here ten years ago, when she was in her twenties. She'd recently had a daughter with her 'Whingeing Pom' husband.

'Well, if you need training for when Rosie is old enough, look no further. I'm skilled. I could do it in my sleep.' He winked.

She laughed. 'Well, I suppose you just did! Who were you building a snowman with?' Emma asked as she readied the blood pressure machine.

'Noah.'

'Ah. Nice. I haven't heard you mention him in a while.'

Mike shrugged. 'Tend to just dream about him.'

'Why don't you tell me about him?'

'He's a good lad. Smart. Smarter than me, at any rate. And better looking, too.' He snorted. 'Believe it or not! I'll tell you what he can't do, though. He can't build a snowman for shit! Stands back and lets me do everything.'

Emma chuckled as she secured the cuff around his arm and began inflating it. The room fell silent save for the gentle hiss of the machine and the soft sound of Emma's stethoscope against Mike's skin as she listened to his heartbeat.

After a moment, Emma removed the cuff and made some notes on Mike's chart. He tried to read her expression, but as always, she maintained a professional poker face.

'Imminent heart attack?' He raised an eyebrow.

She regarded him with a disapproving look and continued making notes.

'Sorry.' He knew she wouldn't want to answer that. 'So what was it?'

'180 over 120.'

He nodded his head from side to side. 'Not bad... been worse, no?'

'It has,' she said. 'But still high.'

'Dangerously?'

She lifted an eyebrow.

There was no point in going over the risks with him again. He'd had the sermon time and time again. They'd reached a point where he wouldn't accept help. Six months ago, they'd told him that his risk of having a heart attack over the next twelve months was at 50 per cent. After three months, he'd quipped that he made it a quarter-way through and the nurse at the time had given him a right earful. Took him to task on his family and his pathetic attitude. When the nurse came again, he discovered that someone had changed the locks. Mike agreed to let a new nurse in only if they didn't pass judgement. Although Emma wasn't a fan of his jovial attitude to mortality, she was more patient with him and engaged him with humorous banter. And she expressed a genuine interest in him, rather than just condemning him like her predecessor had.

'Okay, you game for some exercise?' Emma asked.

'I've a hankering for beach volleyball, but the weather isn't up to much.'

'How about six miles around the block?'

'Six! I'll never be ready for the London marathon on your training plan!'

They laughed.

'Thanks anyway, Emma. I've been up and down a few

times already today. Like running a marathon these days, that is! Is there any chance I could get some more medicine to help me sleep? I'm knackered. Sometimes the aches are that bad. I don't sleep.'

'I'll speak to the doctor again, but I think you're maxed out.'

He sighed. 'I just keep drifting off while I'm supposed to be writing my blog.'

'That reminds me, I just read your latest blog!'

'On the Barguest?'

She nodded. 'I'll be on the lookout.'

'Don't be doing that!' Mike laughed. 'You know what happens if you see it?'

'You see that big, black dog on the streets and moors of Whitby, then you're cursed to die within a year...' Her face dropped. 'Sorry...'

It was the irony.

Mike's dying within a year was a strong possibility, without the Barguest.

He pressed on with the conversation so it didn't turn awkward. 'For what? Anyway, don't you just love folklore? I mean, totally unbelievable.'

'Doesn't sound like you disbelieve it in your blog.'

'Well, if I told everyone it was bollocks, the blog would lose its mystique.'

Emma grinned. 'That's disappointing. I like my authors to be invested.'

'I am! But imagine if I believed it! And I started telling you about its glowing eyes looking into my soul. Talking to me with a voice like thunder.' He made a silly, deep voice. 'Mike Bailey, your time draws near. Make peace with your sins, for soon you shall face judgement. Imagine that? Then, not only would you have to deal with a morbidly obese, depressed man with hypertension, but you'd also have to handle a stark raving lunatic. You get paid enough for that?'

'Certainly not!'

'Precisely. So, better I remain the realist.'

'If you insist.'

'You wouldn't have me any other way, Nurse Emma Holloway.'

The two fell into a comfortable silence, the bond between carer and patient a tangible thing. Emma finished her checks, making notes on Mike's chart. His condition was stable, for now.

After Emma had left, Mike turned his attention back to his laptop, his fingers hovering over the keys. But instead of continuing with his blog, he opened a new document.

A letter to Emma.

As he typed, Mike's emotions swelled within him, a mixture of gratitude, sadness, and a desperate need to ensure that his work would live on.

After, he read through the letter several times, but there was one paragraph that he went back to again and again.

> I once lied to you about those tales. There is more truth in them than we choose to believe, Emma. And I can see it clearly. I never told you that because I didn't want you running from my house. You've been a good friend. The best. And now that bloody Barguest had turned his glowing red eyes and taken me, I wondered if you could keep my blog going? Or at least find someone who could? These stories were never meant to die. It's just a thought, Emma. Here are the details, if you decide you'd like that.

He sent it through to his printer. He'd pick it up tonight

at bedtime, fold it up, write her name on the front and leave it with his belongings for when the time came.

Re-invigorated, Mike returned to his blog; the words flowed from his fingertips like water. He determined he wasn't quite ready to go yet. Not only did he have the stories, but he'd a son to reach out to. He checked his watch. He'd try to phone within the hour.

A sharp knock at the door startled him from his writing.

He reached for his mobile phone and opened the camera app that showed who was visiting.

It was Noah.

Chapter Twenty

Phoebe Turner yanked a bottle from the wine rack. She only realised it was the Château Lafite – the very expensive wine they'd been saving for a special occasion – after she'd pulled the cork.

The bottle would have been a perfect choice tonight if not for the email.

Too late now.

She poured a glass and drank it in three mouthfuls, barely appreciating the rich, complex flavours.

She did, however, appreciate that bullet of alcohol.

After refilling the glass, she sat at the worktop and closed her eyes.

Early morning. Dark still. She watches from the passenger seat, smoking continuously. Black sporty BMW. Sitting in the bastard's driveway. Another one of his many rewards for causing so much suffering. Her stomach churns. She thinks that if she keeps smoking, then she won't throw up. Wrong. She'll be throwing up long into the night—

Jolted back to the present by the sound of David's car outside, she opened her eyes.

'Get yourself together.' She took another large mouthful of wine and opened the front door to greet him.

Seeing him do a little skip in his expensive suit and shoes as he came up the drive should make her laugh. It took every ounce of her willpower to feign amusement.

David had his laptop bag in one hand and a champagne bottle in the other. He'd obviously forgotten all about the Château Lafite.

At the door, her husband threw his arms around her and kissed her. Then he backed away, holding her by her arms. 'My wife. No deal' – he clicked his fingers – 'too big. You're incredible.'

'Thanks,' she said. 'It wasn't just me.'

'I know. There's no "I" in team.' He put the bottle down, took her in both arms again, and spun her around. 'But you're the beating heart of the team. Everything you do for these children blows my mind.'

Phoebe knew David couldn't really care less about children. Never really had. In fact, he struggled to even tolerate them. He'd forced her to agree from the outset that they'd never have kids. Phoebe had learned to accept it. It would allow her more time to help others, and she could hold on to the man she adored. She knew he was genuinely happy right now. And his love for her also ran deep.

Despite the terror gnawing at her insides, she was desperate not to let him down. She wanted him to be happy in her contentment, and she certainly didn't want him knowing about the horrors from her past that had returned this evening.

'Started the celebration without me, I see.' He gestured at her half-empty glass on the table. She'd stored the Château Lafite behind some cookbooks in the top kitchen cupboard, having decided that she'd break the news to him that she'd opened the expensive bottle without him another time.

'I needed a little something to unwind.' She knew that her voice sounded strained. 'It's been a long day.'

'I bet it was. Getting George Standish to cough up! Fucking hell. I mean, how?'

She shrugged. 'Charm.'

'Well, let's crack open this champagne, order some take-away, and then...' His eyes sparkled. 'Have an early night?' He nodded and headed for the stairs. 'Quick change, okay?'

'Yes.'

She returned to the worktop, drank some more wine, and held up her fingertips to find they were shaking a little less. The alcohol was working. She closed her eyes again.

She grips the leather seat beneath her with one hand. Cold and unyielding. She smokes with the other hand.

Felix's front door opens.

He always starts early.

'Put it out,' Julian hisses.

She stubs out the fag. Slips down in the chair.

'Don't worry. He can't see us.'

Felix opens his front door.

Panic seizes her. She reaches over and grabs Julian's arm.

Julian clutches her hand. 'Look at me.' His voice is low and urgent. Long, parted black hair. Intense eyes.

She stares into them. She feels safe. Briefly.

'Remember,' Julian says. 'Remember why.'

She nods. He puts his tattooed hand to her face.

Felix is sitting inside the car.

'What's he waiting for?' Julian asks.

The front door opens again. A young woman steps out.

She tastes bile.

'Shit,' Julian says.

The woman climbs into the passenger seat.
She tightens her grip on Julian's arm. 'Stop it!'
'We can't—'

The pressure of David's hands on her shoulders, massaging her, pulled her back to the present. 'You're tense.'

'I'm tired.'

'You're trembling.'

'Chilly after opening the door for you.' She patted his hands. 'I need the toilet.'

She stood. He took her hand and twirled her so she faced him. His face had collapsed into a mask of concern. She stroked his cheek.

'What's wrong?' he asked.

'Nothing, honestly.'

With leaden steps, she went to the bathroom, heart racing, palms clammy. She closed the door behind her and leaned against it, her breath coming in sharp gasps. At the mirror, she stared at her reflection. Older, wiser than she'd been back then.

She splashed cold water on her face and closed her eyes. The memory surged again. Unbidden. Unstoppable.

She breaks away from Julian. Reaches for her door handle.

'No!' Julian drags her back. Tattooed arms are tight around her.

She opens her mouth to scream. Too late. The explosion rips through the night.

She stares at the fireball. Julian releases her. Flames illuminate his face. His eyes. Something raw in there.

He smiles.

How far has she allowed herself to come?

Yanked back to the present by the doorbell, Phoebe's heart lurched in her chest. She waited a minute for David to attend to whoever it was, and then, after forcing herself to take slow, even breaths, she stood up straight.

Pointing at herself in the reflection, she made herself a promise. *Enjoy this meal as much as you can, a couple of drinks, email back whoever sent the image, find out what they want.*

Feeling some resolve, now that she'd some semblance of a plan, she opened the bathroom door—

Her breath caught in her throat, and she steadied herself against the wall, her legs threatening to give way beneath her.

Talking to David... At the front door...
Fuck!

No. It couldn't be. She had to be imagining this.

'Pheebs!' It was David. It was likely that he'd heard the toilet door. He was coming towards her... and he wasn't alone. 'Pheebs... you've a guest.'

Chapter Twenty One

Rob Johnson sat on a weathered bench at the top of the East Cliff. The sun was setting, casting a warm, golden glow across the quaint fishing boats on the harbour below.

Rob closed his eyes, letting the salty breeze wash over his face, and thought about the person he used to share this bench with as a teenager. The boy with the infectious, deep, throaty chuckle that seemed to bubble up from his very soul.

Bryan Parkes.

Even now, Rob could hear it echoing across the years, and when he opened his eyes, he longed to see Bryan sitting there.

But, of course, he wasn't.

And never would again.

His phone buzzed in his pocket. He fished it out, saw Sarah's name on the screen, and felt a pang of guilt. 'Hey, love.' He forced a lightness into his voice that he certainly didn't feel.

'Where are you? Sophie said she left you over an hour ago and you were about to head back.'

'Sorry. I just needed some air.' He watched some seagulls whirl overhead. 'I'll be home soon, I promise.'

There was a pause, and he could almost see her biting her lip, the way she always did when she was worried. 'Is everything all right?'

No, he thought. 'A little under the weather.'

'Sophie was worried about you. Said you took a strange phone call while she was there.'

'Wasn't anything in the end,' he lied, momentarily jealous of the freedom those gulls were experiencing.

'Are you sure?'

'Yes. A little longer, okay, honey? Just another couple of blasts of sea air, then home. The Magpie for fish and chips?'

'That'll be good. Sophie is desperate for you to come back and practise with her.'

Rob's heart clenched. 'My shining star,' he said.

'Your *anxious* shining star!'

'She's going to glow tomorrow.'

'I hope so. You know how much it means to her, how hard she's worked to prepare.'

'I know she'll be wonderful... I love you, you know that, right?'

'I know, I love you, too. Just hurry, okay?'

'I will.' He hung up, staring at the phone in his hand for a long moment, thinking of himself at sixteen, on this very bench with Bryan.

Two sixteen-year-olds huddled together against the biting wind, the grey clouds above threatening rain. Lost. Both victims of those dark, suffocating moments. Unsure of the next step. But knowing one thing.

They had each other.

'No matter what happens, no matter where life takes us, we'll always have each other's backs. Yes?' Rob's promise.

'Yes. Brothers, forever.' Bryan's affirmation.

It had been twenty-five years since they'd last spoken.

Too late now to talk again.

With a heavy sigh, he looked at the phone number he'd scribbled on the back of one of his own cards. A number he'd grabbed from Harry after Sophie had left.

He dialled it.

'Louise?'

'Yes... you called back.' She sounded excited.

'You knew I would.'

'I wasn't sure. I mean, Dad told me you'd be surprised at first, and then you'd come round, but after your reaction, well, I wasn't sure.'

'I'm sorry.'

'Don't be.'

'Your dad was like a brother to me.'

'He said the same about you.'

'We had a bench we used to sit on when we were young on East Cliff. I'll drop you a pin, okay?'

'Yes.'

Afterwards, she texted that she'd be twenty minutes.

A happy family walked past, the parents swinging their laughing child between them. Rob watched them go, a bittersweet smile tugging at his lips. He pondered whether that father or mother held terrible secrets, if their perfect life was merely a disguise, just like his own. Hiding a battlefield of dark, suffocating moments far back in the mists of time.

Chapter Twenty-Two

During the past months, whenever the day started to wind down, Frank would deliberately start winding himself up, readying himself for those nightly jaunts to try and find Maddie.

However, last night's shit show had left him worse for wear, and he needed to conserve some energy for discovering the truth behind Adrian's death. He'd decided to take a step back from prowling the streets of Leeds for the foreseeable future, unless he heard something from any of his old colleagues monitoring the underbelly of the city.

Still, even with this promise made to himself, he felt anything but calm.

He stared up at the picture of Adrian pinned on the board in the incident room. There was now a narrative behind that sad, haunted look in his gaze. Frank's heart clenched as he recalled Rowena's descriptions of what their father had done.

Cold cruelty from someone who should love you. From someone you should be able to trust more than anyone else.

Did it get any more unjust than that?

'I've got you something, Rylan.' It was Reggie, making his usual 'I'm here, everyone!' entrance.

A chewy toy bone suddenly bounced off the wall beside Frank.

'You've got to be bloody kidding me,' Frank muttered.

He turned in time to see Rylan returning to Reggie with his new toy.

Reggie patted his thighs and Rylan climbed up him so Reggie could pluck the toy from his mouth.

'*Seriously?*' Frank asked.

Reggie shrugged, smiling. His teeth glowing as always. 'Sorry, boss.' He stroked the Lab. 'I missed the fella.'

'If you throw anything across the incident room, then you'll need to prepare to miss him even more. Maybe, forever more.'

Reggie's face reddened. He wandered over and offered the toy to Gerry. She looked down at it and up at him. 'He has three toys. All of them quality assured so there're no chemicals and robust enough to not carry any choking risk.'

'It cost me eight quid.' Reggie proffered the item.

Gerry turned her attention back to her computer screen.

'I hope you kept the receipt,' Frank said.

Frank had wanted to start their briefing positively. Human wrecking-ball Reggie had put paid to that.

He surveyed his team, his gaze lingering on each member in turn. Detective Constable Sharon Miller, with her vibrant red hair pulled back in a neat ponytail, met Frank's gaze head-on, a flicker of determination in her sharp green eyes. In contrast, DC Sean Groves seemed to shrink in on himself, his shoulders hunched and his gaze downcast, sandy blond hair hanging limply over his forehead.

Sharon had grown so much since their last case

together, her confidence blooming. Sean, though, seemed unsure of himself, hesitant. Frank made a mental note to take the lad under his wing, to nurture the potential he saw glimmering beneath the surface. Including Reggie, these were the officers that no one else wanted. Donald Oxley had spitefully assigned him these officers on the last case, but against all odds, they'd delivered and impressed him.

They may've been the ones no one else wanted, but they were the ones he'd specifically asked for. They were his team. His responsibility. And he'd be damned if he let them down.

They were already up to date on the discovery of the body, but he glossed over it quickly, anyway, as it was their first meeting.

'Just over an hour ago, we had confirmation regarding the dental records that this was Adrian Hughes. Lightning fast, I know.' He looked up. 'Someone's smiling down on us for once... Adrian was working at Sunnybrook House on 25th August 1989, but didn't turn up on the 28th or the 29th. Moira Hennessey, now deceased, reported him missing on Wednesday the 30th. Between those dates, more than likely sometime between Friday night and Sunday night, someone stabbed him twice.' He pointed at the photograph of the rusty blade. 'And then concealed him behind the wall of the cellar in the Rusty Anchor.' He moved his finger across to the wall. 'Whoever did it filled it in with new mortar and bricks.'

'A long night,' Reggie said.

'Why do you presume night?' Frank asked.

'To keep it off Rory's radar.'

Frank fixed him with a stare. 'Unless it *was* Rory Calverdale? In which case, he could take his time. He could just keep that door locked until he'd fixed the wall. What better time to call an end to the card games in the cellar, giving himself some space?'

'Donald Oxley won't like us looking at Rory. They're close. And Rory does a lot for the community.'

'Does that bother you, Reggie?' Frank's eyes narrowed.

Reggie reddened. 'No, I was just pointing it out like.'

'Is this going to be a problem for anyone?' Frank looked at their faces. 'Any other close friendships I should know about?'

Everyone shook their heads simultaneously.

'Good,' Frank said. 'I couldn't give a monkey's about Oxley's warning. I don't care if Calverdale is raising enough money to turn Whitby into the capital of Yorkshire, I'll enjoy arresting him. This in mind, I, personally, will keep tabs on Rory. I'll stop by first thing tomorrow and find out if he knew Adrian, for starters.'

He pointed out a picture of Adrian's sister. 'Rowena Hughes was out of the country on the dates in question. We've confirmed this with passport control. She was back on Monday 4th September. Both Gerry and I found Rowena genuine. She painted a picture of a reclusive individual that lost himself in comics and only really left the house to go to work at Sunnybrook, or do a spot of shopping for food or comics. I really think she's telling the truth and believes this. We read nothing in her demeanour that suggests otherwise.'

'But something is off here. He'd gone from a reclusive home bird, to the cellar wall in a disreputable pub. He could have been gambling. What other reason did he have to be down there? Also, he was stabbed twice. Now, Rowena was away a lot. Meditation retreats around the UK in which she'd be gone on a Friday and Saturday night, sometimes twice a month. This gave Adrian ample opportunity to conduct himself differently away from his sister's eyes.'

'Wouldn't such secrecy suggest he may've been up to no good?' Sharon's tone was inquisitive, not judgemental.

'It's a possibility,' Frank said. 'There's something else we need to consider, too.' He sighed and looked down. 'Rowena described how her father sexually abused both her and her brother when they were children.'

When he raised his head, he panned his gaze between their saddened expressions. The weight of Adrian's suffering seemed to settle over the room like a pall.

After he described what Rowena had told him, he said, 'So, there're psychological issues at play here. She referred to Adrian as "damaged" and from what we're hearing, he looked to her for support. Almost like a parental figure. Maybe he felt contented and at ease in her presence. But in her absence... well...' He turned and looked at him on the board. 'Something was happening. Maybe someone else was involved? Maybe he'd someone else to lean on? Someone who was leading him astray?'

Gerry said, 'Often, when people suffer abuse of this nature, they become more vulnerable, and more trusting – of the wrong people.'

Frank turned and nodded. 'We need to find out who Adrian was associating with around this period, other than his sister. So, these are my proposals for tomorrow. Sharon, I'd like you to dig into his social work at Sunnybrook House. The place is long closed, and several employees dead, but there's no doubt he will have encountered many people in his career. Both the children he supported, and the colleagues he worked with.'

She nodded and made a note. She definitely appeared more enthusiastic than she'd done in the last case.

'Tonight, if possible, I'd like everyone to read through the investigation at the back end of 1989 and email any thoughts to Sean, patching me in. Sean, if anything comes to light, please follow up on it.'

Unfortunately, Sean didn't look as enthusiastic as Sharon, and Frank hated the way he slumped in his chair. But this investigation would be a chance for Sean to prove his worth. Frank caught Sean's eye, holding his gaze until the lad straightened in his seat. *There was steel in that one,* Frank reckoned. *Somewhere.*

'Reggie, you've the list emailed in by Rory. Of all those he can remember playing cards with during that era, and people who worked the bar. Could you work your way through the list, referencing Adrian Hughes and see what you get back?'

Reggie nodded. 'Aye.'

'Meanwhile, Gerry and I will continue to follow the evidence. As I said before, we'll start with Rory again. See if he can shed any light on what might've been going on under his nose all those years ago.' He turned and looked at Adrian again and sighed. He let a short silence descend before looking back at his team. 'I feel that we failed Adrian Hughes as a child. The fifties were different, aye, more invisible, no question, but we should still accept some guilt. He was abused and broken, and no one lifted a finger to help him. Then, he dedicates himself to helping other children. If we can offer him something, anything, regarding what happened to him in August 1989, we need to snap at the opportunity, okay?'

His team nodded and made sounds of approval.

Good, Frank thought. *This is for another forgotten life who slipped through the cracks.*

Chapter Twenty-Three

After everyone apart from Gerry and Rylan had left the incident room, Frank's phone buzzed.

He answered. 'Helen. How do?'

'Still on your feet?' There was a teasing lilt to her voice.

He grunted. 'Why shouldn't I be?'

'Well, when I saw you, you looked in need of the emergency room.' She tried to keep her voice humorous, but it was clear she didn't consider this a laughing matter.

'I've the heart of an ox.'

'Ox doesn't live forever... Anyway, good news.'

'One of Hel's Bells?'

A running joke between them, a nod to the countless times Helen's findings had been the key to cracking a case wide open.

'Time will tell. We found something on that paperback cover – *The Hitchhiker's Guide to the Galaxy*. There were indentations on the pages. Looks like Adrian was using the book as a makeshift writing surface. We enhanced the impression. You got a pen?'

'Aye. Go on.'

'Moonrise. Fri. Mar 24.'

Frank's mind raced as he scribbled. 'Sounds like a hotel booking.'

'That'd be my guess,' Helen said. 'Over to you now. I'll email the image, too.'

'Thanks Hel. I really appreciate it.'

'Look after yourself, Frank.' There was a softness to her voice now.

'You know, I never knew how many people cared.'

'Because you're pig ignorant – you always have been.' And then, with those stern words, she was gone.

He immediately went over to Gerry with the information. She messed around with the name Moonrise for a while on Google, Frank watching on.

'Here we go. A small place. The Moonrise Hotel. Based in Scarborough. Twenty-five rooms.'

'Let me.' Frank reached for the phone on the desk.

She nodded, stood and plucked her jacket from the back of the chair.

He raised an eyebrow. 'Eh? Early for you, isn't it?'

'I've a meeting.'

'Another date?'

'Yes.'

'Two in two nights? Getting serious with Tommy boy then?' Frank wondered if he was teasing her because he'd just been teased by Helen.

'It's Tom. And serious? What do you mean by serious, exactly?'

Frank shrugged. 'You're becoming involved, I guess.'

She still looked confused.

'Romantically,' he added.

'You have it wrong, Frank. I'm serious, yes, but only

about assessing suitability. Only then would I become romantically involved.'

Clinical as always. Frank shook his head. 'You know I gave you homework to re-read the investigation?'

'Yes. I've read the investigation several times, anyway. I emailed my thoughts to Sean just before.'

Of course she had.

'Brilliant... I guess it's good for you to have a social life. I mean... the all-nighters here were good, the stuff you uncovered, but socialising is important...'

'My date is *only* ninety minutes,' Gerry said. 'We will discuss our day, and then I want to find out more about his family. Although I've little remaining family, family can be important in stable relationships. I want to know what his family dynamics are. If they've the potential to be a hindrance, I'll shorten the date. Whatever happens, I'll work for at least four hours this evening.' Frank marvelled at her ability to compartmentalise. To schedule her life down to the minute.

'I remember.' He nodded. 'You only need four hours' sleep.'

She returned his nod and left.

Phone already in hand, Frank dialled the number of the hotel that Adrian had potentially written on his book cover.

'Moonrise Hotel. How may I assist you?' The voice on the other end was young and chipper, the sort of customer service cheer that set Frank's teeth on edge.

'This is DCI Frank Black with the Scarborough Police. I need to speak with your manager, please.'

There was a brief pause, followed by a shuffling sound. 'One moment, please.'

Frank waited, his impatience growing with each passing

second. Finally, another voice came on the line, older and more authoritative.

'This is Emily Hargreaves, the managing director. How can I help you, DCI Black?'

Frank leaned forward, his free hand clenching into a fist. He could feel the familiar thrum of adrenaline, the rush of a new lead. 'I'm investigating a crime that happened in 1989. I want to know if an individual stayed at your establishment on the night of Friday, 24th March 1989.'

There was a long pause. Frank could hear the faint sound of keys clacking, the rustling of papers. The wait was excruciating. His heart raced in his chest as he willed her to find something, *anything*, regarding Adrian.

'1989, you said?' Emily's voice was hesitant. 'I'm afraid our record keeping doesn't stretch back that far. At least in this system. We've changed ownership several times over the years, and not all the previous management was as diligent as they should have been.'

Frank bit back a curse. Of course it couldn't be that easy. It never was. 'Anything you can find, Ms Hargreaves. Even the smallest detail could be important.'

'Of course, I understand. Can you give me the evening to speak with the owners and see what we can dig up? I'll be in touch as soon as I have something. Can I take the name of the individual concerned?'

'Adrian Hughes.'

'Thanks. I'll try my hardest.'

'Appreciated.' He hung up, leaning back in his chair with a heavy sigh. The weight seemed to settle more heavily on his shoulders with each passing moment. Another lead, another waiting game. But he'd play it for as long as it took.

Chapter Twenty-Four

Heart pounding, Mike watched Noah on his mobile phone screen. Noah was on his doorstep, wearing a black hoodie, ripped jeans, and scuffed sneakers, alternating between pressing the doorbell and knocking firmly. He hunched his shoulders, clenched his jaw, and radiated tension from every line of his body.

Mike squeezed his eyes closed and shook his phone in his hand. Laurie must have given him his address. Why hadn't she listened to him? What the hell was he supposed to do now?

If Emma was here to take Mike's blood pressure in this moment, she'd call an ambulance!

When it became obvious that Noah wasn't letting this go, Mike pressed the intercom button. 'Noah...'

Noah stopped dead, glaring at the interactive doorbell. 'Dad?'

'Yes.'

Noah shook his head. He balled his hands into fists at his sides. 'Why aren't you letting me in?'

Mike's shame burned like acid in his throat.

'Dad? *Talk* to me!' Noah's voice cracked.

'I'm still here. Noah, son… I'm sorry. I really am… Just… it's not a good idea to come in right now.'

Mike could see the disbelief in his son's eyes. A complete inability to comprehend this. But his son had no clue what state his father was truly in.

I'm a mess, son, he thought. *A bloody mess.*

'I haven't seen you in over a year, Dad.' Noah ran a hand through his hair, frustration clear in every gesture now.

'I know.' The admission sat heavy on Mike's tongue.

'Why? I don't understand!' Noah slammed his fist against the door. 'Let me in!'

Mike took a deep breath. The war between his love for Noah and his disgust with himself raged in his chest, threatening to tear him apart. He needed to stay strong. The urge to open that door and wrap his arms around the boy he missed more than anyone could comprehend was overwhelming, but… the consequences of doing so were unthinkable.

'Mum said you wanted to see me. She gave me the address.'

Confirmation that she'd caused this. *Bloody hell Laurie!*

'Was it another fucking lie?'

Hearing his fourteen-year-old son swear like that made him flinch.

'I'm not well, Noah. At all. You know this. It's complicated.'

'I've friends with sick parents. *Dying* parents. They don't hide away.'

'This is different.'

'Are you even really sick? Or just hiding from me? From Mum?' Noah's face was flushing.

Yes to all of them, son. 'I don't want you to see me like this.' Mike swallowed hard, trying to keep his emotions in check.

'You're selfish.' Noah kicked the door this time, the sound reverberating around the house. 'So fucking selfish. Mum's struggling. Working two jobs. And you're what – sitting on your fat arse?'

Something like that, Mike thought. 'I'm sorry.'

'She says you're pathetic. I try to stick up for you, but what's the point?' He threw his hands in the air.

There's no point, son. 'You can stop sticking up for me.'

His son kicked the door again. The force of it made Mike flinch, even though he couldn't feel the impact.

He stared at Noah on his mobile. God, how he wanted to put his arms around him. Soothe him. Nurture him, like he'd done when he was younger.

But that was never to be again.

'Is there someone else? Another woman?' Noah kicked again, his face twisted with a mixture of anger and pain. 'Someone else in there with you?'

'That's ridiculous. I'd never do that.'

Out of breath now, his furious boy stopped.

Was this it? Was his son about to walk away? Would this be the last time he ever saw him?

'You don't care.' Noah's voice was flat.

Mike bit his tongue. It was best to not answer. Let him leave.

'And you never did care, did you, Dad?'

Hold it, Mike, don't crack.

'You don't love me.' Noah wiped at his eyes with the back of his hand.

Mike rubbed his forehead. It was too painful.

'Never did.'

Don't...

'It was all a lie.'

'It wasn't.' He blurted into the phone. 'I love you. Always did. Always will. More than anything, Noah.'

Noah looked up. His eyes were red-rimmed. 'Then open the fucking door!'

Idiot! He'd started it all off again.

He needed to give Noah more. More reason to walk away. To understand that this wasn't for the best. 'It's not that simple. I'm sick, son. Very sick.'

'Dying?' Noah's voice was suddenly small, childlike.

Yes. But would that be too much to bear? 'I don't know.'

'Mum says you can get yourself out of this rut. Is that true?' There was a glimmer of hope in his eyes.

'I don't know.' The truth was, he'd never tried.

'Don't you want to?'

He sighed. 'Yes, and no.'

'Pathetic.' Noah's words were like a slap to Mike's face. 'If I had a son, I'd save myself for my child.'

Because you're better than me, Noah, and that's good, he thought. *I want you to be better than me... that's all I really want now. All that's left to want.*

'Unless I didn't love them.' Noah was sobbing now, his body shaking. This was getting more and more relentless.

He wanted to say so much but knew it would only prolong this. He wanted to say: *None of my love for you has been a lie. I sat by your bedside every night when you were little, reading you stories until you fell asleep. I taught you how to throw a football, how to ride a bike. These moments meant everything to me.* But it wouldn't achieve anything. Instead, he tried again to just make him understand. 'Something changed, Noah. Something inside me broke. It's hard to explain. Knowing how to heal, and being able to, they're two different things. But it was never anything to do with you.' He used a soft tone, pleading for his son to understand.

'Mum says you don't want to live any more.'

She's rarely wrong your mother, Mike thought, using a towel to wipe his tears away. He watched his son move away from the camera, his steps heavy.

Everything fell silent.

Mike suddenly panicked, even though it was a good thing he was leaving. 'Noah?'

Nothing.

He raised his voice. 'I'll phone you, I promise.'

There was a sharp, sudden crack, like a gunshot in the house's quiet. Something heavy had hit his double-glazed window. It splintered but didn't shatter. A spiderweb of fractures radiated out from the point of impact.

Mike's heart leapt into his throat. He closed his eyes, sucking in air. A shock like that had the potential to finish him. And it wasn't how he wanted to go. With Noah so close.

His boy could end up blaming himself.

Noah was back on the door, kicking it, his face contorted again, his eyes wilder than ever. 'If you don't open it. I'll keep throwing bricks. And I'll take out every one of your windows.'

Mike used the towel to mop up his brow.

Noah sounded serious.

Mike's options were diminishing.

If he allowed him to throw bricks, then not only would someone end up getting hurt, but a neighbour could phone the police and have his son arrested.

His son was bloody smart.

Shit... this was going to end badly. 'Okay, don't.'

'Open the door, then.'

'You'll have to give me a couple of minutes...'

'Minutes. What're you talking about?'

'Just listen, Noah! Will you?' Mike couldn't help but raise his voice now. He was a beaten man and frustrated. The unthinkable was about to happen. His son seeing him.

Unthinkable, or just inevitable.

Deep down, he always knew this day would come.

Mike could have moved faster on the rollator, but he was concerned about heavy sweating and being out of breath. Whatever happened, he'd look a state to his son, but it would be better to try to not make it worse. Even at a slower pace, it was brutal. Each breath a laboured gasp while the rollator creaked and groaned under his weight.

When he reached the door, he unlocked the deadbolt with shaking hands. He cracked it open just enough so he could poke an eye through.

'It may hurt you to see me.' He kept his voice soft. 'Are you sure it's what you want?'

'Yes.' Noah's voice was resolute.

'This has nothing to do with you. I love you.'

'Whatever.'

'No. Say it. Say, "This has nothing to do with me."'

Noah sighed. 'Okay.' He rolled his eyes. 'This has nothing to do with me.'

Mike moved back, allowing Noah space to push the door open. 'Okay. Come in.'

Noah pushed opened the door.

For a long moment, father and son stared at each other, and little happened.

Mike dared to hope it would be okay, but then Noah's eyes widened and he paled.

'I'm sorry, Noah, but remember, it's nothing to do with you or your mother.'

Noah's face twisted.

Mike eased forward.

Noah backed off. His hands raised as if to ward off a blow. 'Stay away.'

Mike paused and nodded. 'Okay, I understand.'

'You're not my father.'

The comment cut into him like a knife. He kept the pain from his face, trying to maintain a sympathetic look.

'What happened?' Noah shook his head. His voice was confused, like a child trying to make sense of a nightmare.

Mike tried to move again, desperate to be close to his boy.

'You're fucking disgusting.'

These words cut even deeper, slicing into his heart. Mike lifted a hand from his rollator and reached out with his trembling fingers to his son.

Noah jerked back as if burned.

Mike lowered his eyes, and leaned heavily on the rollator, his body sagging.

A moment passed, and when the silence became unbearable, he lifted his eyes again.

Tears were running down Noah's face.

'My son.' Mike reached out again, his voice a broken whisper.

'Fuck off.' Noah turned and fled, footsteps pounding on the pavement.

For a time, Mike watched his front path. He fixed his eyes on the spot where Noah had vanished from view, hoping his son would return.

When it was clear that wouldn't happen, he closed the door. The sound was like a final, damning chord, echoing in the house's silence.

He took a deep breath and let out a guttural cry of

anguish. The sound was raw, primal, torn from the depths of his soul.

Then, blinded by tears, he lumbered into the kitchen, lashing out with one arm, sweeping it across the counter. Glasses and plates shattered on the floor, shards of ceramic and glass spraying everywhere.

With trembling hands, he reached for the drawer he'd been in earlier, pulling it open to reveal the pictures of them together. He flipped through the pages until he found the picture he sought: a snapshot of him and Noah, grinning at the camera, their faces alight with joy. Noah's tenth birthday, a rare moment of unbridled happiness.

Mike traced the outline of his son's face, his finger leaving a smudged trail on the glossy paper.

He collapsed against the counter, great, heaving sobs wracking his body. His colossal frame shook with the force of his grief, his tears splashing onto the photograph in his hands. He'd lost everything – his health, his dignity, and now, his son.

Chapter Twenty-Five

PHOEBE KEPT HER HEAD LOWERED, sucking in ragged breaths as David put his arms around her shoulders. 'You all right?'

No, she thought, feeling like she had swallowed broken glass. *That man you just let into this house? Have you any idea, David? Have you any idea what you've done?*

She took a deep breath. How could she blame her husband? He knew nothing of her past. 'I've eaten something funny.'

'I see,' he whispered into her ear. 'Shall I tell this Julian to go?'

Inside, she groaned. It was really happening. Her eyes hadn't been deceiving her. Julian was in her hallway.

'Phoebe, how are you?' And there was Julian's voice. It was unmistakable. Deep, laced with confidence. It didn't sound as if it'd aged a day.

She stood up straight and turned to watch him approach. His once long hair was now shorter, flecked with grey, but still styled in a way that exuded an air of cool defiance. He wore a well-worn leather jacket, its black surface softened by years of use, and a pair of dark jeans that hugged his lean frame.

He smiled. She met his eyes. *Those eyes*, still raw and penetrating, like they'd been on that fateful morning after the explosion.

A chill ran down her spine.

'Julian... what a surprise. What're you doing here?' She fought to keep her voice steady.

'Sorry.' He came closer. 'I didn't hear.'

She realised that in her anxious state, she'd failed to take her voice above a whisper. She repeated herself, forcing the volume up. 'How are you? I haven't seen you in so long.'

He smiled. 'Over thirty years, now, Pheebs, can you believe it? But the day I left, I promised I'd come back one day, didn't I?'

'You did.'

Julian had written to her from prison. Begging for her to visit. He'd tried for five years. Weekly. His letters had been kind.

Until that very last one.

That one had been short. One sentence. Blunt. *I'll see you when I get home*.

He'd kept his promise.

Phoebe opened her mouth to speak, but nothing came out.

David looked between them. 'How do you two know each other, anyway? And where have you been for thirty years?'

Julian smiled at David. 'Travelling.' He then turned his attention back to Phoebe. 'But me and Pheebs have a lot of history. We used to run in the same circles. Back in the day.'

Phoebe's stomach clenched. The same circles. A circle that had led to the death of two people in a fireball.

Phoebe looked at David. She could see the suspicion flicking up in his eyes. Her husband was a very intelligent man, and he knew how to read people and situations very well.

'Phoebe has never mentioned you before.' There was no small measure of intrigue in David's tone.

'Like I said, a long time ago.' Julian winked at Phoebe. 'A very different life, wasn't it, Pheebs?'

Phoebe swallowed hard and nodded. She looked at David. She needed to reassure him and keep him calm. Julian was a dangerous man. 'We haven't seen each other in years. Not since we both left Scarborough. It'd be good to catch up.' She looked back at him. 'Unfortunately, you've caught me off guard. At a bad time. My stomach is off.'

Julian nodded. 'A shame.' He shook his head, widened his eyes and beamed. 'So good to see you. The famous Phoebe Turner, off to conquer the world. I always knew you'd make something of yourself. I always said, didn't I?'

'You did,' Phoebe said.

'Told anyone that would listen. I said, "That Phoebe Turner. Eyes on her. She will shine."'

Phoebe nodded. She flinched when she felt an arm around her waist, despite knowing it had to be David. 'That's my girl,' her husband said.

Phoebe felt the discomfort radiating from her husband, the tension in his body palpable even through the fabric of his shirt. The silence that followed was heavy, weighted with unspoken questions and mounting unease.

Phoebe's mind began racing. What was happening? Where was this going? Was Julian here to hurt her? David? Both of them? Was he going to announce the truth? That she was a murderer evading justice? Or was this just a warning? A preamble to blackmail? A money grab? She took a deep breath.

Could she handle this with money? Really?

They'd a lot of money. For freedom, and Julian out of her life, she'd happily pay.

'Well, it's getting late,' David said. 'And Phoebe has got a stomach bug. If you leave your number, I'm sure she'll be in touch.'

Julian didn't take his eyes off Phoebe's. That raw look. His smile was full of malice. She stiffened against her husband.

Julian nodded, clamped his tattooed hands together, and gave a swift nod. 'Of course. I'm interrupting a celebration.'

Phoebe's stomach turned over. *How did he know?*

'Celebration?' David raised an eyebrow. 'What makes you say that?'

Julian grinned and threw a thumb over his shoulder. 'The champers.'

'Ah yes,' David said. 'Well, we were, but like I said, Pheebs has a stomach bug, so—'

'Anyway,' Julian said. 'I hope you feel better soon, Pheebs.'

'Thank you,' Phoebe said.

Phoebe and David stood there, waiting for Julian to turn and head to the door. He was taking his time, smiling and gazing at the two of them.

Phoebe felt ice water coursing through her veins, the chill of fear spreading through her body like a poison. Julian's evil streak had been a mile wide back then, a darkness that had consumed him and everyone around him. After thirty years in prison, she couldn't begin to imagine how much it had grown, how much more twisted and dangerous he'd become. 'Shall I show you out?' David started towards him.

Phoebe's hand shot out, clutching her husband's arm, halting him. He looked at her. She hoped he could read her expression.

Don't get too close.

David looked back at Julian. Then back at Phoebe. He was confused. 'Is there a need to exchange numbers?'

'No need.' Julian said. 'I've your email, Pheebs. In fact, I emailed earlier to give you a heads-up I was back. Seems you must have missed it.'

David said, 'She's been preoccupied.'

'Funny.' Julian laughed. 'The Phoebe I remember could always speak for herself.'

Phoebe took a deep breath. 'Email me and we'll organise something, Julian.'

Julian unclasped his tattooed hands and clapped. 'Brilliant. We've so much to talk about.'

'Yes.' She nodded, willing herself not to throw up.

Phoebe watched as a change came over David, his patience wearing thin. Her husband was a powerful man, used to getting his way, and this strange power play had gone on long enough. He pulled away, turned and edged towards Julian, chest puffed out. A metre from him, David said, 'Who are you?'

'Julian—'

'No,' David interrupted. 'Who are you really?'

'Leave it, David,' Phoebe said.

He held a hand up to silence his wife. 'No, Phoebe. I want to hear what's happening here.'

Julian regarded David's face. He tilted his head from side to side, examining him. 'I'd listen to your wife if I were you.'

David edged closer.

'David,' she said. 'Leave it. *Now.*'

Julian reached into his pocket.

Her blood ran cold. She edged forward.

David, too, had noticed that he'd gone to his pocket, and glanced down.

His hand was moving… he was reaching for something…

'I'll email tonight.' Phoebe darted alongside her husband. 'I promise.'

Julian grinned, pulled his hand out, and offered it to David. 'Pleased to meet you, David.'

David shook his hand.

'You're a very lucky man.' Julian winked at Phoebe. 'Pheebs.' He then turned and headed away.

Once he'd left, David locked the door and turned to Phoebe, wide eyed. 'What the hell was that all about?'

Unable to hold herself together any longer, Phoebe stumbled forward and fell into his arms.

Chapter Twenty-Six

Louise Parkes sat down on the bench beside Rob. She was the spitting image of her father. Or, at least, the version he remembered. He'd not seen Bryan for twenty-five years. A lot could have changed in that time before his recent passing.

Strong cheekbones and the same determined set to her jaw. Her auburn hair whipped in the wind coming off the North Sea. There was no denying this was Bryan's daughter. When he looked into her green eyes, it was as if he was looking into Bryan's eyes again at sixteen as they declared themselves *brothers forever*.

'I'm sorry, Louise,' Rob said. 'I never knew about you.'

'It's okay,' she said. 'He told me you hadn't spoken since you were both twenty-six years old.'

Rob gazed out over the sea. 'Almost a quarter of a century ago, and it goes by in the blink of an eye.' He looked back at her and nodded. 'He must have been proud of you.'

Louise shrugged. 'He said he was.'

'How often?'

She smiled rather than answered.

'Every day, I bet.' And he spoke from experience. He was so proud of his children for all of their successes and their failings. In fact, he was in awe of them, knowing that they'd never make the mistakes he'd made.

'He never said why you lost contact,' Louise said.

'It's a good question. I'm not sure either of us fully understood it. I stayed in Whitby. For him, it was too painful. He went to Middlesbrough.' He looked at her. 'Did he stay there? All these years?'

She nodded. 'He built a new life, but the past always haunted him. The drinking... the depression... it was his way of coping, I suppose.'

'You know, we only ever argued once, and that was the last time we saw one another.'

'What about?' she asked.

'I don't know, really.' This was a lie. He knew, really. Bryan had accused Rob of forgetting what they'd been through, almost denying it'd ever happened. Rob had countered that he was just trying to move on, to build a better life for himself. In the end, they couldn't reconcile their different viewpoints. 'How did he pass?'

'His liver. He suffered from alcoholism.'

Rob sighed and looked down. *The damage caused by those dark and suffocating moments.* 'I'm sorry.'

Louise reached into her purse and pulled out a worn envelope. 'He left this for you. He asked me to give it to you only after he'd gone...'

Rob took the envelope with a shaking hand. 'Do you know what's in it?'

Louise nodded, tears in her eyes.

'He told you?'

'Yes. Everything.'

God... that was brave! Or was it stupid? He couldn't say

for sure; maybe a mixture of them both. Well, whatever the verdict, he wouldn't be doing the same with his own children. 'It's an awful story for you to hear.'

'He said he wanted me to know why he'd failed me so many times,' Louise said.

'I see,' Rob said.

Louise fixed him with her gaze. 'But he never failed me. Not really. That was just how he felt. He was always so full of guilt. He never deserved that.'

No, he did not. Rob opened the envelope.

Inside were a couple of sheets of paper, covered in Bryan's familiar scrawl. Rob's vision blurred as he read the words, a lump forming in his throat.

Dear Rob,

If you're reading this, then I guess you're sitting alongside my daughter. She's a sight, eh? Beautiful.

I want you to know that I'm glad you've had so much success. Although our argument that night long ago drove a wedge between us, I now see it as a turning point. It freed us from the chains of our shared pain, allowing you to build the life you always deserved. You've made a good life for yourself. I'm glad you did. You deserve all the happiness in the world, my brother.

Rob looked up at the gulls again, willing the tears back. The girl next to him had lost her father. He didn't wish to put his grief on to her. When he was back in control, he continued.

I wish I could say the same for myself. I had moments of happiness, fleeting glimpses of a better life, but the darkness always found me in the end. The memories of what we endured, the scars that man left on our souls, they never truly healed. I tried to bury the pain, to drown it in drink, but it always resurfaced, dragging me back down into that abyss.

Rob closed his eyes and sighed. No one ever forgets. That was the truth. He'd tried, but it was impossible. Some just learn to live better with the rot inside them. *I'm sorry, Bryan,* he thought. *Sorry that I learned to live with it, and you just couldn't. If I could have taken the hell out of you and taken it on myself, I would have done.*

He read the remaining section of the letter, still willing back the tears. It was a tragic tale about a man eventually consumed by darkness, ending rather abruptly with:

In the end, the bottle won. It claimed my health, my hope, and finally, my life. But even in death, I hold fast to the promise we made all those years ago, my brother.
   Your brother,
   Bryan.
   P.S. Ask my daughter for the second envelope.

He looked up at Louise. 'Do you have the second envelope?'

She handed it over and he opened it.

Part of him expected this, but he still stared down in disbelief.

He could barely breathe, and there was a chill running through his body the likes of which he hadn't felt for so many years.

With trembling hands, he held the photograph of a man in his thirties. The bulbous, blood-flecked cheeks and cold, dead eyes stared back at him, a ghost from his past that he'd tried so hard to forget. The blue rosette pinned to the man's lapel seemed to mock him, a symbol of power and respectability that hid the monster beneath.

There was a time when this photograph would have caused a flurry of anger, but for years, he'd worked on suppressing this rage to preserve a contented façade for Sarah and his children.

But now that Bryan was dead, he couldn't help but feel those old embers of anger flaring.

He turned the picture over and read the words. *It's time.*

'No.' Rob tried to hand the picture back to Louise.

'It's not mine,' she said. 'He wants you to have it.'

'I don't want it.' He rubbed his temples. 'And I don't want to do what he's asking.'

She slumped as if her father was taking on the weight of Rob's sudden rejection through her body.

He looked at the words again. *It's time.*

Rob shook his head. 'Why didn't he ever do it himself?'

'The same reason you haven't. He didn't want to drag his family through it.'

And yet, here he was, thrusting this burden upon Rob from beyond the grave, expecting him to shatter the life he'd so carefully built, to expose the ugly truth and face the consequences alone.

'What changed his mind?'

'Me. I told him to. I told him no one can heal, no one can move on without the truth. That leaving an injustice like that burning in our shared histories was abhorrent.'

Rob ran a hand through his hair and sighed. 'Abhorrent is one word for what happened. So, if he agreed, why's he waited and passed it to me?'

'Because by the time he agreed, it was too late. He wrote this letter to you, Rob, only days before he died.'

Rob stared at the back of the photograph. He couldn't face turning it over and looking at that horrendous man again. 'I can't. My family doesn't know.'

'I appreciate that,' Louise said. 'If it helps, I'm glad my father told me everything.'

Rob glared at her. He couldn't stop himself. 'That doesn't help.'

Louise nodded and looked away.

'If it's so important to you, and him, why don't you do it?' Rob asked. 'You could leave my name out of it?'

'I thought about it. I even suggested it to my father. But he says that there will be no appetite for it. The victim is gone. You're not. You're alive. When you expose things, people will be forced to listen.'

'For fuck's sake.' He gritted his teeth and shook his head. He caught her shocked expression from the corner of his eye. 'Sorry for swearing. I should know better. I wouldn't do that in front of my children.'

Louise put a hand on his arm and regarded him with a sympathetic look.

'I can't. I just can't. It will destroy my family.'

She held his gaze, her eyes searching his face. 'Will it? Or will it set you free?'

He closed his eyes and let his head loll forward, replaying that moment in his mind again:

No matter what happens, no matter where life takes us, we'll always have each other's backs. Yes?

Yes. Brothers, forever.

Louise took her hand from his arm. When he opened his eyes, she was standing and looking down at him. She was holding out a small key. 'A safe deposit box.' She gave him the location. 'Everything you need.'

He took it.

She leaned down and pressed a gentle kiss to his forehead, a gesture of comfort and understanding. 'Whatever you decide to do, I understand, and he would too.'

And then she left. He touched the damp spot on his forehead where she'd kissed him and felt Bryan's presence.

For a long time, he sat on the bench, watching the sun dip below the horizon, painting the sky in shades of orange and pink. The gulls continued their endless dance above the waves, their cries echoing across the water like a mournful song.

Sarah phoned; he apologised and lied. Said he'd had problems with the boss at the head office. He suggested she order pizza.

With a heavy sigh, he took one last look at the photograph, the face of his tormentor staring back at him from the past. He slipped it into his pocket along with Bryan's letter and the key, the weight of his decision pressing down on his shoulders.

Rob stood and made his way down the cliff side towards home, towards the light and love waiting for him there.

And as he walked, he could almost feel Bryan's presence beside him, could almost hear his voice whispering in the wind. 'Brothers, forever.'

Chapter Twenty-Seven

The sun was only just dipping below the horizon as Frank entered Whitby Cemetery. He couldn't recall the last time he'd come before closing time, making him feel rather out of sorts, having to use the entrance rather than scaling a wall.

He was also stone-cold sober.

'How do, love?' he asked Mary at her gravestone.

Frank and Mary had been married for thirty-three years. He could always imagine her clear as day. In this moment, she occupied his mind with her warm smile, her soft brown hair framing her face, and those eyes that always seemed to see right through him.

He feared the day when the clarity of how she looked faded from his mind.

'Aye, before you start, love, I look a state... But you'll be pleased to know that Hel has already given it to me with both barrels.'

Mary smiled, her eyes crinkling at the corners, as she accepted him, warts and all. She'd always been so patient with him, even when he'd been at his worst.

'I'll be more careful next time... but I won't stop.' He gave a sharp nod. 'This is on me, Mary. No one else. I failed Maddie. I thought I had it under control. I was wrong.' *And then, like a complete dickhead, I lied to her, and she disappeared into the night like a ghost.*

He lowered his head, sighing, feeling Mary's presence, imagining her soothing words. *You did what you thought was best. That's all we can do sometimes.*

'You give me too much credit, love. Always have done. But, like I said, I'll find her again. I swear to you. I got her off that shite once, and I'll do it again if need be. No matter what it takes, I'm bringing her home.'

In his mind, she regarded him with a knowing look and said, *That's not all, is it, honey?*

He took a deep breath, trying to compose himself as the earthy aroma of the cemetery filled his nostrils. 'No. There's this case, too. Adrian Hughes. His own father abused him, Mary. Broke him in ways no child should ever be broken. The things he went through. And yet someone steps up and disposes of him behind an old wall like an animal. I can't have it.'

Frank could feel Mary's understanding, her shared horror at the cruelty in this world. She'd always had such a big heart, always wanted to help those in need.

He sat in his wife's presence a while longer, pouring out his heart and drawing strength from her memory. As the last of the light faded from the sky, he rose to his feet. 'I love you.' He kissed his fingertips and then pressed them to the cold stone.

Frank tried to resist the urge to visit *his* grave. He certainly couldn't piss on it with all these eyes around and he'd given the prick enough soakings to last a lifetime, anyway. But, as always, he felt compelled to go. He could always make time for a quick muttered obscenity at his resting place.

Nigel Wainwright had earned that privilege.

Not only had the bastard had an affair with Mary, but there'd been others before her, a string of infidelities that had left a trail of broken hearts in their wake. Then, he'd driven them both onto the wrong side of the road, killing Mary, himself, and a young mother in another car.

All that while over the limit.

So, respect the dead?

Ha! Give me a break! After what that man did?

Frank was sixty-four, and probably didn't have too much longer left in this world, and he'd be more than happy to let any Tom, Dick and Harry loose on his grave to do whatever they wanted if he'd departed it in so obnoxious a manner as that man had.

As he neared Nigel's grave, he glanced at a kneeling figure. His stomach dropped as he recognised the woman.

Bollocks!

It was Nigel's widow.

He spun, desperate to leave.

'Frank?'

Too late. Evelyn Wainwright had spotted him.

He couldn't bring himself to acknowledge her.

'Frank.' Her voice was louder. She was getting closer.

He turned, his jaw clenched and shoulders tense. Taking a deep breath, he forced a neutral expression onto his face. 'Evelyn. How do?'

'Why do you keep coming to my husband's grave?' Her tone was sharp, accusatory, with a hint of suspicion.

He feigned surprise. 'Eh? I come to see Mary.'

'Mary's over yonder.' She pointed off into the distance.

'Aye. I guess I've taken a wrong turn.'

Evelyn smirked. 'Except, a year back, I saw you skulking around here before.' She pointed several rows down. 'You see, my brother is here, too. There were times I was with him, and I've seen you standing here, staring down at Nigel's headstone.'

Thank God you haven't seen me at nighttime when the gates are shut. I'd be behind bars by now.

He sighed and held his palms up. 'Collared. Sorry.'

'Why, Frank?'

Frank hesitated, his mind racing. A mixture of truth and improvisation formed his response. 'Well, sometimes I struggle to understand, you know, why it all happened. So, I come to ask him. Yes, it's stupid.' He shrugged a second time, his voice softening. 'I mean, he can't answer me, can he? But, sorry, I won't come again.'

'If I visited your wife's grave, Frank, would I find any answers?'

Don't Evelyn, he thought. *Not now.*

'You see, I have questions too.'

He took a deep breath, steeled himself, and turned. 'Sorry Evelyn.'

He made it a metre before she said, 'I'd love to know why Mary seduced my husband.'

And there it was.

The battle cry.

Shit.

He stopped and said over his shoulder. 'Mary didn't seduce Nigel.'

'Ah... and you know that, for sure?'

He faced her again. 'Aye. Because I know Mary. The question is, did you know your husband?'

Evelyn narrowed her eyes. 'Yes. Nigel wasn't like that.'

Frank bit back the words that threatened to spill out,

the truth about Nigel's past indiscretions, the pain he'd caused to so many. He didn't want to hurt Evelyn, to shatter the illusions she'd built around her marriage, but he couldn't let Mary's memory be tarnished by lies. 'It's best we shut this conversation down now, Evelyn. Everyone lost. No one gained. We shouldn't make the situation worse—'

'Why not? I've nothing left, anyway. We never had children.' She shook her head. 'Your wife ruined my life.'

Frank gritted his teeth and looked down. *Keep it together. She doesn't know the truth, and she'll never see it through the pain.* 'I'm sorry for your loss. If you want to blame anyone, blame me, not Mary. I should have been there for her... more. I wasn't. She was in pain over our daughter, and I was lost in my job. I'm asking you' – he looked back up and met her eyes – 'to put this on me. I made Mary lonely.' *But she'd never have seduced him.*

'What're you implying?' she hissed. 'Are you suggesting I wasn't there for Nigel, then? That he was lonely? I was a good wife to him.'

'That wasn't what I was implying.'

'Good. So, we agree he was seduced?'

Frank pointed at her. He wanted to shout obscenities in her direction. It took every ounce of his willpower to force them back. He shook his head. 'Look. There's a lot of pain here. But not again...' He looked down. 'Please. That's your last warning.'

She snorted. 'Your wife was a temptress and *I'm* on a warning!'

Frank felt his cheeks flush. 'Your husband was pissed. He drove head-on into another car and left a family without a mother. Two children without a mother. And me without a wife. You can't hide from the facts.'

'What facts? He'd had a couple of glasses of wine. You can hardly say he was pissed.'

'He was, and I can!'

'Nonsense.'

'Well, he was pissed enough to ruin three families by swinging his car onto the wrong side of the road.'

She was jabbing her finger in his direction now. 'Fuck you, Frank. Look at the state of you. Telling me you've never had a few drinks and got behind the wheel? You're a fat, washed-up pillock. And looking at your face, it seems someone else agrees.'

Frank shrugged. 'I don't care what you say about me. Just not my wife.'

Evelyn wiped tears away. 'He'd never have cheated on me if not for her.'

The words tumbled out of Frank's mouth before he could stop them. 'He'd had three affairs before.'

Evelyn's face contorted in disbelief. 'Not true.'

Frank felt a sudden, guilty relief at finally unburdening himself. 'I have evidence, Evelyn. Names, dates, places. I didn't want to tell you, didn't want to cause you more pain, but I can't let you blame Mary for Nigel's mistakes.'

'You're lying.' Her voice cracked, barely above a whisper. The fight drained from her posture as her head fell, and she sobbed.

Frank's anger drained away, replaced by a deep, aching sadness. He stepped forward, reaching out a hand to comfort her, but she flinched away.

'I'm sorry for your loss,' he said. 'I really am.'

She nodded and looked up. 'How's your daughter doing?' Her tone was softer now. The question seemed genuine. Was she extending an olive branch? Suffering guilt over her husband's role in taking someone's mother away?

Frank's heart clenched. He didn't know what to say. Discussing the shambles of his life with Nigel's widow wasn't an option, though.

So he lied. 'Fine. She's fine.'

With that, he walked away, his shoulders hunched against the sudden chill in the air. As he made his way back to his car, he couldn't shake the feeling that he'd handled the situation badly. He'd let his anger get the best of him, let the truth spill out in a way that had only caused more pain. And that olive branch, that chance for understanding and forgiveness? He'd let it slip away, too caught up in his own grief and guilt to reach out and grasp it.

But he had to let this guilt go now. Because all that mattered was finding Maddie and getting justice for Adrian. Everything else was just noise, a distraction from the things that truly mattered.

Even so, as he lay in bed that night, staring at the ceiling and trying to quiet his racing thoughts, he couldn't help but dwell on the encounter.

When it came to opportunities to find some measure of peace and closure, how many could he afford to miss?

Chapter Twenty-Eight

The morning light filtered through the curtains. A pale glow settled over the bedroom. Phoebe stirred. Her eyes were heavy with exhaustion after a restless night. When she rolled over to find her husband's side of the bed empty, the events of the previous night came flooding back. A wave of despair crashed over her.

She sat up and put her fist to her mouth, recalling Julian's visit, followed by gut-wrenching sobs and desperate confessions of what she and Julian had done together thirty-five years ago. She'd never shake away that look of pure anguish she saw etched on her husband's face as she laid bare her secrets.

Then, there'd been shouting, David's voice trembling with rage and disbelief, before he'd snatched up the bottle of champagne they'd intended to celebrate with and drained it in gulps.

But the night had ended better than it'd begun. David's anger had given way to a weary sort of acceptance, before he'd gathered her in his arms, whispering soothing words and reassurances.

In bed, Phoebe had clung to him, her body still wracked with sobs, as he stroked her hair and told her he'd handle this.

Through the long hours of darkness, Phoebe had lain awake, her mind racing with thoughts of the lengths David might go to protect her and keep their life together from unravelling.

David had a cloudy history. A past tinged with darkness from his days in the cutthroat world of property development. He'd run with the wrong people, made questionable choices, but he'd clawed his way out of that life, determined to be a better man for her sake.

This morning, in the pale light beneath crumpled sheets, she realised that she'd never felt fear like this.

Fear of what Julian might do. Fear over the consequences of her actions all those years ago. And fear of the lengths David could go to.

The ping of an incoming email broke her reverie, and Phoebe's heart leapt into her throat. With trembling fingers, she reached for her phone, her stomach knotting with dread.

The email was from goodietwoshoes@hotmail.com again.

This time it was a photograph of Larpool Wood. It offered secluded woodland walks on the outskirts of Whitby. She and Julian used to go there together.

In the image, dappled sunlight filtered through the emerald canopy, casting an almost ethereal glow on the well-trodden path. She could almost feel the warmth of his palm against hers, hear the soft rustle of leaves beneath their feet.

That time together had been a lie.

A handsome, rugged exterior had concealed the true

Julian. A man who'd wowed her with passionate opinions and beliefs. She discovered the truth of who he really was much later.

She closed her eyes and recalled Julian's face illuminated by the inferno, his eyes raw, consumed by a feverish intensity. Gone was the lover, full of heart and integrity, replaced by a man driven to the brink by his obsessions, a man who'd let nothing and no one stand in his way. The screams, the acrid stench of smoke, the searing heat... it all came rushing back, threatening to overwhelm her.

Phoebe's breath caught in her throat, her mind already conjuring images of David confronting Julian, of the violence that could ensue. She couldn't let that happen, not after everything they'd built together.

The sound of footsteps in the hallway drew her attention. David appeared in the doorway with two cups of tea.

'I received another email. He wants £100,000. I think we should pay it, David.'

He went pale. 'You responded?'

'No... not yet.'

He sighed. 'Good.' He put the cups down. 'Show me.'

David took a notepad from the top bedside drawer and scribbled down the information from the email.

Phoebe felt the tears welling up again, her composure crumbling. 'David, we should pay him. We can afford it. We could sell the York property and—'

David shook his head. 'You think that will be enough for a man like that? He'll be back before the end of the year.'

'Maybe. But is it not worth trying first?'

David took a deep breath and shook his head. He took her hand. 'I looked into his eyes last night, Pheebs. That man is going to keep coming back until he destroys you.' He lowered his voice. 'We have to get there first.'

Phoebe pulled back, her eyes searching his face. 'What're you going to do?'

He cupped her face in his hands, his touch gentle but firm. 'The right thing.' His voice left no room for argument. 'I'm going to make sure that all those children get the chances they deserve, and I'll sleep easy knowing that I've been part of that.'

'David, I—'

He kissed her, cutting her off.

He pulled back. 'Once he's taken everything from us, he'll see you in jail, my darling. That serves the world, and the children within it, no purpose. It won't be happening.'

Phoebe felt her heart constrict, a mix of fear and relief battling within her. She knew there'd be no talking her husband out of whatever he was planning. He wasn't concerned about the children. That was all said for her benefit – he'd just do whatever it took to protect her.

The room darkened as the sun moved behind clouds.

'This time tomorrow,' David said. 'It will all be a bad dream.'

Chapter Twenty-Nine

For the first time in a while, Frank didn't feel any effects of the alcohol he'd consumed the night before. Was he on the slippery slope of alcoholism? As Bertha rattled into the car park, he convinced himself that it was his throbbing face that was distracting him from the hangover, but vowed to rein in the drinking over the next couple of days just in case.

Even though he was early, he wasn't at all surprised to see Gerry banging away on her keyboard – she was nearly always the first in the building. Rylan came and greeted him before returning to her side, tail thumping on the floor.

'How do?'

She didn't look up and continued typing.

'I'm fine too, thank you,' Frank said.

He knelt and stroked Rylan again. He noticed a chunk of sleep at the corner of the Lab's eye and plucked it away.

'Frank! I must ask you to be careful about touching his eyes. It's a common way for bacteria to get introduced and cause infections.'

Bloody hell – did Gerry have eyes in the back of her head? 'Ah... okay... noted.'

He stood, feeling scolded, but at least glad she'd noticed his existence. 'Any news?'

'Emily Hargreaves from Moonrise Hotel called back late last night and left a message to call back on her mobile.' Gerry didn't look up and maintained her focus on the screen. 'I've just got off the phone with her.'

He checked his watch. 'Bloody hell, Gerry. A bit early! I bet she didn't appreciate that.'

Gerry wrinkled her nose. 'I didn't expect gratitude.'

'Aye... and what did she say?'

'They located some old records and confirmed that Adrian Hughes stayed there on Friday, 4th March.'

'Boom!' Frank clapped. Gerry flinched. 'Sorry... so, we're right. When the cat's away, the mice will play.'

Gerry frowned.

'An expression. Rowena would have been away, I guess, and Adrian was out enjoying himself.' He winked. 'His double life.'

Gerry's expression didn't change. She looked at her notes. 'Other people who stayed there that same night. Laura Bauer, Jan Nowak, and a couple, Tessa and James Garrick.'

'Small crowd for a hotel?'

'Yes. Emily said the same. I checked the weather for that day. Stormy. In fact, they'd had a week of thunderstorms, which is probably why no one was too keen on booking.'

'You can check the weather from 1989?'

'Of course,' Gerry said.

Sometimes he forgot how far this information age had come. He guessed that was what made him outdated. He'd never have considered being this thorough!

'Would you be able to get in touch with them, Gerry?'

She looked up for the first time. 'I thought you wanted me to come with you to see Rory again?'

'I'll be fine. This is a strong lead. You try to get in touch with these four guests. If they're alive, let me know what they can remember.'

Gerry nodded.

'How was the date?' Frank asked.

'Tom didn't show.' Gerry typed with her expression unchanged. Frank wondered whether she was putting on a brave face.

'Shit. I'm sorry,' Frank said.

'Why are you sorry?' she asked, still typing.

He shrugged. 'Must have been disappointing?'

She stopped typing.

'Embarrassing even?' he continued.

'Nothing of the sort.' She looked at him. 'It saved me time asking irrelevant questions. His absence gave me all the answers I needed.'

'Yeah. What a prick, eh?'

She furrowed her brow. 'How so?'

'Standing you up?'

She shrugged. 'He wasn't interested. It was important information.'

'Yeah, but he could have phoned. That would be the usual social convention.'

'How do?' It was Reggie, fortunately, here to interrupt this rather awkward conversation.

Frank turned around. Reggie was in his Lycra running gear.

Frank's eyes widened. 'Bloody hell! Bit early for that!'

Reggie rolled his shoulders. 'Best time to run, first thing.'

'I didn't mean too early to run. I meant it was too early

for me to see you like that! Christ! I won't need my coffee any more. Bloody wide awake now!'

As Frank headed out, he made a mental note to grab him and Gerry lunch on his way back from interviewing Rory again. A small gesture, but one he hoped would convey his appreciation for her dedication, and that he sympathised with her for being stood up, even though she didn't seem to care less.

Chapter Thirty

Mike Bailey ran his finger through the greasy residue smeared at the bottom of his air-fryer. Grimacing, he eyed up the ball of fat on his fingertip. 'You're disgusting.' He sucked the grease from his finger.

After, he stared down at the empty family-sized packet of sausages, wondering if he should cook the second packet in his fridge. He made a resolution to wait. Otherwise, he'd be ordering in more food before afternoon.

Using his rollator, he worked his way back to his sofa. Having stuffed his face before the exertion, he had to pause a few times as his stomach churned. Eventually, he made it to the sofa and eased himself down, his days of flopping down long behind him. It would break the sofa, and probably him, too.

Mike was always exhausted, but this morning it had got to where he simply felt wired. Last night in bed had been *so* bad. The memory of Noah's horrified reaction had tormented him. The effort to reconnect on the doorstep had left his boy with more scars than he'd already had.

Mike cursed Laurie, Noah's mother, for giving out his

address, before realising he was blaming the wrong person. There was only really one person to blame in all of this.

Despite feeling wired, and believing sleep a mere fantasy, Mike managed a nap, albeit a restless one. These days, the Barghest was always looming in his dreamworld, its glowing red eyes boring into Mike's soul.

The sound of the doorbell jolted Mike awake.

Heart pounding, he glanced at his mobile screen. The guilty party. He hoped she wasn't here to beat him with a stick over yesterday. It was she that had sent him, for fuck's sake!

He regarded his ex-wife on the screen with a sigh. Laurie used to take pride in her appearance; these days she always appeared pale and dishevelled.

More wreckage left in your wake, Mike.

He pressed the intercom button on the phone. 'Laurie, I—'

She cut him off by pounding on the door. 'Just fucking open it, Mike.'

He sighed. He may as well. She'd already seen him like this several times. Besides, he felt annoyed at her for sending Noah around, and he was determined to tell her so. The other times she'd visited, he'd worked his way to the door. But right now, he felt too exhausted to move.

'There's a key,' he said. 'Under the fifth pot beneath the kitchen window.'

The key was there for food and parcel deliveries. His nurse, Emma, didn't need it, though. She had her own. Would he have to move his key now? Would Laurie tell Noah? Well, he couldn't take the risk, although he suspected the chances of Noah ever returning probably stood at zero.

Laurie came in silently and sat on a single chair opposite him. She was yet to look at him. Her head was hanging low. When she finally looked up, her eyes were red and puffy from crying.

He was sympathetic, but he couldn't hide the frustration he was feeling over what she'd done. 'Laurie, that was a mistake.'

She narrowed her eyes. 'Your son? Desperate to see you? A mistake?'

Mike sighed. He didn't do anger these days, really. Not just because it would probably kill him, but because he simply had little energy. So, he kept his voice gentle. 'Did he tell you what happened?'

She shook her head. 'No. He said he was going to come and see you, and then hasn't come home.'

Mike's breath caught in his throat. 'Shit... I...'

She shook her head. 'Stop. He phoned. It's not that. He's at a friend's.'

'Thank God—'

'It's this.' She threw something in his direction. It landed on the sofa beside him. 'I found *these* in his room.'

He plucked a small resealable plastic bag filled with tablets from the sofa beside him. He held them up in a shaft of light from the window. Each pill had some kind of cartoon character stamped on it.

Mike's stomach churned as it'd done earlier on the journey to the sofa. He felt his blood running, ice cold, and the hand clutching the pills shook. 'Oh no. Oh God.'

He looked up at his ex-wife, who was sobbing now, tapping her foot on the ground and wringing her hands. 'You see? You see what's happening? It's spiralling.'

'Are you sure these are his?'

She glared at him. 'They were in his top drawer.'

Mike stared at the pills again. There must have been over fifty. 'They can't all be for him.'

'Are you serious, Mike? What's wrong with you?'

He shook his head. 'Sorry... I'm tired...'

'He's dealing, Mike. Your son is a drug dealer.'

He closed his hands around the resealable bag, hiding it from view. 'Stop. Just stop. Please.'

She snorted. 'Why? So, you can turn a blind eye to this, you pathetic, self-pitying bastard.'

'No, I just don't feel so good.' Mike's chest was tightening, his breath coming in short, shallow gasps. His knuckles turned white, and he hoped he was turning the pills to dust. His heart raced, and cold sweat beaded on his brow.

Laurie's words echoed in his mind, each syllable a dagger to his heart. Pathetic. Self-pitying. Bastard. The weight of his failures pressed down on him, crushing the air from his lungs. He wanted to scream, to deny it all, but the truth of her words settled like a lead weight in his gut.

Tears pricked at the corners of his eyes as he struggled to regain control, to steady his breathing and slow his thundering pulse. But the panic had taken hold, its icy fingers wrapped around his throat, squeezing until black spots danced at the edges of his vision.

'I'm sorry,' he muttered between ragged breaths. 'I'm so sorry.'

The rest of the conversation passed in a blur behind his panic attack. Only after she'd left, and he was coming round, was he able to reconstruct moments of it...

Him pleading and begging for forgiveness. Him promising that he'd do what he could to help his son.

Her sharp tone had never faltered. She'd laid all the blame at his feet. Then she'd delivered a final call-to-arms and left. 'If you truly wanted to save your son, you'd get help.'

It was only after she'd left that he delivered his weak excuses to the now empty chair.

'It's not that simple... I've tried, Laurie... I'm trapped... it's not as easy as you think...'

Tears in his eyes, he regarded the bag in his trembling hand again, and then struggled to his feet and onto his rollator, pinning the pills between his palm and the handle.

His body straining, he journeyed to the bathroom. His muscles burned and his lungs heaved as he fought against the limitations of his own flesh.

But even as his physical form faltered, Mike forced himself on.

Get with the programme, Mike. Noah needs you.

Now, more than ever, he had to break through these walls of his own making. Shatter the chains of apathy and self-pity that had held him captive for so long.

Yet even as this determination surged through his veins, Mike felt the familiar tug of hopelessness, the insidious whisper that told him he was too far gone, too broken to ever truly change. It was a voice he knew all too well, a constant companion in his darkest moments.

With each agonising step, Mike waged an internal war, his desperation to save his son battling against the ingrained patterns of thought that kept him mired in his own misery. He wanted to be the father Noah deserved, to rise above his own pain and be the guiding light his child so desperately needed. But the ghosts of his failures loomed large, a seemingly insurmountable barrier between the man he was and the man he longed to be.

In the bathroom, he stared at the tablets in the small bag. He considered swallowing them whole.

A morbid vision flashed through Mike's mind, vivid and unbidden. Noah, standing by a fresh grave, his youthful face etched with grief and anger. Eyes which were once so full of life and laughter, hollow and haunted. And Mike, now a helpless spectre, watching his son slump away, seeking that path of self-destruction.

Like father, like son.

The vision hit Mike like a physical blow, stealing the breath from his lungs and sending a spike of icy fear through his heart.

No. Finding Mike dead in this bathroom wouldn't make this situation any better. It'd be another burden for his boy to carry.

He unsealed the small bag, tipped it over the toilet bowl, and watched as the pills disappeared into the swirling water.

Fuck your failure, Mike. No more. Do you hear? No more.

In the dark recesses of his consciousness, the Barghest's eyes glowed, a haunting reminder of what he was up against.

Chapter Thirty-One

Rory was busy stacking glasses behind the bar. 'Frank! Just in time. I got my new La Marzocco Linea Classic coffee machine!'

'Your what?'

'A coffee machine known for precise temperature control and consistent espresso extraction. Fancy testing my java?'

Even though Frank understood nothing of what Rory had just said, coffee sounded nice. 'Yeah, go on then.' He looked around the pub, suddenly nostalgic for the days when he could have complemented the coffee with a roll-up.

As Rory operated the machine, steaming the milk and pulling the espresso shots, he first asked Frank about his bruised face.

'It might not look it, but it's feeling better,' Frank lied.

'How's the investigation?'

'Moving along,' he said. *Just.*

'Sorry, Frank, give me a tick to concentrate – only the third time I've used it. Don't want to mess it up.'

Frank tapped his foot. He considered stopping him and telling him there was no need to go to so much effort over his coffee. He wondered why people bothered waiting in a pub! It was quicker and easier to have a pint pulled.

'Almost there,' Rory said. 'You know, it barely seems five minutes since we last spoke.'

You worried about something, Rory? Frank thought.

Rory turned around, holding the fresh coffee. 'You're going to love this, Frank.'

Frank pulled a photograph from his inside jacket pocket. 'Swap you.' He put the picture down on the bar, and Rory placed the coffee cup beside it.

Rory picked it up and squinted at it. He pushed his glasses down from his head and brought the photo closer. Then, he nodded.

Did he recognise him? A surge of adrenaline whipped through Frank.

Rory looked back up and held the picture high. 'Is this the victim?'

'Aye.'

'Yes. He used to come into the Anchor. A long while back. Didn't know him personally, like.'

'Does the name Adrian Hughes mean anything to you?' Frank slid the coffee cup towards himself. The rich aroma wafted up to greet him.

'Afraid not.' He looked at the picture again. 'Adrian Hughes, eh? Now what happened to you in my pub?'

'Good question.' Frank lifted the cup to his lips and took a sip. Bold, smooth flavour. 'That's fine coffee.'

'Damn right it is.' Rory winked.

'Can you remember when Adrian Hughes came into the Anchor?'

'Bloody hell, Frank!'

FORGOTTEN LIVES

'Roughly. Did he play cards? Stands to reason he could have died in that cellar.'

'In the eighties?'

Frank took another sip of coffee. 'I could get used to this.' He nodded appreciatively at the cup.

Rory nodded, clearly proud of his java.

'Could you be more specific than eighties, Rory?'

He raised an eyebrow. 'I'll try. If you trust my memory.'

'I do.'

'He wasn't a regular, but I remember seeing him a few times. Mainly for the cards. It was to the back end of the eighties as I remember old Jed Harris moaning about how he'd rinsed him for that week's dole cheque. Classy, eh? I remember Jed dying not long after.' He tapped his chest. 'Heart issues. That was around 1988, or perhaps 1989... I spoke to my wife last night, as I promised. Now she recalls we stopped the games at the end of August, as I thought yesterday. Do you know when he disappeared yet?'

'Then.' Frank eyed up Rory with narrowed eyes. '30th August.'

Rory's face darkened. 'Shit. I don't like the way you're looking at me.'

'Well, let's look at this from my perspective,' Frank said. 'Adrian Hughes was reported missing on 30th August 1989. We suspected he actually disappeared over the previous weekend – 25th August to the 27th. And now I discover that you closed down the cards cellar and locked the door right after that weekend? Quite a coincidence that, wouldn't you say?'

'Well, I didn't specifically say that weekend.'

'But it's the last one in August. And you said there was no more cards after that.'

Rory gulped. 'You honestly believe, Frank, that if I killed this Adrian, whoever—'

'Hughes.'

'Yes, Adrian Hughes. A man I never even really knew – that I'd keep him in my own cellar?'

'And then give it to the council to come along and find it?' Frank asked, assisting Rory in painting a stupid portrait.

'Precisely. Would I really be that thick?'

Frank shrugged. 'Wonders never cease. And, believe me, that wouldn't be the stupidest thing I've ever encountered.' *Although quite high on the scale, admittedly,* Frank thought.

Rory fixed him with a stare. 'It wasn't me. No chance. I barely knew the man!'

'But seems strange. That being the final weekend. Coincidental.'

'I can't explain, except to say it'd been coming a while. The wall was shite, as I told you. After a weekend, I just put an end to the risk.'

Frank finished his coffee, nodding. 'Delicious.'

'Best had be. The machine cost £10,000.'

Frank stared at his coffee like it was something from another world. *Jesus.* 'Guess treating myself to one of these machines is out of the question then.'

'Cheaper if you go refurbished,' Rory said.

'Still be out of my price range, though. Rory, what *do* you remember about Adrian Hughes?'

'Not much. Although I remember a couple of instances of him coming in with a much younger lad. An odd pair they made. Back in '89, some of my staff weren't always diligent enough to check the identification of our youngest patrons. These days, he wouldn't be served anywhere around here, though.'

Frank nodded. 'You say it was an odd pairing?'

'Aye. I reckon over twice his age.' He raised an eyebrow suggestively.

Frank frowned. 'So you thought they were involved?'

'They weren't kissing or cuddling or owt, but I remember some of my other punters having a grumble over it. They obviously thought so. I didn't want to make assumptions, like.' Rory held up his hands defensively. 'But you didn't see many, ah, alternative lifestyles back then, if you catch my drift. Especially not in a place like the Rusty Anchor.'

'Did the young lad play cards too?'

'No, but I seem to recall him accompanying Adrian down there.'

Frank nodded slowly, digesting this new information. 'I see. And did you ever interact with Adrian directly? Get a sense of who he was?'

Rory shrugged. 'Not really, to be honest. Like I said, he seemed a quiet one. Was on his own, or with this young lad. And he played cards. All I can tell you really...'

'Can you remember anyone having a run-in with him?'

'You mean, did I fall out with him and put him behind my cellar wall? No.'

Frank nodded. 'How about the lad? Any altercations with him?'

'Nothing.' Rory's response was sharp. He was becoming more defensive.

Not that Frank cared. He wasn't Donald Oxley.

Frank leaned forward, his elbows resting on the bar. 'Rory, if there's something you're not telling me, now's the time to come clean. Anything you know could be crucial to this investigation.'

'I've told you everything I know, Frank. I didn't have any problems with Adrian or the lad.'

Frank held Rory's gaze for a long moment, searching for any hint of deception. But Rory's eyes remained steady, his expression resolute. Frank leaned back in his seat wondering if Frank's pressure would worm its way back to the chief constable. 'Could you give me a description of the lad with Adrian?'

He sighed. 'I'll give it a shot.'

Frank took out his notebook to make notes.

After that, Frank declined a second cup of coffee. It was delicious, but he needed to get back.

In his car, Frank considered the fact that Rory had closed the cellar on that same weekend. It was too coincidental. He didn't believe it was Rory, though. Frank's gut instinct, honed over years of police work, told him Rory wasn't their man.

For one, Rory's reaction seemed genuinely surprised and concerned when confronted with the timing. If he'd been involved, Frank would have expected more nervousness or rehearsed responses. Moreover, Rory's willingness to share information about Adrian and the young lad didn't align with someone trying to cover up a murder.

There was also the practical aspect. As Rory had pointed out, keeping a body in his own cellar for decades, then handing the property over to the council, would be an incredibly risky and foolish move for a murderer. Frank had encountered some dim criminals in his time, but this level of stupidity seemed unlikely, especially for someone who'd managed a successful pub for years.

So if it wasn't Rory, what did that suggest? Had someone convinced Rory to shut up shop that very weekend? It hadn't sounded that way. Rory, himself, was fairly adamant that he'd been the one to make the decision, so could someone have subtly influenced him, leaving very little trace on his memory?

Frank rubbed his chin, pondering.

If not Rory, then who? And how did they manage to time things so perfectly with the cellar's closure?

Also significant was this younger man who'd accompanied Adrian.

Potentially too young to be in the pub, but a suggestion that he was Adrian's boyfriend.

There was no doubt now that Adrian Hughes had a secret life which he'd hidden from his sister.

Frank tried to stay positive by telling himself that secret doesn't always mean bad. But he'd be lying if he said he wasn't starting to feel concerned.

Chapter Thirty-Two

Rob had never been blind to his trauma.

He'd just done a bloody good job of hiding its existence from everyone, while it'd lingered in the darkest, quietest recesses of his mind, draining him.

Still, to date, he'd managed. Admirably, in his opinion. He'd built a career and a family.

A robust unit.

Or so he'd thought.

Now, following the death of Bryan, and his meeting with Louise, that robust unit felt more like a house of cards.

And it teetered on the brink of collapse.

It'd been so long since he'd experienced flashbacks to those dark, suffocating moments. But here they were. In all their glory. Visiting him in those brief seconds between wakefulness and sleep, where the mind went into a spin. Until that crushing, suffocating weight of Gideon's heavy body was too much, and he was dragged upright, sweating and shouting in the here and now.

Sarah had never seen him like this. She hugged him in

the early hours, wanting to know what was wrong. In the end, he'd given up on sleep and headed out for a walk, sparing his family those tormented cries.

After Rob had used the key and his passport to retrieve a brown envelope from the safe deposit box at the bank, Rob took it and walked to the stone pier to open it. It was still early. Apart from some fishing folk bobbing around on the water, he was alone.

He gazed up at the Gothic ruins of Whitby Abbey looming atop the cliffs. He breathed deeply the briny scent of the sea and opened the envelope.

A TDK cassette tape. The black plastic casing was scuffed, the label faded with age. Rob ran his thumb over the raised letters, feeling the bumps and ridges beneath his skin.

A circle of gulls squawked, making him jump, and he almost dropped it into the sea.

That may've been for the best. This unassuming little rectangle held the power to change everything, to bring the darkest secrets of his past screaming into the light.

He recalled Bryan's words as if it were yesterday. 'I recorded everything.'

Rob turned the tape over in his hand, the weight of it far greater than its physical mass. He'd never listened to it. Had never really needed to. He'd experienced Gideon Blackwell's nasty instructions and cruel voice firsthand. It was recorded in his brain, forever. As evidenced by the worst night's sleep he'd had in the longest while.

Rob closed his eyes, the sound of the waves fading into the background as he thought of his family.

Sophie. A star on the stage, her passion for theatre burning bright. He remembered the pride that had swelled in his chest as he'd watched her take her first bow, the way her eyes had sparkled with joy and triumph. She'd a future ahead of her, a world of possibilities just waiting to be seized.

Nathan, his middle child. A budding scientist with a mind as sharp as a razor. Rob marvelled at the boy's intellect, at the way he seemed to soak up knowledge like a sponge. Nathan had already won countless accolades for his academic achievements, and Rob knew he was destined for greatness.

Lily, his youngest. A gentle soul with an artist's heart. He thought of the countless hours she'd spent hunched over her sketchbook, her tiny hands bringing to life the wonders of her imagination. She'd a rare gift, a sensitivity and depth of emotion that Rob sometimes feared would be her undoing in this harsh world.

'Don't you understand, Bryan?' he asked out loud. 'It isn't just me and you any more. Two lonely kids on a bench.'

The past could be powerful. Potentially too powerful for the present. How would the shame and scandal from a lifetime ago affect the lives today of the people he loved?

What would it do to Sophie's budding career, to have her father's sordid history splashed across the headlines? How would Nathan and Lily fare at school, with their classmates whispering and pointing, their innocence forever tainted by the sins of their father?

Wasn't his decision made?

He drew his hand back, ready to throw the tape into the churning sea. 'I'm sorry, Bryan.'

Brothers forever.

'But I can't. You're asking me to define my family's legacy with this. They've so much potential. Their futures are so bright. I'd rather go in the water with this fucking tape than risk all of that.'

He could almost see the sadness in his lost friend's face, the expression Bryan had worn during their conversation all those years ago, sitting together on their special bench.

'Why didn't you do it back then? Why didn't you bring him to justice?'

But Louise had been clear on that. By the time Bryan had realised it was the right thing to do, he was too weak. Besides, he'd have known all along that his story would fall flat. Bryan was a washed-up drunk. There'd have been no appetite for taking down former MP Gideon Blackwell over a man so tainted. Somehow, this evidence would be buried. Yet Rob was different. He was a success. People listened to him. Imagine if he told the truth about what had happened to them? People would listen. The world would demand justice.

'But what happens when the truth about who I was gets out?' he shouted into the wind. 'I could lose everything. My family could lose everything.' He gritted his teeth, preparing to throw the tape.

Then, unbidden, some words from Bryan's note echoed in his mind.

I left you in peace all these years. I gave you the freedom you wanted and deserved. But now I'm gone. I'm gone and what happened to me paralyses my daughter. Inside, I know, it still paralyses you. It leaves everything wrong. Gideon hasn't been judged. What he did destroyed me. And despite all your claims, I believe he destroyed part of you, too.

He has been a shadow.

He still is a fucking shadow.

Time to shine the light, brother.

Rob clutched the tape to his chest and wept.

And then an idea struck him.

He turned from the pier, a compromise clear in his mind.

Did he need light to eliminate a shadow?

More darkness could work just fine.

Especially if it would keep his own demons buried.

Chapter Thirty-Three

Frank picked up two bacon butties on the way back.

When he presented a greasy paper bag to Gerry, she regarded it in the same way she'd regarded Reggie's toy bone the day before.

'Go on.'

She shook her head.

'At least look at what's inside.'

'I can't touch that bag,' Gerry said.

He took the bacon sandwich out for her. 'Look. Don't be deceived by the bag. Fluffy bap. Crispy bacon.'

She shook her head again. 'Saturated fat and sodium levels are too high. Not to mention the carcinogenic compounds formed during the curing process… you shouldn't be eating them. No one should eat them.'

Frank regarded her. Tom had been a mean bastard standing her up, no question, but he'd dodged a real bullet. Imagine being partnered with Gerry, and never again being able to enjoy the taste of bacon?

He sighed, looked down at Rylan, and considered offering the bacon to him. Of course, he couldn't, because

Gerry would undoubtedly put an end to his existence. Instead, he held it in the air. 'Anyone for a bacon sandwich?'

Reggie, who was now out of the Lycra, patted his stomach. 'No thanks, boss. I had lychee for breakfast.'

'Eh?' Frank was taken aback. 'What? Actually, don't, Reggie. Best I don't know.'

'I'll take it, boss.' Sean held his hand up.

Frank put it in his detective constable's hand, looking back at Gerry with a smug expression. But she'd already moved on. He looked back at Sean. 'On one condition, though. It wakes you up, lad. Guess what: my no-slumping rule comes into force today.'

'Oh.' Sean looked up at him sheepishly. 'What's that?'

'It means that if I see you hunching over a desk after treating you to a butty that cost me £3.99, I'm going to tie a one metre ruler to your back. *Tightly.*'

'Yes, boss.' Sean corrected his posture. Maybe a little too much.

'Aye, good, but don't slip a disc, like.'

Frank called the room to attention and filled everyone in on his visit to Rory. 'Identifying that young man is going to be key and...' He looked at Reggie. 'We have an issue with Rory. I'm not saying I fancy him for the murder, but the man closed his card cellar immediately after Adrian met his end there. There's something missing here. Something he's forgotten about or is holding back.' He kept his eyes on Reggie. 'However, keep that within these four walls for now.'

Reggie nodded, knowing he was being addressed. He was closer to Donald Oxley than the rest of them and had been out drinking with him. Still, although Reggie irritated the piss out of him, he trusted him. No chance he'd be sitting here otherwise!

'So, Reggie,' Frank said. 'Step up on that list of cardplayers and staff that have worked at the Anchor over the years. Quiz them all to death on Adrian Hughes. Throw his picture out like confetti. And let's find out the identity of the mysterious lad. Someone knows something.'

Reggie nodded. 'Few are alive. Lots of those cardplayers were already on their last legs.'

'I'm sure you'll hit a purple patch soon… Gerry?'

Gerry looked at her screen as she delivered her findings. 'I've been in touch with the guests from the Moonrise Hotel who stayed on Friday 24th March, 1989,' Gerry said. 'Laura Bauer and Jan Nowak don't remember seeing or interacting with Adrian at all. But Tessa and James Garrick recall him very well.'

Frank leaned over his desk, eyes widening.

Here she goes. Gerry Carver. Breakthrough central.

'They emigrated to Australia in their sixties. Tessa hasn't been too well, so I spoke with James alone via Zoom. James Garrick recognised the photo and remembered seeing Adrian that evening. He was in the foyer, sitting with Tessa, waiting for Adrian to finish up at reception, so he could check in.' Gerry panned her eyes around her audience for the first time. 'He was with a much much younger man. At first, James Garrick thought they were father and son.'

Good lord, Frank thought. *Is this the same lad Rory was just on about? The one Adrian was dragging to the Anchor with him?*

'The young man started quarrelling with the hotel manager. It got very heated. I guess this explains why it stayed so vivid in James' memory. Turns out, they'd already banned the young man from staying there. James recalls

Adrian being almost silent throughout the entire altercation. Standing back while his companion accused the management of treating him like dirt. Eventually, both Adrian and his angry companion left with their bags.'

'So, Adrian never actually stayed there?'

'Yes.' Gerry nodded. 'But there's more. James knew the manager. A Felix Cotton. So while James was checking in, he quizzed Felix over the argument. Felix revealed that the young man was a male escort, offering sexual services, and so couldn't stay in the hotel.'

'Bloody hell,' Frank said. 'Could we get in touch with Felix?'

'He passed in 2017.'

Shit. Frank turned and glanced at the picture of Adrian and then back again at his team. 'He was using male prostitutes. Jesus.'

'Explains why he kept his trips out secret from his sister,' Reggie said.

'Who was this young man?' Frank asked. 'Was it the same one in the Anchor? We need to find this out, folks, as soon as we can.'

'I've something else,' Gerry said. 'I spoke to one of Felix's colleagues from the time. He doesn't remember this incident specifically, but he remembers a local agency. This young lad wasn't the first sex worker to cross their threshold. There'd been a few around this period. They were all working for an agency called *The Sapphire Companions.*' She turned back to her computer screen. 'The agency closed down in '92. The owner and manager, Kath Fielding, did a stint in prison for tax issues.'

'Rather than soliciting sex?' Reggie snorted.

'They never found her guilty of soliciting sex, and they

never proved that the agency offered anything but companionship for social events and so forth.'

Frank put his hands on the table, leaned in, and fixed Gerry with a stare. 'Gerry, tell me she's alive and kicking.'

'She's alive.'

'Well done.' Frank tapped the table with the palm of his hand.

'She's in the Whispering Willows Care Home.'

Frank stood up straight, nodding. 'Well, let's hope they're taking better care of her than she took of those young men in the eighties.'

He smiled in Gerry's direction, but she'd already turned her attention back to the computer.

In that moment, he even forgave her for rudely dismissing his well-intentioned, if rather ill-advised, breakfast offering.

Frank called time on the briefing so Gerry and he could see Kath, but Adrian's secret life was really bothering him. He didn't want his team to be in any doubt. They kept going and gave it their all.

'Okay, if he used prostitutes, which seems to be the case, it makes him no less worthy of our focus and attention. If anything, it makes him more so. Remember what happened to him as a child, remember how damaged he was. We owe it to him and his sister to get the full picture. Okay?'

They all grunted their affirmation.

Did they agree?

Who knew?

Right now, he didn't even know if he agreed with himself.

Chapter Thirty Four

THE OPULENT FAÇADE of Whispering Willows Care Home stood in stark contrast to the grim purpose of Frank and Gerry's visit. The sprawling Victorian mansion, nestled amidst meticulously manicured gardens, catered to the wealthy elite in their twilight years. Frank couldn't help but feel a twinge of disgust as they approached the entrance, knowing that a significant portion of Kath Fielding's ill-gotten gains had likely funded her stay in this lavish establishment.

Because of her failing health, it took the best part of the day to organise this meeting, but they eventually made the appointment. Whispering Willows didn't allow dogs anywhere near, so Reggie had agreed to look after Rylan, but not before Gerry sternly warned him off giving the Lab any toy bones.

While being led through the plush corridors, Frank steeled himself, pushing aside his personal feelings. He'd already asked Gerry to lead the interview. He feared being too clouded by judgement, especially after speaking to a sex worker the other night and fearing that his own daughter may've gone the same way. Gerry's matter-of-fact approach was necessary.

They found Kath sitting up in her room by the window, her frail hands deftly manipulating a worn deck of cards. The lines etched on Kath's face spoke of a life lived hard, but her eyes still glinted with a sharpness that belied her age. She looked in better health than the earlier phone calls had led Frank to believe.

'Patience,' she said.

At first, it sounded as if she was admonishing them for their keen approach, but then Frank realised she was merely referring to the game.

'Learned it rather late in life. In prison.' She looked up at them for the first time. 'Keeps my mind sharp. If not for cards, it would have turned to dust long ago.'

Frank, who'd had more than enough card talk in this investigation, introduced Gerry and himself. They both settled into chairs around the table she was playing on.

'I've paid my dues.' She laid the cards down in a neat pile, her movements deliberate and precise. 'I refuse to be judged again.'

Refuse away, but what difference will it make? Frank thought. *Considering what you did, I reckon everyone you meet has a go at judging you. Even if they don't say it to your face.*

'We just need information to assist with a murder investigation,' Gerry said. 'This isn't about your responsibility or guilt.'

'Guilt?' She raised an eyebrow. 'I had a few issues regarding the court's decision on my guilt with those tax charges.'

'Like we said,' Frank interjected. 'Just a few questions.'

Gerry placed a photograph on the table in front of her. 'Do you remember Adrian Hughes?'

She gave it a brief glance, her expression impassive. 'Yes. As I confirmed earlier when you phoned. Did you think I would've accepted this meeting if I didn't? I want to help.'

Sure you do, Frank thought. *But you wouldn't have been able to stop us. We would've got access to you eventually.*

'How did he die?' She looked at Frank. He saw the morbid curiosity glinting in her eyes.

He was in no mood to satisfy that question with an answer.

'Someone murdered him.' Gerry steered the conversation back to her without giving specific details. 'What do you remember about Adrian Hughes?'

Kath sneered at Frank and turned to Gerry. 'That he was a regular client and that he always asked for the same person.'

'And who would that be?' Gerry asked.

'His name was Robert Wake.'

Frank wrote the name down. He pressed the pen hard on his notebook.

'And how old was he?' Frank wanted to hear the words come from her mouth.

'Sixteen.' Matter-of-factly. As if discussing the weather.

'Very young, eh?' Frank narrowed his eyes.

'Old enough to work.' Kath shrugged.

Frank dug the pen harder into his notebook.

'Do you know how we can get in touch with this Robert Wake?' Gerry's voice was calm, and must have sounded ridiculously professional next to his.

'Yes. He runs a car dealership.' She gave the location. 'About five years ago, before I came here, I went with my granddaughter to buy a car. When I recognised him, I left her to it before he spotted me. Fortunately, she doesn't share my family name, or she may not have got such a sizeable discount.' She smiled.

What a shame that would have been, Frank thought.

'Can you tell us anything else about the relationship between your employee, Robert Wake, and your customer, Adrian Hughes?' Gerry asked.

'Only that it suddenly soured. That's why I remember it, you see. Which is just as well, since I've no actual records.'

Frank took a deep breath when he detected the ghost of a smile on her face.

'How did it sour?' Gerry asked.

'Well, it lasted a while. I'm guessing around a year, but I can't be precise. They met every couple of weeks. But then Adrian became possessive, or so Robert claimed. I'd no idea.'

Unable to help himself, Frank said, 'Adrian asked for Robert every time and you didn't suspect he was being possessive?'

Kath shrugged. 'It was common for customers to want the same escort.'

'And what did Robert say to you?' Gerry asked.

'He said that he wouldn't see Adrian any more. That he was taking it far too seriously.'

'And what happened?'

She nodded sharply, her eyes hard and unyielding. 'I told him to do his job.'

'And you thought that was the right thing?' Frank asked.

'Absolutely. He was being paid.' Her words were clipped and final.

Hearing her justify herself made Frank's heart hammer in his chest. He took a deep breath, allowing Gerry back in.

'Your company offered a service to men and women. Someone who could accompany them to events and offer them company in restaurants. Correct?'

'Exactly right.' She nodded.

'Not sexual relationships?' Gerry asked.

Kath feigned a confused expression, her eyes wide with mock innocence. 'We offered a service for lonely or single people who needed company. If anything else was going off, I knew nothing about it.'

Liar, Frank thought.

'Did you know if Adrian and Robert were having a sexual relationship?' Gerry kept the pressure on.

Kath sighed. 'I couldn't answer that. I can't be accountable for everything my employee did outside of the workplace.'

Frank shook his head. He couldn't take much more of this bollocks! 'Did you feel you had any responsibility for Robert's well-being?'

'We paid him well.' Her tone was dismissive.

'So, his mental health wasn't important?'

She chuckled. A low, grating sound that went through Frank. 'Come now, DCI. It was a different world back then, as well you know!'

'Maybe, but I don't remember it being quite so barbaric.'

She rolled her eyes.

'So, what happened when you demanded that Robert continue seeing Adrian?' Gerry's voice cut through the tension.

'He went and quit.'

Good for him, Frank thought. 'Are you surprised?'

Kath shrugged.

'Do you know what happened to Robert after that?' Gerry asked.

'Of course not. Once he was off the books, he was off the books. Then, as I've said, five years back, I saw him in that showroom, looking quite the part! He made quite a life for himself.' She smirked. 'I like to think I played some part in that.'

Frank felt a surge of anger at the levity in Kath's voice, as if the whole sordid affair was just a mildly interesting anecdote to be trotted out at dinner parties. The casual way she spoke of the boy's trauma, the way she brushed aside her own complicity in his suffering, made Frank's stomach turn.

'Jesus,' Frank said. 'The lad was sixteen years old. Have you no shame whatsoever?'

'As I said before, we paid well. It was a good job. Offering company while fine dining and going to cocktail parties! I'm sure it wasn't all bad.'

'You can't be serious right now. Sixteen! You put him in harm's way.'

'Behave!' Kath waved him away. It was a gesture that spoke of a lifetime of rationalisations. 'A sixteen-year-old boy? They're bloody strong. Have you forgotten when you were young, DCI? I ensured all our girls were over eighteen.'

'Have you tried justifying this to your granddaughter?' Frank asked.

'She doesn't ask.'

'Because you were buying her a car?'

'Because she knows the truth.' Kath sighed, trying to

convey a long-suffering patience. 'Anything else I can help you with before you go?'

'Did Adrian ever request anyone else?' Gerry asked.

'Yes... but only after Robert left. I can't remember how many times. Not quite as many. Eventually, we lost his business. I guess he felt betrayed over the Robert situation. Always a shame, really. Losing a regular.'

Frank guffawed. 'You lost the business because someone stabbed him and sealed him behind a wall.'

Kath raised an eyebrow and Frank immediately regretted satisfying that morbid curiosity she'd shown earlier.

'At the end of August in 1989,' Gerry said.

Kath nodded. 'So long ago... so that's the real reason we never heard from Adrian again. Interesting.'

'Who was the young man Adrian requested after Robert?' Gerry asked.

Kath sighed and shook her head. 'My memory is failing me. I only remember Robert because of our set-to over it all. To be honest, we'd a lot of employees back then.' She fixed Frank with a stare. 'But I'd tell you if I could remember.' She sounded sincere, but he couldn't help but doubt her words.

'Can you recall if Adrian ever requested companionship for the Rusty Anchor pub?' Gerry asked, her pen hovering over her notebook.

She gave it a moment's thought, her brow furrowed in concentration. 'It sounds familiar. But the pieces don't always join in my head any more.'

'How about the Moonrise Hotel?' Frank asked.

Kath shrugged. 'I'm sorry.'

Frank realised it was the first time that Kath had apologised for anything since they'd entered the room.

After another series of questions that yielded nothing, Frank stood up and left without saying goodbye, leaving Gerry to the pleasantries.

Back in the car, an Audi checked out from work because of Gerry's aversion to Bertha, Frank said, 'She's a piece of work, but at least we've a name. Robert Wake. But if her memory is accurate, we've another young man to identify. It was more than likely this second young man in the Rusty Anchor with him.'

Gerry researched on her phone, using the car showroom information given to them by Kath.

'Robert Johnson,' she said, 'manages this showroom. Has done for ten years.'

'Kath said five years back, so let's confirm he changed his name from Wake to Johnson before we speak to him.'

Gerry nodded.

While Gerry made the phone call, Frank reflected on the first moment he'd seen Adrian's remains, and the drive he'd felt to find the truth and get justice.

If Adrian had indeed hounded sixteen-year-old Robert Wake, and paid him money for sex, then everything Frank had felt until this point would come under severe scrutiny.

But it was important to hold judgement in check until he had all the facts.

And if it turned out to be the truth, could he find any mitigating factors? Any shred of context that could explain, if not excuse, Adrian's actions?

Maybe Adrian had never known that Robert was this young?

Or maybe Adrian, broken by his own experience of abuse, couldn't form proper relationships and felt drawn to prostitution?

But how much mitigation could he be allowed? At what

point did understanding and empathy give way to accountability and consequence?

Whatever came next, one thing was obvious.

The revelations were getting murkier and murkier, and Frank really didn't like it.

Not one bit.

Chapter Thirty Five

For the past few hours, Rob had been sitting in his car near Sir Gideon Blackwell's grand Georgian house on the outskirts of Whitby. His phone had rung several times from an unknown number. A DCI Frank Black had left a message. A request to speak to him regarding an old investigation.

A matter of urgency.

Not now, he'd thought, rubbing his temples. *Whatever it is, DCI, I can't do that now. There's already too much going on.*

Sarah had also left several messages pressing him on when he was coming home to get ready to go to Sophie's play.

He'd considered ringing her, telling her not to worry, that he'd be back soon, but the truth was, he didn't know if he would be.

In all honesty, he didn't know what he was doing.

The world was in a spin.

Another text message from his wife just intensified the situation.

> The police have been round. A DCI Frank
> Black! They need your help with
> something. What's going on?

Good question, he thought. *I've no idea.*

After it had turned dark, he moved his car closer to Gideon's looming property. Its windows glinted in the moonlight like watchful eyes.

Gripping the steering wheel, he tried to comprehend what had brought him to this place, but his mind was a whirlwind of conflicting emotions. Anger at the man in this house; concern for the family he adored; and guilt over his obligation to Bryan.

His phone buzzed in his pocket, and he glanced down at his smart watch to see a message from his wife.

> Sophie's performance is about to start!
> Where are you???

Rob closed his eyes and saw what should be happening.

Him, in the audience, watching as his daughter shone. The proud father. Clutching the hand of the woman he cherished. Loving husband.

This was who he was. Who he'd always wanted to be.

He opened his eyes and gazed back at Gideon's home. Those intimidating windows suddenly blurred into the eyes of that middle-aged predator back in the late eighties, staring at Rob as he demanded that he lie down on a bed.

He left his vehicle and walked down the winding driveway, sneering at Gideon's house. A monument to the monster's success. A symbol of the power he'd once wielded that had earned him a knighthood.

Former Conservative MP, Gideon, had been a controversial figure – lauded by some for his efforts to revitalise

FORGOTTEN LIVES

Whitby's tourism industry, reviled by others for his staunch support of austerity measures that had left countless families struggling to make ends meet.

Rob rang the doorbell, his heart pounding in his chest as he waited for a response. A moment later, the door swung open to reveal Gideon himself, seated in a wheelchair, half of his face frozen in a permanent grimace. Rob had read somewhere about his stroke, but he'd didn't know the extent of the damage it'd caused.

'Can I help?' Gideon's speech was slurred and difficult to understand.

Rob forced a smile. 'Sir Gideon Blackwell, I'm a friend of your son, Neil. I was hoping I could come in and talk to you for a moment. My name's Rob Johnson.'

There was no recognition. But why would there be, after all these years?

This savage individual had wasted no time getting to know the people he consumed.

'What's it about?' Gideon asked.

'A business proposition. Neil said you'd be interested.'

Gideon thought about it, then with his one good eye narrowed, nodded and backed his wheelchair away from the door, allowing Rob to enter.

The interior of the house was just as grand as the exterior, all polished wood and gleaming marble. Rob followed Gideon into the lounge and observed the expensive furnishings and various modifications made to accommodate Gideon's mobility issues – the lowered shelves, widened doorways, and handrails running along every wall.

'Would you like a drink?' Gideon gestured towards the well-stocked bar in the room's corner. 'Whisky, perhaps?'

Rob nodded. 'Yes, please.' He watched, dry-mouthed, as

Gideon steered his motorised wheelchair over to the bar, his movements slow and clumsy.

How the mighty have fallen, Gideon!

Rob's top lip curled upwards as he remembered Gideon yanking his arm forcibly up behind his back and pressing him firmly down, face first, onto the bed, suffocating him...

Seeing this once-powerful man reduced to this – a shell of his former self, probably dependent on others for even the most basic of tasks – carried some satisfaction.

Would this have been enough for you, Bryan?

Of course, it wouldn't be enough. And Rob realised something else, too. He realised that seeing Gideon again like this, after all these years, wasn't enough for him either.

As Gideon poured the drinks, Rob wandered around the room, his eyes darting from one expensive trinket to another.

Rob's gaze fell upon a set of intricately carved ivory figurines, their delicate features a testament to the skill of the artisan. A gold-plated globe sat upon a mahogany stand, the continents etched in painstaking detail. On the mantelpiece, a series of crystal decanters glinted in the soft light, their contents undoubtedly as rare and costly as the vessels that held them.

He spun a tale about his friendship with Neil.

'Neil and I go way back.' Rob maintained a casual tone. 'We were at Oxford together, you know.'

Gideon paused in his efforts to pour the whisky, his good eye narrowing. 'Is that so? Neil never mentioned you.'

Rob laughed, the sound hollow even to his own ears. 'Well, you know how it is. Youthful indiscretions and all that. I'm sure there's plenty about his Oxford days that Neil hasn't told you.'

He watched as Gideon wrestled with the heavy crystal

decanter, his hands shaking with the effort. The amber liquid sloshed dangerously close to the rim of the glasses, but somehow, Gideon filled them without spilling a drop.

'We had some good times, though.' The lies flowed easily now. 'Late nights at the pub, chasing girls, that sort of thing. I remember this one time.'

As he spun false anecdotes, his dark thoughts continued to whisper.

The stroke has partially destroyed this man, but is partial really enough?

Is anything but complete destruction enough?

Even if he can't move, he can remember, can't he? Lose himself in the memories of what he did to us? Enjoy himself...

He broke off from the anecdotes, acknowledging what this monster was.

Gideon had invaded him. Both him and Bryan. Treated them like meat. Not just once, but again and again. For several months. Hired them as escorts, so their word would mean nothing. And when he'd grown bored with them? Who'd come next? He didn't know, but it'd certainly happened.

This man was a true predator.

Gideon had eroded their self-worth. Reduced Bryan to a shattered husk. Rob may've rebuilt, developed a life worth having, but even so, his insides still ached from the damage caused.

Looking at the pathetic man now, he could never have imagined such an easy opportunity. Never in his wildest dreams.

He was helpless. If he was to have an accident, would anyone question it?

It could be as simple as a fall.

Gideon was coming towards him in his motorised

wheelchair now, a tray clipped to a holder on the side, holding the two crystal glasses of whisky.

Rob's fingers twitched. But how much more rewarding would it be to curl his fingers around the disgusting man's throat. Watch the light leave his eyes.

'Speaking of Neil...' Rob accepted the glass of whisky from Gideon. 'He's doing well for himself. In our group, no one expected him to go on and be the most successful. Shouldn't have doubted his skills as an architect.'

Gideon nodded, a flicker of pride crossing his ravaged features. 'Yes, he's always had a talent for design. Even as a boy, he was forever sketching building models. I knew he'd make something of himself.'

Rob sipped his whisky, the smooth burn of the alcohol doing little to quell the rage simmering in his gut. 'Must be nice to have a son like that. Someone to carry on the family name, to make you proud.'

Rob's phone buzzed in his pocket again, another message from Sarah flashing across his watch.

> She's on stage now! She's beautiful!! This will upset her so much. Please, hurry.

'So,' Gideon said. 'What's this proposition?'

And then the combination of knowing that he was drinking with a man who'd stolen so much from him and Bryan, and that he'd let his daughter down, provoked a surge of anger. A white-hot fury that threatened to consume him. He looked at Gideon, and felt the urge to lash out, to make him pay for all the pain he'd caused. 'There isn't one.'

'I don't understand.'

Rob drank the whisky in one mouthful.

'I think it's time for you to leave.' Gideon's words were

barely intelligible. 'I don't know who you are, but you're not a friend of Neil's.'

Rob saw Gideon moving towards the far wall, where there was a conveniently placed panic button at a height he could easily reach. Rob lunged forward, grabbing the back of Gideon's wheelchair and jerking him to a stop.

'It's too late.'

He went around to the other side of the wheelchair and looked down at Gideon. Gideon's one good eye widened, fear and confusion mingling in its depth. The functioning side of his mouth opened to speak, but before he could utter a word, Rob's phone buzzed once more, and he looked at his watch.

> I cannot believe you're missing this. For pity's sake!

Rob felt the rage inside him burning hotter than ever, consuming every rational thought. His gaze fell on the fireplace, the stone hearth taking on a new, sinister meaning. He circled behind the wheelchair and spun it around to face the fireplace.

Rob could almost see it play out in his mind's eye – Gideon's skull cracking on the unforgiving stone hearth, blood pooling around his lifeless body.

'It's what you deserve,' he said out loud.

Chapter Thirty-Six

THE LAST OF Phoebe's colleagues bade her farewell and left the building, their voices fading into the night. Outside, darkness had fallen like a thick, suffocating blanket, but Phoebe couldn't bring herself to leave, not yet, even though focusing on work seemed an impossible task.

It had been over an hour since she'd been supposed to meet Julian in Larpool Wood. With each passing second, the knot in her stomach grew tighter, the sense of dread more palpable. She'd received no word from David about what had transpired at the meeting point, and the silence was deafening, a void that her imagination rushed to fill with a thousand horrifying possibilities. Phoebe knew, deep down, that she'd get an update when she returned home, but that it wouldn't be the full picture.

David would simply tell her it was over, that she needn't worry any more. It wouldn't be enough, and she'd tell him so. How could she ever stop worrying if he wasn't completely transparent with her? Her husband's past was far from savoury. He didn't like to talk about it, in the same way she didn't want to talk about hers, but she had her suspicions.

Still, to this day, she couldn't believe how fortunate she'd been. Following the deaths of Felix Delaney and Theresa Long, the police had never connected her to Julian Sims or to the crime.

David would do anything to keep that from happening. If the truth ever got out about what happened in 1990, she'd go to jail.

Deep down, she knew Julian Sims wasn't walking away from that meeting.

With a shaky breath, she looked at the various awards lining the walls of her office, testaments to her success, her philanthropy. The 'Visionary Leader' plaque from the National Council for Voluntary Organisations, the 'Outstanding Contribution to Education' certificate from the Department for Education – each one a reminder of the good she'd done, the lives she'd touched. And yet, in this moment, they felt hollow, meaningless in the face of the shadows that threatened to engulf her.

Unbidden, her husband's words from that morning echoed in her mind.

This time tomorrow, it will all be a bad dream.

But would it really?

Could anyone truly erase such vile stains from their past?

Bury sins that clung to you like a second skin?

She looked at her phone. The screen remained dark and silent, mocking her with its blankness.

Stomach churning, she headed to the bathroom.

Her workplace felt eerie in its emptiness, the halls that had once buzzed with life now as silent as a tomb. Most of the lights were off, the motion sensors having long since given up on detecting any sign of movement, and Phoebe's footsteps echoed loudly in the deserted hallway, each one a jarring reminder of her solitude. Every shadow seemed to hold a threat, every flicker of movement a hidden danger. The faint hum of the ventilation system sounded unnaturally loud in the stillness. A few times, she paused with her hand clutched to her chest, her heart racing as she scanned the darkness, certain she'd seen something lurking just out of sight.

When she finally reached the bathroom, the automatic lights flicked on, harsh and blinding after the gloom of the corridor. Phoebe leaned against the sink, her reflection staring back at her from the mirror, pale and haunted. She closed her eyes...

And there it was, the memory that never failed to send a shiver down her spine. Julian's face, illuminated by the inferno, his eyes raw.

Gasping, she opened her eyes, turned the tap on, and splashed cold water on her face. The icy water felt like needles on her flushed skin, but the shock of it brought her back to the present.

But the thoughts wouldn't leave her, the questions that had plagued her for so long. If she hadn't run the next day, if she'd stayed with Julian instead of seeking the sanctuary of her parents, what path would her life have taken? Would she have been dragged down into the darkness with him, consumed by the same madness that had driven him to such desperate acts?

The sudden ring of her phone jolted Phoebe out of her reverie, the sound unnaturally loud in the bathroom's stillness. With trembling fingers, she fumbled in her suit pocket, her hands shaking as she finally extracted the device and answered.

'Pheebs?'

'David, thank God.'

'Listen to me.' His voice was tight with panic. 'You need to get in your car and come home. Right now.'

'What's happened?' Her voice sounded small, even to her own ears, a fragile thing in the vastness of the empty room. 'David?'

'No time, Pheebs. Just come home! I'm begging you.'

Her mind reeled. He spoke in a clipped and urgent tone that she'd never heard from him before. But she wouldn't be passive. After what had happened in 1990, she'd vowed never to be that person again. 'What's happened?'

'They fucked it up, Pheebs. He got away.'

The reality of the situation sank in, and with it came a wave of fear so intense it nearly brought her to her knees. 'Okay.'

After hanging up, she stared at her phone in shock, and couldn't move. She thought about the vast, empty building she was alone in. No longer a sanctuary but a trap, a labyrinth of dark corners and hidden threats. She looked around the silent bathroom, heart hammering in her chest.

With an immense effort of will, she pushed herself away from the sink, taking a deep breath and trying to steady herself.

In the mirror, she noticed one of the cubicle doors was almost closed.

Phoebe's heart leapt into her throat, her pulse pounding in her ears as she stared at the door, every muscle in her body tensed for fight or flight.

'Hello?' she called.

Nothing. The seconds seemed to stretch into eternity as she stood there, hardly daring to breathe.

Then, she lowered down to her knees and looked beneath the cubicle door, expecting to see feet.

When she saw nothing, she instructed herself to get it together, rose, and lurched for the bathroom door.

Marching back towards her office, heart thundering, she took in the moving shadows in the darkness. They seemed to multiply with every step. Each one a potential assailant, a spectre from her past, come to drag her away. She willed herself to stay calm. Her mouth was dry though, and her tongue stuck to the roof of her mouth.

After she grabbed her bag from the office, she exited her block, pausing only long enough to check that all the doors were securely closed behind her. She jogged to the lift. Out of breath, she pounded the button while staring left and right down the empty corridor. 'Come on... come on...' The wait was interminable, each second dragging by with agonising slowness, and she found herself glancing over her shoulder again and again, certain that at any moment, Julian would materialise out of the shadows.

The doors opened. 'Thank God.' She slipped inside the lift.

She hit the button for the underground car park over and over. Her heart really did feel like it was going to burst from her chest. 'For fuck's sake, close.'

The doors shut. As she descended, she leaned against the cool metal of the lift wall, feeling the dampness of her shirt clinging to her skin, closing her eyes, catching her breath. 'It's okay.' In her mind's eye, she pictured where she'd parked. She'd reversed in and was against the wall just to the left of this lift.

You'll be in your car in a matter of seconds.

She opened her eyes. The lift doors opened with a soft ding. Phoebe stepped out into the car park. Automatic lights flickered overhead. The harsh fluorescent glow conjured a range of eerie shadows on the concrete walls. Her workplace had been eerie enough on the third floor, but this was a whole new level. The near deserted space was still and oppressive. Three vehicles remained, including her own. She headed left to her BMW, glancing up at the CCTV camera mounted in the corner, its unblinking eye a slight comfort. He wouldn't risk anything here, would he?

With a deep breath, she took out her keys and pressed the button. The soft beep of the locks disengaging echoed around the cavernous expanse.

She reached for the handle—

And then, out of the corner of her eye, she glimpsed movement on the other side of the car. Someone was rising from a crouch, a dark figure unfolding itself from the shadows.

Phoebe's breath caught in her throat as she yanked open the door, desperate to put a barrier, any barrier, between herself and the unknown threat.

She'd barely got one foot inside the car before the figure, dressed in a balaclava and tracksuit, had rounded the front of the vehicle and yanked her head back by her hair.

Her assailant tugged, dragging her from the vehicle. The pain in her scalp brought tears to her eyes. 'Get off me!' She dug her nails into the fingers tangled in her hair.

The figure slammed her against the closed back door of the BMW, knocking the wind from her lungs.

She gulped for air, blinking away the spots that clouded her vision.

Then she recognised the eyes peering out from behind the balaclava. *Raw. Illuminated by a car on fire.* 'Julian—'

His hand closed around her throat, cutting off her words and her air.

He leaned in close, his breath hot against her ear as he hissed, 'All those years, I kept quiet.' He squeezed harder, his fingers digging into the soft flesh of her neck. 'I didn't think I was asking for much. You got a life. I didn't.'

The world was dimming around the edges. Her temples throbbed as her lungs screamed for air. She clawed at Julian's hand, but it was useless against his iron grip. 'And then someone takes a shot at me in the forest?'

Phoebe heard the words but was too consumed by panic and desperation to comprehend them. She focused on a single, lonely thought in her mind.

Survive.

Fuelled by pure adrenaline, acting on instinct rather than conscious thought itself, she brought her knee up, slamming it into Julian's groin.

He grunted in pain, his grip loosening just enough for Phoebe to break free, gasping and choking as air rushed back into her starved lungs.

Julian stumbled backwards, and she struck again. This time, his knee. He crumpled to the ground. She rolled along the side of the vehicle, allowing herself to fall in through the open door. She drew her legs back, righted herself in the seat, and slammed the door shut with enough force to rattle the windows. With shaking hands, she hit the automatic locks. They engaged with a satisfying clunk.

She hit the ignition button. The engine roared to life. Confused, yet overjoyed that he'd yet to make a reappearance, she pressed down the accelerator—

There was a loud crash as Julian landed on the bonnet.

Fuck you.

She pressed harder on the accelerator, sending the car surging forward. She looked up, straight into those eyes again, poking out of the balaclava. More hateful than ever before.

And why wouldn't they be?

He'd spent his entire life in prison, not betraying her once, and she'd sat back when her husband sent someone to end his life in Larpool Wood.

She hit the brakes.

Julian flew from the bonnet. His body rag-dolled through the air until his head smashed into a bollard. He crunched to the ground, face down.

Phoebe simply sat there, hands white-knuckled on the steering wheel, staring at him through the windscreen.

She tried to steady her breathing, but it was very hard to do so.

Lying in that twisted heap, Julian looked almost boneless.

She waited, expecting some flicker of movement. If she saw so much as a twitch, she'd put her pedal to the floor and disappear into the night, leaving him broken and bleeding in her wake.

But there was nothing, only the steady hum of her BMW's engine, the rasp of her own laboured breathing.

Slowly, hardly daring to believe it was over, she edged the car closer to him, turning as she did so, until she was alongside him. He was lying on his right cheek, so she could see his left eye through the balaclava. The eye stared ahead, glassy and vacant. A puddle of blood was spreading out around his misshapen head, dark and glossy in the harsh light.

She could taste bile.

Oh God. What had she done? He was dead.

Why hadn't they just paid him?

£100,000. Or this?

She gritted her teeth. *They should have just fucking paid him.*

And now she had a real problem.

She couldn't possibly drive away, leave him behind. There were CCTV cameras everywhere, cold mechanical eyes that had borne witness to the killing.

With trembling fingers, she dialled David's number. 'It's me.' Her voice was thick and choked as she continued gasping for air.

'Are you coming—'

'Stop, David! Listen... he's dead. I... I killed him.'

'*What?* Jesus, what—'

'He attacked me in the car park. He was wearing a balaclava, but it was him! It was an accident. He was on my bonnet. I tried to get away. He hit a bollard...'

'Pheebs, slow down...' He tried to keep his voice calm, but she could hear the undercurrent of panic.

'There's CCTV. I'm fucked.'

'One moment.' There was a long pause as he thought. 'Okay, Pheebs, listen to me carefully.' David's voice was calm, controlled, a lifeline in the chaos that threatened to consume her. He instructed her on the best course of action. It sounded reasonable, except—

'Yes, but what if they find out I know him?'

'Why would they suspect that? He was wearing a balaclava, so you never saw his face. And, if they give you his name, give nothing away in your expression. Do you understand?'

'Yes.' The word was little more than a whisper. 'Yes, I can do that.'

'Good. I love you, Pheebs. We'll get through this. I love you.'

'I love you, too.'

For a brief, hysterical moment, Phoebe wondered if this was all some twisted dream, a product of her fractured psyche finally shattering under the weight of so many secrets, so many lies.

But the blood on the ground was real. The body lying broken and still, that was real too.

With a shaking hand, she dialled 999, her heart pounding like a drum as she waited for the operator to answer.

Chapter Thirty-Seven

Whitby Abbey. Weathered stone. Towering arches.
   Red eyes boring into his back.
   199 steps. Aching calves.
   His heart pounds.
   Salty wind. Crashing seas. Crying gulls.
   His breath comes in ragged gasps.
   Whitby's old town. Deserted. Winding alleys.
   The echoing paws on cobblestones.
   Church Street. Old fishermen's cottages. Red-tiled roofs. Weather-beaten walls.
   Hot breath burns the back of his neck.
   The Swing Bridge. Safety. Over the River Esk.
   Almost there.
   A chance.
   No chance.
   The spectral hound's massive form blocks the way.
   Glowing red eyes fix on his face.
   Jaws open.
   A yawning chasm of darkness—

The Barghest lunges.

Mike's eyes flew open, darting frantically around the dim, unfamiliar room. Shadows pressed in on him from all sides, suffocating and disorientating. His heart raced, pounding against his ribcage. 'Where am I?'

He turned his head from side to side, his movements sluggish and uncoordinated, then looked down at his heavy chest, rising and falling rapidly with each laboured breath.

Slowly, concerned faces came into focus around him, their features blurred and indistinct at first, like figures in a fog.

'Emma?' His throat was raw, his mouth dry as dust. He squinted, trying to make sense of the scene before him.

'It's me, Mike. I'm here.' Emma's voice was thick with emotion as she clutched his hand, her fingers warm and reassuring against his clammy skin.

He could see tears in her eyes. 'Thank God, Emma. What's happened? Where am I?'

'Mike...' Emma's words seemed to come from far away, muffled and distorted. 'Mike... you've had a heart attack.'

He managed a small nod, his gaze darting around the room once more, taking in the sterile white walls, the beeping monitors, the tangle of tubes and wires connected to his body. A wave of dread washed over him, cold and inexorable.

'Is it my time? Is this the end?' His voice cracked, barely above a whisper.

Emma's lips moved, her expression urgent and pleading, but her words faded into the background, drowned out by the rushing of blood in his ears. The room spun, darkness creeping in at the edges of his vision like gathering storm clouds.

As Mike felt himself slipping back into unconsciousness, he could have sworn he saw a pair of glowing red eyes watching him from the shadows – the Barghest waiting to claim his soul.

Chapter Thirty-Eight

Despite the revelations from Kath's interview, the day had quickly fizzled out.

Rob Johnson, formerly known as Robert Wake, hadn't been at work, or at home. Nor was he answering his mobile.

Frank had visited the Johnson residence earlier. Sarah, Rob's wife, assured Frank that her husband would return home soon because he wouldn't miss their daughter's stage performance of *Romeo and Juliet* for anything. She told him she'd pass on the message and asked what it was regarding. Frank had been deliberately vague. 'Nothing to worry about. We just need his help with an investigation.'

As Bertha bounced his weary body along the road home, Frank realised that the lack of progress had left him feeling restless and unsatisfied. His victim's emerging character also plagued him. It was hard to reconcile Rowena's description of the gentle, comic-loving brother with the man who exploited vulnerable young men for his own gratification.

This train of thought took him to Maddie. Like Adrian, she had hidden parts of herself from those close to her.

The urge to dull his troubled mind with a drink was strong, but he'd already vowed to put a stop to that. He reminded himself of the reason. *If I don't get control of it now, then it'll get complete control of me. Then, what am I good for? Granted, I'm due for the scrap heap, but when I finally lie down upon it, I want to do so with dignity...*

He'd treat himself to some painkillers, though. He glanced at himself in the rear-view mirror. His eye was still black, and his lip still puffed up. In a way, the lip was the worst part. It made smoking roll-ups more difficult.

Although reducing roll-ups would be a fine move, he wasn't in a rush to do that. The drink first. He was too long in the tooth now to go all or nothing!

He gave some consideration to stopping by to see Mary, but the encounter with Evelyn was still raw and vivid in his mind, and he didn't want to risk a rematch.

Proud of himself for not opening the fridge for a beer when he arrived home, he celebrated with three pieces of toast smothered in butter, two paracetamol, and then smoked his way through three roll-ups in the garden.

As the night wound on, a gnawing emptiness inside him intensified. Deep down, he knew it'd be impossible to fill it without alcohol, but he stood resolute. When it became too much, he found himself drawn to Maddie's room, hoping to fill the emptiness with memories of her.

The room was a snapshot of Maddie's life before her disappearance. Empty water bottles stood on the bedside table, a testament to Frank's desperate attempts to keep her hydrated during her detox. The top drawer of her dresser was open, revealing unopened packets of crisps. Supplies he'd left for her when he'd locked her in, determined to help her shake off the chains of her heroin addiction.

Frank's heart clenched as he saw her bed, still made, the sheets unchanged since the last time she'd slept there. He closed his eyes, a vivid memory washing over him. The night he'd come into this room, and, in a rare moment of vulnerability, Maddie had asked him to stay with her.

'Daddy? Daddy, I'm cold.' Her voice had been small and frightened, like when she was a little girl. 'Daddy, I'm cold. Mummy isn't here. Can I sleep with you?'

Just as he'd done then, he lay down on the bed. Except this time, when he tried to put his arm around his daughter, there was nothing there.

He opened his eyes and sighed.

Tears ran down his cheeks, soaking his pillow.

Closing his eyes once more, Frank lost himself in the evening's memory. He'd stroked her hair until her breathing evened out and she'd fallen asleep.

'I had you back,' he whispered, his voice choked with emotion. 'I had you back, Maddie. You came back to me for comfort and protection, and—'

The words caught in his throat, the pain of her absence a physical ache in his chest.

He kicked off his shoes, clutched her pillow close, and sobbed.

'I'm so sorry, Maddie. It was wrong of me to take your phone. I was just trying to keep you safe. Please. I can't lose you again...'

As exhaustion overtook him, Frank found himself halfway between this world and the dream world. In that hazy space, he could almost feel Maddie's hand slip into his, her voice soothing in his ear. 'Shh, Dad, it's okay. I know you were looking out for me. You saved me from myself. I never would've got clean without you.'

With those comforting words echoing in his mind, Frank drifted into a restless sleep, clinging to the memory of that precious night, when his love had been enough to shelter Maddie from her demons, if only for a little while.

Chapter Thirty-Nine

Rob Johnson was still not answering his mobile phone, so Frank contacted the showroom. The receptionist informed him that Rob had called in to say he was sick.

You're one evasive bugger, Frank thought.

He contacted Gerry, who was already at HQ. 'If you can leave Rylan, then I'd appreciate you at the interview with Rob.'

'Reggie is here, so Rylan can stay with him. I'll get a taxi.'

Within the hour, Frank and Gerry stood side by side at Rob's front door.

She regarded his face as they waited. 'The swelling is going down.'

'Aye,' Frank said. 'I smoked my first roll-up today without wincing.'

Sarah Johnson answered. She recognised Frank from the previous day. Her eyes were red, and she looked as if she'd been crying.

'He's in bed,' she said. 'He's not great.'

'It's important.' Frank held Sarah's gaze, his expression unwavering. 'We can't wait any longer.'

No chance he's giving us the slip now.

'Come in then.'

'Thank you,' Frank said.

They hovered in the hallway until Rob made an appearance five minutes later. His dressing gown hung loosely from his shoulders. The sour smell of sweat and sickness clung to him, and his eyes were bloodshot, set deep in his pale, clammy face.

Maybe he's ill after all, Frank thought.

Frank decided not to get too close. The last thing he wanted was to be laid up in bed with all of this going on.

Frank held up his badge. 'DCI Frank Black, and this is DI Gerry Carver.'

'No need.' Rob waved the badge down. 'My wife said you'd been in touch.' His voice was hoarse.

Frank nodded. 'Yet, you haven't called back?'

'Sorry.' Rob held up his hands. 'Been feeling like shit. This stomach bug. Been staring into a toilet bowl most of the night.'

Frank nodded. 'Must have come on suddenly? Your wife says you were out yesterday evening, and she said you were going to your daughter's play?'

'Yes, it did. I never made it to my daughter's play. Like I said, I've spent a long spell in the bathroom. And I just couldn't face returning your call.'

'Well, no worries,' Frank said. 'We're all here now. Is there somewhere we could talk?'

Rob's eyes darted between the two detectives. He swallowed hard, his Adam's apple bobbing in his throat. 'You really want to catch this? Perhaps we could schedule an appointment for later this week?'

'No, it's pressing, sir,' Frank said.

'What's it about exactly?'

'Private may be best.' Frank could see Sarah milling around in the lounge, close to them.

Rob's face drained of what little colour it had left, his forehead damp with perspiration. 'It all sounds rather intimidating. Should I call my solicitor?' He swayed slightly, looking as if he might be sick at any moment.

'That's your right, of course... Although, I cannot understand how we've been intimidating.' Frank leaned in so Sarah wouldn't hear. 'I'm just giving you a chance to keep this more private... Mr Wake.'

His eyes widened. Although still ashen, his expression was suddenly more alert. It seemed his former name was a good antidote to that heavy fog that had been over him.

'Okay.' He looked over his shoulder, towards his wife, who was texting somebody on her mobile. He pointed up with a trembling finger. 'I'll take you to the office. The kids are all out.'

Chapter Forty

Rob showed them to his office, a spacious room with a large mahogany desk and floor-to-ceiling bookshelves lining the walls. Several framed photographs adorned the walls, depicting Rob shaking hands with various celebrities and dignitaries. Interspersed between these images were dozens of children's drawings, each one lovingly preserved behind glass. It was a shrine to Rob's success and his role as a family man, a carefully curated display designed to project an image of respectability and wholesome values.

He gestured down at his dressing gown. 'I'm going to put some clothes on and just check Sarah knows to give us space.'

Rob returned a few minutes later, dressed in a crisp white shirt and tailored charcoal trousers. This gave him a more composed look, but his face was still ashen and damp with perspiration.

Frank pointed at a child's drawing, feeling a twinge of nostalgia. 'I remember this time well.'

'I frame everything my children have ever made for me.

There's more in my office in the showroom... and a great deal more in storage upstairs.'

That seemed a little overkill to Frank. Too showy, perhaps? Still, he didn't want to criticise or condemn a man who took fatherhood seriously. 'You're very proud of them...'

'Very. And they are of me.' He turned back to the office door and closed it. 'A proud family. That's how I want to keep it.' The door latch clicked. He turned back and looked at the two detectives. 'Nobody here knows about Rob Wake. My mother, God rest her soul, is long gone. As far as everyone knows, my father was a bastard, and my mother raised me. Then, I got lucky and became an apprentice to a mechanic when I was seventeen. This is all true, I hasten to add.' He sighed. 'Look, I implore you to keep it that way. Whatever I can do to help. Whatever. But please... I'm begging you.'

Frank nodded. 'I hear your plea, Mr Johnson. And we're not ignorant of your situation, but you don't know why we're here. In fact, I'm intrigued why you're not more curious about what's brought us to your door. Most people don't ignore phone calls from the police, especially ranking police detectives.'

'I explained that earlier. I've been out of it. Besides, I assumed it was to do with my identity after your revelation downstairs. And if that's the case, I assure you, DCI, that everything is legitimate. I followed all the correct channels and—'

'Let me stop you there.' Frank had his hand in the air. 'We're not here about identity fraud.'

'Oh.' Rob raised his eyebrows. 'Now, I'm confused. So, what're you here about then?'

'Shall we sit?' Frank asked.

Once they were all sitting, Rob opposite them and behind his desk, Frank got to the point. 'We're here about a murder. DI Carver?' He gestured at Gerry, signalling that it was time for her to come in with the facts and evidence.

Gerry met Rob's eyes; her expression was unreadable. In an interview, this was one of the rare moments when she willingly stepped out of her comfort zone, knowing that direct eye contact was essential to gauging a suspect's reactions. She explained the gruesome discovery of Adrian Hughes's body at the Rusty Anchor.

Rob was sinking into his chair before Gerry had even finished, as if the weight of her words were physically crushing him.

The mere mention of this ghost from Rob's former life was enough to shake the foundations of his carefully constructed new identity.

'When?' Rob choked out, his voice barely above a whisper.

'We suspect it happened in 1989 between Friday 25th and Sunday 27th August,' Gerry's tone was clinical and detached.

Rob took a deep breath and straightened himself in his chair. 'A long time ago, then.'

'Aye,' Frank said. 'But not long enough to stay buried.'

'How did he die?' Rob asked.

'He was stabbed twice. It's impossible to know which of the two knife wounds killed him.'

Frank raised an eyebrow. Gerry's statement seemed oddly specific, almost pedantic. Did it really matter which blow had been fatal? Someone brutally murdered the man and left him to rot in a makeshift tomb. But Gerry was precise, her mind always grasping for the most accurate version of the truth.

'Were you aware that Adrian disappeared?' Gerry asked, pressing on.

Rob shook his head. 'Not exactly... no... how much do you already know about me? About Rob Wake?'

Gerry explained all of their findings regarding Sapphire Companions and their conversation with Kath Fielding. Whenever they brought up her name, he sneered. It seemed there was no love lost there then.

'How did you first come to work for Sapphire Companions?'

Rob took a deep, shuddering breath. 'It was a low point. A really fucking low point.' He looked between their faces, his cheeks flushing with shame. Frank noted Rob had lowered his voice, terrified his wife may hear. 'I had a dreadful childhood. My dad was a drunk, and he beat me and my mum, black and blue.' He sighed. 'I'm sure you've heard it a thousand times.'

'Doesn't matter how many times we hear it,' Frank said. 'It isn't acceptable.'

Rob nodded. 'Anyway... when my father died, he left my mum with a mountain of debt.' Rob's voice took on a bitter edge. 'Illegal debts, you understand. She'd no choice. These people weren't going away. She tried, but she was struggling to make ends meet. I told her I'd work and pay my way. But apprenticeships don't pay all that much, really. So, when I was sixteen, I found out about Sapphire. I wasn't sure what the requirements were, but I was sporty, and well-built for my age. I was good-looking as well. At least, I assumed so. I'd never been short of interest from girls.' He rubbed his damp forehead. 'I didn't know, okay?'

'What didn't you know?' Gerry asked.

He dropped his hands and rolled his eyes. 'You know what! You want to make me say it?'

'It's best to be clear, Mr Johnson,' Frank said.

He lowered his voice. 'I didn't know sex was part of it. When I stopped by, they said it was an escort service, you know? Accompanying men and women to events, being a pleasant companion. I assumed it would be just women. I know, naïve, huh? The money was too good to pass up.'

Frank felt a wave of sympathy wash over him. The desperation in Rob's voice was palpable, and he could almost see the scared sixteen-year-old boy behind the successful businessman's façade.

Leeches like Kath Fielding feed on desperation, he thought.

'So, they never mentioned sex in the job description?' Gerry's question hung in the air.

'No. They weren't about to implicate themselves with that, were they? Still, you soon got the message. It starts with these customers offering you sizeable amounts of money at the end of the evening. You know, the sort of money that a kid in my situation needed.' He clenched his hands on the table. 'You think it's off the books, which it is, so you agree, close your eyes and think of the payday. Only later, Kath would have one of her heaviest office employees confront you for 60 per cent of that windfall. Turns out that there're no real secrets. The clients were transparent with the company – it was just never written down. Sixty per cent! Rather soul-destroying, eh? I'd never felt so degraded. And I wasn't the only one.'

I bet you weren't, Frank thought, inwardly sighing.

'But you continued?' Gerry's tone was neutral, but her eyes were sharp. She was assessing him.

Rob nodded.

'Why?'

'Forty per cent of that was better than 40 per cent of

fuck all! And like anything, it got easier. Are you disgusted by me?'

'No,' Gerry said.

'We're disgusted with the people who manipulated you into this, Mr Johnson,' Frank said.

He looked at Frank and nodded. 'Thanks. Means a lot to hear that.'

'Did you get your mother out of debt?' Gerry asked.

Rob nodded. 'Yes. And then I quit.'

'How long did it take you?' Frank asked.

'Less than a year. A lot less. I started around my sixteenth birthday in...' He did a quick calculation in his head. 'It would have been in September 1988. I was done by April 1989. That's definite because I started my apprenticeship then. So, seven or eight months.'

Four months before Adrian died in the Rusty Anchor, Frank thought.

'Was your mother not curious?' Gerry asked. 'About where the money came from?'

'Of course. But I told her not to ask. Obviously, she then assumed it was drugs, but better that than the truth! She hated it. Was desperate for me to stop.'

'But she still took the money?' Frank raised an eyebrow.

'Yes.' Rob narrowed his eyes. 'I forced it on her. Told her I'd see those we were indebted to myself if she wanted. She was terrified of that. Thought I might get in a brawl with them. Get myself seriously hurt. To be honest, she was probably right.'

He sighed and looked off in space, deep in thought. 'You should have seen Mum's face the day I told her I'd signed up to be an apprentice. That my days of playing *Scarface* were over.' A ghost of a smile played across his face. 'She was over the moon.'

'How many clients did you have over that period?' Gerry asked.

'I can't remember.' Frank heard the sincerity in his tone of voice. 'Too many, I guess.' His eyes filled with shame, and he looked down. 'Men and women. Usually much older.' He snorted. 'Some celebrities.' He sneered and nodded. 'Politicians.' He shrugged. 'I guess I could destroy many people with what I know.' He looked back up at Frank. 'Or at least destroy myself in the process of trying.'

'Apart from Adrian, who we will get to shortly, did you have repeat customers?' Gerry asked.

He nodded. 'That was common. A few tried to get you to slip off the books and partner up with them. A few people I knew went down that road. I never saw the point. Kath was already riding roughshod over me. Why bother trading her in for someone else who'd only do the same thing?'

'Who told you about this Sapphire in the first place?' Frank asked.

Rob thought about it. 'I found a card in a phone box.'

Frank made a note. Did the time he took to answer match up with the response? He sensed he'd stalled there to concoct his lie.

'Okay, Kath Fielding told us you reported Adrian to her for becoming obsessive,' Gerry said.

'Ah, she did, did she?' He sneered over the thought of her, and not for the first time. 'Surprised she remembered. She didn't seem to give a shit back then.'

'Could you talk us through what happened with Adrian?' Gerry readied her pen above her notebook.

'First, I don't know what you're thinking, but I didn't kill him. As I've said, I was done and dusted with that game by April 1989, and you said he was murdered in August? I was a full-time apprentice. I'd rather you didn't approach my first boss, Steve Wicks, for an alibi, but you can if you must.'

'Thank you,' Frank said, thinking, *Although it's not really an alibi, is it? You could still have murdered him in the evening, outside of work. And who's to say you didn't continue freelancing? Must have been tempting following the sudden drop in income when starting an apprenticeship.*

'At first, Adrian seemed all right, to be honest. Quiet, you know? Some of them' – he screwed up his face – 'some of them had their hands all over you. Adrian wasn't like that. He seemed a good regular.' He flinched. 'Christ, I can't believe I'm talking like this. It was a lifetime ago. It seems like a different fucking person, you know?'

'I understand it must be hard,' Frank said.

Rob's expression darkened. 'Anyway, it soon became clear that something was really off about Adrian.'

Apart from the fact that he was paying sixteen-year-old sex workers? he thought. He kept his expression neutral, though, nodding to show that he was following Rob's train of thought. 'How so?'

'It started with the way he was looking at me... I know... sounds ridiculous. But he'd stare at me. For long periods.' He patted his chest. 'Boring into you.' He rolled his eyes. 'Hard to explain. Like I said, he kept his hands to himself in public, but when we were alone, he held me more tightly. I kept having to tell him to ease up.'

Suddenly, there was a creak outside the door. Rob's head snapped towards the sound, his face draining of what little colour it had left. They all waited in silence until they could hear fading footfalls on the stairs close by.

He sighed. 'Sorry... I didn't hear Sarah come up.'

'Back to what you were saying,' Frank said. 'Was Adrian ever violent with you?'

'No, not exactly. The tight hugging wasn't aggressive. He'd stop when I asked. Like I said before, he was gentle. Physically, at least. But there were ways in which he wasn't gentle, I guess. He became intense. Possessive. He began asking questions about my life, who I was seeing, what my plans were. If he thought I was seeing other clients, he'd become sad, so I attempted to deny it as frequently as possible. He was desperate to know how he factored into my plans. At first, I thought he was falling in love with me, but then I realised he was trying to own me.'

'We've a record of you and Adrian being asked to leave the Moonrise Hotel on Friday 24th March 1989,' Gerry said. 'Do you recall that incident?'

He nodded, impressed. 'Wow. How did you dig that up?'

'Adrian had left a note of the appointment in his belongings.'

Rob raised an eyebrow. 'Really? Odd. I remember, yes.' He nodded. 'We were due to spend the night there, and I was going to tell Adrian that this was it, and I wouldn't see him any more. However, we were told to leave the hotel. I'll never forget how that manager spoke to me. Calling me a rent boy... accused me of spreading AIDS... laughing when he called me a "lad of the night". If I didn't feel degraded enough by the life I was leading already, he made damned sure I did right then. After we left the hotel, I was emotional, angry, and just told Adrian straight away that it was over. That I didn't want him coming near me.'

Frank heard Gerry's pen moving quickly over the paper.

'He kept trying to book me. So, I told Kath I couldn't see

him any more, and she gave me hell. She told me to do my job. She didn't seem to care that I was becoming increasingly paranoid, and his interest in me was becoming obsessive. Over the next week, I saw him lingering around my house, where I lived with Mum. Up till then, I'd only seen him on some weekend evenings at pre-arranged venues. It scared the shit out of me seeing him there in broad daylight.'

'Did you tell Kath this?' Frank clenched his own hands beneath the table.

'Yes. And she didn't care, but I still refused to meet him.'

Frank felt his heart sinking. A sixteen-year-old boy. A child, really. That's all he'd been.

'A couple of weeks passed,' Rob said. 'And then he showed up on my doorstep.'

Bloody hell.

'Twice,' Rob continued. 'The first time he told me he missed me and begged me to see him. When I refused, he said he'd kill himself. He came back two days later, except this time Mum opened the door. She'd witnessed me demanding he leave two days earlier, and so chased him off with a broomstick. And that was the last time I ever saw him.'

Frank leaned back in his chair, studying Rob's face, searching for any hint of deception. A heavy silence settled over the room, broken only by the ticking of a clock on the wall. *All's well that ends well, eh?* Frank thought. *I don't think so.*

'The very next day, Kath came to me and demanded I see him or I'd lose my job. I told her to stick her job. I'd settled my mother's debt. I refused to be controlled any more. Best decision I ever made. I changed my name, not out of necessity, but because I wanted to refresh and start again. I found that apprenticeship with Wicksy within a month.'

Frank raised an eyebrow. 'Wicksy?'

'Steve Wicks.'

'Ah.' Frank nodded. 'Was your mother not confused about the name change?'

'Of course. But I told her to leave it well alone. She'd then assumed it was to do with my life as a drug dealer.' A wry smile tugged at his lips. 'She was happy to let it go.'

'Did you ever visit the Rusty Anchor?' Gerry asked.

Rob shook his head. 'Knew about it. Bit of a trek from here. I'm fairly certain I never went there.'

'Fairly certain?' Gerry pressed.

'*Certain*. I was only sixteen, probably not even heard of it then!'

'Probably?' Gerry's tone was sharp, cutting through Rob's evasive language.

'Definitely!' A note of defiance crept into Rob's voice.

Gerry made notes. The scratching of pen on paper suddenly seemed unnaturally loud. Frank knew what was coming next, so he held off and let Gerry bring it in. She pinned Rob with her gaze. 'The landlord recalls Adrian coming into the pub with a young man. The young man in question would have been around your age.'

Rob shrugged. 'Wasn't me.' He glared at Gerry. 'I'm *positive* and *certain* that I've never been.'

'Would you mind giving us a picture of your younger self, at sixteen, so we can clear that with the landlord?' Gerry asked.

Rob nodded. 'Of course. There'll be a photo with my mother's belongings in the attic. But I'm telling you that his murder has nothing to do with me.'

'If you could email that over later, that would be fantastic,' Frank said.

'So, if it wasn't you, Mr Johnson,' Gerry continued, 'who else do you think could have been going into the Rusty Anchor with him?'

Rob shrugged. 'Beats me. Like I said, he gave up after two visits to my home. Maybe he moved on and found someone else?'

'True,' Gerry said. 'Could he have been seeing someone else while he was seeing you?'

'Of course,' Rob said. 'He wasn't exclusive to me! I made him no promises. I'm sure he was finding company wherever he could.'

'And do you know of anyone else that you worked with at Sapphire, about your age, who could also have had Adrian as a client?'

Rob shook his head. 'It isn't like a normal workplace. We didn't have social gatherings or anything. I met Kath, and she gave me work. And was a complete bitch when I needed her. Excuse the language. And that's it, really.'

Frank felt like they had enough for now. He slid a card over the table. 'For you to email the picture.'

'Of course.'

'If anything else occurs to you, please get in touch. Especially anything to do with a young man that could have been with Adrian. Oh, one more thing. Do you play cards?'

Rob blinked, clearly thrown by the sudden change in topic. 'Cards. No. Not my thing at all. Why?'

'It seems Adrian enjoyed playing cards in the cellar at the Rusty Anchor.'

Rob nodded. 'I see. They played cards in the cellar, there?'

'Aye. And that's where we found his body, remember?

The landlord claims that the young man in question used to accompany him to the games.'

Rob nodded thoughtfully. 'Interesting. I wish I could help more.' He shook his head and spread his hands in a gesture of helplessness.

'If you're telling us everything, then your help is appreciated and invaluable.' *But you're not telling us everything, are you?*

He stared at Rob until he flinched. There was a tightening around his eyes.

'Any more questions, DI Carver?' Frank asked Gerry.

'Yes...' Gerry said, her attention still focused on Rob. 'Two.'

She paused for effect, waiting for Rob to acknowledge her. 'Okay.'

'Your place of work isn't an alibi for the 25th to the 27th of August 1989. The card games were at night. Do you have an alibi?'

'Eh?' Rob said. 'How could I? Really?'

Frank knew it was an almost impossible question to answer after so many years, but it had a way of unsettling potential suspects, putting them on the back foot. 'Well, what were you up to around then, sir?'

'I was working hard. Trying to make a good impression. I was working weekend days, so I would've been getting early nights. So, I'd have been with my mother, but that won't help you because, as I pointed out, she's gone.'

Gerry nodded. 'Second question. What did you know about Adrian's personal life?'

'We didn't talk about him often. It was always about me.'

'So, you didn't discuss his occupation?' Gerry asked.

'He was a social worker.' Rob shrugged. 'Liked to help kids… ironic, really, don't you think? I was just a kid, really.'

'Were you aware of his family situation?'

'No.'

'His history of abuse?'

Rob's brow furrowed, a look of genuine surprise crossing his face. He leaned forward slightly, his voice lowering. 'He was abused?'

'Unfortunately, so.' Frank nodded. 'According to his sister, yes.'

He shook his head. 'I didn't know. Was the abuse bad?'

'All abuse is bad,' Gerry said.

'Yes, I know… sorry… just surprises me.'

'Why?' Gerry asked.

Rob shrugged. 'I don't know. He just didn't seem angry. I always assumed people who've been abused are angry. Tied up in knots, you know?'

'Not always,' Frank said.

Gerry was in no mood to let this go. 'You do seem rather shocked by this, Mr Johnson.'

'Of course. Like you said' – he narrowed his eyes, on the defensive – 'abuse is bad. No one should be abused.'

'Does it make you feel any different towards him now? Sympathetic, perhaps?' Frank asked. 'Guilty, maybe?'

Rob's head snapped towards Frank, his expression one of shocked indignation. 'I don't know what you mean. Anybody who's abused deserves sympathy, don't they? If you're asking me if I would've still stopped it dead in its tracks, then, fuck yes, I would've done. This wasn't the life for me. And he was knocking on my fucking door. Have you not been listening?'

'I'm sorry, sir.' Frank decided it was best not to push him further.

Gerry, however, wouldn't be reading that. 'Have you ever suffered abuse?'

Rob's face darkened, his eyes flashing with anger. 'What's that got to do with anything?'

'Just establishing common traits among all those involved in—'

'If I was abused, I'd discuss it with a doctor before discussing it with you, DI. Is that okay?'

'Okay, Mr Johnson.' Frank opted to close down this escalating exchange. 'Thank you for speaking with us at length.'

As they walked back to the car, Frank turned to Gerry. 'What do you think?'

'Inconsistent,' she replied without hesitation.

Frank raised an eyebrow. 'How so?'

Gerry ticked off points on her fingers. 'First, he was vague about whether he'd heard of the Rusty Anchor, switching from "fairly certain" to "definitely" never been there. Second, his reaction to Adrian's abuse history seemed off - surprise, then immediate defensiveness. And third, his body language changed noticeably when we asked about his own potential abuse history.'

Frank nodded, impressed. 'Good observations. I caught some of that, but not all. I'd be interested to see if Rory recognises him in that photograph he's sending.'

Gerry nodded. 'He won't. Rob wouldn't be so forthcoming if there was any danger of that.'

'You're right.'

'There was one blatant lie, though.'

'Go on.'

'There were two golfing trophies on the wall to the right of the room.'

'Okay... I'll take your word on that. How are those trophies relevant?'

'Not those trophies, rather the one just behind them. It was in the shape of a pack of playing cards. I took a quick look on the way out. Third prize in a national poker competition.'

Frank felt a bolt of adrenaline. 'I thought he didn't like cards?' He glanced at Gerry suspiciously as they climbed into the car.

'Why are you staring at me, Frank?'

He smirked. 'Why do you think? Come on. How could any human being possess such sharp observational skills?'

'You won't find the answers by looking me up and down.'

'You've eyes like a bloody hawk, Gerry. Mine are useless in comparison.'

'I know that. So can I take this opportunity to remind you to put your glasses on? I noticed you veering too close to a cyclist earlier.'

'Oh.' He pulled his glasses down from the top of his head, settling them on the bridge of his nose with a grumble. As he pulled out into traffic, Frank couldn't help but feel both impressed and unnerved by Gerry's uncanny perception.

Chapter Forty-One

Hands trembling, Rob Johnson watched the two detectives drive away through his office window. Since Louise's phone call two days earlier, his life had spiralled into chaos, and it was showing no sign of improvement.

As soon as their car disappeared, he rushed towards the bathroom beside his office and closed the door before he experienced the first retch. He made it down to his knees before the second retch, and his stomach heaved out breakfast.

After, Rob sat on the bathroom floor, his back against the wall, panting heavily.

What a fool he'd been...

All those years believing that the past was escapable.

You're a fucking idiot, he thought to himself.

He closed his eyes and let his mind drift back to the previous evening and his confrontation with Gideon Blackwell in his lounge. Rubbing at his forehead, he recalled the moment he'd considered thrusting the wheelchair towards the fireplace, sending the frail old man face forward onto the hearth. *And shattering his skull*, a dark voice whispered in his mind.

Would that have eased some of the pressure he now felt? Or would it have intensified it?

He recalled turning Gideon around. The vicious rapist shrivelled up in his chair. Too weak… too pathetic… so unlike the strong younger politician who'd once wrestled him face first onto a bed.

It was hard to believe it was the same man.

Despite the damage caused by the stroke, Rob could see the confusion on his face. 'You really don't remember me, do you?'

'No. I do not.' Gideon tried to speak with authority, but his slurred words and fading health were clear in every syllable.

'How many of us were there?' Rob's top lip curled up.

'I don't know what you're talking about.'

'Don't you dare. Don't you fucking dare! My name is Rob Wake, and I was sixteen. *Sixteen.* When you almost broke my arm. *Sixteen.*'

'Sixteen doesn't make you a child,' Gideon said.

White-hot fury surged through Rob, and before he could stop himself, he slapped Gideon across the face with the back of his hand.

Rob took a step back, watching the bastard shaking off his stinging blow.

You could easily kill him, he thought to himself. *But don't make this all worse than it already is.*

'I remember you now, Rob.' Gideon reached up to stroke his stunned cheek. 'You'd the most wonderful eyes. Blue. The lightest shade.' He looked up at Rob. 'Still do.'

Disgust rolled in Rob's gut. 'As if you could see my eyes while I was pinned down? You're a sick rapist.'

'I seem to remember you coming back. I seem to remember most of you coming back.'

'We were *desperate*. We were children!' Rob clenched his teeth, turning away. It would be easier to claim that he couldn't believe what he was hearing, but of course, he could. The man was insidious, and in his younger years, had been capable of these awful things. He swung back. 'How many other children did you take advantage of?'

'I think you should leave now,' Gideon replied.

'Have you no shame?'

Gideon took a deep breath, refusing to move his eyes from Rob's. When he eventually exhaled, he said, 'More than you can imagine.'

Rob had never expected those words. He reeled back, a cold sensation running through him.

Regret? From this monster?

He'd really not expected to be confronted with that.

Denial, yes. The man was a politician, after all.

But regret? No, never.

'If someone had done to my son what I did to you,' Gideon said, 'it would have been unacceptable.'

'So, why?'

Gideon shrugged. 'One of the oldest excuses, I guess.'

'Power?'

Gideon shook his head. 'In this case, no. It may've started there, but it should have ended before it did. No. The other excuse. Helplessness.'

'Bollocks.' Rob's voice came down in volume to a hiss. The anger was boiling within him. 'You could have stopped yourself.'

Gideon nodded. 'Maybe. It's possible. If you were looking at me, like you're looking at me now—'

'Judging you?'

'Yes... perhaps.'

And then something occurred to Rob, and he had to hold himself back from doubling over as the disgust recoiled in his guts again. 'That's why you turned us over? So you couldn't see our faces. You made us faceless.'

Gideon looked down.

Bile rising in his throat, Rob shook his head, turning again, talking to himself more than he was to Gideon now. 'I should have destroyed you years ago. Keeping silent. It was selfish of me. How many more suffered? And what closure did we ever really get? We wanted our lives back.' He turned to face Gideon again. 'But your shadow never left us.' He pulled out the TDK tape and turned back to face Gideon. 'But you've been on borrowed time. And this... this is a parting gift from Bryan. Another sixteen-year-old. He—'

'I remember Bryan, too. He spoke very softly... gently. I still sometimes think about his voice.'

Rob jabbed a finger in his direction. 'Think about this. That boy with the sweet voice drank himself to death because of you. Because of that damage.'

Rob saw the shame in his damaged face again.

'But he left a parting gift for you. For everyone.' Rob took the TDK tape from his inside pocket. 'The truth about Sir Gideon Blackwell. Do you want to hear it?'

Rob expected Gideon to recoil in shock. View the TDK tape like a doomsday weapon. But there was little change in his demeanour. 'Unnecessary. I know what's on it.'

'He spent his life in misery because of you. His daughter gave me this. She wants to expose the man who destroyed her father. It affected her life too.'

'So sad.'

'You think?'

'It's no excuse. Nothing can justify it. But there was a reason I only ever used prostitutes. To avoid—'

'Don't even say it,' Rob cut in. 'If you're even going to suggest that we weren't innocent, too.'

'I know, I—'

'You paid for a service, all right? You paid to torture children.'

Gideon nodded. 'I'm sorry.'

'I don't want apologies. You certainly won't get forgiveness. You almost broke my arm. I still have nightmares about the physical pain you caused me. I felt like I was suffocating on your pillow. And yet, I let you do it again!'

Gideon sighed. 'Use the tape.'

'I will.'

'Good. You know my son doesn't talk to me any more.'

'I don't care.'

'It tears me up. That's why I let you in, you know. I knew you weren't here to discuss my son, really. In fact, I think I knew you meant me harm. But desperation leads to choices that—'

'Don't talk to me about desperation.'

'Use the tape, Rob, I really want you to. I'll probably be dead before that tape ever makes the papers. It would be unjust, I know. But I've had four strokes already. Each one comes faster than the last. I'm fragile.'

Rob shook his head. He hadn't expected this. Expected Gideon to wriggle out so easily.

'One final cheat, eh?' Rob's lips twisted in a bitter smile. 'Dying before facing up to what you've done.'

Gideon lowered his face. 'You may not believe me, but I've thought about the things I've done every day of my life. I won't die happy, content. I'm miserable.'

Rob shook his head and turned away, torn between

disgust and a strange, fleeting pity. Was this the desperate attempt of a man to inspire sympathy, or was it the truth… extreme self-pity from a man who'd destroyed the lives of others?

But with Gideon's impending death, Rob realised he had a chance to keep his own carefully constructed life from crumbling. Exposing Gideon would serve no purpose if he was going to die soon anyway. The risk of ruining his own reputation and destroying his family life suddenly seemed too high a price to pay. He decided he'd talk to Louise, Bryan's daughter, and explain this twist of fate, emphasising that Gideon would die bitter, twisted, and lonely.

A sharp knock at the bathroom door jolted Rob back to the present. He spun around to see his wife, Sarah, standing in the doorway, her face etched with concern. In his haste to reach the toilet, he'd forgotten to lock the door.

'Rob?' Sarah's voice was soft. 'What's going on? Please talk to me.'

'My stomach… it's not getting better.' The lie tasted bitter on his tongue.

She sighed. There was disappointment there. She knew she was being lied to. 'What did the detectives want?'

'Just a mix-up. They're investigating the murder of someone I know nothing about.' More lies. Each word felt like a betrayal.

Sarah stepped into the bathroom, her eyes searching his face. 'Please.'

He couldn't make eye contact as he lied again.

She held up a TDK tape.

Rob struggled to his feet, his heart pounding in his chest.

'I was hanging up your coat, and it fell out of your pocket. I'm sorry.'

'Did you listen?'

'I thought it might be music, an old tape you found in your office or something. I was curious...' She trailed off, her eyes filled with worry. 'I dug out the old cassette player from under the stairs.'

With shaking hands, Rob considered snatching the tape from her grasp, but what was the point? It was too late.

Tears glistened in Sarah's eyes. 'Who's that on the tape?'

He put his head against the bathroom wall.

'Who is it?' Sarah pressed, her voice trembling. Her hand was on his back. 'It isn't you. This had nothing to do with you, did it? Tell me it didn't.'

'Please,' Rob whispered, tears stinging his own eyes. 'Please... you don't want to know. It's awful.'

Gently, she took his hand, her touch a lifeline in the darkness. 'I do... I really do. Let me in.'

And with those words, the last of Rob's defences crumbled. Through his choked sobs, he told her everything, clinging to her as the weight of his past threatened to drag him under.

Chapter Forty-Two

REGGIE WAS EAGER, so Frank concluded his briefing on the Rob Johnson interview and gave him the floor.

'It's been challenging. Many of our eighties' card players have either passed on or have dementia. I noticed lung cancer was a cause of many deaths. Some family members even went as far as mentioning that smoky cellar as being a death trap.'

'Appropriate words,' Frank said.

'Yes, I thought that, too, but didn't say so,' Reggie said. 'Caught up with two though who were larger than life, despite being in their early nineties. Terry O'Neil and Bill Hawkins.'

Frank wearily cracked his back, thinking, I could do with finding out what their secret is, then.

'Both Terry and Bill remembered Adrian well,' Reggie continued.

'Well?' Sharon questioned. 'I thought he wasn't the most memorable character?'

'He wasn't, which was what made him memorable,'

Reggie said. 'Best poker face in town, apparently. So quiet he didn't give a thing away. It didn't make him too popular. Bill said he used to do well for himself at the poker night until Adrian joined in. Then, he struggled to make ends meet.'

'Probably would have been a good excuse to stop,' Sharon said.

'Yes,' Reggie said. 'He was fully aware he was addicted. Now both Terry and Bill remember him having a young man with him. This young man never got involved. In fact, he looked bored out of his mind. Also, according to Terry, he was barely old enough to shave. Bill went as far as asking Adrian if the young man was his son. Adrian declined to answer, preferring instead to focus on the cards. From how sheepish he was, Bill didn't believe it was his son. Now, I've been thinking it was this Rob fella after our breakthrough with Sapphire, but you've put paid to that with your interview.'

'Not necessarily,' Frank said. 'Just because he quit Sapphire and became a car mechanic doesn't rule him out. We've also just received the photograph by email from the man of the moment himself, so we can show that to Rory. You could also show Terry and Bill, too, Reggie.'

'I will do.'

'Waste of time,' Gerry said, without looking up at the others.

Frank felt a flicker of irritation at her dismissive tone. He kept his voice level, but there was a hint of steel in it. 'No harm in trying, Gerry. But since you seem so certain, why don't you share your doubts with the rest of us?'

'Firstly, he willingly gave us his photo. He must be certain he won't be identified. Secondly, there's the trophy. I doubt someone skilled at cards would just be sitting back at a card game, looking bored out of his mind.'

'Maybe Rob felt too intimidated by Adrian, and was just too scared to get involved?' Reggie suggested.

'But Rob didn't suggest Adrian was intimidating,' Gerry countered.

'Rob may not have been a cardplayer back then?' It was a rare interjection from Sean. 'Maybe he learned everything he knew about cards from watching Adrian in the Anchor?'

Fair point, Frank thought.

'Time will tell,' Frank said, ending the conversation. He doubted Gerry was wrong about Rob's innocence. Her track record spoke for itself. But this discussion was wasting time.

'Sharon. What've you found?' Frank already knew what she'd discovered but wanted her to share it with the team. The discoveries were fantastic. Further vindication that he'd chosen wisely in keeping the same team on.

'Adrian applied to foster a child in November 1988.'

Frank noticed Gerry turn her attention from the computer to the room. He hadn't filled her in, so this revelation would certainly have piqued her interest. It was nothing she wouldn't have discovered herself if she hadn't been busy with interviewing Rob, even so, she'd probably be second-guessing why she hadn't unearthed this information prior to Sharon, especially given her long nights and dedication to her work.

'Lucy Bailey worked as a cook at Sunnybrook House between 1980 and 1988,' Sharon continued. 'As a single mother, she sometimes brought her son Mike to work with her, mainly on weekends when he wasn't at school. He spent some time with other children his age under adult supervision, of course. Lucy passed away suddenly on the

2nd of November 1988, and Mike's father had disappeared long ago. Mike would have been twelve years old. Seems Adrian had a relationship with Mike during his visits. Adrian put forward both himself and his sister, Rowena, as Mike's potential foster parents.'

'Rowena never mentioned that,' Gerry said.

Frank read the irritation on Gerry's face. In a way, it was good. An irritated Gerry would be a powerful one in the days ahead.

'I'll be following up on that with a call to Rowena, shortly,' Frank said. 'On the face of it, it looked a great opportunity for Mike Bailey, didn't it? A social worker and a primary school teacher offering to foster him. Doesn't get better than that... So, what went wrong, Sharon?'

'Well, I've got a copy of the application and the decision on the fostering.' She then described how it worked. In 1988, the fostering application process was primarily paper based. The local council's social services department would have handled the application, with a panel of experts making the final decision. As part of her research, Sharon submitted a request to the council's archives, citing the ongoing investigation as grounds for accessing the historical records.

'It was Mike Bailey himself who ended up killing the application. He told a panel that his relationship with Adrian wasn't good, and he wanted to live with his uncle, Carl Moss – the younger sibling of Lucy. Problem was, his uncle wasn't keen at first. He changed his mind, however. There's a brief mention of the financial incentives of fostering swaying Carl's decision... nevertheless, the panel concluded that Carl was family, and was the best option. Especially, when you throw in Mike's admission that

Adrian "scared" him.' She made quotation marks with her fingers.

'Scared him?' Reggie said. 'How?'

'No mention. Mike mustn't have elaborated.'

'Our bloody horse-whisperer scaring him?' Reggie couldn't get his head around it.

'Just because he's quiet,' Gerry said, 'doesn't mean that he's gentle.'

'And that he's not intimidating,' Frank added.

'Guess so.' Reggie shrugged.

'Good work, Sharon. Now, Carl passed, unfortunately, what year was it again?'

'In 2014 after a brief illness, but I've located Mike Bailey.' Her expression became more sombre. 'And that's not good news either. He's been having major health issues. Morbidly obese to the point of becoming housebound. He's currently in hospital after suffering a heart attack only last night. I spoke to the doctors earlier. With his blood pressure and condition, he's a ticking time bomb. They were surprised that he survived this episode. Poor man.'

'Aye,' Frank said. 'Did they seem open to us speaking to him without making a fuss?'

'The doctor pleaded with us to leave it a day or two for Mike to settle. I convinced him to let us speak to Mike tomorrow.'

'Sharon, you're a gem.'

'Excellent work, Sharon. Now, Sean, what've you got?'

'I've found three individuals willing to speak to me. Jane Thompson, Tom Roberts, and Lisa Parker. All of them were at Sunnybrook House when Mike was there. I'll be talking to them tomorrow.'

'Great work.' A rare smile tugged at Frank's lips.

He turned to look at Adrian's picture.

We're getting there, he thought.

The altruistic social worker... an innocent man stabbed and concealed behind the cellar wall...

Yet so many question marks...

Time for you to come clean, fella.

Chapter Forty-Three

THE NEXT MORNING, after parking, and while they were heading into the hospital, Gerry said, 'I've packed your lunch.'

He did a double take, a roll-up hanging from his mouth. 'Eh?'

'I know things were different when you were younger, Frank. Schools didn't educate effectively on healthy eating...' She pointed at the roll-up that was now in his hand. 'Or smoking.'

'School, eh? Now that was a long time ago. I've eaten a lot since then and I'm still here... maybe, they got it right after all?'

Gerry shook her head. 'No. I couldn't sleep last night, Frank. I thought it was the details of the case that were plaguing me. When I gave it proper thought, it was my concern for you that was keeping me awake. You really don't look well.'

'Shit, Gerry, are we back on this?' He pointed at his eye. 'The swelling is going down. I'll be as good as new in a couple of days.'

'No. It's health in general... your weight... your wellbeing.'

'Jesus, are you and Helen swapping notes?' Frank pounded his chest. 'Heart like an ox.' He took a deep drag on his roll-up and tossed it onto the ground. He coughed into his fist.

His phone rang. After answering it, he heard Sharon's voice. It was a welcome relief. At least Sharon didn't scrutinise his health every five sodding minutes.

Still, the information she delivered sent his blood pressure soaring.

Chapter Forty-Four

Frank mumbled to himself as he navigated the labyrinth of the hospital corridors, wincing at the stench of disinfectant. 'I loathe hospitals.'

As soon as he said it, he knew his comment was a mistake.

'Then, in order to avoid them, I'd advise—'

'Gerry!' He bit back some coarse language when he caught two nurses at the end of the corridor regarding him with narrowed eyes.

He grumbled an apology to Gerry for raising his voice, and then they found the ward. A doctor was waiting for them there. They showed their badges.

'Detectives.' The doctor's voice was low. 'He's been informed of your visit. Mike is in a delicate way. His heart is weak, and his blood pressure remains high. He was fortunate last time. He might not be so fortunate again.'

'Noted.' Frank gave a sharp nod. 'You have my word. We'll tread carefully. If he's not our man, we'll be out of his hair quick enough.'

The doctor thanked them, eyeing up Frank's facial wounds suspiciously, and led them to the room.

As they entered the room, Frank's steps faltered, his breath catching in his throat.

Mike's body spilled out over the edges of an oversized hospital bed. Mike's face appeared round and puffy, his cheeks had a mottled red colour, and his eyes seemed sunken, almost disappearing into the folds of his skin. Machines beeped and whirred around him, monitoring his vital signs, a tangle of wires and tubes snaking across his bulk.

Frank tried to recall ever being this close to someone suffering so extremely from obesity, but realised he'd only seen it this advanced on television. He swallowed hard, a mix of pity and unease twisting in his gut. He immediately began feeling guilty for being so critical of his own weight.

The nurse sitting beside Mike rose. She touched his hand. 'I'll see you later, Mike.'

He smiled up at her. 'Thanks, Emma.' He winked.

Frank noted the fear on Emma's face. They were close.

'Don't worry,' Mike said. 'I'm not done yet.'

Yet.

Frank pondered the doctor's words outside.

One didn't need to be a medical professional to know that Mike's time could be up any day.

As Emma passed them, she paused and her eyes narrowed as she regarded Frank. 'He's a good man.'

Frank nodded. *Heard you loud and clear*.

She left the room.

Mike fixed his eyes on them as they approached. When they were closer, Frank noticed a faint wheezing sound that the machines had drowned out from a distance.

Frank reached for his badge. 'I'm DCI Frank Black, and

this is DI Gerry Carver. I'm sorry to hear what happened. We understand you're weak, so we don't want to take too much of your time. The doctor has spoken to you already?'

'Yes.' Mike's voice was thin and reedy. 'About Adrian Hughes. You found his remains in a pub cellar wall.'

'That's correct.' Frank pulled a chair close to the bed. It was heavy, so he couldn't raise it off the floor enough, and the legs squealed. He apologised for the noise and lowered himself into it. Gerry took up position on the other side of the bed, which already had a chair ready. She prepared her notebook.

'The doctor and the nurse,' Frank said, 'they've got your back. It must be a difficult time. It's nice to see you in the best possible hands.'

Mike let out a weak laugh. The sound rattled in his chest long after he'd finished. 'Look at me. Hardly matters any more, does it?'

Frank flinched. He looked away and steeled himself.

No time for sympathy. *Keep wearing your poker face, Frank.*

But when he looked back, he realised that this was going to be impossible. There was profound sadness in Mike's eyes, the likes of which he'd never seen before.

He glanced up at Gerry, who looked impassive, wondering if she was at least considering the same question as him.

What could drive a person to such a state?

'What would you like to know?' Mike asked.

Frank didn't want to go in too hard, for obvious reasons. Asking him straight out if he'd killed him was a definite no-go.

'When did you last see Adrian Hughes?' Frank asked.

'When I was twelve. When my mum died.'

'That would be November 1988?'

'Around then, yes. I never knew Adrian Hughes had disappeared until the doctor told me about his body earlier.'

Frank nodded, making a note, thinking how strange it was that nobody, apart from his work colleagues and sister, had been aware of his disappearance. In 1989, Adrian vanished off the face of the earth, and yet, Rob, who claimed to have been stalked by him, hadn't even noticed. And now, Mike, who'd almost ended up in his care, hadn't the foggiest, either. It just didn't ring true.

'We know Adrian worked at Sunnybrook House, and that your mother was the cook there.' Frank nodded, making a note. 'Can you tell me about that?'

'Sure.' Mike's gaze drifted. 'I used to go to Sunnybrook sometimes, mainly on weekends or during school holidays, with my mum. The people who worked there were caring and knew my mum struggled with childcare. When I turned eleven, I could have just stayed at home, but I enjoyed going. There were other boys there, too. I could play football with them.' He widened his eyes. 'I wasn't always like this, you know. We'd also play games. Cluedo, Monopoly, that sort of thing.' He winked. 'I even had a girlfriend once. But then, she was fostered. After that, I wasn't allowed to know where she went. That was a bummer.'

'A shame,' Frank said.

'That's life,' Mike said. 'But she had the loveliest smile. I still remember it now.'

Frank smiled. 'Cherish those memories. The older you get, the more they fade.' As soon as he said it, he felt somewhat insensitive. Had he been thoughtless? Would Mike even have the chance to grow old?

'Believe me, there're some memories I'd rather forget.'

Frank looked at him. *And what do you mean by that?*

Noticing Frank's scrutiny, Mike suddenly added, 'Like my father disappearing when I was six. My mother dying when I was twelve, and—' He broke off.

Was there something else there? Something which had been on the tip of his tongue?

'And how well did you know Adrian? At Sunnybrook?'

'He was there a lot. Quiet man, but he'd join in the games sometimes. Not football, just board games, mainly. He liked comic books. So did I. We talked about them, occasionally.'

'Any comics in particular?'

'Marvel, I guess. Spider-Man and the like. I can't say it was ever something I carried on with after that time.'

Gerry leaned forward. Frank knew she wanted to ask some questions. He thought about his promise to the nurse and the doctor. Go easy, Gerry, he thought to himself. 'Would you say he took an interest in you, Mike?'

Mike screwed up his face. He was on the defensive. 'He was fond of all the children. That was his job. That was his life's calling.'

Frank noticed that the beeping on one machine had sped up. He looked up. Mike's blood pressure was 180/120 and his heart rate was 110 bpm.

'Was he fonder of you than the other children?' Gerry asked.

'What would make you say that?'

'Well, he tried to foster you, along with his sister, Rowena,' Gerry said.

Mike sighed. Frank watched the heart rate and blood pressure monitors. No change.

'I guess he'd have fostered us all if he could have done,' Mike said.

'But he only tried with you.'

'I guess that's because I wasn't actually in care at that point. I think he was hoping to keep that from happening to me. That made me an anomaly, I suppose. It wasn't the case with the other children. He couldn't foster them all.'

'Do you think he'd have offered you a suitable home?'

The beeping intensified. Frank noted that Mike's heart rate had increased to 120 bpm. 'How could I answer that? I didn't go.'

'No, you didn't,' Frank said. 'And why was that?'

Mike looked to Frank. 'Because my Uncle Carl took me in.'

'And you thought that was the better option?' Gerry asked.

'Of course. Wouldn't you? He was my uncle. My mum's brother.'

'Makes sense,' Frank said, making a note while eyeing the monitors. It was fascinating. Could the changes in pulse and blood pressure show anything? Could someone use them like a lie detector test? Probably not. Still, it was interesting to gauge Mike's reactions.

'I was depressed. My mum had just died. I didn't want to live with people I hardly knew.'

Gerry was still leaning in. She looked at Frank. He nodded, giving her the go-ahead. 'In the records, it says you reported that Adrian scared you. Can you elaborate on that?'

Mike's blood pressure increased again. His chins wobbled as he shook his head. 'I just made that up. Stupid, I know. He was always a quiet, reserved man.' The words tumbled out in a rush. 'I was scared. I was a child. My mum had died, and I just wanted to be with my uncle, who was always kind to me.'

'Our report suggests,' Gerry said, 'that your uncle didn't want you at first.'

Frank balked at the directness of her statement.

Mike glared at Gerry for the first time. 'That's not true.'

'It may not be.' Frank glared at Gerry. 'It's one social worker's assessment. They may've been mistaken.' *But more than likely not,* he thought.

Still, he didn't want to give this man another heart attack, and they'd yet to make the biggest revelation of all.

'I was told nothing like that,' Mike said.

Frank nodded. 'You wouldn't have been. Tell me about your uncle, Carl Moss.' He hoped that some fond memories might calm Mike down.

Mike nodded, his breath coming too fast for Frank's liking. 'Uncle Carl, yeah. It was... it was fine, living with him. He wasn't very paternal, okay, that's fair, but we had fun. He always chatted with me, played games with me, watched television and stuff. I was never an inconvenience, you know? I suppose the only criticism was that he wasn't too strict, you know? He didn't mind what time I got in at night. And when I started missing school, he didn't force me to go, just tried to talk me into it. When he got in trouble for it, I did the right thing and went back. He'd always come to my aid, you know?'

Frank felt it was time to share what Sharon had told him earlier. 'Do you know where your uncle worked?'

'In various pubs over the years,' Mike said.

'Can you remember the name of them?' Frank asked.

'Not really.'

The heart monitor picked up its pace again. Mike's breath became more laboured. There was no point in leading him into confessing what he already knew. It was pushing him too hard. 'Your uncle worked at the Rusty Anchor pub, didn't he?'

'Yes.'

'Where we found Adrian Hughes... and it was around the time he disappeared, too.'

The machines were blaring. Mike's heart rate had shot up to 160 bpm.

Frank took Mike's arm. 'Deep breaths. It's okay.'

'I don't feel so good...' Mike's face drained of colour, leaving him a sickly grey, his lips trembling.

Frank looked over at Gerry. She, too, looked concerned now.

He didn't know whether to ease off or press on. If he eased off, he might never get the answers. But the consequences of pressing on... well... they didn't bear thinking about.

Gerry spoke first. 'As far as you're aware, did your Uncle Carl know Adrian, Mike? Could Adrian's presence at the pub have had anything to do with your uncle?'

A shrill alarm burst from the machine. Mike wheezed. 'I can't...' He closed his eyes, and his head slumped to one side.

Chapter Forty-Five

W<small>HITBY</small> A<small>BBEY</small>. Weathered stone. Towering arches.
Red eyes boring into his back.
199 steps. Aching calves.
His heart pounds.
Salty wind. Crashing seas. Crying gulls.
His breath comes in ragged gasps.
Whitby's old town. Deserted. Winding alleys.
The echoing paws on cobblestones.
Church Street. Old fishermen's cottages. Red-tiled roofs. Weather-beaten walls.
Hot breath burns the back of his neck.
The Swing Bridge. Safety. Over the River Esk.
Almost there.
A chance.
No chance.
Adrian blocks the way.
Eyes, which were once kind and gentle, now glint with a predatory hunger.
Mouth open.

A yawning chasm of darkness—
Adrian lunges, his fingers clawing at Mike's flesh, dragging him back into the nightmare of his past.

Chapter Forty-Six

THE DOOR BURST OPEN, and two nurses and a doctor rushed in. Frank and Gerry found themselves ushered out.

Outside, they exchanged looks. 'I'd ask you what you think,' Frank said, 'but I think it's fairly obvious. We need another run at him.'

They could hear shouting and commotion coming from inside the room. Another nurse and doctor were heading in.

'If it's possible to have another run at him,' Frank inwardly sighed.

They lingered until the alarms had stopped, at least.

A nurse came out.

Frank stopped him. 'Is he okay?'

'Stable... again...'

Good.

'Okay,' Frank said to Gerry after the nurse had left them. 'We're not getting back in there soon. For now, we need everything we can find on Carl Moss. We also need to speak to Rory again, and soon. We're beyond coincidences now. Adrian Hughes wasn't just in that pub to play cards and show off a young escort. I'm certain of it. He attempted to foster Mike, but Mike rejected him because of Carl, a man who worked at the Anchor. It's connected... it has to be.'

'I wouldn't disagree,' Gerry said.

When they were back in the car, Frank turned to Gerry. 'When I see someone like that, with a body ravaged by grief and self-neglect, there's only one conclusion.'

'What's that?'

'A burden. An overwhelming burden. Enough to drive you to this shadow of an existence.'

Chapter Forty Seven

Frank ended the call and let out a loud sigh of relief. Everyone in the incident room looked up from their computers. Even Rylan's ears perked up, the Lab's brown eyes fixed on Frank with an almost human-like curiosity.

'Mike Bailey?' Reggie asked.

'Aye. We didn't kill anyone.'

Gerry frowned. 'I don't understand. I don't see how it would've been our fault—'

Frank snorted, a sound caught between amusement and exasperation. 'You can be certain of one thing, Gerry. It would have been our fault. It's always our bloody fault. I've already had more than one frosty look from Donald since we came back.'

Gerry nodded, then reached down into a bag at her feet. She put two Tupperware containers out in front of her. He recalled her offer to supply lunch.

Frank put down the phone and approached, eyeing the offering suspiciously. 'Lunch?'

'Yes.' She opened one container. 'All natural.'

'Christ,' Frank muttered, peering inside as if it might

bite him. 'Are you sure? It's dazzling. Should food glow like that?'

'Fresh tomatoes and fresh lettuce. Organic. And only from a specific grocer—'

'I was being sarcastic, Gerry. I know it's a salad. Thing is, Gerry, I'm not a salad fella.'

'That makes no sense, Frank. You can't define yourself by a food group.'

'Watch me,' Frank grumbled. 'Yeah... look, if my food didn't live and breathe once upon a time, I'm not partial to it.'

Sean, who was overhearing the conversation, laughed.

She shook her head. 'You need variety in your diet, Frank.' She handed him a napkin, wrapped around a knife and fork.

Frank took the container. 'Thanks, I guess.'

Gerry nodded, a hint of satisfaction in her eyes. She stood.

'Where are you going? If I have to eat it, you do, too!'

'With pleasure! But first, I need the bathroom.' With that, she was gone.

As soon as she was out of sight, Frank rummaged around the salad with a fork, poking at a piece of cucumber as if it were evidence at a crime scene. He saw Rylan eyeing him up. 'What do you say, boy? Want to share?'

He held a tomato out with his fingers, checking Gerry wasn't watching through the door. She'd have him for not only skimping on the salad, but for feeding her dog.

Not that it mattered. Rylan sniffed the tomato and turned his head away, unimpressed.

'Traitor,' Frank mumbled. 'We're on the same page, aren't we, fella?' Frank chuckled, setting the container aside. 'Both of us, more sausage roll than salad roll.'

He looked over at Sean, who was hunched over his computer. 'You want this, Sean?'

'No thanks. Just eaten.'

'Please.'

'Nah, I'm full.'

Damn it. Frank eyed the bin, wondering if he could get away with a quick disposal.

Sean suddenly sat up straight. 'Boss?'

'Yes.' Frank felt a tingle of excitement. 'Have you changed your mind?'

'Boss, I think I've got something.'

Frank raised an eyebrow. 'What? What is it, Sean?'

'Back in 1988, a young woman named Phoebe Turner was working part time at Sunnybrook House. Apparently, Adrian Hughes reported Phoebe to the boss for drinking on the job. That was October 1988. The next day, she lost her position because of it.'

Frank pushed the container aside with enough force to nearly send it skidding off the desk, his appetite for justice suddenly far stronger than any hunger for food. He walked over to Sean. 'So, the accusation was true?'

'They searched her belongings and found vodka. Open and shut. Apparently.'

Frank looked up at the picture of Adrian, his faith in the innocence of his victim at an all-time low. 'Unless it was planted.'

'Why would he do that?'

'Well, we can't ask him... but we can ask her. Can you find her for me?'

Gerry returned from the bathroom.

Frank filled her in on Sean's discovery.

'We need to talk to Rory again.' Frank stood up. 'And by then, we should have Phoebe's address to pay her a visit.'

Gerry nodded, already gathering her things. 'What about our lunch?'

'Later,' Frank lied, his mind drifting to the heavenly aroma of fresh-baked goods from Botham's of Whitby. The old bakery near the steps in town was calling his name, and who was he to ignore such a siren song?

Chapter Forty-Eight

As Sharon drove to meet the first of the three former child residents of Sunnybrook Home, she struggled to still her whirring mind and focus on the road. Beside her, Reggie was desperate to engage her in conversation. She said little back to him, but it didn't deter the stubborn DS from trying over and over.

At one point, she caught a whiff of his aftershave. Christ, did he bathe in the stuff?

She cracked the window. The sound of air rushing in quietened him down for a few minutes. He spent the time looking at some nonsense on his phone and chuckling to himself. He didn't share the same sense of foreboding she did – but then again, why would he? He hadn't spoken to any of them on the phone.

During each conversation, Sharon's senses had been raging. There was something here. Something unpleasant. A resignation in all of their voices that the day was finally here. The truth was to come.

Sharon feared it, but Reggie was none the wiser. She

expected his shock when they finally revealed the part of them that was dark and broken.

After winding the window up, she considered warning him, but suspected she'd sound irrational. Her concerns were based on instinct and not evidence.

Sharon and Reggie pulled up in front of a modest, red-brick house on a quiet, tree-lined street.

'Can I take the lead, sir?' she asked.

Reggie looked surprised. After all, he was her senior. 'You sure? I've done this a thousand times.'

So bloody condescending. Her default was to challenge him rather than pander to it, but she wanted the lead. If she was right in her suspicions, then these people would need calm and understanding. She trusted her own people skills and expressions of empathy, and she hadn't known Reggie long enough to trust him. So, she pandered. 'Please, sir. It's a learning curve.'

'Aye, of course.' He smiled and winked.

The pride he felt over showing generosity nauseated her, but she didn't want to be distracted from the issue at hand, so she exited the car without discussing it further.

A woman in her late forties opened the door to them. At first, she appeared at ease, but after viewing their badges, a sad, haunted look came into her eyes, and she gave a swift nod. 'Lydia Thompson, we spoke on the phone?' Sharon said.

'Come in.' Lydia turned away, her shoulders hunched slightly.

I wasn't wrong, Sharon thought. *Something is coming.*

She exchanged a look with Reggie as they stepped in. A raised eyebrow. She guessed what he was thinking. *What's up with her, then?*

As they stepped inside, the scent of fresh-baked cookies wafted from the kitchen, a jarring contrast to the heaviness in the air.

Photos of smiling children adorned the walls of the lounge. The place was full of joy. But Sharon could sense that beneath the surface, Lydia was anything but joyful.

'Sorry I had to be so specific about the time you came here.'

'No problem, Lydia, you're doing us a huge service, seeing us on short notice like this.'

She sighed. 'I just didn't want anybody else to be home.' She gestured for them to sit on the sofa while she perched on the edge of an armchair, her hands clasped tightly in her lap. 'I'll get to it. Adrian Hughes. Just saying his name... well...' She broke off. She looked pale, suddenly.

'Take your time,' Sharon said.

'It's okay. Look, here's the thing. I buried it. All of it... I mean, I know it happened. It isn't like I've forgotten. It just doesn't have the right clarity, you know?' Her voice trembled. 'Until about ten years ago, when it returned with more clarity. I couldn't feel confident in believing in it entirely. I'd repressed it for so long. But I had treatment, and it came right out. Adrian Hughes abused me when I was a child.'

'I'm so sorry.' Reggie's voice was uncharacteristically soft, and Sharon suddenly felt guilty for judging his empathy levels earlier in the car.

'It started with little things. He'd find reasons to be alone with me, to touch my shoulder or my hair. He read comics to me. I was only eleven and I didn't understand what was happening. Both my parents had abandoned me. You know how it feels when an adult wants to spend time with you after such abandonment?'

'I can only imagine. I'm so sorry that happened to you.' Sharon could feel her heart breaking for both the young girl Lydia had once been, and the tortured adult she now was.

'I can tell you exactly how it makes you feel.' Lydia's eyes had a distant look in them. 'Like it gives you a second chance at being worth something.'

A lump formed in Sharon's throat.

'And as time went on, it got worse,' Lydia continued, her hands trembling in her lap. 'His hands would wander. He said it was our special secret.'

Sharon felt the weight of Lydia's words hitting her like a physical blow. Beside her, Reggie shifted in his seat.

'And I never doubted him. I always believed him. He had a way. A quiet way.' Lydia leaned forward and whispered, 'And for the first time in my life, I felt worth a damn. How bad is that? He made me feel grateful for what he was doing. And the sad thing is, since I was abused, I've never felt that way again. No sense of worth. My husband tries so hard, and yet, he cannot make me feel how I should feel. Special. Cherished.'

Sharon swallowed. She thought of her relationship with her father. They'd been so close. They'd stayed up until all hours when she was in her teens watching classic crime dramas like *The Sweeney*. She'd felt special. Cherished. And as a result, now felt guilty.

'Even when the touching became painful, I didn't want to say anything. I didn't want to upset him, hurt his feelings, get him in trouble.' She lowered her head. 'Ten years ago when the psychiatrist brought the truth out, and I recalled it all with clarity, I came forward to expose Adrian. Turned out Sunnybrook was long gone. And he'd long gone, too.'

This was news to Sharon. 'Can you remember who you reported it to?'

Lydia shook her head. 'I can't remember. I remember them being fairly confident that he was dead. Suicide, they said. There didn't seem to be much of an appetite to drag things up. They said it would be hard to investigate with the time that had elapsed, but they would if I wanted to. I thought about it for a time. Spoke about it with my husband. But I figured it would be a traumatic ordeal for my family and children.'

It took every ounce of Sharon's willpower to hold back an expression of disgust. How could her colleagues, predecessors, whoever they were, have considered it the right move to leave this horror in the silence? Had the other two child residents of Sunnybrook she was about to speak to come forward as well, only to be shut down? It was heinous to consider the lack of appetite to bring the dead to justice, even if it meant helping those still living with the damage.

'But I found peace another way,' Lydia continued, fixing Sharon with a stare. 'By forgiving him.'

Sharon felt a cold fury building in her gut – *did a man who preyed on such vulnerability deserve forgiveness?*

'I forgave him for the illness that caused him to do whatever he did to me, and the others. And yes, it gave me some peace.'

'What else do you remember of Adrian Hughes?' Sharon asked, almost afraid of the answer.

'That one day he was just gone,' Lydia said. 'And not long after, someone fostered me. Around Christmas 1989.'

Rather than make a note, Sharon reached out and took Lydia's hand. 'I'm so sorry, Lydia. What you went through was unimaginable...' She took a deep breath. As she exhaled, she said, 'With the discovery of his body, I think the truth is going to come out now.'

A single tear rolled down her cheek. 'It's for the best, I think. Even though he's gone, the truth matters, doesn't it?'

'Yes.' Sharon squeezed Lydia's hand. 'Yes, I couldn't agree more. And I'm in awe of how strong you are.'

'I lost a lot of time because of that man.' Lydia looked up at the pictures of her family. 'But I found a love for those around me like you wouldn't believe.'

As they left Lydia's house, Reggie was uncharacteristically quiet. Once in the car, he finally spoke, his voice a mixture of anger and disbelief. 'We're trying to find the killer of a fucking monster! Don't know about you, but I'm more inclined to give him a medal than arrest him.'

Sharon understood Reggie's sentiment, having had similar thoughts herself during the interview.

'Wait till Frank hears about the man he's fighting for justice for!' He pulled out his phone. 'I'm calling him.'

Sharon glanced at Reggie, seeing the bewilderment etched on his face as he bashed his mobile screen. She knew that Frank, like her, would have expected this revelation. Frank was a weather-beaten old copper who'd seen it all – he'd know that monsters often hide behind respectable facades.

She listened to Reggie leave a message for Frank on voicemail.

As they drove to meet the second person, who could very well turn out to be another of Adrian's victims, Sharon's mind raced.

Had the person who'd taken Adrian's life been a victim? Could it even have been Lydia?

Or did they have a vigilante on the cards – someone trying to rid society of one of its scourges?

The car filled with a tense silence, broken only by the rhythmic thumping of windshield wipers against a light drizzle that had fallen. It felt as if the very sky was weeping for Lydia and the others like her.

Sharon couldn't shake the feeling that they were standing on the edge of a very dark rabbit hole. And they were about to tumble right in.

Chapter Forty-Nine

Frank and Gerry entered the Whitby Arms, Rylan alongside them. Rory looked up from behind the bar, his face breaking into a grin. He hadn't looked that happy at the sight of Frank before, so he could only assume the landlord's overjoyed expression was because of the Lab.

'Rylan!' Rory came around the bar.

Rylan stood up straight, let his tongue loll out, and panted. He was probably recalling the offer of a biscuit days earlier.

'No feeding your lad, right?' Rory glanced at Gerry.

'That's right.'

Frank sidled away as he recalled his earlier sin of trying to feed Rylan a tomato earlier.

'Can I offer you both a coffee?' Rory said, already reaching for the mugs. He winked at Frank this time. 'From the new machine?'

Frank's mouth watered at the memory of the rich, smooth brew he'd enjoyed last time. He was tempted, but caught Gerry's disapproving look. Caffeine was on her hit list, too, and by not eating her salad, he'd no credit in the bank.

'It's okay, Rory.' Frank waved off the offer. 'You give your fancy new machine a rest. Did you check the picture we sent over in an email?'

'Literally ten minutes back. It wasn't the young lad that Adrian came in with. Sorry. I know it was a while back, but the lad you sent over looked burly. Strong. Like a rugby player. The lad I remember was stick thin.'

Frank nodded. Maybe Rob was telling the truth then. Maybe he'd never seen Adrian again after he'd come to his house the second time.

'You haven't stopped by just for that, have you? Sorry to waste your time if—'

'No,' Frank cut in. 'There's something else, or rather someone. Do you recall Carl Moss?'

'Of course, aye. Not likely to forget him. Worked for me for a fair time. Not just that. He was a mate, you know? Top bloke. His death a while back hit me hard.'

Frank nodded. 'Can you remember the dates he specifically worked for you?'

'Bloody hell. On and off for fifteen odd years!' Rory exclaimed. 'He was a builder, so when business was bad, he'd work with me for a time. Did some long stints if I recall?' He gazed off, a reflective look in his eyes. 'Aye. Top bloke. Did all the extension work on our home, too. Cheap as chips.'

'And was he working at the Rusty Anchor on 29th August 1989?'

Rory waggled his finger. 'Now, now, Frank. Take it from me, right now. Carl was no killer. Gentlest man you ever met. Calm. Measured. Guy was like a hippie, you know? Long hair. Chilled out.'

'But was he working here around then?' Gerry asked.

'Let me think... possibly... aye... I remember discussing that cellar wall with him, and he'd offered to fix it up at some stage, so he must have been around that era. But look... Carl? No chance. What's put him on your radar?'

'He's Mike Bailey's uncle.'

'Yeah. That's right. Lovely lad. Least he was back then. Haven't seen him in a fair while. What's the relevance here?'

'You recall Carl fostered his nephew?'

Rory nodded. 'Aye. Remember it well. Tragic what happened. You know, Carl was worried about the responsibility but that lad was no bother. And' – Rory winked – 'that lad was the best glass collector you ever saw. Rapid, like—'

'Hang on,' Frank interrupted. 'He worked for you? At the Anchor?'

'Well, not exactly. He was only thirteen, or fourteen... he wasn't on the books, officially, like. Long time ago now. Struggling family, Frank. I hope you'll not be slapping my hands for that now.'

Frank waved such a suggestion away. 'What happened?'

'What do you mean, what happened?' Rory said. 'I gave Carl a few extra quid when Mike helped.'

Frank looked at Gerry, who'd been uncharacteristically quiet up to now.

Mike had never mentioned working at the Anchor. Why not? Was it because his spiralling heart rate and blood pressure had cut him off? Or had he been deliberately keeping it back? He could hardly have claimed to never have seen Adrian Hughes again after the failed attempt to foster him if he was working in the same pub that Adrian played cards in.

'How often did Mike work here?'

'It wasn't a constant thing. Lad had school, you know? But he popped up, occasionally. Weekends were busiest, so it was good to have a hand around then.'

'So, he could have been in the Anchor at the same time that Adrian Hughes was?'

'I guess so,' Rory said. 'But what's that got to do with the price of apples?'

'Adrian Hughes tried to foster Mike.'

'Eh?' Rory looked completely baffled.

Frank explained it to him.

Rory nodded. 'Aye, that all seems rather odd.'

'Can you recall any interaction between Mike and Adrian?'

Rory thought about it for them, but it was clear from the outset that this was all news to him. He shook his head.

'What was the relationship like between Mike and Carl?'

'Good. If I remember right. Like I said, Carl was a top bloke, but he had his ways, like. A free spirit, you know? Carl treated Mike more like a good friend than a nephew, or even a son. Like equals. Nice to see, really.'

'How about Carl and Adrian?' Gerry asked. 'Did anything ever happen there?'

There was a slight widening of his eyes. *Bingo*, Frank thought.

'Come to think of it, there was something. An odd one, actually.' Rory clucked his tongue. 'This one time Carl got angry with Adrian at the bar and told him to leave. Adrian did as he was told. I thought at the time: "What was all that about? The man doesn't say bloody boo to a goose." Carl wouldn't talk about it. I told him I couldn't bar Adrian unless I knew what he'd done. But no one ever mentioned it again. Adrian came back at some point. But no, Carl wasn't a violent man. That was the only time I ever saw him wound-up.'

Frank thanked Rory for his time and led Gerry and Rylan out of the pub. His mind was whirling with the new information. Mike had lied to them. He'd been at the Rusty Anchor, likely around the time of Adrian's disappearance.

Lost in thought, Frank made his way to Botham's of Whitby, where he picked up a pasty and wolfed it down outside the shop, smoking as he did so.

'It doesn't look comfortable smoking and eating simultaneously.'

'It's not simultaneous. I breathe out. Have a mouthful, swallow, then take another puff. And I find it comfortable, thank you.' He took a defiant drag on his cigarette.

'I see. Does it affect the taste?'

'To be honest, I ate it that quick I barely tasted it anyway.'

As they walked, Frank's phone started to buzz. He recalled it buzzing in his pocket while he was interviewing Rory. Checking the screen, he noticed a voicemail message from Reggie, but before he could listen to it, Sean's name flashed on the screen. Frank answered immediately. 'How do, Sean?'

'Boss, I've got something big.' Sean's voice was tight with excitement.

'As do we,' Frank said.

'Bet I got you beat, boss. Phoebe Turner, the woman that Adrian had fired from Sunnybrook, killed someone last night.'

Frank's mouth fell open, the last bit of pasty tumbling to the ground. 'Jesus.' He looked at Gerry, who was making a rare moment of eye contact, her expression full of curiosity. 'Fair play, Sean. You got us beat. Elaborate.'

Chapter Fifty

Gerry reluctantly agreed to leave Rylan at Frank's place, unattended, with a bowl of grain-free kibble (which she always carried in her bag) for a maximum of two hours. Frank assured her he'd be mindful of the time, suppressing a sigh as she started a timer on her watch. Was he really that unreliable?

She also insisted on putting on some music to relax Rylan. Frank showed her his collection.

'Do you have any Mozart?' she raised her eyebrows.

Frank shook his head. 'I'm not as sophisticated as Rylan. Will Led Zep cut it?'

Ten minutes later, Frank and Gerry pulled up outside Phoebe Turner's sprawling Victorian home, the gravel crunching beneath the car's tyres.

Frank eyed the manicured gardens and imposing façade. 'Quite the estate for a charity CEO, eh?'

Gerry, who'd been scanning the background information on her phone, said, 'It's her husband's property business that's made them millionaires.'

'Well, good on her, either way. She's going to need some

serious dough for the lawyer. Ready to tread carefully?' The snort that followed was of pure derision, a jab at his earlier conversation with Chief Constable Donald Oxley.

He'd been his usual buoyant and motivating self. 'Frank, she's facing charges of manslaughter! With the Julian Sims case under active investigation, be sure to tread carefully. You discuss her connection to Adrian Hughes, nothing else, understand?'

'What if the connection to Adrian Hughes somehow ties into Julian Sims?'

There'd been a lingering silence, in which Frank could almost hear Donald's teeth grinding.

Eventually Donald said, 'It doesn't,' and hung up, abruptly.

'That man really fills me with "get up and go", know what I mean, Gerry?'

A shake of her head had shown that she didn't quite understand what he meant.

Now, as they approached the front door, Frank considered Phoebe's background. She'd come a long way since drinking on the job. Multiple awards, glowing press coverage. 'Every child deserves a chance to shine,' she'd proclaimed in one interview. 'It's our duty to provide opportunities for all, regardless of background.' Hardly a candidate for two violent murders. However, the CCTV footage of her dispatching Julian Sims would be argued away as a terrified response to a mugging.

Just before knocking, Frank recalled that he'd forgotten to listen to Reggie's voicemail when Sean had distracted him with news of Julian Sims' death. He was out speaking to former child residents of Sunnybrook with Sharon. He'd obviously found something of note, but it was too late to call him back now, the door was opening.

David Turner's dismissive attitude was clear from the start. After showing his identification, Frank said, 'It's not about the charges against your wife. It's unrelated.'

'So, what's it about?'

'Can we speak to her directly, sir?'

Cue angry, rich husband who was used to having everything his own way. 'She's in no state for this!'

Frank leaned in, so he'd be able to smell the tobacco on his breath. 'Here or the station, Mr Turner. And alone, please.' He leaned back, keeping his eyes locked with David's. 'Yes, alone would be best.'

He stepped back, allowing them entry. Frank suspected it was the bruises that mottled his face that had been the intimidating factor rather than his gruff tone of voice.

Phoebe sat hunched on the sofa, hair dishevelled, eyes red-rimmed. She clutched a glass of wine like a lifeline. 'I gave you everything at the station.' She was slurring her words. 'I haven't even slept yet. And you're back again!'

'It's not about last night,' Frank said.

'Someone mugs me, tries to strangle me, and I'm the fucking criminal?'

'It isn't about the incident in the car park.' Frank drew a deep breath.

She gulped a large mouthful of wine. 'I don't have my solicitor. I don't want to talk.'

It was useless. She'd switched herself off. Frank decided to change tack. 'It's about Adrian Hughes.'

Phoebe looked up. 'Sorry?'

Now that has got your attention, Frank thought.

'We found his body,' Gerry said.

Her mouth hung open, and she looked between them.

'You remember him?'

'Yes... of course. Jesus. But that was *so* long ago.'

Frank nodded. 'May we sit?' He gestured to the chairs opposite.

As they settled in, Phoebe took off her watch so she could scratch the top of her wrist. Frank noticed a tattoo on the top of Phoebe's wrist: a series of interlocking geometric shapes that formed a stylised eye. It would have looked out of place with her usual polished appearance, but somehow suited her current dishevelled state. She put her watch on the sofa beside her, opting not to put it back on.

'We discovered his remains several days ago. We suspect he died in August 1989.'

'About the last time I bloody saw him.' Phoebe gulped again. After swallowing, she must have realised how that must have sounded. 'Shit... I didn't mean it like that. I just meant it was a long time ago, around that time. I didn't murder him.'

'We didn't say he'd been murdered,' Gerry said.

Phoebe gulped again. This time, she didn't have wine in her mouth. 'Sorry... I just assumed. I mean, why else would you come?'

'We could be here to rule out suspicious circumstances,' Frank said. 'But we suspect he was murdered.'

Phoebe pressed a fist to her forehead. 'And now you think I'd something to do with it? Because of all that bullshit last night? What does that have to do with anything?'

'We have assumed none of that,' Gerry said.

'Good, because my head is killing me.'

Frank regarded the line of empty wine bottles in the kitchen.

'So why are you here?'

Frank said, 'You worked at Sunnybrook House with him and he—'

'Had me sacked,' Phoebe interjected. 'Because he was a lying bastard.'

Gerry consulted her notes. 'Dismissed. After—'

'Sacked, dear,' Phoebe said. 'Get this right. They searched my belongings, said they found alcohol – which they didn't; and if they did, it was planted. Then, they escorted me off the premises. You know they held my arms? Manhandled. I was out of control, apparently. A danger. Complete bollocks of course. The reality was I wasn't even drinking.'

Frank's eyes fell to the glass in her hand.

She snorted and shook her head. 'I took my job seriously. I did then, and I do now. Speak to anyone who knows me properly.'

We might just end up doing that, Frank thought.

'Did you fight the charge?' Gerry asked. 'If they held your arms, you could have complained.'

'You know what year this was?' Phoebe regarded Gerry as if she was stupid.

Tread carefully, lass, you couldn't be further from the truth!

'Of course,' Gerry said. 'It was 1988.'

'Your rights in a workplace aren't what they are now. And there were children involved, I guess. So, when they struck, they struck hard. *Incorrectly* struck as I maintain.'

'Assault was still assault in 1989,' Gerry said. 'If someone hurt you—'

'You're not listening, dear.'

'Can I ask that you refrain from calling me dear?'

Phoebe narrowed her eyes. 'What would you prefer?'

'Detective Inspector or DI. You can shorten to detective by all means. I can also tolerate officer. Not dear.'

Phoebe then smiled. 'Actually, I quite like you.'

'Irrelevant,' Gerry said. 'This interaction is purely professional.'

Phoebe leaned forward and put the glass on the table. 'Okay. Here's the thing.' She sliced the air downwards with both palms as if trying to restore focus and order. 'I was told that they wouldn't pursue an investigation *if* I didn't make a fuss. I could have ended up with a serious blot on my name. A ban from working with children. In the end, I thought my long-term prospects were better without going to war with them.'

Frank nodded, made some notes.

Out of the corner of his eye, Frank noticed Gerry sketching something in her notebook. He tried to catch a glimpse, but she'd angled it away.

'Why did Adrian make those accusations if they weren't true?'

'*And* plant alcohol on me?' she added, a sneer across her face.

'If you say so,' Frank said. 'Why?'

'Because I knew... he was bad news. Overly friendly with the kids. Unprofessional.' She smiled at Gerry, clearly linking back to her professional comment moments back. 'I caught him with kids sitting on his lap as he read them those comics. One time, I caught him hugging a twelve-year-old girl. Yes, she was crying, but he was kissing the crown of her head. Is that right?'

'No,' Gerry said.

'It was rhetorical, DI. I approached my manager, Moira, expressed my concerns. She spoke to Adrian, and within two days, I was gone. Moira must have bought the fact that I was an alcoholic and made it all up. Adrian had wriggled out of it.'

'If that's true, it sounds like he'd something to hide.'

Phoebe gave a swift nod. 'Seems a fair interpretation.'

'Did you ever see Adrian again after that?' Gerry asked.

'No.'

'Did you ever go to the Rusty Anchor?'

'The pub? Not that I recall. Why?'

'That's where Adrian's body was recovered.'

'Ah.'

'After you lost that job, didn't you remain concerned about the welfare of the children in his care?' Frank asked.

Phoebe flinched over this. She looked down. 'Of course.'

'You never considered it more important to try to prove your suspicions rather than protect a future career?' Frank pressed.

Her face reddened. She drained her wine glass. 'I wouldn't have succeeded. They would've simply destroyed me.' Phoebe's voice was fierce, almost defiant. 'I'd my ambitions, my drive to help more children. I never wavered.' She looked up. 'I've helped thousands of children.'

Frank nodded. *At the expense of how many others?*

He made more notes, asked a few more questions, but it was clear Phoebe had nothing else to offer. Her mind kept circling back to the events of the previous night, her responses becoming more erratic and evasive.

At the door, Phoebe suddenly clutched Frank's arm, her eyes wild; no sleep and a tonne of alcohol had left her unhinged. 'Please, last night... with Julian. I was protecting myself. It wasn't my fault.'

Frank gently disentangled himself. 'That's for others to decide, Mrs Turner. We'll be in touch if we've further questions.'

Outside, Frank turned to Gerry. 'What do you think?'

'I think she knew her victim last night.'

'How can you be sure?'

'She said, "Last night... with Julian." It sounded too natural. She could have said with her mugger, or with Julian Sims.'

Frank saw her point. 'Good spot.'

Does anything get past her? he thought, and not for the first time.

Chapter Fifty One

After Reggie and Sharon had updated Frank and Gerry back at HQ on Adrian's abuse of three former residents at Sunnybrook, Frank stormed into his office, slamming the door behind him. The blinds rattled as he yanked them down.

His fist came down hard on the desk, sending papers flying and his mug – 'World's Greatest Dad' – dancing perilously close to the edge.

'Bloody hell,' he growled, catching the mug before it toppled. Twenty years, that mug had been with him. Twenty years of morning brews and late-night contemplations. Losing it now would be a right kick in the teeth, especially with everything else going on.

He leaned back in the chair, closed his eyes, and massaged his temples. In his mind's eye, he saw them – the victims. Grey, hollow-eyed, shuffling like zombies. And looming behind them, Sunnybrook House, a monument to suffering.

He'd known, hadn't he? Deep in his gut, he'd felt it

coming. So why wasn't he prepared for this? Why did it feel like a sucker punch?

He thought back to his last case involving Charlotte Wilson. A musician. Young, sweet, and innocent. Her death had clawed at him for answers. But not all victims are the same, are they?

This was justice.

And this wasn't the first evil bastard he'd been forced to get it for.

The door creaked open, and he didn't need to look up to know it was Gerry. Her presence was as predictable as it was, at this moment, unwelcome. He cut it off at the source. Standing, pointing down at the table, he declared, 'He was a fucking monster.'

She didn't respond. She merely closed the door and then regarded him.

'Have you anything to say?' Frank asked.

'You didn't ask a question.'

'Oh, for the love of – well, was he a monster or not?'

'I know you're speaking figuratively, but you need to define a monster for me.'

He waved her away. 'Forget it.'

She approached the desk. She stood opposite him, placed her hands on the edge, and then looked up at him.

He watched her eyes flicker.

Searching through your data banks, eh, Gerry? he thought. *Determining which of your learned responses will pacify the beast in front of you?*

He sighed, feeling guilty for even thinking such a thing. 'Look, Gerry, I'm sorry. It just doesn't sit right, does it? How can we justify using all our resources, what little we have – all our energy – to get justice for a serial destroyer of lives?'

'Because we've a duty to find the truth. You know that a victim's character is irrelevant.'

'Aye.' He growled and sat down. 'Aye, but this isn't just any old wrong'un we're talking about,' Frank growled. 'This bastard was a predator, Gerry. Used his position to get at kids. Doesn't this investigation feel like a complete betrayal to his actual victims? And who knows how many victims there even are? What if these three are the tip of the iceberg?' 'I don't know... I need to think... I mean, how in God's name are we supposed to fight tooth and nail for the likes of him?'

'It's the right thing to do. Also, understanding what happened to Adrian might help us prevent similar cycles of abuse in the future. And by thoroughly investigating, we might uncover more of his victims and help them too. It's not just about Adrian; it's about everyone involved.'

He rubbed his temples. 'I guess. I'm just disgusted by what he is.'

'Remember also Frank that if Adrian had got justice when he needed it; if maybe his mother, or Rowena, had exposed the father, then perhaps Adrian's trail of destruction would never have happened.'

'Are you suggesting that we owe him?'

'Well, in a way, maybe we owe him for that time? He was innocent *then*. And we didn't help him *then*.'

'No... no... just because he was abused doesn't make it acceptable that he did the same thing. He lost any claim to sympathy in my book.'

'I think you're angry, Frank. I believe that when you're calm, you'll see things differently.'

He slammed his fist again, and he glared at her. 'How do you know what I think?'

She took a step back. She didn't like raised voices and

aggression. Did anyone? Although it was part of her autistic diagnosis, and Frank, again, felt a pang of guilt for not respecting it. He saw his cup had survived the second hop. It wouldn't survive a third.

'Frank. People aren't always born evil. You know that. They can be shaped. We can give Adrian justice for the horrendous things that ruined who he was, and eventually, led to his demise. Meanwhile, we find the truth of what happened to those damaged by this vicious cycle. Ultimately, we end the cycle. It's what we do.'

'Tidy everything up, you mean? Not cutting it off at the source. It's always so retrospective!'

''By solving this case, we might prevent future abuse. Think about it - if we can understand how Adrian went from victim to perpetrator, we might be able to identify warning signs in others. We could help break the cycle before it starts.'

He sighed and closed his eyes. 'Okay, I need a moment alone.'

After he heard the door close, he opened his eyes.
Bollocks!

He leaned back in his chair, his mind swirling with the complexities of the case. Maybe she was right, and the emotional weight of it all was pressing too heavily on him. He'd make it up to her in the morning when he felt better, but for now, he needed to be alone with his thoughts.

Chapter Fifty-Two

THAT NIGHT, Frank drove Bertha into the heart of Leeds, then into the shadowy maze of streets around it, until he was lost in a labyrinth of decay and despair. The old Volvo's engine grumbled, a familiar sound in an unfamiliar place. Abandoned buildings loomed like rotting teeth, their windows shattered and their walls tagged with graffiti. The streets were littered with the detritus of broken lives - used needles, empty bottles, and the tattered remains of forgotten dreams.

There were so many faces. So many people lost. Damned.

And in so many faces, he saw Maddie.

Each time he thought he recognised her, he pulled to the side of the road, his hands shaking as they clutched a roll-up, watching. His heart pounded, a mix of hope and dread coursing through his veins.

Was that her there, on the corner, her hair cut short?

Or was that her, in the yellow raincoat, hunched in the doorway?

Or, God forbid, was that her, arguing with her heavy-handed boyfriend?

Each and every time, the answer was the same.

No.

Not once did he step from his vehicle. It was for the best. His face, still a mess of bruises and cuts, would only frighten those lost and damned people on the street. Many of them came from a life of violence, and many still lived within it. His face would be a reminder of the violence that lurked everywhere. He couldn't risk their reaction.

Past one in the morning, Frank drove back to Whitby and parked beside the cemetery. He was desperate to be close to Mary.

Still, he couldn't bring himself to go in.

Tonight, his shame felt too great.

Instead, he sat there, chain-smoking, staring into the darkness, wondering if Mary was even here at all. The acrid smoke filled the car, a poor substitute for the warmth he longed for.

Bones. That's all she was now. Same as Adrian Hughes. Same as Charlotte Wilson, the lass with the beautiful voice.

Bones.

'Except not forgotten, love,' he said out loud. 'You may not be here any more, but as long as I'm here, you won't be forgotten.'

Eventually, despite his desperation to be close to someone he loved, he realised he couldn't be and started the engine.

He drove home wondering if he'd ever be close to someone he loved again.

Or was his baby girl gone forever?

Chapter Fifty-Three

Gerry struggled to make eye contact most of the time. When required to address an audience, she'd force herself to look from person to person, fighting anxiety. With people she was close to – her parents, who'd since passed, and her closest colleagues, Frank perhaps – she tried her hardest, but it wasn't comfortable.

However, when it came to interviewing witnesses and suspects, it was different. She didn't feel any concern about being judged. In fact, she was often the one doing the judging! There was only one other area in which she felt comfortable with eye contact.

And that was in a confrontation with authority.

In this situation, she was being led by frustration. Being judged was the furthest thing from her mind.

Without confrontation, eye contact with DCI Marcus Holloway was a complete no-go. He was brimming with confidence, enjoyed dominating situations with piercing eyes, and as was intimidating as they come. She usually kept her eyes down, despite knowing that it made her seem timid.

Still, Marcus was a favourite with top brass in North Yorkshire, so it was best to avoid confrontation. However, as their negotiations wore on his arrogance really grated on her. Some arrogance was good. Yes, she agreed. She, too, possessed her fair share. You needed to be confident. But *this?* No, this was way too much.

'So, let me get this straight.' Marcus leaned back in his chair, lacing his fingers together. 'You want access to everything we've found out about Phoebe Turner thus far?'

'That's correct.'

'Even though we've determined that they're two separate investigations?'

Determined? Who determined this? Him? How? In her eyes, there was plenty of doubt. 'I think it will help.'

'Why?'

She still hadn't looked up. 'We're under-resourced as it is. Phoebe may've been involved with the death of Adrian Hughes in some capacity, and you've had a small team on her for a couple of days.'

Holloway leaned forward. She gave him a quick look. He looked as if he spent a long time styling his salt and pepper hair.

'My team is the best,' Marcus said. 'If anything relating to your investigation comes up, you'll be the first to know. But nothing has. As yet.' He leaned forward. 'So, isn't that just confirmation that our operations are unrelated?'

She'd expected this. If she hadn't been armed with something, she wouldn't have bothered making the visit. Until this point, she'd wanted to avoid embarrassing him, but it seemed like she'd no choice. Maybe it was the only form of communication he really responded to. Time to challenge him. Her frustration levels were maxing out. She fixed him with her eyes. 'I don't believe your investigation is moving in the right direction. If you'd found what I'd found, Phoebe would already be back in custody.'

Both of Marcus's eyebrows shot up. After a moment of silence, he snorted and shook his head, breaking off eye contact with her. He was clearly not used to being challenged. 'What could you have possibly found out that my team hasn't?'

'First, sir, I want you to promise that I can have access to your information.'

He thought for a moment, laughed and met her eyes again. 'If you can tell me something we don't already know, then you can have as much access as you want.' A wry smile tugged at the corner of Holloway's mouth. His confidence had returned.

'Do I have your word?' Gerry asked.

'Do you want a signed document, DI? Look, I'm a busy man. I've never known answers to come from another department on a silver platter... especially a team run by DCI Frank Black.' He sneered. 'So, my patience is wearing a little thin.'

Without a word, she pulled out her tablet from her bag and queued up a video. 'CCTV footage from the car park where the incident took place.'

'Seen it,' he grunted without looking. 'Obviously.'

She turned it and placed it on his desk. 'As you can see, it provides a clear view of Phoebe Turner engaged in a phone conversation.'

'So?' he shrugged. 'She was calling emergency services.'

'Have you had it lip read?'

'Ha! Why would I use money on that? I've heard the recording. The recording is crystal clear.'

'I know,' Gerry said. 'I heard it, too.'

'Good on you. Now...' His eyes trailed down to where she was pointing.

The time stamp: 21.37.

'What time was the emergency call logged?' She asked.

She stared at him fully now as his expression darkened. He was sensing embarrassment. If it wasn't obvious to him that this DI in front of him was about to unleash something, then he really had disappeared into his own ego. 'I'll have it double-checked.'

Gerry persisted. 'According to your own records, the emergency call was logged at 21:40.' She fast-forwarded the video, the digits on the time stamp blurring until they settled on 21:40. 'So, unless the time stamp is wrong, that's the emergency call.'

'Let me see that.' Marcus dragged the slider back and forth. 'Shit.'

'So, she phoned someone before the emergency services,' Gerry said.

'Shit,' he repeated.

'Your team missed that,' Gerry's voice was neutral despite the weight of her revelation.

He regarded her with narrowed eyes. 'Yes. Happens. *Occasionally*. I'll have it looked at. Thanks for bringing it to my attention.'

'I suggest a lip read and the towers,' Gerry said. 'Find out who she called.'

He glared now. 'I've been doing this a long time, DI. Longer than you, in fact.'

'Yes, I know.' She tried to add a tone of disbelief. His darkening expression suggested he got the message.

'But we wouldn't bring her back into custody based just on that, DI,' he said. 'No. It's probably her husband. Sometimes, people phone family members first when panicking.'

Gerry nodded. 'Yes, but I'm not finished.'

She heard him take in a deep breath.

She dug out her notebook and showed him the sketch of a series of interlocking geometric shapes that formed a stylised eye. She'd drawn it the previous day at Phoebe's house.

'What's that?'

'A small tattoo on the front of Phoebe's wrist. She covers it with a watch.'

'Okay. And is it relevant?'

'Yes,' Gerry said. 'I imagine she keeps it hidden with that watch. So, I'd be surprised if you or your team saw it. But she was both exhausted and inebriated when we went to see her and she slipped up.'

He nodded, looking reassured by Gerry's admission of good fortune. 'We can't always catch everything.'

Gerry reached over to her tablet and found the webpage she'd ready.

Marcus's eyes bulged. 'Fucking hell.' He sat up and dragged the tablet towards himself. It was the Wikipedia page on a historic activist group called the Animal Freedom Foundation. Their logo looked identical to Phoebe's tattoo. 'No way. It can't be. Her? Ms Charity 2024? She can't have been involved in the AFF.'

Gerry simply nodded and found it remarkably easy to keep eye contact. More so than in a very long while.

'The Animal Freedom Foundation?' Marcus was struggling to let it sink in.

'Well, on the outside, the AFF seemed moralistic,' Gerry said. 'The morality might have attracted her from the outset. But they were, ultimately, militaristic. They were responsible for bombings, acts of vandalism, spates of violence—'

'Yes, I know what the AFF did. Obviously, Phoebe's former involvement is something to think about.'

That was the understatement of the year, Gerry thought, before saying, 'Go to the next page.'

He scrolled to the next page. There was an image of a much younger Phoebe marching, holding a placard saying, 'No More Torture in the Name of Science!'

Marcus rubbed his temples.

She also filled him in on the way she'd said Julian so casually at the door the previous day, as if she'd always known him. 'Julian Sims was the leader of the AFF. He served over thirty years for planting a car bomb that killed the scientist, Felix Delaney, and his partner at the time, Theresa Long. So, this is no coincidence.'

'I agree,' he said. 'Phoebe's lying. It wasn't a random mugging, after all.'

Then his manner changed. His embarrassment lifted, and he suddenly had a glow on his face that she hadn't noticed before. 'That was impressive.'

'You'd have got there eventually.'

'Yes. No doubt. But that was lightning fast.'

'I only sleep four hours a night.'

Marcus smiled. 'You're quite something, aren't you?'

People had said this to her before. She always responded in the same way. 'I just followed all the logical links as presented to me.'

'You fancy moving over to another team at some point? We may not have impressed you this time, but we're usually very effective. Someone with your skills would find plenty to enjoy.'

'I'm okay, sir. Thank you anyway.'

He sneered. 'Must be quite archaic over there with Black?'

'Actually, I find him forward-thinking and passionate. That's something rather refreshing in a man his age and at the end of his career. He can sometimes lead with emotion, rather than calculation, which I've pointed out could one day lead to a grave outcome, but there's no doubting his methods can lead to success as well.'

'Dinosaurs were very dominant and successful until their grave outcome.'

He waited for her to smile. She didn't. She understood the sarcasm – she just didn't really understand the point of it, really. They were all on the same team, weren't they? 'I think you'll find it was an environmental cause that wiped out the dinosaurs, sir, not emotion.'

He laughed out loud. 'At least think about it.'

'Okay.' It was a white lie. Her parents had taught her to use them. Usually to protect people's feelings. Here it helped in shifting the focus on. 'So, your files. Can I see everything you have on Phoebe now, please?'

'I signed nothing.' He paused and held up the palms of his hands in mock surrender.

She remained impassive, expecting this to be an attempt at poor humour.

'I'm joking,' he said.

Yes, poor humour.

'I gave you my word. The same word that tells you that you have a place with me, Gerry. Now, I'll get Cassie up here to take you to her office and give you access, while I have Phoebe picked up.' He guffawed. 'But I doubt we've found anything more than you could find on your own!'

'Oh, I completely doubt it too.' Gerry looked him straight in his piercing blue eyes. 'It's a time saver. That's all it is.'

Chapter Fifty Four

Rob's eyes swept across the living room, taking in the tapestry of their family life – framed photos, children's artwork, and well-worn furniture that whispered of love and laughter. His gaze lingered on each of his children: Sophie, his talented actor; Nathan, the budding scientist with a razor-sharp mind; and Lily, his gentle artist.

The weight of his secret pressed down on him, vice-like, around his chest. He gripped Sarah's hand, anchoring himself. If he was hurting her, she didn't let on.

The children's eyes were wide, brimming with curiosity and an expectation that made Rob's heart race. He'd never seen them quite like this, hanging on his every breath.

Sophie, always the confident one, said, 'Dad, we're listening.'

He smiled. 'I know you are, honey.' He looked at them all. 'You're all such good listeners. You're all so special to me, and you're special to each other.' He looked at his wife and smiled. She'd a tear in the corner of her eye. He winked. 'Your mother made sure of that.'

'You didn't do such a poor job yourself, either.'

He took a deep breath, nodding as he turned back to face his children. His heart hammered against his ribs as he met each of their gazes, acknowledging the love and trust he saw there.

Now or never, he thought. 'I need to ask for your forgiveness...' His voice trembled. He rolled his shoulders back, steeling himself. 'I've kept the truth from you for far too long. But your mother, ever the best of us, has made me realise that this is the only way I'll ever find closure.' He squeezed her hand again.

The children exchanged glances, seeking comfort in each other. Rob felt a flicker of pride at their unbreakable bond – a testament to the family they'd built. He swallowed hard and then, in a breathless rush, he told them about his troubled childhood, about the abuse he'd suffered at the hands of Gideon Blackwell and about his time as a teenage prostitute.

The stunned silence that followed was deafening, yet inevitable.

Panic clawed at Rob's insides, but he'd resolved to be patient. He lowered his gaze, giving them time to process.

'Oh Dad,' Sophie whispered.

He looked up at her. 'I'm sorry.'

'Stop saying sorry.'

He nodded and lowered his gaze again.

He heard her soft footsteps approaching, then felt her arm settle over his hunched shoulders. Her light touch was a balm, and for a moment, he dared to hope that the burden was lifting.

He looked Sophie in her tearful eyes. 'I'm going to the police.' He gave a swift nod. 'I have evidence. I know it will bring scrutiny to our family, but Gideon needs to face the consequences of his actions. He can't die thinking he's escaped what he's done.' He looked between the faces of his two other children and offered them swift nods, too.

He felt Sophie's lips brush his cheek as she leaned into his shoulder. 'You're so brave, Dad.' Her voice was ringing with conviction. Rob fought back tears, wanting to keep this moment stoic, matter of fact. But real life rarely cooperated with such plans. This was raw, and his family closed ranks around him, embracing the tragedy as their own.

'We're all behind you, no matter what,' Nathan said, sitting beside him.

Then Lily was at his knees, laying her head on them. 'I love you, Dad.'

He cried then, surrounded by his family, their love and support enveloping him. The burden lifted, if only temporarily, but it felt monumental.

After the children had left, Rob embraced Sarah, pressing a kiss to her forehead. 'You were right,' he murmured. But even as the words left his lips, an unshared memory surfaced – the cellar of the Rusty Anchor. The final, damning secret he'd kept buried.

Chapter Fifty-Five

ALTHOUGH MIKE HAD NARROWLY AVOIDED a second heart attack, the interview with DCI Black and DI Carver had left him utterly drained. Each time he woke, he'd try to read, but the steady beep of the heart monitor quickly lulled him back to sleep. During one of his more lucid moments, as he watched the morning light filter through the curtains, Emma arrived for a visit.

He smiled. 'Sorry, I forgot our appointment at the gym.'

His attempt at humour fell flat. Emma's face remained stoic, devoid of even the faintest grin. Something was amiss.

She sat beside him and took his hand in hers. She hadn't even spoken yet, but the gravity of her silence spoke volumes. 'What's wrong?' Mike asked.

She shook her head and looked down.

'Sorry if I gave you a second fright, but I'm okay now.'

'It's not that.'

'What is it then?'

Emma remained silent, her gaze fixed on their intertwined hands.

'No need to worry. I've experienced hell and made it back. I feel it can only get better from here on—'

She looked up at him, her eyes brimming with a sadness that made his words catch in his throat.

'Okay, now I'm worried.' Mike's heart rate picked up slightly. 'As you can probably tell by the beeping.'

She shook her head. 'That's why they won't tell you… why they don't want me to tell you…'

He took a deep breath, exhaling slowly. *No need to panic,* he thought. He already knew his health was buggered – no point in freaking out about it now. 'Look… if you're here to tell me I'm never getting out of here, then that probably isn't breaking news. Maybe, just tell me about your plans today… maybe, you could stop by here at lunch—'

'It's not about you.'

He raised an eyebrow, disorientated by her words. For so long, everything had revolved around him – his diet, his blood pressure, his heart, his duty as a father. This shift in focus was jarring. Then he felt his stomach churning. 'Emma, what's happened? Is it you? Has something happened to you? Your family?'

She shook her head. 'My family is fine.' Her voice was barely above a whisper.

If it wasn't her, or her family, that left only one possibility. Mike's heart rate climbed again. Emma stood up, panic etched on her face. 'I made a mistake. I'm a fucking idiot.' She pulled her hand away, but Mike reached out and grabbed it. 'It's okay…' Mike closed his eyes, willing himself to be calm, taking slow deep breaths. If he didn't, then he wouldn't get the news. And when he got it, he knew he had to accept whatever it was, no matter how devastating it might be.

Eventually, his heart slowed slightly again.

'Keep hold of my hand.' His voice was barely audible over the beeping of the machines. Emma sat back down, their fingers firmly intertwined. He focused on his breathing, finding a fragile peace within the chaos. 'You wanted to tell me whatever it is because it was the right thing to do,' he said, his eyes still closed. 'I appreciate that, Emma. And I want you to feel you're doing the right thing.'

He kept his eyes closed, concentrating on his breathing, on her hand in his, on the fact that in order to know and deal with whatever it was, he had to stay calm.

'It's your son,' Emma said. 'Something's happened to Noah.'

Chapter Fifty Six

Frank lumbered into the incident room, clutching two pre-packaged salads he'd snagged from the petrol station. He made a beeline for Gerry, perched in her usual corner.

'Peace offering.' He plonked them down on her desk. 'For being a moody bastard. And look, I'm going to eat one, too.'

He'd chosen a Caesar for himself – there had to be some bloody flavour – while Gerry's was as plain as her expression.

She eyed the offerings. 'Thank you. You're forgiven. I understand you've been having a difficult time. I'll also try to be more patient when attempting to improve your lifestyle.'

Frank nodded, a small smile tugging at his lips. Trust Gerry to deliver acceptance like she was reading from a script.

'But, for future reference,' she said, 'I don't eat pre-packaged food.'

Frank's eyebrows shot up. 'It's bloody organic.' He

jabbed a finger at the label on hers. 'It cost me an extra two quid.'

'Yes, Frank, but I cannot eat pre-packaged food. The preservatives and additives can trigger my sensitivities and disrupt my digestive system. Also, in a salad, the maximum number of ingredients I can tolerate mixed is two. There are five ingredients in this one.'

Well, piss on that, Frank thought. *If you're not eating yours, then neither am I. Might as well have grabbed a bacon butty.*

'Anyway,' he said, changing tack. 'I got your message that you were going to see Holloway. What was that all about? Pompous git. I wish I'd caught you on the phone to warn you off. Not my cup of tea, that man.'

'He doesn't like you, either.' Gerry was as matter of fact as ever.

Frank snorted. 'I guess we won't be sitting with each other at the Christmas social then. Shame.'

'Actually, he referred to you as a dinosaur.'

'Dinosaurs were a powerhouse for a long time.'

'I don't think he was using humour in that manner.'

'You think?'

'He also offered me a job.'

'Bloody piss ant.'

'What's a piss ant?'

'Don't know. Just tell me what you said.'

'I told him no.'

'Strange. I thought you'd be champing at the bit to get out of here after me playing the arsehole card last night.'

'Why would I want that?' Gerry asked. 'You're one of the most dedicated and passionate detectives I've ever worked with. Your methods may be unorthodox but they get results. I have no intention of leaving this team.'

Frank felt his face heat, a rare blush creeping across his cheeks. He glanced around, noticing his other colleagues' curious looks. Rylan chose that moment to nuzzle his hand. 'Rylan likes you too, which is also a massive plus.'

Clearing his throat, Frank steered the conversation back to business. Gerry explained the reason behind her visit. That the death of Julian Sims wasn't down to a mugging gone wrong. Phoebe Turner had history with the AFF, a group that was behind some violent incidents and one murder.

'Jesus wept,' Frank said. 'And butter wouldn't melt, eh? She was all about the children. Wonder if that scientist blown up in that car had children?'

'Well,' Gerry said, 'Most of what they gave me in return was useless... until I got to this.'

She handed him a printout.

Frank's eyes nearly popped out of his head. 'Jesus Christ. It can't be.'

Gerry nodded. 'Yes.'

'We need to speak to Phoebe again right now. Does anybody we ever talk to tell the fucking truth?' He looked around the room, taking in the shocked faces at his sudden outburst. 'Don't look at me like that... dedicated and passionate, remember?' He shot a smile at Gerry. 'Garnished with a little unorthodoxy.'

Chapter Fifty Seven

DCI Marcus Holloway confronted Frank at the door of the interview room, his chest puffed out like a peacock in mating season.

Marcus was a tall, broad-shouldered man who threw weights around the gym regularly. Not in the mood for the pissing contest, Frank invaded Marcus's personal space and waited for him to step aside.

He didn't.

'You've spoken to the chief constable?' Frank asked.

'Yes.'

'So why are you in my way?'

'I just want to warn you not to fuck my case up.'

A wry smile tugged at his lips. 'Okay, I guess with a warning comes consequences – what are the consequences? Gerry' – he waved her over – 'can you write the consequences down, so I can keep coming back to them while we're in that room? At sixty-four, I can be a rather absent-minded dinosaur.'

'Smartarse,' Marcus said, stepping to the side.

Frank couldn't resist one last jab. 'To be honest, I don't

understand your attitude. If not for my loyal team member' – he paused, letting the emphasis on 'loyal' hang in the air – 'you wouldn't have Phoebe in that room. You'd still be chasing your tails. Have you found out who she made the first call to yet?' He raised an eyebrow. 'Don't worry, son. In the same way we all have to shit, we all have to make mistakes... don't be embarrassed by it. Just maybe be grateful.' He winked.

Marcus sneered. 'Good luck. You're going to need it. She has a solicitor and is playing the "no comment" card.'

Frank looked at Gerry. 'And here I thought that we were all on the same side and you'd be rooting for us.'

He heard Marcus mutter something that sounded suspiciously like 'wanker' as they entered the sterile interview room.

Phoebe was unrecognisable from yesterday. She sat at the table, prim and proper, looking like she'd stepped out of a bloody fashion magazine. Her face was a mask of composure. She'd a haughty look on her face, one that suggested that she'd had a gutful of the police.

A solicitor, who looked like he'd been poured into his suit, sipped from a coffee cup and took deep breaths as he made notes. Frank noticed the buttons on his shirt straining. It made him look down at his own shirt, which fit well.

You may be fat, Frank, but at least you know what you are, he thought to himself. *No need for sausage-casing suits here.*

Frank realised he'd need to remind her that his agenda differed from those who'd already confronted her in this room. They weren't here to go back and forth over the possibility of manslaughter. It was still likely to be unrelated, although it couldn't be totally written off. 'Hello again, Mrs Turner. We're not here about Julian Sims—'

'You said that yesterday,' Phoebe interrupted. 'Yet...' She looked at Gerry. 'You drew the tattoo on my wrist, and now look where we are.'

Marcus had obviously told her it was Gerry that had pieced her narrative together. *Bloody fantastic,* Frank thought, *very helpful of you, Marcus. Remind me to send you a fruit basket.*

'Mrs Turner, we were curious. Ultimately, it may not apply to our investigation, but we've a duty to report on it.'

The solicitor looked up from his notes and met his client's eyes. It was a 'told you so' kind of look. One that said, 'It doesn't matter what they ask you, what it's about, say nothing.'

'Look,' Frank said, trying to salvage the situation. 'We're not taping this.' He nodded up at the camera. 'Or filming it.' Although this wasn't confirmed, and could get him in hot water, he'd simply erase the tape afterwards. God help anyone who stood in his way.

He nodded at Gerry, who slid the printout over the table. The solicitor handled it first, peering over the rim of his glasses. He handed it to Phoebe, who looked it over, her eyes widening, her expression changing for the first time. The solicitor stared at her, completely confused by what it was.

'The thing is,' Frank said, 'we know you were distraught last night. In a state of shock. Our conversation around Adrian Hughes would probably be a blur... At one point, we asked you about the Rusty Anchor. We'd like you to reconsider your answers to the question.'

Phoebe opened her mouth to speak, but the solicitor held his hand up, gesturing for her to remain quiet. 'I'm confused about what this is,' he said.

Gerry leaned forward. 'It's a Halifax mortgage application, dated 13th March 1989.'

'And what's its relevance?' the solicitor asked.

'The two names on the application,' Frank said. 'Phoebe Sawyer and Carl Moss. Sawyer is your maiden name, isn't it?'

'No comment,' Phoebe said.

'It's a fact,' Gerry said. 'It doesn't need a comment.'

'Could you tell me the point of this?' the solicitor asked.

'Well, we're kind of hoping that your client could give us the point,' Frank said. 'I mean, we're just after help at the moment. This doesn't relate to your job remit.'

'My job remit is to protect my client, DCI.'

'Aye.' Frank grinned and looked at Phoebe. 'Carl Moss worked at the Rusty Anchor for a considerable length of time, and it correlates with the time that Adrian Hughes fell victim to murder and hid in a cellar wall.' Frank pointed to the paper. 'Phoebe. You were in a relationship with Carl?'

She stared straight ahead. 'No comment.'

'When did you meet?'

'No comment.'

Frank could feel his irritation building.

'The application was withdrawn,' Gerry said, 'before it was approved or rejected. Does this show that your relationship ended?'

'No comment.'

The solicitor leaned in and whispered into her ear.

'Did Carl have anything to do with the AFF?'

She shook her head.

'Was that a no?'

The solicitor glared at Phoebe.

'Did he know about your involvement with the AFF?'

'No. The AFF came after...' She looked down.

'After what?' Gerry asked. 'The end of your relationship?'

The solicitor took hold of Phoebe's arm. She pulled herself away and looked at him with irritation.

'We're just here for the truth,' Frank said. 'It's coming, Mrs Turner. I was really hoping you could put yourself on the right side of that.'

Nothing.

Frank leaned forward, his voice low and serious. 'If this is nothing to do with you, and yet you refuse to help, then how will that look in your other situation?'

She sighed and looked up. 'I want to speak to my solicitor alone.'

The solicitor whispered in her ear again.

'No,' Phoebe hissed at him. 'I need to speak to you alone.'

The solicitor nodded and looked at Frank with a face like thunder. 'You heard.'

Frank and Gerry stood.

'I'll let you know shortly what my decision is.' Phoebe was trying to give off the air of someone who held all the cards.

Of course, she didn't, but Frank bit his tongue. He'd prefer to get to the point sooner rather than later. 'Thank you, Mrs Turner.' It stuck in his throat on the way out. 'Let us know when you're ready.'

Chapter Fifty-Eight

Beep-beep-beep

Once a hypnotic burden, lulling him in and out of consciousness, the monitor had transformed into a reassuring symphony of life.

Because he had to keep going now.

After the news Emma had given him, he simply had no choice.

Beep-beep-beep

Even after learning that Noah was fighting for his life, Mike's blood pressure and heart rate hadn't spiked like they had during the detectives' visit. He'd been laser-focused on staying calm, knowing that not panicking – and staying alive – was the best way to be there for Noah.

Beep-beep-beep

Last night, another kid involved in county lines had stabbed Noah, his fourteen-year-old son. A turf war turned bloody. The other boy, someone else's child, was in custody. Noah had spent the night in surgery with lacerations to his liver. Against the odds, his son had fought to survive and had done so.

Granted, he wasn't out of the woods yet. He'd had a blood transfusion and was still out of it in the ICU, but the doctors had some hope. Apparently, when he'd been first admitted, they'd had very little.

Beep-beep-beep

So, that sound was now the most reassuring sound in the world. An auditory reminder that he was still here, still fighting.

And while he waited, he relived all those memories of his boy. Building snowmen in the garden, Noah's laughter ringing out as they rolled the massive snowballs. Teaching him to fish, the pride on Noah's face as he reeled in his first catch. The memories brought a smile to his face and kept that beat steady.

I'll be here when you wake, son.

I'll be here.

So, for the first time in what felt like an eternity, Mike Bailey was deliberately fighting for his life. Emma had left almost an hour ago. She'd promised to return as soon as there was any news.

He made her promise to come back and tell him if Noah woke or, God forbid, he passed. That he'd continue his own fight if she promised him this, and she did.

Beep-beep-beep

Yes. The Barghest remained. But he gave it no attention. He lingered somewhere at the side of Mike's mind. Instead of his own blood, Noah's now dripped from its teeth. Its intentions were obvious. It wanted to remind him of his own failures, crush him with that fact that he'd let his son down in every way that mattered.

Beep-beep-beep

But you won't win. After all, you don't really exist, do you?

It's time for you to go.
I need every ounce of strength for my boy.
For Noah.
So get ready, Barghest, our final reckoning is close.
I'll stare deep into those red eyes and vanquish you.
Be a father to my boy.
The father he should have had all along.
Beep-beep-beep.
If he wakes up, that is.

Chapter Fifty-Nine

The solicitor, Peter Booth, was a picture of distress. His face had gone ashen, arms crossed tightly over his chest. Every word from Phoebe sent him on another loop of his emotional rollercoaster. One moment he'd narrow his eyes, shaking his head in disgust; the next, his gaze would dart around nervously, lips trembling.

'I met Carl about a year before I got mixed up with the AFF.' Phoebe's voice was steady, but her fingers fidgeted with the glass of water in front of her. 'I was working at Sunnybrook, then. He came in sometimes to collect Mike when his sister was working a long shift. We talked, he was funny and we just kind of hit it off. It never felt serious. I don't think either of us wanted that. Carl certainly didn't want serious. He was happy with a very simple life. I was twenty-two, or thereabouts. Young, and full of ambition. Ultimately, though, his lack of ambition doomed us from the outset.' She smiled, nodded. 'There's nothing wrong with being unambitious if it keeps you happy, I guess, and Carl was happy. *Very*. But that's not how I saw the rest of my life panning out... still, to begin with, I was head over heels. This was in 1988, a couple of months before I lost my job at Sunnybrook.'

Frank leaned forward, his interest piqued. 'So, you were going to the Rusty Anchor as far back as 1988?'

Phoebe nodded. 'But rarely. I lived at home with my parents, and Carl had a bedsit. We'd mostly hang out there when he wasn't working. The first couple of months of the relationship were fun. It was only after I suspected Adrian Hughes was up to something at Sunnybrook that I became more agitated. I wasn't drinking... well, no more than usual... but I was struggling to sleep. And my parents weren't interested in listening to my paranoia – they'd never been all that interested in me full stop in all honesty. Carl was easy come, easy go, so I didn't burden him with it, simply because he wasn't the kind of person you burdened with anything. Live the best life possible with the least stress.' She broke off for a mouthful of water. 'So I became a bit obsessed with Adrian Hughes. Not because of him having me fired. No. I was worried about what he was up to. It hurt yesterday, DCI, when you said I was more concerned about my career. It wasn't that at all. I just had no evidence. So, I spent the next few months trying to get some. I started to follow him.'

Frank's eyebrows shot up, and he exchanged a quick glance with Gerry. This was getting interesting.

'Good lord,' Peter murmured under his breath. The solicitor looked like he was about to have a heart attack, clearly thinking his client was self-destructing.

Phoebe glanced at her solicitor. 'Look, before I say anything else, I want to make one thing clear. I didn't kill Adrian. This is all about how much I care about children. I followed him because I was worried. That's the truth. I saw him in the Anchor at a later date, but I still never communicated with him. All I wanted was a shred of proof, something. Anything that could show he was up to something. If I'd got it, I would've sacrificed my career, gone to the police, and taken Sunnybrook to task over protecting him, too.' The glass trembled slightly in her hand. 'But I got nothing.'

'Nothing at all?' Frank asked, his voice tinged with scepticism.

'Well, nothing to do with children. I found things out about him. His social incompetence wasn't an act. He was an awkward man in all walks of life. He rarely went out. Mainly to shops. Some weekends, he'd go to a bar or restaurant. He met young men, but not underage men. I became intensely obsessed. It was the same a year or so later with the AFF. Things just consuming me—'

Peter coughed. Then his eyes darted between Phoebe and the detectives, panic written all over his face. The prospect of her confessing her guilt to murder was chewing on him.

Phoebe waved him off. 'Something inside me just gets switched on, you know. And then I'm off... driven. Imagine my surprise one night when I followed him to the bloody Rusty Anchor! Where Carl worked!'

'And?' Frank leaned forward again.

'He played cards. Downstairs. Probably the reason I'd never spotted him in there before while I was visiting Carl.'

'When was this?' Frank asked.

'Beginning of 1989, I think.'

'Who was he with?'

'Alone. To begin with. He didn't bring someone with him until much later.'

Gerry, who'd been quietly observing, spoke up. 'Did you ask Carl what he thought of Adrian?'

'Yes. I pointed out that he worked at Sunnybrook with his sister, but he couldn't recall ever seeing him when he used to collect Mike. He said he was a rather odd bloke. I think those were his words. I think he even asked his sister about him one time, and got a similar answer. People thought Adrian was peculiar. Unfortunately, it was only really me who thought that something more sinister was going on. Carl said he was quite a regular card player. At least two weekends a month.'

'Did you ever see Adrian interacting with anyone else during those visits?'

'Only at the bar. He spent most of the time in the cellar,' Phoebe replied, shaking her head.

'I assume he must have seen you?' Frank asked.

'Not really. Like I said, I didn't go in often and, when I did, I was careful. I can't say for sure that he never saw me, but I never spoke to him, or ended up face to face with him in an awkward situation. Typically, I'd sit in the snug, which remained unseen when entering through the front door. I knew he was there, though. I could see out the front from where I sat, and I always kept my eyes on who was coming in. My intention was never to be caught unaware. He probably would have walked straight past me, but I didn't fancy risking any awkward conversations. Over time, I became less obsessive. He met young men for dates, and sometimes stayed in hotels with them, but he never brought them to the Anchor. I began to believe, and hope, that I may've been wrong about him and young children.'

'What happened regarding the mortgage application in March?' Frank asked.

'What it says on the tin, really. Carl had a lot of money saved on account of some inheritance from his father and said he wanted to live with me. I spent most nights with him at the bedsit, anyway. It was cramped. So, we applied for the mortgage.'

'But then withdrew the application in May?' Frank asked.

'Yes,' Phoebe said. 'Because things were getting fucked up.'

'How so?'

'Well, first, Carl's sister, Lucy, died out of the blue and Mike was suddenly staying in the bedsit with him. I knew Mike from my time at Sunnybrook; not really well, but we'd spoken. A pleasant lad. Always attempting to socialise with other kids. Some of those children were really struggling. Yet, he always tried...' She looked off into space. 'I wonder what happened to Mike. You know, he always had a distant look in his eye. He was eager to help and be friendly, but he'd his own demons. His own problems.'

'You just said you didn't know him really well?' Gerry said.

'Not in Sunnybrook. But I got to know him in the months after her death. You see, Carl was his only living relative. At first, Carl saw everything as temporary. That somehow Mike would find a new home he'd love. Mike wanted to stay with Carl, but I don't think Carl could face up to this. He spent a few months in denial. His life was carefree and he liked it. He also believed that he'd be a disastrous father figure. I tried not to get too involved at this point. Until... well, until I heard Adrian was trying to foster him. Good lord...' She looked between the detectives' faces. 'Can you imagine my horror? Well, I got involved then, I can tell you!'

'You told him your fears?' Frank asked.

'Not exactly, no. It turned out that one of Carl's chief concerns over fostering his nephew was that it would drive me away. That sharing a house with him and a teenage boy wouldn't be my bag. Truth be told, it wasn't. But I still convinced him I could live with the both of them. Whatever it took. I couldn't let Mike go to Adrian. I just couldn't. Not with all those doubts I'd had about him. Eventually, Carl was happy to oblige. Remember, he knew he could be a strange bloke from serving him in the Anchor, so I think he was relieved he could face up to this responsibility, eventually.'

'However, it then turned out that Adrian's application was being taken seriously. He was a qualified social worker, after all. The alternative, Carl, was a barman who lived in a bedsit. He was about to buy a house with a girlfriend of less than a year; although I'd been told my sacking hadn't gone onto a permanent record, I couldn't be absolutely certain that the information hadn't filtered through to the relevant departments somehow. An off-the-record comment would be enough. So, it didn't look good. I pulled out of the house, and Carl got a home on his own so he could live with his nephew if he got custody. At first, it was still touch and go, but then it was Mike himself who put a stop to Adrian's claim. He announced Adrian was intimidating and wouldn't live with him. Neither Carl nor I pressed Mike to say that.' She paused and looked into Frank's eyes. 'I know what you're thinking.'

'Do you?' Frank asked, his voice neutral but his eyes sharp.

'You're thinking what had Adrian been up to with Mike?'

Frank's jaw tightened. 'I prefer to stick with the facts for now.'

'Well, it was precisely what I thought, DCI. Adrian Hughes was all wrong. Mike's concerns were another warning flag.'

'Anyway, Carl got custody and Mike moved in. I continued living with my parents. Mike collected glasses at the Anchor. Officially, he was a tad young to be doing that, but it earned him pocket money and helped Carl out, who now had a mortgage, so it seemed a good thing. This was around mid-year.'

'And Adrian?' Frank asked.

'He continued to come and play cards.'

'Did Adrian ever speak to Mike?' Gerry asked.

'I only knew of the one time.' The glass in her hand shook hard now. 'Until that point, their paths had never crossed. Although Mike worked weekend nights, Adrian was mainly down in the cellar. It was easy for them to stay out of each other's way. However, one night, Adrian was ordering from the upstairs bar. This was unusual, as they usually brought drinks down to them. Carl was serving while Mike was stacking the fridge behind him. I don't know what was said. Carl wouldn't tell me. But there was an altercation. Carl escorted Adrian out of the pub. He did it calmly though, as was his usual demeanour. In retrospect, it may've been better if Carl had gone in all guns blazing. Barred him. Because about two weeks later, he came back. I think this was around July, and he wasn't alone this time. He brought someone with him.'

The young man? Frank thought, his pulse quickening. *The sex worker from Sapphire? Did Phoebe know who he was?*

Phoebe continued, 'This wasn't the one I saw him with

fairly regularly months earlier while I followed him. This lad was slighter. He looked *even* younger, to be honest. It worried me somewhat. *Nauseated me*. I can't recall Mike's path crossing with Adrian again, even so, I wouldn't have had him anywhere near the place. But then that was Carl all over, really. He never wanted to kick up a fuss, so he wasn't about to ask Rory to bar him.'

'Did Mike ever tell you what happened between him and Adrian?' Gerry asked.

'I tried hard. I wanted him to open up to me. I was desperate to know the truth. You can be sure, if Mike had ever told me what I suspected, I would've convinced him to go to the police. Eventually, however, things went wrong with Carl. We were never really suited for each other. I heard about his passing a while back, and I felt more overwhelmed on that day than the day we split up. Cried for days. I think separating from Carl felt exciting at the time, but years later, I realised it was maybe his strength that made him so gentle. Maybe it was his resilience and calmness that made him the best of us. It was only when he died did I wonder if I'd made a mistake all those years ago. In fact' – she looked at her solicitor – 'I wonder if the mistake is going to be more costly than I could ever imagine.'

'What happened after you separated?' Frank asked.

'Phoebe,' the solicitor interrupted. 'We discussed this.'

She held up a hand. 'I'll finish Peter. That's what we discussed.'

Peter the solicitor glowered.

Phoebe said, 'I asked to stay in touch with Mike, but Carl didn't think it was a good idea. Carl knew my suspicions about Adrian, but he'd never given them much credence, and I'd never elaborated. It'd never been black and white enough for him. Just suspicions, he said. After

July, I never went back to the Rusty Anchor, and I never spoke to Mike, Carl or Adrian again.'

The solicitor nodded, as if to suggest that was it. 'Well done, Phoebe... now—'

Frank wasn't about to let this go. He leaned forward, his voice intense. 'Do you think Carl could have killed Adrian?'

Phoebe shook her head. 'I've thought about it since you told me about the body, but I can't see it. Carl just didn't have that in his character. Even that night he threw Adrian out – well, he was so calm.'

Frank pressed on, his instincts telling him there was more. 'Even if Mike told his uncle what had happened, and it was as you suspected?' *After all, such revelations could drive the sanest, calmest individuals into a frenzy.*

Phoebe thought about it. 'No... I can't see it. He may go to the police, but confront him, fight him? Kill him?' She shook her head firmly. 'It just wasn't who he was.'

Frank made a mental note. He wouldn't be striking Carl from the list. No chance. He was still the strongest suspect.

'I don't suppose you ever spoke to that young man Adrian brought into that pub?'

'Of course I did.'

Frank's eyes widened. He couldn't hide the sharp intake of breath that followed. This could be the breakthrough.

'I took him to one side and asked him about Adrian,' Phoebe said. 'At first, he didn't want to talk to me. I mean, why would he? He didn't know me from Adam.'

Frank felt his heart racing. 'At first?'

'Yes... I told him straight out what I suspected. And... I saw it in his eyes, immediately. I was right. I'd always been right.'

Frank felt the blood rushing to his temples. 'What did he say?'

She sighed. 'Nothing then. He came over all grey and said he couldn't speak now. I wrote my home number down. I told him to ring me.'

'Did he?'

'Once.'

'And what did he say?'

'He said that Adrian had told him things. Things he'd done.'

'Go on.'

'He wouldn't be specific...'

Shit! Frank thought, his hopes momentarily dashed.

'But he said he was going to record him, and then get back to me.'

'And?'

Phoebe sighed and then shook her head.

Frank felt like hitting the table. There was no sentimental mug to break here, but he might shatter his dignity, so he held back. He clenched his fists instead, his nails digging into his palms.

'If not for what happened next.' Phoebe looked down. 'The distraction with the AFF. My meeting... Julian...' She looked at the red-faced solicitor and sighed. 'I may've gone back and chased it up. But I left it. It's almost shameful now, looking back. It's shameful, in fact. I should have gone back and seen him.'

Frank felt like his heart was going to burst from his chest. 'What was his name?' He was leaning so far forward, his large stomach was crushed against the desk.

'It was so long ago...' She closed her eyes, pondered. Then they burst open. 'Bryan!'

It was something, but not enough. *His surname... I need that. Please think.*

She looked deep in thought, but then slowly shook her head.

Frank forced back a cry of *Bollocks!* and let his shoulders sag.

She suddenly looked up. Her eyes widened, a spark of recognition lighting them up. 'Bryan Parkes.'

Frank felt his heart missing a beat.

Chapter Sixty

KATH FIELDING, the former owner of Sapphire Companions, hesitated when Frank mentioned Bryan Parkes over the phone. Her voice wavered as she confirmed he'd been sixteen at the time. Whether Bryan became Adrian's regular, following Rob's resignation from Sapphire, she wouldn't confirm. But Frank sensed there was more to the story than her failing memory allowed. She also couldn't recall whether the Rusty Anchor was a place that Adrian took any of his dates, either.

Before arriving at Bryan's sun-bleached terraced house, Frank and Gerry had pieced together a grim picture of his life. Born in 1973 to a single mother who struggled with addiction, Bryan had been in and out of care homes for most of his childhood. His adult life read like a textbook case of someone failed by the system: soliciting in his early twenties; a string of petty thefts and robberies in his thirties. The list went on: assault charges, drunk and disorderly, drink driving. He'd bounced between jobs: courier, factory hand, pizza delivery driver. A brief marriage in his late thirties had produced his daughter, Louise, who'd lived with him since she was eight. She was now nineteen, living in this house. Frank's gut twisted as he contemplated what kind of life Louise might have had.

As they approached the front door, Frank braced himself for the worst. He'd seen this cycle too many times – broken parents raising broken children.

Frank knocked on the door. To his surprise, Louise answered, a young woman who seemed to defy her circumstances. Her sophisticated attire and composed demeanour were at odds with the troubled history Frank had imagined.

'DCI Frank Black and DI Gerry Carver.' Frank held up his badge. 'We're sorry for the recent loss of your father, Bryan. We'd like to ask you a few questions. Would that be okay?'

She nodded. 'Of course. Could I ask what it's about?'

Frank opened his mouth, but Gerry, ever direct, beat him to it. 'We're investigating a murder,' Gerry said. 'We recovered a body in a public house called the Rusty Anchor. It's our belief that the murder may've occurred in August 1989, and there's a strong possibility that your father was present.'

The colour drained from Louise's face, and Frank inwardly winced at Gerry's bluntness.

'Louise,' Frank said, his tone gentler, 'we're not here to accuse your father of anything. We just wanted to see if, maybe, you knew something that could help us with our inquiries.'

'From 1989?'

'I know,' Frank said. 'A long shot... nice place, by the way,' he added, hoping to ease the tension.

'My father was house-proud. He believed that the way you kept a house reflected who you were. Come in.'

As they entered, Frank's eyebrows rose at the modern

decor – sleek lines, minimalist furnishings, and a cool grey and white colour scheme. It was a far cry from the chaos he'd expected based on Bryan's history.

In the kitchen, Louise busied herself with the kettle while Frank and Gerry took in the high-end appliances and glossy marble countertops.

'I wish I could make my kitchen look as nice as you have, Ms Parkes,' Frank said.

'Louise,' she corrected, a small smile touching her lips. 'And this is all my father's work. He was good with his hands. Like I said, he was a proud man.' She sat down and took a deep breath and sighed. 'He didn't like me caring for him. In fact, he didn't like anyone caring for him. And he was in a lot of pain. But he was always gentle... right until he passed. I hope I'm as compassionate with those around me when my time comes.' Her eyes glistened with unshed tears.

'It sounds like he was really fortunate to have you with him,' Frank said.

'He wasn't fortunate. He deserved everything. Whenever I needed him, he was always there for me.'

Frank nodded, feeling a pang of guilt as he thought of Maddie. Here was a man with a troubled past who'd managed to be there for his daughter, while Frank...

'Your father was an alcoholic.' Gerry said.

Louise nodded.

'Many alcoholics struggle in family relationships and society,' Gerry continued.

Louise's jaw tightened slightly. 'My father struggled. It doesn't mean he didn't succeed. In some areas, at least.'

'But you must have known about his pain?'

'Of course.' A tear slipped down Louise's cheek. 'There were demons. His nightmares were like nothing you could imagine. Shouting, sweating. And the drinking, at night, was awful. But he never laid a hand on me. He was only ever kind and interested in me. I never missed a day at school, and he fought my corner hard in every difficulty I encountered.'

'Sounds like a wonderful man,' Frank said.

'He was,' she insisted. 'Although no one ever believes it.' She shrugged. 'I'd love to see others hold up as well as my father had done with the things he'd experienced.'

Frank leaned forward. 'Could you tell us about any of those experiences?'

'Gladly. Although he never wanted me to do it. He never wanted me to absorb the horrors of his life into mine. But you're here, asking, so I'll tell you. Sir Gideon Blackwell.'

Frank felt his stomach drop. 'The former MP?'

'Yes. That man raped my father. Several times. Violently.'

Frank struggled to keep his expression neutral, even as rage boiled inside him. 'I'm sorry,' he managed, his voice tight.

'When was that?' Gerry asked.

'When he was fifteen.'

Frank clenched his fists under the table, willing himself to maintain composure.

'My father wasn't the only one Gideon abused. There were others.'

'How did your father meet him?' Frank asked.

'Through Sapphire Companions,' Louise said.

Frank's mind raced back to his conversation with Kath Fielding, her callous dismissal of the boys' vulnerability. He tamped down the urge to storm out and confront her again.

'The truth always comes out, though, doesn't it?' Louise

said. 'I told him that. But he didn't see it as reassurance. His only concern was protecting me. I tried to convince him to expose Gideon… he had evidence, you know… but he wouldn't do it.'

'What evidence?' Gerry asked.

'Recordings.'

'Where are they, Louise?'

'I've given them away. To someone else.'

'Who?'

Louise lowered her head. 'I can't.'

'Why not?' Frank asked.

'Because I promised my father. I couldn't attach myself to it. He didn't want me bringing the evidence forward. He expected someone else to do it. Someone who owed him.'

'Who?' Gerry pressed.

'Please,' Louise said. 'Let me honour his wishes.'

'This is a murder inquiry,' Gerry said. 'Which means you have a duty.'

'But by doing this, now, I'm doing everything he didn't want. I'm involving myself. I value the promises I made to him.'

Frank shot Gerry a look, silently asking her to back off. 'Okay, can we ask a few more questions?' He kept his tone gentle, sensing Louise was close to revealing more.

'Leaving Gideon Blackwell aside for the moment. Did your father ever talk about his past? His time at Sapphire Companions, or his relationship with Adrian Hughes?'

Louise shook her head. 'No. He only ever told me about Gideon. I'd heard him screaming his name at night in his sleep. I knew about Sapphire, but nothing much else. He didn't like to talk about that time in his life. To be honest, he never really talked about much of his life. He worked hard to bring me up and drank hard. He became desperate, broke the law, but then he'd always get himself back on the straight... he feared going inside... feared leaving me alone.'

'Did he ever mention the Rusty Anchor to you?' Gerry asked.

She shook her head. 'Sorry.'

'Do you think that there was anything else that plagued him, in the same way that the incidents with Gideon Blackwell plagued him?'

Louise flinched, and Frank leaned forward, sensing they were on the verge of something important.

She reached for a tissue, dabbing at her eyes. 'There was something. He told me he'd tell me one day. When it was close to the end. Unburden himself. But he never did. He got too weak, and even near the end he said he couldn't... he just couldn't. I think he was terrified of destroying how much I adored him.'

Frank's mind raced. Could Bryan have been involved in Adrian's death? He glanced at Gerry, but her expression remained impassive.

'I was wondering if you had a picture of your father when he was younger,' Frank said. 'Something we can use in our inquiries. I'm so sorry to have to ask, but he may've been present when this murder took place, and this will help us eliminate him.'

'Of course.' She left the room, her footsteps echoing in the quiet house.

Frank looked at Gerry. He whispered, 'The secret he never told her? Do you think he killed him?'

'He's involved,' Gerry said. 'We need the identity of the man he trusted.'

'I agree. We won't leave without it, Gerry. She wants to tell us. It'll come.'

'Really? She seemed adamant.'

'She does.' Frank leaned back in his chair, his expression thoughtful.

Louise returned, a worn photograph in her hand. As Frank took it, his breath caught in his throat.

Two young men grinned out at the camera – their arms slung around each other's shoulders.

One was burly and strong; the other was thin, waif-like, almost malnourished.

'This is Rob Johnson, isn't it?' Frank pointed at the bigger lad.

Louise gulped. 'Yes.'

Frank's mind whirled. The pieces were falling into place.

'Was he also raped by Gideon Blackwell?'

Louise froze, her face pale. Frank studied the image, his heart heavy. Two lives, two destinies, forever altered by the cruelty of a powerful individual. And at the centre of it all, Adrian Hughes, another predator who'd plundered Sapphire Companions of broken souls.

'You gave the evidence to Rob, didn't you?' Frank asked.

After a long moment, Louise nodded, her voice barely above a whisper. 'They thought of each other as brothers.'

Chapter Sixty-One

OUTSIDE, in the car, Frank looked at Gerry. 'For the love of a brother, no waters run too deep.'

'Sorry?'

'An Egyptian proverb. I remember hearing it once. I had a brother as a small boy. He passed young. We need to speak to Rob again. I think he knows the truth of what happened to Adrian in the cellar.'

'Do you think Rob killed Adrian?'

Frank rubbed his chin. 'I don't know, Gerry. But he's been holding back, that's for certain. The way he tried to avoid us... how can we not be suspicious?'

He started the car, the engine rumbling to life. As they pulled away from Louise's house, the weight of their discoveries settled heavily on Frank's shoulders.

'You know,' he said, breaking the silence, 'when I first saw Louise, I expected to see a broken young woman. Someone carrying the weight of her father's troubles. But she was... different.'

Gerry glanced at him. 'I often find people predictable, Frank, but sometimes there are surprises.'

'Aye, people can surprise you. What do you make of this connection between Rob and Bryan?' he asked.

Gerry was quiet for a moment, considering. 'Without talking to him, it's difficult, but why give the evidence to him? The bond is obviously strong. He knew about Gideon Blackwell.'

Frank nodded. 'And could well be involved himself, too. Was he also one of Gideon's victims? It's a bloody mess, Gerry. A right bloody mess.'

They drove in silence for a while, the landscape rushing past their windows. Frank's mind was racing, trying to connect the dots between Rob, Bryan, Adrian, and Gideon.

'We need to tread carefully here,' he said finally. 'Rob's got a family, a successful business. We don't want to go in guns blazing. But let's speak to him. And, after that, Gideon.'

Frank phoned Rob and, expecting the cold shoulder, was surprised when he picked up almost immediately.

Rob agreed to tell him everything he knew, but only on a particular bench, and only alone. He didn't want to be interrogated. He wanted to keep the conversation out in the fresh air, and not sweating in a stuffy environment. Frank had sensed a strange undercurrent in Rob's voice on the phone, a tension that went beyond the gravity of the confession he'd promised.

As Frank drove, he couldn't shake the image of those two young men in the photograph, arms around each other, smiling despite the horrors Bryan had endured. Rob, too, perhaps. And how did these horrors connect to a late-night card game in the Rusty Anchor?

Chapter Sixty-Two

Up ahead, Frank could see Rob Johnson sitting alone, his broad shoulders hunched against the chill of the whipping winds, gazing out over the North Sea. The sky was a leaden grey, heavy with the promise of rain, and the waves crashed against the rocks below with a relentless fury, their spray carrying on the biting wind. After killing a second roll-up, Frank drew in a deep breath, savouring the salty air rather than a stew of carcinogens in his lungs.

Frank settled onto the bench beside him, the rough wood cold and damp beneath his hands. He looked across at Rob, who continued to stare straight ahead. Rob's hands were clasped tightly in his lap, and Frank noticed a smear of what looked like blood across the back of one. 'Mr Johnson?'

'Rob, please. I'm about to tell you terrible things. I wanted to be away from the house. My family. I hope you understand that.'

'Of course. Is that blood on your hand?'

Rob stared down. 'Yes. Must be. I cut myself shaving this morning. Keep wiping at it.'

Frank's eyes narrowed slightly. Rob was clean-shaven,

but he couldn't see any obvious nicks. His instincts tingled, sensing that there was more to this than a simple shaving mishap, but he let it slide for now.

'This place was special to me and Bryan,' Rob said. 'Do you have a special place?'

'Did. Long time ago now. With my daughter, Maddie. A duck pond. We'd go there when she was feeling low, when the world seemed too heavy for her young shoulders. There was a willow tree. We'd sit under that tree for hours, just talking, watching the ducks. And this is where you came with Bryan?'

He nodded. 'My brother.'

Frank recalled Louise's words – they thought of each other like brothers.

Rob's eyes were watering – either from the sharp, bitter wind off the seas or his sadness. Frank couldn't be sure which, but he suspected it was a bit of both.

There was a long moment of silence. Rob gazed into the distance, as if he'd lost himself in the depths of his own memories. Frank was patient. He was well aware of the struggle to express truths that he'd kept inside for a long time.

Finally, Rob took a deep, shuddering breath. 'On this bench, we'd tell each other everything, Frank. Two sixteen-year-olds, eh? Not what you'd expect from the usual sixteen-year-old! But at that point, it felt like we'd lived so many painful lifetimes. And we shared so much pain. All because of one man in particular... Gideon Blackwell.'

Frank's stomach churned at the name, bile rising in his throat. Over the years, he'd heard whispers about Gideon Blackwell, dark rumours that were never quite substantiated. But the look in Rob's eyes, the raw agony that flickered there, left no doubt in Frank's mind that the rumours were true.

'At first, we were too ashamed to tell each other. It happened frequently to both of us. Our tales were similar. Pushed by Kath Fielding to go back again and again. Four times before he grew tired of us.'

Frank gritted his teeth. The thought of that woman using children for a profit. She'd got off so lightly. A short jail sentence, and now the best care in the world, as she saw out the rest of her days. The injustice of it made his blood boil.

'But, here, eventually, we shared our pain. I think it was that which allowed us to survive.'

Frank reached out, laying a hand on his shoulder, a silent gesture of support. He could feel the tension thrumming through Rob's body. He held it there for a couple of seconds and drew his hand back.

'I can't believe Bryan's dead.'

'I'm sorry, Rob. Truly.'

Rob's lip trembled, and he looked away, blinking furiously. 'All those years, all that pain... and in the end, it was the alcohol that got him. The one thing he couldn't escape.'

'Gideon's time is up,' Rob said after a moment, his voice hardening. 'It's over.'

Frank felt concern stirring within him. There'd been a lot of finality in those words. He recalled the blood on Rob's hand, the strange tension in his voice on the phone. Had something happened?

He was about to ask about Gideon when Rob spoke again. 'I'm sorry for not telling you what happened to Adrian Hughes. I was trying to protect Bryan, but I know it's too late for that.'

Frank's heart raced. Being so close to the truth filled him full of adrenaline. 'Tell me now, Rob.'

Rob closed his eyes, his face contorting as if in physical pain. Then, with a shuddering exhale, Rob talked. 'They're fractured... my memories. But I'll tell you what I can, what I know for sure...'

He paused and ran a hand over his face, fingers trembling slightly. Frank waited, holding his own breath, knowing that whatever Rob was about to say would change everything.

'Bryan came to me that night. The end of August. About three in the morning. A weekend. I can't remember which day. Covered in blood. He was shaking, his eyes wild, like a man possessed.' Rob looked at him, and Frank felt his blood run cold. There was some blood smeared up Rob's left cheek, the same blood that Frank had noticed moments ago on his hand.

'Adrian had admitted to Bryan that he'd abused younger boys. And after what happened with Gideon, it triggered something in Bryan. He'd always carried a knife for protection. After the other cardplayers had left, Bryan couldn't hold back any longer. He threatened Adrian with it in the cellar, and before he knew it... well... you know the rest.'

Frank's mind reeled over the fact that the truth was coming, yet there was now another issue at play. A more pressing one. 'Rob. Stop and listen to me. There's blood on your hands. Your face. It's not from shaving. What's happened?'

Rob flinched and looked away.

'Is anyone hurt? In danger?'

Rob covered his eyes with the palms of his hands as he continued. 'No... no... you wanted to know about Bryan.

Then listen! He was terrified, lost, *after* he came to me because he'd nowhere to go.'

Frank stood and got out his phone. He needed to call this in. Something was off here.

'After everything he'd been through,' Rob continued, still covering his eyes. 'I couldn't bear the thought of him spending the rest of his life in jail over this bastard, so I...' He dropped his hands. 'What're you doing?'

'I'm calling for help, Rob. Okay? That blood. It's not yours, and you need to tell me whose it is—'

A siren in the distance drowned out the crashing sound of the North Sea and the whistling air.

Rob said, 'I went to Gideon's before you called me.'

'Why?'

'To tell him I'd decided. That I was going to hand the evidence over. I was going to destroy him. I went round the other night and left him with some doubt. Today, I wanted to leave him with no doubt.'

The police car streaked down the road towards them, lights flashing.

'Is that Gideon's blood?' Frank could feel a sinking feeling in his gut.

Rob nodded, his eyes haunted.

The doors opened and two officers stepped out.

They approached. The taller of the two, a broad-shouldered man with a buzz cut, had his hand on his taser, ready to draw at a moment's notice. His partner, a wiry woman with sharp eyes, gestured for Frank to step back, her other hand resting on her baton. Rob held up his hands. Frank could now see some blood on his sleeves and shirt collar.

'Rob,' Frank said, sensing the willingness of the officer to shoot. 'Lie down.'

'I'm unarmed,' Rob said, complying. The officer knelt,

his knee pressing into Rob's back as he snapped the cuffs around his wrists. With a grunt, he hauled Rob to his feet, the metal of the cuffs glinting in the grey light. After the officers read him his rights, Frank stepped forward and addressed them. 'How did you know we were here?'

Rob answered before the officers. 'After you contacted me. I'd already left Gideon. A neighbour saw me. I kind of knew this was coming. I phoned my wife and told her where I was going. My intention was to prevent her from getting into trouble.'

'Did you kill Gideon?' Frank kept his voice steady despite the dread coursing through him.

'No.' Rob shook his head. 'No.'

Frank looked at the officers. 'What's happened?'

'All we know is that there was a single gunshot wound to the head.'

'Suicide,' Rob said. 'I got there. The door was unlocked. I went in and found him like that!'

Frank looked back at the officers.

'We don't know, sir. Like I said, that's all we know, and we were merely asked to collect him as a matter of emergency.'

Frank fixed Rob in his gaze. 'If you didn't... well... how did you get all this blood on you?'

'I saw him there.' There were tears in his eyes. 'Shrivelled up on the floor beside his wheelchair. Panic overcame me. I went there the other night, see, to tell him Bryan was dead, and I was going to hold him to account. I was worried that I'd get the blame. So, when I saw him lying there, blood around his head, I tried to help him into his chair, thinking the same thing. That this would come back on me.' He groaned. 'It was only when I knelt and clutched him that I saw the gun, and then realised the blood was from a bullet hole... in the side of his head. He was stone dead. And I'd never have touched him if I'd known.'

'Jesus.' Frank ran a hand over his face. 'Why didn't you call the police right away? What made you choose to come here first? Why?'

Another police car had come up behind the other.

Rob shrugged.

'Look.' Frank turned to the two officers. 'I need another five minutes.'

They looked at one another dubiously. 'Sir...'

'No really. Five minutes in the back of the vehicle. This isn't about Gideon Blackwell.'

'Sir, I...'

'I insist,' Frank growled.

The officers looked at each other and then relented.

Chapter Sixty-Three

IN THE BACK of the vehicle, Frank had to wait for Rob to stop crying.

'I've ruined everything...' He blew his nose and then wiped his eyes, his voice hoarse. 'My family... I only ever wanted to do the right thing. You have to believe that. And now... Jesus, now, I'm going to jail for something I didn't even do!'

'You won't go to jail *if* you didn't kill him, Rob. The truth will come out. You can be certain. But Rob, I just need your head back in the game a moment longer. You didn't finish your story. Bryan killed Adrian. Is that right?'

'Yes.' Rob's voice steadied as he continued. 'He didn't plan to. He threatened him with the knife, told him he should give himself up to the police. At that moment, his anger against Gideon just came out. That he'd never had the bottle to stand up to him. It almost felt like a second chance to fight back. But Adrian was dismissive. Waved him away. And then he just lost it. Lashed out with the knife. As soon as he'd done it, he realised his mistake. He dropped it immediately. Too late, I guess. Only takes one blow.'

Frank could almost see it – Bryan, his face twisted with rage and pain, the knife flashing in the dim light of the pub cellar. And Adrian, his eyes wide with shock and horror, his life's blood spilling out onto the cold stone floor.

'Christ,' Frank muttered, rubbing his temples.

'He came to me and was in my arms. Inconsolable... terrified... lost. He came to me because he'd nowhere else to go.' He thumbed his chest. 'I was his brother. And I know this for sure... that man didn't deserve to go to jail. Adrian Hughes? He'd abused children in that home for young people, detective. Openly admitted it. Do you realise this?'

'Aye.' Frank sighed. 'But that's not the point here.'

'It should be the only point,' Rob said.

'That,' Frank said, 'is your viewpoint. Society is built on a different one. What happened next, Rob?'

He lowered his voice. 'I helped him destroy his clothes, got rid of any evidence that might tie him to the crime.'

Not good, Frank thought. 'But the body?'

'I asked Bryan the same thing.' He rubbed his forehead aggressively.

'And?'

Rob closed his eyes as he rubbed. 'My head. My head feels like it's going to split into fucking two.'

'Finish, Rob,' Frank said. 'It's important.'

'Why should I? Bryan deserves justice. I do, too. Now both of us are on the verge of burning.'

'Tell the truth,' Frank said. 'Tell the truth and I swear to Christ, I'll see it through to the right outcome.'

Rob gulped. 'Someone else was involved, okay?'

Frank took a deep breath, his mind reeling.

'Someone who helped him hide the body,' Rob continued. 'In the wall.'

'Who?'

'Now this is the truth.' He dropped his hands and forced his eyes open despite the obvious discomfort on his face. 'He wouldn't say.'

Frank shook his head. 'Rob...'

Rob glared at him. 'Listen, or we're done. He wouldn't fucking say, okay? Said that if the roles were reversed, it would be the same. That I wouldn't say.'

'Carl Moss?' Frank said. 'It was Carl who helped him?'

'Listen, I don't know that man, and I swear on my family, I don't know who it was.'

Frank took a deep breath and closed his eyes. They'd got the killer, but who helped with the disposal? The mystery deepened, even as some pieces fell into place. Something occurred to him. He opened his eyes. 'You said he lashed out, and as soon as he'd realised his mistake, he dropped the knife.'

'That's right,' Rob said.

'Adrian was stabbed twice.'

Rob paled and looked away.

Frank's mind raced back to Gerry's earlier observation about the two knife wounds. It hadn't seemed significant, but now... He marvelled at her ability to consider angles that others might dismiss. 'You know something else, Rob?'

He sighed. 'Look, it was years later before Bryan even told me there'd been a second person. That night, Adrian had come back at Bryan like a man possessed after he'd stabbed him. His hands were around his throat. If not for another person, he'd have been done for.'

'So, someone else delivered the fatal knife wound?'

'Apparently. But, look, he never told me who it was. You have to believe that. He merely said that this other person was another of his brothers. And brothers never betray one another. Who was I to argue with that?'

After, Frank stood alone on the windswept cliffs, the case taking on additional dimensions in his mind. Bryan Parkes, the boy abused by Gideon Blackwell, turned killer. Rob Johnson, the loyal friend burdened with the dark secret. And the mysterious third man, the one who'd dealt the final blow to Adrian Hughes and helped hide his body.

The stabbing had taken place after hours. Had Carl Moss been there after hours? Tasked with locking up? It could have been Rory or another staff member, but the idea of Carl as a builder made more sense. He'd know how to close that wall.

Frank took a deep breath.

If it had been Carl, then both killers were dead and wouldn't face trial for the murder of Adrian Hughes. The relief that washed over him surprised Frank. It was followed quickly by guilt. He was a detective, sworn to uphold the law, not to judge who deserved justice and who didn't. And yet...

Chapter Sixty-Four

AFTER FRANK HAD CONTACTED Gerry to fill her in, he spent the journey back to HQ trying to learn more regarding Gideon Blackwell's death, but he found most avenues of inquiry busy. The discovery of the body was still fresh, and information was scarce. It was impossible for him to know for certain at this stage how bleak the outcome was for Rob Johnson, but deep down, Frank believed him. There'd been a raw honesty in that man's eyes.

He turned his attention to Carl Moss.

It made perfect sense.

He contacted Rory. Frustratingly, the call went straight to voicemail. He left a message asking him to call back. He was eager to discuss the weekend of 25th August, 1989 again to establish what time the pub had closed on those weekend nights and reopened the subsequent days. Establishing a timeline for the actual murder and the later concealment of the body might just fix Carl in the frame. Frank also mentioned Carl by name, and asked whether he'd had his own key to lock up with, or whether he used Rory's and then dropped it back off with him afterwards.

Once at HQ, he felt less edgy. The end was near. If they could confirm it was Carl, then both killers were dead. There would be no need to drag anyone through court and jail them for ridding the streets of a predator. Although Rob was guilty of hiding the truth, Frank wouldn't be pushing for his arrest. Ultimately, it may be unavoidable, but he suspected there wouldn't be any appetite from his superiors to prosecute this man.

When he walked into the incident room, something thudded into the doorframe above his head.

'What the—' He broke off when he saw Rylan bounding towards him. At first, he thought the Lab was going to send him crashing to the ground, but Rylan veered to the right, snatched up a toy bone, and returned to Reggie, who stood at his desk, wide eyed, his teeth clenched.

'Reggie?' Frank growled.

'Sorry.' Reggie bent down, red-faced, picked up the toy, and put it on the desk.

Frank looked around the room. No sign of Gerry or Sharon. Sean had his head lowered, but Frank could see the grin he was trying to hide.

Frank walked over to Reggie's desk, put two hands on it, and eyed up his DS. Reggie sat down, looking very uncomfortable.

Frank took a deep breath and looked between the two of them. He picked up the toy bone and passed it between his hands as if it were a mace, and he was deciding which of them to bludgeon with it. 'And when something breaks,' he said, his voice low and dangerous. 'Who's paying?'

'Won't happen again, sir,' Reggie said.

'That's what you said last time, Reggie. Yet, it's still happening. So, who's paying?'

'Me, sir.'

Frank smiled. 'Why didn't you say?' He turned and hurled the bone across the room. Rylan shot after it like a furry missile. 'Good boy.'

Admittedly, Frank thought, *that feels good.*

Chapter Sixty-Five

Sharon returned, and Frank briefed everyone on what he'd learned from Phoebe, Louise, and Rob. The team listened intently, their expressions a mix of shock and relief as Frank recounted Gideon's death. The sense of closure felt welcome in the air.

Gerry entered. Rylan trotted over to greet her. She knelt, stroked his head, and then strode briskly to her desk, a file clutched in her hand.

'How do, Gerry?' Frank called from across the room.

He watched her curiously. It was unusual for Gerry to be away from her desk or Rylan for so long.

She sat and opened the file.

'Gerry?' Frank prompted.

'Helen called while you were with Rob Johnson,' Gerry said, not looking up.

'And?'

'Forensic analysis of the mortar used in the repair work on the pub's cellar wall revealed a unique chemical composition. The spectroscopic signature suggests a proprietary blend of Portland cement, fly ash, and silica fume, with traces of a distinctive accelerant. It's a formula specific to a local Yorkshire supplier popular with builders. Three builders' shops: Builders Hub, Yorkshire Building Supplies, and Hanson's Hardware. I contacted these stores. Not all of them kept meticulous records… predictably. All except Hanson's Hardware. Carl Moss purchased this exact product on 26th August, 1989, along with a fresh set of bricks.'

Frank felt a surge of adrenaline. This was it. Carl Moss was the second man.

He turned to face the board and spoke. 'On the evening of the 25th, or rather the early hours of the 26th, the card game ended, and the players left, escorted out by Carl Moss. Carl must have returned to the cellar and witnessed the end of the struggle, with Bryan desperately trying to fend off a wounded Adrian. He was being choked, according to Rob. Carl must have grabbed the knife and stabbed Adrian.'

'Sorry to play devil's advocate boss,' Reggie said. 'But it seems extreme. Wouldn't he have tried a loose brick over his head first?'

'There'd been an altercation between them, remember? It had something to do with his nephew, Mike…' Frank turned. 'Whatever this was could have provided an excellent opportunity for him to stick the knife in? Literally as well as figuratively?'

'Or,' Sharon said, 'Maybe emotions were just high. There would have been blood, or perhaps Adrian could have been holding Bryan's throat very tightly. Like with a dog biting, that can be hard to break.'

Frank nodded at his audience. 'Yes. I've a feeling there may be some details we will never know. However, we now know that Carl must have headed out first thing on

Saturday morning to get the mortar and bricks and repaired the wall. I wonder if Carl convinced Rory to put an end to those games that very day, and the door was locked. Maybe Carl promised to get to the wall in due course, and then just conveniently forgot to mention it for a time until it fell from Rory's radar? Rory's recollection of all this is vague. He recalls being concerned about the damaged wall, and I guess Carl just stimulated those concerns to get the cellar closed down.'

Frank turned back to the board, his eyes fixing on Adrian's photo. His thoughts were a mixture of satisfaction and melancholy. *I promised to get to the truth, and I did. But I'm glad that no one is going to answer in court for what happened to you. You ruined lives, Adrian. I understand that you, too, suffered, but I cannot let it justify what you did to others.*

He heard everyone congratulating each other behind him. Just then, his phone buzzed in his pocket. He turned around to see Reggie clapping and announcing a pub visit, then retreated into a corner to answer the call. He put a finger in one ear while trying to listen.

Frank greeted a colleague from Leeds.

What he heard next hit him like a physical blow.

He stumbled, his free hand groping for the edge of his desk to steady himself. He took a deep breath, grabbed his keys and staggered towards the exit.

He sensed Reggie behind him. 'Frank, pub?'

'Not now.' He kept walking. His mind was reeling, emotions he couldn't name firing up inside him.

'Frank, what's wrong?' Reggie persisted.

Frank felt a surge of irritation and clenched his fist. *Easy, Frank.* 'I'll call you later.'

Outside in the corridor, Gerry caught up to him.

'Gerry, please... not now.' He stumbled on.

'Something's happened. What is it?'

'I don't know, yet.' He brushed away tears and quickened his pace.

She reached out and grabbed his arm.

He stopped.

'Tell me,' she said. 'That's what colleagues do.'

He turned.

'I saw you take the call,' Gerry said. 'I saw your expression change.'

Of course you did, he thought. *You never miss a thing. But if what I just heard is true, does any of it matter any more?*

He looked up at her, his eyes haunted. 'They found a girl matching Maddie's description. She's dead. Drug overdose. Leeds. I'm heading to the hospital.'

'There are a lot of girls matching Maddie's description.'

'Yes...' Frank felt his chest tighten with dread. 'But how many of them would have her purse?'

Frank's voice broke on the last word, the reality of what he'd just said crashing over him like a wave. Gerry's hand tightened on his arm, a silent anchor in the storm.

Chapter Sixty-Six

Mike's eyes widened. 'Is Noah awake?'

'In and out of consciousness.' Emma squeezed his hand.

Mike struggled to sit up, his massive frame protesting with every movement. 'I want to see him.'

There was a long pause. It spoke volumes. Emma's gaze dropped to the floor, avoiding Mike's desperate eyes.

'He's my son,' he insisted.

'I know.' She met his eyes. 'He's not out of the woods yet. He needs rest, Mike.'

A flicker of anger sparked in his eyes. 'And they think I'll antagonise him?'

'No... I don't think so.'

'Has his mother seen him?'

Another long pause. The silence confirmed his suspicions, each second feeling like a knife twisting in his gut. 'Where is he?'

Emma's reply was soft, almost apologetic. 'ICU, ward 3.'

'And where's that?'

'Same corridor as this one. The other end. About five minutes.'

Five minutes!

'So close.' Mike's voice was barely above a whisper, choked with longing and frustration.

She squeezed his hand again. 'Does it help to know he's close?'

'Of course,' he lied.

Because five minutes, for Mike Bailey, at 215 kg with a heart on the verge of giving up, might as well have been the other side of the world.

Chapter Sixty Seven

MEMORIES FLOODED IN.

A pink blanket. A squirming, soft bundle. A shock of black hair.

Tiny clenched fists. Long drinks from her mother.

What matters any more?

Nothing. Not the long hours at work. Not the weight of the world outside these walls. None of it.

All that exists is the three of us.

Cocooned together.

'She's got your eyes, Frank.'

Breathless, Frank leaned on Bertha. The hospital – a concrete monolith – loomed. 'Come on.' He jogged and made it to the front door. He doubled over, sucking in air, and almost vomited. The purse. It couldn't be hers. It had to be a mistake.

Sun-dappled grass. Chubby legs. Arms outstretched. An amusing toddle. A gummy grin. The world is perfect. Scooping her up. Laughing. Crying. Marvelling at the miracle. 'Dada.' Our cocoon.

Forcing back tears, fighting through sweat and exhaustion, Frank navigated the hospital corridors. The linoleum glowed under the glare of sickly fluorescent lights. Doctors and nurses brushed past him with blurred faces and muffled, distant voices. One stopped to ask him if he was okay. Frank didn't know. He was barely aware of the words he used. Everything was in a daze. He'd never felt so heavy.

Curious questions. A hungry mind. A will to know and belong. Her hand locked in his. Eyes searching him. He could give her what she needed, what she longed for. A place in the world. Their perfect world. Everything together. Cocooned. Perfect. A mug with 'World's Best Dad'.

Sinking down into the depths of the hospital, he rested against the wall of the elevator. He was uncertain if his face was covered in sweat or tears any more. He wasn't sure it really mattered. It was so hard to push aside memories of his mistakes now. Had he fought too little when she used to come back so late at night, stinking of alcohol and weed? Were the shouts enough? Were the punishments sufficient? Or, maybe, it'd been much too much? Had he fought *too hard*? Had he pushed her away?

Kicked the can down the road until this fucking moment?

Shadows in her bedroom. Different alleys and different journeys. Shaking hands. Desperate choices. Need. A splintered cocoon. Outside, the world was not so perfect. And her voice was no longer her own. 'I'm sorry, Dad, I'll do better, I promise.'

There was nothing left in his body. He rang the buzzer. 'DCI Black.' He placed his head against the wall.

'I'm sorry, Mary,' he said, out loud.

There was a clunk. The mortuary door opened. Frank peeled his head away from the wall. *Welcome to the end of everything, Frank.* A doctor looked at him. He wore a face mask, but the pity in his eyes was intense enough. Frank didn't need to see the whole facial expression. 'This way, please, DCI.' The words seemed to come from under water. The mortuary door felt cold and unyielding. The sweat that covered him only intensified the chill. Inside, the air was heavy with the scent of decay and disinfectant. It gripped him tight. The doctor gestured to a table in the centre of the room, a sheet-draped form lying motionless upon it. *She's got your eyes, Frank.* 'God, no,' he muttered. 'Please don't let it be her.'

Heavy at the door. Turning, pacing, wanting to come in. Yet, wanting to walk away. Back home. To where it all started. Needing help. Back with Dada. World's Best Dad. Come in, Maddie, let's get you well. 'Don't fuck this up, Frank.'

The doctor pulled back the sheet. Pale and still. Features slack. Gone. A shell. Frank stumbled backward, spotting the chair just in time... Down he went. *Down and heavy.*

Chapter Sixty-Eight

For over an hour, Mike stared at the ceiling, the rhythmic beeping of the machines no longer lulling him to sleep. Despite everything that had happened, he felt more alert than he had in months.

Wired, in fact.

After telling him about Noah's location, Emma had delivered a parting warning. 'You still have to be prepared, Mike. Confidence is higher, but there's no certainty yet.'

And yet, with the possibility of his son's death still looming, they'd denied him the opportunity to see Noah. His boy. His flesh and blood.

The only thing of him that was worth anything in this godforsaken world.

How dare they hold me back?

If, God forbid, Noah died, then he'd never see him again. Who got to make such cruel decisions?

He was relieved that his son was fighting, that his chances were better than ever, but he couldn't shake the thick shroud of despair that grew more suffocating by the minute.

And with such melancholy, old demons were inevitable.

And what better demon to make an appearance than Adrian Hughes?

As a child who'd recently lost his mother, Mike had blamed himself for what Adrian had done to him behind closed doors.

So, he'd never told a single soul.

He'd been a vulnerable, lonely child, and he'd looked up to that demon as a kind man. A compassionate man that'd always had time for children struggling with the hand they'd been dealt in life.

But he wasn't. Really, he was a manipulative man. An abusive man.

The guilt, the pain and the anguish had always been too much.

And what had he, Mike Bailey, done with the pain and the anguish? The false guilt that this was in some way his fault?

Internalised it, that's what.

Like many others before him, and many others would in years to come.

The consequences were always destructive, but for him, they'd been particularly stark. It'd eaten him up, consumed him, and turned him into – he held up his warped and fleshy fingers in front of his eyes – this monster. And that may've been all right. Maybe. If it'd been only him that had suffered for being spineless. But no, that wasn't to be the case, was it?

Because rot spreads.

And someone in ICU Ward 3 was suffering because of his weakness.

He looked at the beeping monitor.

I don't want to be spineless any more.

With a grunt, he heaved his massive frame upright, fighting gravity, ignoring all his burning muscles and bones. Every rib felt as if it would split, and his limbs trembled without mercy.

I don't want to be weak.

Fumbling with clumsy, swollen fingers, Mike tore at the wires and tubes that tethered him to the machines.

Alarms blared. He gritted his teeth and swung his legs over the side of the bed. Ahead, he sighted the rollator. It may've been mere feet, but it may as well have been miles.

Fuck it, he thought. *No one will tell me whether I can hold my son's hand or not.*

Tensing himself, he slipped from the bed, expecting to fall. There was a thud as the floor took his excessive weight, and his legs quivered. But he'd stayed upright, albeit with the aid of a bedside table.

Behind him, the machines raised hell.

Someone tore open the curtains. He could see several familiar faces. Nurses. One doctor. He didn't care. He'd already started the journey.

Sweat poured down his face, stinging his eyes and dripping from his chin. His breath came in quick gasps; the effort of moving his massive frame from the bed to this upright position had been more than he could bear. He knew his heart could give out at any moment. That he could hit the floor dead.

But no, he thought. *You've lain down and taken it for far too long. This is about Noah now. It's about what you owe to your son.*

He could hear the professionals pleading with him, their voices urgent, their hands gentle but firm as they surrounded him.

'Get away from me!' He lurched away from the bedside table, half-expecting to go flat onto his face...

His hands found the rollator.

It'd seemed impossible.

For Noah, I can do anything. Anything.

A kind young nurse named James begged. He'd his hands in front of him, joined as if to pray. He was trembling all over. 'You're not strong enough, Mike. You could hurt yourself.'

'James, you've... been good... to me...' Mike sucked in air. 'But you need... to get out... of my... fucking... way.'

He edged forward on the rollator.

James stood his ground.

Mike took a deep breath and thrust his body weight onward. The wheels took him. Realising there was a real danger of them both hitting the floor now, James skipped out of the way.

As he rolled, he could hear the nurses talking behind. Someone suggested Emma, but she was doing her rounds in town. It wouldn't be long before they tried to sedate him, but they'd need to get some strong orderlies to hold him up and stop him from splitting his head in two on the floor.

Gasping, he pressed on. Slow progress, but some progress. He made it to the end of the ward. The sharp scent of antiseptic assaulted his nostrils, mingling with the stale odour of sweat and desperation. A doctor came up alongside him. 'What're you doing, Mr Bailey?'

'Going... to see... my son.' He was panting so hard that forcing the words out was near impossible. *Is this what it feels like to drown?* he wondered, his lungs burning with each laboured breath.

'I understand. If we get you back into bed, we'll help with that, see what we can do.'

'No... don't... trust... you.'

He was losing energy, but he sighted the end of the ward. The door to the corridor was ajar. No one had thought to shut it and lock it. Such a simple solution.

They hadn't bothered because they didn't think Mike would make it.

They were probably right.

'Unless you stop now,' the doctor said. 'You may die.'

I've been dead a long time. Mike grunted and pushed with all his might. *Time to live.* He made it a good metre or so, exhaling. He sucked in another deep breath and went for a consecutive metre.

At that point, the doctor had determined that shutting the door was a good move. Mike's anticipation caused him to swerve his rollator slightly, catching the doctor's foot and sending him scurrying into the wall. Mike then threw himself into the last couple of metres to reach the door.

His eyes widened when he saw the sign in the corridor.

Ward 3 of the ICU. Along the red line to his left.

He could feel his heart beating in every part of his body. He guessed it could be reassurance that it was still getting blood around his hefty and failing body. It wouldn't be for long, though. He could already feel the pain. A searing, white-hot agony that radiated from his chest, down his left arm.

Every inch of him screamed in protest, begging him to stop, to rest.

But he couldn't. Not now. Not when he was so close.

Come on... for your son. You failed Noah before. Not now. Not when it matters most.

He heard a crowd gathering behind him, calling his name, demanding his attention. Keeping his eyes ahead, he tried to blank them out.

Knowing that his body was on the verge of catastrophic failure, he sent his focus to stronger moments in his life. Happier memories. To try and spur him on.

Noah's laughter. A small hand clasping his own. The wonder in Noah's eyes as they watched fireworks explode across the night sky, the boy's face painted in shades of red, green, and gold. Each precious moment, each flicker of joy, kept his mind whirring, enabling him to push forward even as his body screamed for rest, and sweat drenched his face and white gown.

Ahead were more nurses and doctors now. The murmur of their voices, the squeak of their rubber-soled shoes against the linoleum.

They distracted him from his memories, and he felt himself back in his heavy body. He leaned over the rollator sucking in air. His vision blurred, the edges darkening. He closed his eyes.

Noah... Noah...

By thinking his name over and over, he desperately tried to hold on to his son, who waited for him minutes away.

Noah... I'm coming—

There was a hand on his shoulder. The grip was tight. *Inappropriate.*

He saw Adrian Hughes smiling from the corner of his office. A board game set up. Come and play, Mike.

'Get the fuck away from me!' Mike shouted at the top of his lungs. He shrugged off the hand and his eyes snapped open.

An orderly took some steps backwards, showing his palms. 'I'm sorry, Mr Bailey, but this is enough. We're here to escort you back to your bed.'

'Just... try.' He widened his eyes, a surge of defiance rising within him.

And then he was going again. Sucking in breaths. Lurching as he exhaled. Once... twice... three times. Each step was a battle, a war waged between his iron will and his failing body.

The ICU couldn't be more than a couple of metres away.

Please, he begged his body. *Please*.

But his vision tunnelled, and he'd lost complete control of his respiration now.

He didn't need a doctor now to tell him that his heart was about to burst.

A stabbing pain shot through his left knee, nearly sending him tumbling to the ground. He gritted his teeth, gripping the rollator with white-knuckled intensity.

Another hand grabbed him again.

'Get...' He couldn't get the next word out.

Someone took his other shoulder.

He managed two words this time. 'My... son!'

'Please, Mr Bailey. Don't make this difficult.'

Mike released the rollator and jerked his right arm up.

He contacted the orderly's face.

There was a gasp from the onlookers.

Mike couldn't believe his hands fell to the rollator again. Not that it mattered. His arms trembled, the muscles quivering with fatigue. There was very little left.

Through tunnelled vision, he saw the door of the ICU. It couldn't have been more than a metre...

There was another hand on his other shoulder.

Again, he struck, but this time, he missed. He lost balance, so when he brought his hand back again, he failed to catch the handle and slumped forward. His body, pushed beyond its limits, refused to right itself. He lost control of his knees. His whole body weight collapsed into the rollator.

He went into a spin, crashing down onto his back, his vehicle coming down on top of him.

When he opened his eyes, his vision swam, black spots dancing at the edges. He glanced down at his massive heaving chest. He could feel his heart pounding in a frantic, erratic rhythm within it.

'Noah...' he said.

He closed his eyes and imagined Noah's face, pale and drawn, but alive. Waiting for him.

'Noah...'

He allowed himself to imagine a future where he was healthy, where he was there for Noah in all the ways that mattered. He saw them fishing together; the sun glinting off the calm surface of the lake. Noah's face, no longer gaunt and haunted, but full of life and laughter. He envisioned them laughing together, sharing stories and dreams, and repairing the bond that years of neglect had broken. It was a beautiful dream, a glimmer of hope in the darkness, and Mike clung to it with all his might.

Chapter Sixty-Nine

THE JOURNEY from Leeds hospital to Whitby hospital had done little to clear Frank's head. He still felt disorientated and saddled emotionally by his experience back in the mortuary. However, a returned phone call from Rory had changed everything regarding the Adrian Hughes' case and the conclusions they'd already reached.

What greeted him in the hospital corridor dragged him from his own chaos, though the scene before him was no less frantic.

Up ahead, a gathering crowd blocked the corridor.

Frank increased his pace. The cacophony of raised voices grew louder with each step, a discordant symphony of urgency and concern. The sharp scent of antiseptic mingled with the cloying odour of fear and desperation, making his stomach churn.

Doctors, nurses and orderlies rushed back and forth, both alongside Frank, and ahead of him. A large man lay in the centre of it all. As Frank drew closer, he realised that the large man was the person he was here to see. Mike Bailey, sprawled on his back, his arms flailing, demanding everyone get away from him.

Frank, still exhausted from his descent into the pits of the previous hospital, took a deep breath and used a burst of adrenaline to drive himself forward, pushing his way through the throng.

A metre or so from Mike, Frank saw two doctors circling around him; both held syringes. They were looking for an opening. To Frank, it looked barbaric, like predators rounding on prey.

Orderlies were also darting in, trying to seize Mike's arms. Their intentions were clear. They wanted to pin his arms for the injections.

'Stop!' Frank ripped his badge out, held it up. 'DCI Frank Black, Scarborough Police. What's going on here?'

Silence fell. The doctors and orderlies froze, turning to look at him with expressions of surprise and confusion. Mike stopped shouting.

Frank turned, looking from face to face, willing someone to speak.

'My son!' Mike suddenly shouted.

Frank turned and looked down at him. His wide red face shone. Sweat, tears, or potentially both. 'Someone stabbed him.'

Frank felt as if someone had punched him in the gut. He went to his haunches, clutching his knees, fresh memories from the hospital before overwhelming him.

His heart clenched as he relived the suffocating fear, the sickening dread, the hospital's sterile corridors...

Every fibre of his being straining towards the mortuary...

A voice pulled him from his memories. 'I'm James.'

Frank looked up into the face of a junior nurse. 'Just a minute, son.'

He closed his eyes and took a deep breath, willing the nausea to pass, but he was still struggling.

The pale, still face on the mortuary table... features slack in death.

It may not have been Maddie, but it was a life cut short all the same.

Another tragedy.

And a reminder.

Here was a life that could so easily have been his daughter's, if he didn't find her in time.

He gritted his teeth. *Pull yourself together, Frank.*

He rose, groaning, his back popping, and addressed the nurse. 'James, what's happened?'

'Mr Bailey's been trying to get to his son's room in the ICU, but he's in no condition to be moving around. No condition, whatsoever—'

'So, you want to make him worse by pumping him full of that shite?' Frank pointed at one doctor wielding a syringe.

'For his own safety,' the doctor said.

Frank squared his shoulders. He looked between the two doctors, his gaze steady and unwavering. 'Is he a danger to his son?'

'No, of course not, but to himself!'

'Then stand down.' Frank's voice was low but firm. 'If he's done nothing wrong, you've no right to come between a parent and their child.'

'I have a duty of care,' the doctor said.

'Then care, man.' Frank shook his head. 'If he can see his child, touch his child... do you know what a gift that is? Have you any idea?' Frank's voice cracked, tears welling in his eyes as he looked down, remembering his arms around Maddie as she trembled in her bedroom all those months ago. He looked back up. 'Not forgetting what it might actually mean for his child?'

A stunned silence settled over the corridor.

Frank narrowed his eyes. 'Help him up.' His tone would allow no argument. 'Give him a few minutes with his son...'

The doctors looked at each other.

Frank took a deep breath and growled. 'I insist.'

The orderlies hesitated, looking to the doctors for guidance. After a long, tense moment, the doctor with the 'duty of care' nodded. 'He can have five minutes.'

Frank moved to Mike's side and knelt, his back in knots. 'Help me, then.'

Together, Frank and the orderlies heaved Mike to his feet. Frank clenched his teeth as every one of his ageing muscles burned. James righted the rollator and they got Mike over to it.

'Come on,' Frank hissed at the other orderlies. 'Let's get this over the line.' They took up positions on either side of Mike, supporting him. Frank was underneath Mike's right arm, while another orderly was beneath his left, and the two doctors and James helped from behind.

Slowly, painfully, they resumed Mike's journey. Half-carrying, half-pushing him. Frank glanced around, noting all their faces set in determination as they helped bear Mike's weight. Such a turnaround from moments before. Everyone was suddenly with him, rather than against him. Frank could feel Mike's body trembling against his own, every laboured breath a testament to his unwavering resolve.

'Stay with us, Mike,' Frank murmured, his voice low and encouraging. 'Eyes on the prize.'

'Noah,' muttered Mike.

'Yes, Noah. A little further. Seconds away, fella.'

Mike's gasps were ragged and strained now, and his head was bouncing with the movement.

The journey became harder as they entered the ward, but Frank wasn't sure if that was down to his own fatigue, or the fact that Mike was fading fast. He imagined it was a combination of both.

At that point, two nurses came up alongside them, wheeling a bed. 'Good thinking,' Frank said. 'Okay, lads, ready.'

Frank turned to stare into Mike's eyes. They were half-closed.

The DCI clutched the large man's damp cheeks. 'Look at me, Mike.'

His eyes fluttered open.

'Your son is metres from you, fella. You need to get yourself onto this bed.'

'Thank... you...' Mike said.

'Enough with the thanking, get yourself bloody going.'

Together, they worked Mike over to the bed. It took a few people to hold the frame, preventing it from moving about under the sheer weight that was coming, but eventually, they had Mike sitting on the side. The youngest and strongest of the orderlies took his legs, while the other supported his back as they laid him down.

Frank put his hand on Mike's wide chest. 'Home free, fella. Home free.'

Frank stood to one side as the nurses pushed him towards a room. Once it was inside, Frank turned and looked at the crowd, nodded, and then followed the two doctors.

A woman ran past him and brushed against him. 'Sorry,' she said.

'Ma'am?'

She turned. 'Sorry... I need to see him. I'm his nurse. Emma Holloway.'

He recognised her from the interview the other day. 'I remember.' He went into the room alongside her.

There was a bandaged young lad in the bed alongside Mike. He had machines wired up to him, but he kept his eyes open and looked to his right at what was happening.

Mike, meanwhile, had his eyes closed, lying back. A doctor was checking his vitals.

Frank gulped. *Were they too late?*

Emma grasped his arm.

Come on, fella.

The doctor looked up, relief etched on his face. 'He's still with us. Let's get him rigged up.'

Frank sighed, allowing the doctors and nurses to go past him so they could collect some more equipment to monitor Mike's vitals.

Emma dropped her hand. 'What happened?'

Frank opened his mouth to explain it when Mike's eyelids began fluttering.

'Mike?' Frank said, striding forward. The doctor allowed him access.

Emma followed behind. 'He's tired... maybe don't.'

He looked back at her and read her expression.

We don't know how many more chances he has left.

She nodded. 'Allow me.' She slipped around Frank and took Mike's hand.

'Your son, Mike. He's here. Noah's to your left.'

Mike didn't open his eyes, but there was a faint smile on his face.

Frank went over to the young man, who was looking both exhausted and confused.

'You look like you've been through the wars, young man.'

Noah gulped. 'What... happened?' His voice was barely more than a whisper. He was weak, and far from well himself.

'Something I'll never forget.' Frank smiled down at the boy. *And something I'm sure you'll never forget when you hear all the details.*

'I don't understand.' He sounded very weak.

'He got to you, Noah. That's all you need to know for now. He got to you because he loves you more than anything. Now you need to rest.'

He turned with tears in his own eyes.

I wish I could get to you, Maddie.

Chapter Seventy

Frank was standing outside Noah's room when his phone rang.

'Reggie?'

'Boss, I'm in the hospital car park, looking for a space,' Reggie said. 'I'll be there in a minute.'

Frank rolled his shoulders, trying to straighten his back. It was sore from helping Mike. 'No need.' His voice was heavy with exhaustion.

'Eh? Why? What's happened? You said we were wrong on Carl Moss, and that—'

'False alarm. We were right all along.'

'But boss, I—'

'We *were* right, okay?' Frank interrupted, his gaze drifting into Noah's room through the window. Mike and Noah were both asleep. Their beds had been pushed closer together now, so they'd been able to hold hands for a time. Even out here, Frank could hear the machines on either side of the patients beeping steadily, a reassuring rhythm that seemed to echo the beating of Frank's own heart.

In the room, Emma moved to the centre to separate

their hands to prevent cramping. She then tucked the blankets around Mike's sleeping form, her movements practiced and efficient.

'So, you don't need me?' Reggie asked.

'Oh, I need you. All that remains is the report. And that's where you come in.'

There was a moment of silence on the other end of the line, broken only by the distant sound of traffic.

'Reggie?'

'Thanks, boss.' There was frustration in his voice.

'Don't worry, you're good at it. Now, you did do as I asked, didn't you? When I told you to come here?'

'Yes, boss. I didn't tell anyone. I kept it quiet.'

'And it's to stay that way.'

Another pause, longer this time. Frank could almost hear the gears turning in Reggie's head as he mulled over the implications of Frank's words.

Frank broke the quiet. 'You know this is for the best.'

'I know, boss. But Gerry?'

'What about her?'

'She may figure it out.'

'She won't because I never told her what Rory said to me.'

'Are you sure this is the right move?'

Frank's gaze settled on Mike and Noah, their chests rising and falling in unison.

'Never been surer about anything.' His voice was barely above a whisper.

Later, as he nursed a coffee in the hospital canteen, Frank's mind drifted back to the moment that had brought him here. Rory's phone call, responding to Frank's earlier message about Carl locking up after the card nights.

'What you said got me thinking. I remembered something. I'm sorry I didn't think of it before, but it was such a long time ago. But it may be relevant.'

And it had been relevant. *Very relevant.*

'There was this one time I had it out with Carl over locking up. I caught Mike slipping the key through my door at home during the early hours. Mike admitted that his uncle wasn't always locking up on weekend nights after the card games. That he'd sometimes be too busy being out on the tiles.'

The revelation had almost stopped Frank's heart dead in his chest.

'I gave Carl a right rollicking,' Rory had continued. 'Hardly responsible parenting, eh? Mike was far too young to be up that late, never mind locking up. Yes, I was pissed off, but honestly, it never came up again as we then stopped the card nights. I'd been planning to stop them for a while, anyway. He seemed happy with the idea. Guess that's why it slipped my mind in telling you earlier. Until your message about the key, it just never factored in my recall.'

In the quiet of the canteen, Frank closed his eyes, the scene playing out in his mind with vivid clarity. He could see Adrian and Bryan in the cellar, their voices raised in anger. The glint of the knife as it plunged into Adrian's chest. Adrian, bleeding, his hands wrapped around Bryan's throat, squeezing the life from him. And then Mike, the only other person in the pub that night, bursting in, trying desperately to pry Adrian's fingers from Bryan's neck. In the end, he'd had no choice. He'd picked up the bloody knife and driven it deep into Adrian's flesh, ending the struggle once and for all.

It might not have happened exactly like that. Mike might have done it from anger and bitterness. Phoebe had suspected that Adrian had abused Mike in the past at Sunnybrook.

Although this wasn't certain, one thing was. The body of that serial abuser had been hidden behind that wall. And Carl, after learning the truth from Mike, had returned the next day to buy the supplies and seal Adrian away forever.

But now what?

No longer was everyone involved in Adrian's death gone. One person remained.

If Phoebe had been right, and it seemed more than likely that she was, then Mike was yet another person who'd suffered trauma.

A person who may've wanted to die, who'd been ready to let go.

A person who'd fought through agony and despair to reach his son, to hold him one last time.

Frank was in no mood to bury Mike Bailey.

There were sleeping dogs. And this was one that he definitely needed to let lie.

Epilogue

Alone in her jail cell, Phoebe opened the envelope, her fingers trembling slightly. While unfolding the crisp white paper inside, a small photograph came loose and fluttered to the ground. She bent to pick it up, her eyes widening as she took in the image of a young woman, dressed for her graduation, standing in front of the Radcliffe Camera at Oxford University.

Amelia Okonkwo's face was alight with pride, her dark eyes shining as she held up her degree.

Phoebe's mind drifted back to the day she'd first met Amelia. Amelia had been a child from a disadvantaged background, who'd won a full scholarship to Oxford from Phoebe's charity, Brighter Horizons, to study science. In this letter, Amelia outlined her dreams of becoming a researcher, of finding cures for the world's deadliest diseases. She specifically mentioned her ambition to develop new treatments for malaria, which still ravaged many communities in her parents' home country of Nigeria. Over and over, she thanked Phoebe and Brighter Horizons for giving her the opportunity to pursue her passions.

Phoebe clutched the letter to her chest and smiled, a bittersweet ache filling her heart, and lay back on her bunk.

Later that evening, the walls of her cell seemed to close in on her, suffocating her and she wondered then if she'd ever emerge from the weight of her own actions – the deaths of Felix Delaney and Theresa Long in that fiery car explosion – or the years of lying, or her failure to expose Adrian Hughes. In fact, her prison sentence for the manslaughter of Julian seemed rather light considering her sins.

She kept the letter under her pillow as she slept.

At least she could be proud of this.

Children like Amelia who'd been given a chance they wouldn't have otherwise had.

Something to hold on to. Some light in the darkness.

⁓

Sophie Johnson stood centre stage under the spotlight. Her voice was clear, strong and true. Rob smiled. *True. Truth.* How he'd needed that in his life for as long as he remembered. And now here it was, in all its glory. The lightness was indescribable.

Sophie's performance as Elizabeth Proctor in *The Crucible* was captivating. Her portrayal of a woman struggling with the weight of lies and the pursuit of truth resonated deeply with Rob. As she delivered her lines with unwavering conviction, Rob felt a profound connection to the themes of honesty and redemption unfolding on stage.

Beside him, his wife Sarah squeezed his hand. He whispered in her ear, 'I'm proud of her.' She fixed him in a stare and mouthed, silently, 'I'm proud of you.' He nudged a tear away, and then turned his smile to the person on his other side. Louise Parkes. Her eyebrows were raised. She whispered, 'She's so good.'

As the final scene drew to a close and the audience erupted in applause, Rob felt a lump form in his throat. He stood with the rest of the crowd, clapping until his hands ached.

It had only been a month since he'd been able to put the Gideon Blackwell suicide behind him once and for all. Camera footage had exonerated him. Cameras outside Gideon's home showed him arriving on the first visit. On that night, Gideon had shown him out, or at least had been at the door, ushering him away following the confrontation. The second visit had also been caught on Gideon's cameras. This was when he'd found him dead. The pathologist ascertained that Gideon had been dead for over twenty-four hours at that point, and the gunshot wound was clearly self-inflicted.

Since then, life had been on an upward turn.

After the show, they waited for Sophie in the lobby. She burst through the doors, her face flushed with excitement. Rob went to her and embraced her. 'Did you see me, Dad?' Rob held her close, breathing in the scent of her hair, the warmth of her embrace.

'Every second.'

'And?'

'I loved it, sweetheart. You were amazing.' Sophie pulled back, her eyes shining. Then, she noticed Louise by her mother. And she looked confused. Sarah led Louise forward. 'Sophie, there's someone I'd like you to meet,' Rob saw the shyness in his daughter's eyes. 'Someone very special to us all.'

'I think I know.' Sophie moved closer to Louise. 'Are you Bryan's daughter?'

'I am,' she said. 'And you were amazing.'

'Thank you.' Sophie flushed. She smiled at her father and then looked at Louise again. 'I'm so pleased to meet you, *cousin*.'

Rob took Sarah's hand and held it tightly. *Thank you, Bryan*, he thought. *I'm so happy we found a way back to each other*.

As he watched Sophie and Louise chatting animatedly, a warmth spread through Rob's chest. The weight of secrets he'd carried for so long seemed to lift, replaced by the joy of this new connection, this extension of family.

And for the first time in longer than he could remember, Rob felt a sense of peace settle over him.

∽

The sun beat down on the crowded stadium.

On the track, a line of young men crouched at the starting blocks, their muscles coiled and ready.

In the stands, Mike Bailey sat in his wheelchair; the surrounding air was thick with the smell of sweat and anticipation. His entire focus was on Lane 4.

Bang!

The runners exploded from the blocks. Their legs pumped. Talented young men flew down the track.

But it was Lane 4.

That was what mattered.

All that mattered.

Mike gripped the armrests of his chair as he watched Noah pull ahead of the pack.

Ten metres to go, five, three, one metre...

He couldn't help but think of his own 'race' down that hospital corridor all those months ago. The memory of that desperate journey, fuelled by love and determination, flooded back to him.

When Noah crossed the finish line, his arms raised in triumph, the crowd erupted in cheers and Mike, with a strength he'd worked tirelessly to regain, made the effort to rise from his chair, so he could clap and holler for his son.

During the awards ceremony, as Noah made his way to the podium, the gold medal glinting around his neck, Mike's mind flashed back to that day in the hospital, to the moment when he'd opened his eyes to find his son's hand clasped in his own.

It was in that moment he'd made a promise. A vow. He'd be there for his son, no matter what. And that had started with his health, a journey that had been as challenging as it was rewarding.

Noah stepped up to the microphone, and Mike felt a lump form in his throat.

'I want to thank my dad. Without him, I wouldn't have trained, and I wouldn't be here.'

Mike's vision blurred with tears.

When the event's organiser asked Noah what motivated him during the training, he responded with, 'Easy. Seeing Dad fight every day, seeing him lose 65 kilograms and keep going, no matter how hard it gets. What he goes through with nutritionists and physical therapists... well, my training is nothing in comparison.'

Mike felt a hand on his shoulder. He looked up to see Emma standing beside him, her eyes shining with tears. 'Amazing,' she said.

'He is.' Mike wiped a tear away.

'I was talking about you.'

'No.' He waved her away. 'This is his moment.'

'Is it?' Emma asked. 'I think you deserve it too.'

Mike smiled. 'His moment,' he emphasised. 'And he can have as many as he wants. And through every single one, I'll be the happiest man alive.'

As the cheers of the crowd washed over him, Mike couldn't deny that he still felt the presence of those glowing red eyes. However, instead of feeling the Barghest's breath on the back of his neck, Mike now sensed it lurking at a distance. He knew it would always be there, but he also knew that he had the strength to keep it at arm's length now. With Noah's *moments* coming thick and fast, Mike felt equipped to face whatever challenges the beast may have for him in the future. True, the Barghest might never fully disappear, but it no longer held the power to consume him, and that made him smile.

From ear to ear.

~

Gerry stood in her kitchen, meticulously arranging the place settings. She consulted her watch. Fifty-seven minutes until Tom's arrival. She'd plenty of time to prepare the food.

He was three minutes late, but that was an acceptable margin, so after opening the door, she determined not to mention it.

Tom stood on the other side, a bouquet in his hand. He smiled as he saw her. 'You look beautiful.'

Gerry nodded, accepting the compliment as a factual observation. 'Thank you,' she replied, stepping aside to let him in. 'And thank you for the flowers.'

As they made their way into the living room, Tom's gaze fell on a framed photograph on the mantelpiece. It showed a younger Gerry, her arms wrapped around an older couple, their faces lined with laughter.

'Are those your parents?' Tom asked, his voice gentle.

Gerry nodded. 'They passed away a few years ago in a boating accident.'

Tom's face fell. 'I'm so sorry.' His hand reached out to squeeze her shoulder. 'That must have been incredibly difficult.'

'It did shock me. It was a statistically unlikely event. The probability of both parents dying simultaneously is quite low.' She sighed. 'They were good people.'

Tom nodded, his expression one of understanding.

As they settled at the table, Tom complimented Gerry's cooking. She nodded. She found praise for cooking ridiculous. She merely followed recipes with precision. The outcome was never in doubt. Still, she wanted to keep the atmosphere nice, and etiquette was the real challenge for her here.

Overall, she couldn't deny that the conversation between them was flowing easier, and she was feeling less and less need to probe him. It was a positive sign. So, as they finished their meal, she said, 'I've a question for you.'

Tom raised an eyebrow. 'Okay,' he replied. 'It has been a while. Go on.'

Gerry fixed Tom with a steady gaze. 'Are you ready to have sex?'

Tom choked on his wine, his eyes widening in shock. He coughed, sputtering as he tried to catch his breath. 'Sorry?'

Gerry tilted her head, her expression one of mild confusion. 'I asked if you're ready to have sex,' she repeated, her voice matter of fact. 'I find you attractive, and I believe we've a strong connection. It seems like the logical next step.'

Tom stared at her, his mouth opening and closing like a fish out of water. 'I... well... yes, of course,' he stammered, his face flushing red. 'I just wasn't expecting... I mean, you caught me off guard.'

Gerry nodded, making a mental note. 'I see. You're surprised. In the future, I'll provide a warning before broaching topics of a sexual nature. Is five minutes sufficient preparation time?'

'Well, I can't argue with that,' he replied. He took a deep breath. 'I'm ready.'

As they made their way upstairs, Rylan padding along behind them, Tom glanced over his shoulder at the dog. 'Does he have to come with us?' he asked, his voice uncertain.

Gerry paused, her hand on the bedroom door. She looked back at Rylan, then at Tom, her expression serious. 'Yes,' she replied, her voice firm. 'Rylan is an essential part of my life. He provides emotional support and helps me navigate social situations. If you want to be with me, you need to accept that he's part of the package.'

Tom nodded. 'Of course. I suppose Rylan is okay. I suppose I should be grateful you're not inviting Frank to join us.'

'Why would I do that?'
'You talk about him a lot.'
'He's my colleague.'
'That's fine, Gerry, I meant nothing by it. Just humour.'
'I see. Sometimes I struggle a bit with humour.'

He took her hand. It made her feel uncomfortable at first, but she steeled herself and adjusted to the feel of his skin against hers.

As they entered the bedroom, Gerry turned to Tom. 'I should inform you that I've prepared a checklist of sexual activities I'd like to try.'

Tom's eyes widened, a mix of shock and intrigue on his face. 'That sounds exciting, but shall we start with the basics?'

Gerry nodded. She felt strangely excited. Before this evening, she'd considered them 87 per cent compatible. That number was growing by the minute.

As she undid her shirt, she watched Rylan settle into his bed in the corner.

She wondered if Frank would be proud of her progress in human interaction. She'd tell him all about it tomorrow.

After all, that was what colleagues did.

∽

The claw tore into the roof of the Rusty Anchor pub. Bricks and mortar flew. Dust billowed up, obscuring the crumbling structure. Frank stood at a safe distance, having opted to forgo the cumbersome safety gear. He was in no mood for such precautions today.

As the old pub crumbled, he thought of Rowena Hughes' face when he'd explained the reasons behind her younger brother's death. He didn't give the details of his serial abusing at Sunnybrook, instead focusing on the relationship with the young male sex worker that had gone wrong. She was nobody's fool though, and she realised he'd kept many secrets from her, many of which would be unsavoury.

These revelations shook her deeply, but she hadn't let them destroy her. Both she and Frank had spoken at length about how blaming herself for Adrian's choices was a fool's errand. Yes, she could have spoken up about what her father had done to her brother, spared him years of misery, but she'd been too scared to even speak up for herself. Children couldn't be blamed for being trapped in that cycle of pain. And there was no guarantee it would have made a difference, anyway.

The claw struck again. Tiles cascaded down, shattering on the ground below. The pub groaned as its structural integrity weakened further. Frank found himself grappling with difficult questions. Did Adrian's treatment at the hands of a monster inevitably turn him into one himself? There were no easy answers to questions like these. Was looking back in this way pointless? Just as the Rusty Anchor was being reduced to dust, was the past also irreparable? Were all their efforts to uncover the truth ultimately futile?

Frank turned away from the demolition, ready to move forward. You couldn't make the world a better place by dwelling in the past. It was time to let go of pain and focus on the future.

He paused, his gaze sweeping over the vast expanse of the North York Moors. The open landscape seemed to mirror his own feelings of guilt and uncertainty. He thought of Mike lying in that hospital bed, holding his son's hand, and how it had led Frank to keep a secret that could destroy his relationship with Gerry if she ever found out. It went against everything they stood for as police officers. But Frank knew he'd made the right decision. Mike deserved a chance to heal and rebuild his life. And if that meant keeping the truth buried, if it meant shouldering the burden of that knowledge himself, then so be it.

He glanced behind himself one last time. The old pub was no more. Sometimes the kindest thing we can do is let the past stay in the past.

As he climbed into Bertha, Frank's thoughts drifted to his own daughter, Maddie. She wasn't in the past. She was very much in the *now*. Lost somewhere in the vast world. He'd find her no matter the cost. He wouldn't allow her to become another dark, buried secret, like all the others.

In the cellar of a derelict pub.

Continue to discover the dark truths of Whitby's Forgotten Victims. DCI Frank Black and DI Gerry Carver return in *Forgotten Souls*...

No soul is quiet, yet the cry of the forgotten soul is impossible to ignore.

When the sea yields a grim discovery on Whitby's coast, DCI Frank Black hears the haunting cry of Greg Lyle - a vulnerable 13-year-old boy fascinated by sea creatures, last seen walking his beloved dog, Buddy, twenty-six years ago. Alongside his autistic companion, DI Gerry Carver, Frank pursues this cry through a labyrinth of shattered homes, hidden identities, and religious obsessions.

In Greg, Frank recognises Gerry's vulnerability. In Simon Lyle, he sees reflections of his own failings as a father. As buried truths surface, Frank's resolve only strengthens.

He will answer the cry of this forgotten soul. Even if it costs him his own.

FORGOTTEN LIVES

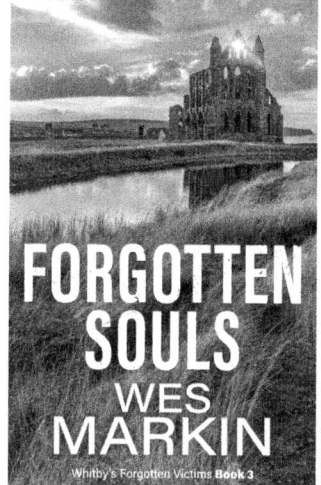

Scan the QR to Pre-order!

Free and Exclusive read

Delve deeper into the world of Wes Markin with the
FREE and **EXCLUSIVE** read, ***A Lesson in Crime***

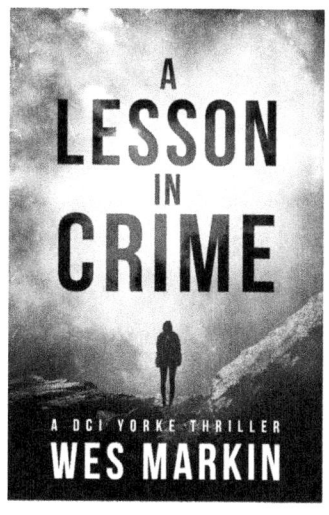

Scan the QR to READ NOW!

JOIN DCI EMMA GARDNER AS SHE RELOCATES TO KNARESBOROUGH, HARROGATE IN THE NORTH YORKSHIRE MURDERS ...

Still grieving from the tragic death of her colleague, DCI Emma Gardner continues to blame herself and is struggling to focus. So, when she is seconded to the wilds of Yorkshire, Emma hopes she'll be able to get her mind back on the job, doing what she does best - putting killers behind bars.

But when she is immediately thrown into another violent murder, Emma has no time to rest. Desperate to get answers and find the killer, Emma needs all the help she can. But her new partner, DI Paul Riddick, has demons and issues of his own.

And when this new murder reveals links to an old case Riddick was involved with, Emma fears that history might be about to repeat itself...

Don't miss the brand-new gripping crime series by bestselling British crime author Wes Markin!

~

What people are saying about Wes Markin...

JOIN DCI EMMA GARDNER AS SHE RELOCATES TO KNA...

'Cracking start to an exciting new series. Twist and turns, thrills and kills. I loved it.'

Bestselling author **Ross Greenwood**

'Markin stuns with his latest offering... Mind-bendingly dark and deep, you know it's not for the faint hearted from page one. Intricate plotting, devious twists and excellent characterisation take this tale to a whole new level. Any serious crime fan will love it!'

Bestselling author **Owen Mullen**

Scan the QR to READ NOW!

Also by Wes Markin
ONE LAST PRAYER

"An explosive and visceral debut with the most terrifying of killers. Wes Markin is a new name to watch out for in crime fiction, and I can't wait to see more of Detective Yorke." – *Bestselling Crime Author Stephen Booth*

The disappearance of a young boy. An investigation paved with depravity and death. Can DCI Michael Yorke survive with his body and soul intact?

With Yorke's small town in the grip of a destructive snowstorm, the relentless detective uncovers a missing boy's connection to a deranged family whose history is steeped in violence. But when all seems lost, Yorke refuses to give in, and journeys deep into the heart of this sinister family for the truth.

And what he discovers there will tear his world apart.

The Rays are here. It's time to start praying.

The shocking and exhilarating new crime thriller will have you turning the pages late into the night.

"A pool of blood, an abduction, swirling blizzards, a haunting mystery, yes, Wes Markin's One Last Prayer for the Rays has all the makings of an absorbing thriller. I recommend that you give it a go." – *Alan Gibbons, Bestselling Author*

One Last Prayer is a shocking and compulsive crime thriller.

Scan the QR to READ NOW!

Acknowledgments

Returning to the atmospheric streets of Whitby for this second instalment has been a joy. The town continues to surprise and inspire me, offering up new mysteries with each visit. Its rich history and brooding landscapes have once again provided the perfect backdrop for Frank and Gerry's investigations.

I am deeply grateful to my readers who have embraced Frank and Gerry, allowing them into their lives and following their journey. Your enthusiasm and support have been the wind in my sails, propelling this series forward.

As Frank and Gerry delve deeper into Whitby's secrets, I find myself increasingly in awe of their resilience and determination. Frank continues to chart his own course, often surprising me with his actions and insights. His evolving relationship with Gerry remains a source of fascination.

My heartfelt thanks go out to my family: Jo, Hugo and Bea. Your unwavering support, patience, and ability to keep me grounded (and laughing) are the bedrock upon which these stories are built.

I owe a debt of gratitude to the incredible book bloggers and reviewers who have championed this series. Your passion for books and willingness to spread the word about fresh stories is the lifeblood of this occupation!

To the people of Whitby, thank you for welcoming me and this series into your community. Your town's unique charm, from its ancient pub cellars to its windswept moors, continues to be an endless source of inspiration.

Last, but not least, to my readers: thank you for joining Frank and Gerry on this journey. Your willingness to follow them down dark alleys and into the shadows of the past makes all of this possible.

I look forward to our next adventure in Whitby, where the cry of a forgotten soul awaits Frank, Gerry and the team...

Review

If you enjoyed reading **_Forgotten Lives_**, please take a few moments to leave a review on
Amazon, Goodreads or BookBub.

Printed in Dunstable, United Kingdom